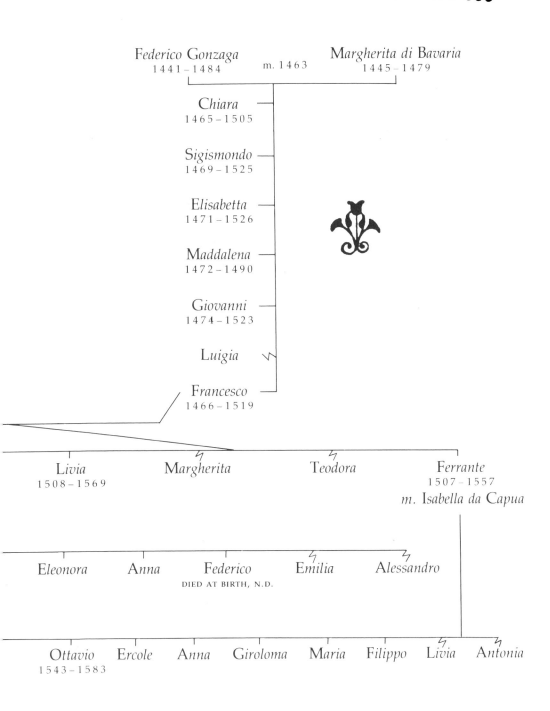

Federico Gonzaga
1441–1484   m. 1463   Margherita di Bavaria
1445–1479

Chiara
1465–1505

Sigismondo
1469–1525

Elisabetta
1471–1526

Maddalena
1472–1490

Giovanni
1474–1523

Luigia

Francesco
1466–1519

Livia
1508–1569

Margherita

Teodora

Ferrante
1507–1557
m. Isabella da Capua

Eleonora

Anna

Federico
DIED AT BIRTH, N.D.

Emilia

Alessandro

Ottavio
1543–1583

Ercole

Anna

Giroloma

Maria

Filippo

Livia

Antonia

Private
Renaissance

Also by Maria Bellonci

Segreti dei Gonzaga
Tu vipera gentile
Lucrezia Borgia
Delitto di Stato

translated in English

Lucrezia Borgia
The Prince of Mantua

Private Renaissance

A NOVEL

MARIA BELLONCI

TRANSLATED BY

WILLIAM WEAVER

WILLIAM MORROW AND COMPANY, INC.
NEW YORK

Library of Congress Cataloging-in-Publication Data

Bellonci, Maria.
  Private renaissance.

  Translation of: Rinascimento Privato.
  I. Title.
PQ4807.E47R513 1989   853'.914   88-13710
ISBN 0-688-08188-6

Printed in the United States of America

First U.S. Edition

1 2 3 4 5 6 7 8 9 10

BOOK DESIGN BY BARBARA M. BACHMAN

Contents

Private
Renaissance

I

The Measure of Youth

Room of the clocks
the year 1533

MY SECRET IS a memory, at times fearsome in its action. Isolated and motionless, on the verge of motion, I stand in the center of swirling currents that spiral around this room, where my hundred clocks tell different times in different tones. If I raise my head, I see them gleam, and to each fiery glint an image corresponds. I am always pulled outside myself by the storm of living. What is time, and why must it be considered past? As long as we live, only one time exists: the present. A yearning power grips my entrails; constructive or destroying, I cannot say; it is without any rule, at least apparently.

Evening is falling. The candelabra glow, all alight. I have dismissed my servants, as I often do now. I can clearly discern the jagged writing of the letter lying open on the little table. A calm anger rises from my heart to my head and bursts in the daze of questions that follow it. How can this man count on my obedience, indeed, on my complicity? "I must ask this favor of you: Do not write me; do not take advantage of this hyperborean distance in order to cease fearing me." And then: "I feel a culpable vanity thinking how you have always fled me." I, write him? I, flee him? I, subjected to judgment? And yet, reading those sentences, I cannot help perceiving an inner fraught tremor that combats my intransigence and almost defeats it.

These letters from the foreigner born in England, which have always seemed to me without ambiguity and often guilelessly filled with stories, splendid or delicate, never to be considered dangerous or suspicious because of any magnetic attraction hidden in their depths. But the moment ticks by and urges me to a strict, thorough examination of myself, of the transformations that define a human being insofar as one can be defined. The clock strikes and begins a measure of hours, and to me it seems a signal.

I arrange my years, successively present. The first period of my life is surely a development of natural instinct; though marked by many doubts, life went its own way. Of that time I recall disjointed images and a rush of energy that somehow entitled me to be invincible. Later came the test that completely overwhelmed any motion of rights in reality, and a sharp break divided the first part of my girlhood from the second. It was April, in that round-numbered year, 1500; with it there struck us, like a dreadful summons, the horrible rout of the Milanese under the impact of the armies of France, of Louis the Twelfth.

I T I S T H E harsh dawn of a foggy spring. I am in bed. My nurse, Colomba, suddenly wakes me, saying things too frightful to be true. I spring down from the bed, pull a fur-hemmed robe around me, and run—for something within me refuses walking—into the next room just in time to see the gaunt head of the horse of my brother-in-law Signor Giovanni Gonzaga, appearing from the circular staircase that leads into my apartment in the castle. The horse's head does not conceal the rider but, drawing back, repels him into a distant, haunted vision. Both horse and rider are covered with dust and mud, both are at the end of their strength, and Signor Giovanni, letting the reins go slack, slips down the animal's flank, caught barely in time by his groom, who has been following him. Youngest of all my brothers-in-law, Giovanni now seems very old, perhaps because of the dust that whitens his hair; he is drunk with fear and weariness, his every feature distraught, and yet he is shrill, irate. And his voice is almost unrecognizable when he announces, in broken phrases, the things he has suffered and that we are yet to suffer.

"It's the end for the Moro!" he cries, in a hoarse voice, "It's the end for all of us, and you, first of all, Isabella. They caught him, disguised as a Swiss soldier, among the Swiss infantry. Those mercenaries had refused to fight, and they were heading for their homes. He, Ludovico, your Moro, was marching in their midst, on foot, trusting to luck, but a man from Lausanne recognized him and identified him to the French. They also captured Galeazzo of San Severino; they'll take the pair to France as prisoners. Cardinal Ascanio fled with me; I left him behind, near Piacenza, looking for some refuge, a hiding place. Everyone is fleeing Milan. Those taken alive have their throats cut and are disemboweled. And now what about us? All I could think of was getting to Mantua, to warn everyone, you, first of all."

His neck slumps to one side as if it were broken, and his voice dies in a breathless gurgle. Behind me, my ladies stir but dare not approach me; they peer in at the far end of the room, they rush off down stairs and steps, and they fling open doors, they call and weep, summoning the whole castle. With a gesture I give an order to Signora Violante, who is standing motionless, under Master Mantegna's "Trionfi," annihilated like the prisoners in that picture. She understands it and vanishes. Signor Giovanni abruptly recovers himself; he strides toward me furiously.

"I have rushed to you, Isabella, because what we're about to go through is your doing. If we do not support one another, we are lost. We cannot run off, leave the way clear for the French, with no thought of what might happen to our people and to the city. We must think of our defenses, my brother the marquis must give me instructions at once; he is the one who recklessly sent me off, as you advised, or rather, insisted. Here I am; look at me. Perhaps Cardinal Ascanio will ask for asylum here; you guaranteed him unconditional assistance, you offered him even your person, to protect the Sforzas. You, dear sister-in-law, are the most suspect in the eyes of the French. They call you la Sforzesca, and they growl threats. They mean to take you hostage, with your daughter and the child you are carrying; they would like to drag you to France. Isabella, bear this firmly in mind: For the Sforzas it's all over. Give up any idea of defending them. They are not people to help, and they never will be again."

An icy stone blocks the breath in my bosom. Signor Giovanni was cruelly prophesying, battering me without respite. I had just enough breath to remind him that it was his duty to go at once to the rooms of the marquis, his brother, and at the same time I urged the groom to succor his master with drink and bandages. Thus I got rid of him. I have long known that men yell like that merely to release their passions.

But I was not able to take in the full gravity of his words, even though I kept reminding myself of this misfortune that was befalling our lands and perhaps all of Italy. It was true, entirely true, what I had said to Cardinal Ascanio in the days of splendid illusion, illuminated by the good fortune of the Sforzas. Everything that was theirs seemed, then, superb, and rightfully so, deifying. To the Duke Ludovico, il Moro, the legendary Moor, we owed our stunned joy in his existence. It was enchanting to hear him discourse upon government, new cities, the life of his people. I alone knew the extent of his subtlety, to which the others submitted unconsciously. The invention of the science of government was for him a web of rapid actions, a supremely mechanical exercise, controlled by his hand. He had once defined the king of France as his general, the pope as his chaplain, and Venice, his warehouse. And these assertions which might have seemed dictated by a spirit made insensitive by power appeared, on the contrary, true and definitive.

I stood up, overcome by the present. And what about us? Again I heard the words of Giovanni. What would become of us? What would become of me, the Moro's only real ally? Should I now consider it a piece of luck that my husband had so hated Ludovico? It was so. Francesco's jealousy and rancor toward Sforza now became an unsteady basis of hope. Everything I had believed in was giving way. I felt I was clutching at a dry bush to keep from plunging into a ravine.

All my ladies had abandoned me. Soon Francesco, having listened to his brother, would burst into my rooms, and with his Mantuan voice, broad and resonant, he would attack me fiercely for my long sympathy for the Sforzas. Should I respond to his accusations or be silent, meek like a woman lacking spirit? There was no part of my body that did not throb and ache. I folded my hands over my belly, to protect the child I bore inside me. I could not weep.

In the gray dawn mist a shadow had come closer to me. And before I could recognize the shadow as it took on human substance, someone spoke to me: "Being afraid serves no purpose; this is a maxim of yours, my lady."

It was the voice of all my days, the voice of Pirro Donati, calm, with its tone of soothing explanation that connected the most disparate things and gave encouraging plausibility to all speech. Pirro Donati: his presence at that moment steeped me into a kind of pause, and from that pause rose an enlivening possibility. I had first seen him when he arrived as a page from Ferrara (I was six years old then) in the suite of the ambassador Beltramino Cusatro, who came to draw up the contract of my marriage to Francesco Gonzaga. Even then Pirro evidenced a maturity quite rare in a boy who had just completed his twelfth year. I found him again in Mantua when I arrived there a bride and after that became accustomed to seeing him always in my rooms in the castle, the first among my gentlemen.

In that blanched light with streaks of dull gray I could discern the familiar trim face, the tawny eyes with an occasional paler glint, the brow broadened by a first loss of hair at the temples, the thin, straight nose, the calm mouth, wise with words of reassurance.

"You have heard?" I murmured.

There was no need for more. He did not speak of Signor Ludovico, did not try to lighten the stone I carried in my breast. As always, he looked beyond the moment and proposed something to me. In fact, with a serenity only slightly vibrant, he said: "There is no immediate danger, my lady. The French are in Milan, enjoying their victory; they are busy looting and collecting ransom. And do you really believe the pope can allow them to settle in Italy? The emperor surely cannot allow it, and the Venetians, even more, would not allow it. Have you forgotten the league against the other French king, against King Charles? Things will change, as they have always changed, but meanwhile, it is necessary to act."

I was in such a state that I could admit the suggestion of a message, perhaps a letter to be written. But to whom? I stiffened. Without replying, I pretended not to notice that he was drawing me to my feet and, with a light touch on my shoulder, leading me away.

"Listen to your women; they are beginning to scream again," Pirro continued. "They do not understand what their duty is. I will go and scold them; they must put you to bed. Remember your condition and your absolute need to rest," and peering at me, he said further, "There is something to be done. Do it," and he insisted, in a lower voice, "Lock the doors."

I did not immediately perceive how appropriate this advice was, but I followed it. Pirro led me into my great bedroom, warmed by a log that was making a hill of embers in the fireplace, and delicately he made me sit down on a stool. One by one, my women all came back, undressed me, and covered me with heavy blankets under the impassive design of our nuptial emblems that poured, dancing, down from the vaulted ceiling. The fire was stirred into silence, I received a hot tisane that failed to calm me. Pirro had disappeared.

"There is something to be done"; "a maxim of yours"; "Lock the doors": the sentences pounded in my head; slowly I grasped them, and a warrior instinct ran through me. I had to defend my child; I had to remain sealed in my room as in a fortress; it would be impossible for anyone to enter and accuse me; no one would be able to broach in my presence the huge, sanguinary disaster announced by Signor Giovanni.

In a wan voice I called my nurse, Colomba: "I am ill, Nurse, ill. Send word at once to Castelli, my physician; hurry." I let a groan escape me, to ease the pain.

I was still moaning, finding in that pretense a kind of relief, when Castelli, white and bearded, entered, filled with self-importance as his glorious moment had arrived. He examined me, asked questions, frowned, and issued instructions: Rest; silence; no one in the room except the nurse and two of my women. The door locked against everyone. There was risk of miscarriage, his expression said; care had to be taken. In a brisk shuffling around me, order was established. A few minutes went by, and someone knocked impetuously at the door.

"The lord marchese!" the nurse said, frightened.

"No one must enter," Castelli decreed from inside, grandly. "I will go speak with him."

He went out, leaving the door ajar, and after a brief exchange in two tones differently determined, he came back to me, shutting the door again. As a precaution he chose to remain in my room, and he took his place sedately on a backed bench by the fireplace, a book in his hand. The nurse was dozing; the women had vanished. Beneath the vaulted ceiling that silence spread, tense, ever ready to reecho, that silence that had assumed so many different tones in the ten years of my married life. I almost seemed to hear the music of the fifes and drums that had accompanied my waking the morning after the wedding. Among the festive company there was Elisabetta, Francesco's sister, and many young relatives of the house of Gonzaga; but I looked at none of them. I looked up, peeking through the sheets at the cascade of emblems, the *F* and the *IS*, initials of our names, that descended from the ceiling toward me or rapidly rose, rampant. My heart was about to burst with joy; endless increase seemed to lie before me then. But now the happiness of those interwoven letters appeared counterfeit, actually a threat, and worse, a confused threat. I have never liked confusion; reason demands that each thing and each time have its place; otherwise, life is a blur. In little, light moves, as if restraining myself, I returned, I skirted the words of my brother-in-law Giovanni. I refused to enter into their reality, and yet they were true.

The Sforzas. Nobody knew better than I what the Lombardy of the Sforzas had been under Ludovico the Moro, and from this certain knowledge I arrived at the glowing spot in my soul, always ready to burst into flame. Like a cruel, proud flash, a thought crossed my mind. Perhaps today's misfortune would not have occurred if a hostile fate had not touched me at a vital point where I still felt a loss beyond compensation, for Ludovico Sforza had asked me as his bride from my father, and if the messenger had arrived in Ferrara even only a few days earlier, the nuptial contract between me and Francesco would never have been signed. Without a moment's hesitation, my father offered the Moro my sister, Beatrice; she was, after all, an Este as well, my little dark sister, who, with her heavy cheeks and olive skin, so resembled her ancestor King Ferrante of Aragón. She wore two locks dangling at either side of her face to make its oval seem less broad. Beatrice in Ferrara had been taciturn, keenly observing me in every act, and I was still amazed at the extraordinary metamorphosis I had then witnessed. Once she was in Milan, married, she proved a genius in the art of winning her husband through her insistent seductions, enacted one after the other.

I myself saw the first of the many. The Moro was no more than curious about her; he had too many women around him, chosen among the most beautiful and the most endowed with amorous grace and lively wit. But he considered me a queen. He had lost me by a few days, I should have been his destiny; this was what he seemed to say to me when he came toward me on the evening of his wedding feast in the Milanese castle, walking across a gently sloping lawn, white with intact snow, scattered with roses. Ludovico was radiant in his glory, his good luck, his wealth; he led me to admire the loggia of the ball court frescoed with the bellicose feats of his great father, Francesco Sforza. With smug majesty he took delight in leading me then, in the compliant winter season, through his sumptuous apartments. He showed me the plan for a new city, with five thousand houses, drawn up by his engineer, Leonardo da Vinci, and also his dearest possessions: the chests brimming with ducats, with splendid gems in finely worked filigreed settings, and the rarest French and Italian volumes that rows of amanuenses were intent on copying, and those Greek and Arabic Bibles that I also proposed to read, convinced that I could possess everything, learn everything.

I had to stifle the cry of protest of my twenty-six years, till then brimming with sensational hopes. I no longer relied on the obedience of the natural order, the idea of an inevitably victorious fate, but I could not tolerate the idea of error. "I must reread *De casibus*, my beloved Boccaccio," I said to myself, recurring to books in my usual way; the errors and the misfortunes of the great would enlighten me. But I could not prod my imagination. I was more overwhelmed than weary; my eyes wide open to that faint dawn that was shading into a grayish day, I suffered a kind of urgent lucidity that impelled me. With a shudder I sank into a doze, and almost aloud I uttered the name of Ludovico.

He! How had he managed to err?

"When it is a question of the State, there is no one to look to save relatives. Take care of yourself now, Isabella." I hear the realistic voice, with its tight northern vowels, of my father, Ercole, who was not wrongly called the West Wind. The Moro was, on the contrary, rich in feeling, warm and vital, even if a certain Visconti chill lurked in his depths. When my sister, Beatrice, died (she was only twenty-two), his mourning was theatrical, inventive. He remained shut up in the vast Milan castle, in a dark room, illuminated only by the dim circle of a single candle, as he litanied the praises of his lost wife. And he inveighed against Isabella of Aragón, who had been the true duchess of Milan, my sister's great rival. He kept saying: "There she is, walking up there on the floor above, to let me hear that she is alive, that she has won. She is alive, she has won, and she mocks me."

It is probable that the Moro's errors began with that ostentatious grief and perhaps, more seriously, even before, with that nephew of his. I had met Gian Galeazzo in Milan, and to me he had not seemed mindless, as Ludovico said of him with contempt; his character was mild, tending to the soft and playful, but that was how he had been educated, or rather betrayed day after day, in that limbo among horses, dogs, and the childish amusements his invalid life demanded. An affectionate husband, after his marriage he had three children in rapid succession. My thoughts hover around Isabella of Aragón and her story, a subject of gossip in all the courts of Italy and Europe. And now I feel clearly the suspicion that Ludovico's mania for aggrandizement did not help him. What good did it do him, to steal his nephew's power? His political errors began with that moral error that gradually made them more determinant; kings, and all rulers, distrust usurpers.

But the Sforzas had really been the masters of Europe. Even then it had seemed a privilege to be able to study from a close vantage point the politics of Ludovico the Moro; he ranged beyond the Alps, holding many strings and skilled at pulling them as no one else was. Who but he had called the first French king, Charles the Eighth, into Italy, with the promise of the conquest of the kingdom of Naples? Who but he had managed then to foment a league to drive the king back to his ultramontane possessions and, at the same time, negotiate peace with him personally, defying all the confederated Italian states? Later, to rid himself of tiresome enemies, he financed a war fought by the Burgundians against the emperor Maximilian and drove the sultan Bajazet to unleash the Turkish horde on Venice. And to raise money, he increased the taxes of his rich State with no fear of the populace. He had made the Milanese rich; now they should pay their part.

He never ceased to surprise me with his way of impassively entrusting himself to the unexpected, of waiting for the right time
and drawing it out to exhaustion in tiny skirmishes, since he
considered the temporizing strategy of the Italian condottieri a
valuable heritage. Nothing slipped through the fine mesh of his
intelligence.

And none of this had been real. Maximilian must have come
to an agreement with the Burgundians, the Turks had left the
Venetians room enough for their plan of conquest against Milan,
and these were no longer the days of condottieri skilled in defensive tactics now that from the north serried ranks of French
and Swiss troops were descending, armed with bombards and
culverins, and trained in destructive war.

And yet the Moro was a true chief of state, great lord of our
time. When he came to Mantua to deliver to Francesco the ill-
starred baton of Captain General of the imperial troops (I could
see now it was ill starred), he brought with him an escort of eight
hundred people, mostly gentlemen of Lombardy. What a chore
it was, in those days, to prepare lodging. I, in particular, was
responsible for Ludovico himself, and I never ceased pondering
the colors of the apartment, no longer mourning black, but still
no brilliant hues. How long I hesitated before choosing finally
that deep gray. Ludovico wrote me brotherly love letters with
declarations of this sort: that he loved me more than any other
relative, his own children included. These were days of exalted
living at our court, and Mantua shone in that special June light
that spreads its scented spring under the skies. I paid no heed to
Francesco's ill humor. I heard him move about the castle and say
in a loud voice that the Moro could have sent him the captain's
baton by messenger and have spared him all the debts he now
had to incur. "Stubborn wife," he repeated to me, in private, at
every moment, "don't you realize that it's all useless and that
King Louis will take Milan whenever he wants?"

This forecast reechoes, and I tremble at my obstinate heedlessness, for I knew everything that Francesco knew. I must forget
those days that beclouded my alert faculties. Secret days that I
have never wanted to go back to, for I would not imitate those
silly females who live on past images and make personal tales
out of them.

For the guests' entertainment I devised a Diana's hunt, to be
held in the Wood of the Fountain, with all my ladies, mounted,
dressed in antique garb. At our appearance there was a furor of
applause from the people of the court. It was a cloudy morning,

and we became lost in the great, shady forest, Ludovico and I. The air darkened; suddenly it rained. We were near a little lake, just avoiding the nets that separated the area of the hunt from that of the leopards, restless in their enclosure. He and I were alone, on the bank of that pearly lake, motionless beneath the pelting rain; we had taken refuge in a fisherman's hut. What happened? Ludovico, in a gentle tone, quoted Dido and Aeneas: *"Speluncam Dido dux et Troianus eandem devenient. . . ."*

"Is not Virgil the father of destinies in Mantua?" he asked me, laughing.

I also laughed, unusually subdued; the Moro's strength radiated and pressed me, heavily. I was not aware that my laughter resembled the foolish laughing of my girls when they were surrounded by men bent on amusing them. Voices of hunters who had sighted us rose in the woods, and a little later there were people at the hut with blankets and lengths of waxed canvas. But the weight of that victor, which I had felt upon me, remained.

I ASK myself if what I feel now is remorse, and for what? I refuse to think: "My God, forgive me." I open my eyes wide and call my women, who hurry to my bedside, with Lady Violante at their head. I ask to be dressed; I put on a comfortable, soft dress that does not conceal my condition but rather accentuates it. By now it is night; the great double-arched windows stand out against the dark sky. Since dawn the whole day has gone by; I am hungry. They bring me food, and I eat, drinking my white wine from Sirmione. I realize the moment has come, and I order the doors to be unlocked.

Francesco enters and, driven by his own impetus, finds himself in the center of the room, where he stops, a bit dazed. Behind him I see my brother Cardinal Ippolito, who has come, surely in a great haste, from Ferrara. I see my brothers-in-law Monsignor Sigismondo and Signor Giovanni restrained and anxious; still farther back are the rolling eyes of our buffoon, Frittella.

"Excellent, there are difficult witnesses," I think, and I run eagerly to Francesco, flinging myself on his sturdy chest.

"Francesco! Oh, Francesco! What a horrible disaster! What abysmal misfortune. You were right when you didn't want to join forces with Ludovico. I alone am guilty of having trusted him; I alone drove you to it, led you astray, deceived you. But I was deceived as much as you, or more."

These and other words. I utter a flood of words, barely punctuated by the weeping I repressed for so many hours while I was thinking, and my own words drive me into a scene of despair. I observe myself: I am proceeding along two parallel lines, one quite alert and controlled, the other all fire and distraught grief, bursting from the depths of my soul.

I ask forgiveness, I believe; I assume the blame for infinite errors caused by excessive trust. All around, nobody moves. I feel Francesco's heart beating in great thuds beneath my head, which is resting on him, and I redouble my tears until a fit of exhaustion seizes me, and my husband conducts me to my seat. I peek through my hair, which has fallen over my face, and I glimpse sympathetic expressions. I dry my tears, as Francesco, speechless, overcome, looks at me. He knows me too well not to suspect I am acting, but on the other hand, he is enchained by the fury of that sorrow and feels obliged to comfort me. For this scene has wellsprings of such vehemence, so sincere and desolate and conflicting, that I myself could not have doubted it. Even my brother the cardinal, master of the most subtle feigning, has moist eyes. It is that moisture that tells me I have won. Meanwhile, everyone starts speaking to me, and Francesco, to recover his composure, calls the physician Castelli aside and has a serious, intense conversation with him, nodding thoughtfully at the man's words.

Another sudden flood of tears catches even me by surprise, and Francesco rushes to me. I am so vulnerable, so weak and young, with my long golden hair regally loose, that this time he embraces me and comforts me with sly references to certain amorous games that are only ours. My brother-in-law the prothonotary pronounces religious words that guarantee the infallible intervention of Divine Providence. Signor Giovanni speaks little, and with embarrassment; my brother cardinal d'Este tells me much about Ferrara and my father, the people of our childhood; he mentions all my brothers and, first of all, my sister Beatrice. It is late when they go out, and I notice the fat white hand of the physician Castelli motioning them to rest assured. I no longer feel any fear, only a great stir, as if a giant hornet were buzzing inside my drained head.

AS FAR as my health is concerned, I have always been a delicate lioness, in my mother's words. Spells of illness actually served me as periods of rest, after and during days of excessive combativeness. Soon I was entirely forgiven and loved all the more for having been victim of Ludovico, that monster of treachery, and the court, and the chancellery, and the people heard me reiterate my determination to be a "good Frenchwoman." At first these two words seemed to me a lying epitaph, but I had no time to explore my conscience because in May my prayer was finally answered. Accompanied by a cloud of prayers of our saint, Suor Osanna Andreasi, on the sixteenth of May of the year 1500, the beginning of the century, our first male child was born: Federico. He was handsome, this son of mine, and truly deserved his gold-trellised cradle and every sort of good omen. What triumphant delight I felt in displaying him, naked and perfect in every limb, to the envoys who came to see me. Francesco was mad about his heir and would have liked to see the child grow up in his own arms; he laughed at him with his tawny laughter, in the storm of all the merry voices. In this happiness I quickly recovered from the childbearing, and I began to look around me.

Pirro Donati came, and we consulted each other. Ignoring the exhortations of Signor Giovanni, I sent people, very circumspect, to Milan for reliable news, but their reports on returning were not good. The French had discovered a traffic of messages just before Ludovico's capture, and they were muttering about dark conspiracies. They trusted no one, least of all me. The prothonotary Sigismondo, my second brother-in-law, receiving information from ecclesiastical sources, declared desperate the condition of Ludovico Sforza, prisoner of His Majesty. Stubbornly hostile to us, these French continued to threaten dragging me and Federico through their muddy cities. A white fury filled my mind.

"*Bonne française, bonne française,* be careful," I would mutter to myself perhaps as my comb crackled in my hair, and silent, I would angrily contradict my words. Books helped me recall examples of pride humbled by victors. Histories were full of examples; it was enough to mention the gold of Brennus, the Caudine Forks. I felt keenly argumentative; we had no ducats, but I ordered precious dresses, on credit, one, of Alexandrine satin, with gold curlicues embroidered on gold. The pale blue was enlivened by the gold; it shone like a sky pierced by the sun's rays.

In his usual conciliatory manner Pirro Donati insisted on reminding me several times of the name of Chiara Gonzaga, who lived in France, widow of Gilbert of Bourbon, duke of Montpensier. She was Francesco's older sister, a great friend of King Louis. We put our faith in her, lady of every grace and consideration, but formerly, when she had spent some time with us, I had not found her a woman much interested in talk about political maneuvering. We sent her letters with renewed hope, and she re-

vealed a quick and shrewd talent, confronting the king, leaving
him no respite, and guaranteeing for all of us. It was Chiara, in
fact, who suggested an important name to me, that of Cardinal
de Rohan, my worst enemy. Now he had established his court
in Milan, this cardinal, who was a very great lord, haughty by
nature, of sharp, lofty wit. I thought how to arrive at him directly,
without intermediaries; with many missives and envoys to people
in his circle we finally hit upon an approach.

He was an impassioned lover of Italian painting, especially of
the noblest; he admired the great masters and, above all, our
Andrea Mantegna, native of the land of Padua but for many years
in the service of the house of Gonzaga. In great haste I summoned
the supreme master, old but still gifted and youthful in his art,
and as gruff as ever. Partly through persuasion and partly through
some severity (not much, however, because Mantegna was not
an easygoing man), I commissioned the work of him: a Saint John
with the portrait of the kneeling cardinal, copied from a medallion.
First Rohan had someone else write me. Then he wrote me himself, still mentioning my so-called Sforza inclination, to which I
replied with feigned annoyance, commanding him to appear in
Mantua and ask my pardon. I informed Francesco of my plan.
He flung up his hands in desperation, as if to repel such reckless
audacity; but I knew how courtly these Frenchmen are with us
women, and our audacity makes them all the more gallant. Mantegna's picture proved perfect, and the cardinal was so tamed
what with letters and painting that he began to sing my praises
on all sides. And so, fighting our battle through art and politeness
and the recommendations of our kin, we managed to win the
pardon of the king of France, who had come down to Milan with
a great court of nobles and knights to take possession of the
conquered state.

As the northern sky cleared, a more dangerous storm gathered
in the south. The time of public sorrowing under the Borgia name
was approaching. In that endless year of 1500 on the chessboard
of Italy tormented games were engaged between lords and other
men, untrained in the philosophy of government and rule, who
suddenly found themselves playing a central role in a buccaneer
ascendancy. It was our lot to live through all the evil time of the
Borgias with them, those Italianized Spaniards, the worst breed
the world has known. The head of this family, Rodrigo Borgia,
vice-chancellor of the Church, had had himself elected pope through
many subterfuges; he had numerous relatives and children, and
of these, his favorite was Cesare, formerly a cardinal and now,

decardinalized, the captain of great armies, a man spurred by incredible ambition.

In the first year of the century Cesare Borgia had seized all of Romagna except Faenza. Meanwhile, the king of France wanted to obtain the Borgia pope's consent to a divorce from his ugly, sterile queen in order to marry the beautiful Anne of Brittany, who would bring as her dowry her rich region, and so the monarch supported the adventurer with incredible favors and intimacy. More and more arrogant and insidious toward those who governed the Italian states, unequaled in his impertinence, this son of the pope menaced us: the Valentino, as he was called, after the duchy of Valentinois given him by King Louis. With every stratagem, we tried to hold him at bay, but his rough, imperative behavior kept us awake at night. And I could no longer restrain Francesco and his straightforward speech as he inveighed against the Borgias and even against the French king, who seemed to mock our silent dismay. I tried to calm my intemperate husband with words of elementary political equilibrium, observing concretely that the Venetians would never be content to have a strong and threatening papacy at their borders. Shifting to allegorical speech, I told Francesco that we should entrust ourselves to the god Kronos, the old god of time, who allayed distress, but Francesco shrugged. I had better luck when I appealed to his devout spirit and told him of the prediction made by our Suor Osanna: The sainted woman had firmly defined those Borgia devils as a straw fire destined to burn out quickly.

Amid the conflicting reports it was more difficult than ever to maintain order, and it was a sorrow to see all the homeless people who came to us seeking refuge. We lacked the heart to send them away. Perhaps we also failed to realize how dangerous our game was, only slightly less dangerous when it was a matter of succoring women. In fact, the two women of Ludovico the Moro turned up in Mantua. Cecilia Gallerani, now Contessa Bergamini, came for a brief period, and, for years, Lucrezia Crivelli, Beatrice's rival; pregnant again, Lucrezia arrived with her little son. We housed her at Canneto sull'Oglio, in a castle of ours, a lonely place with soaring falcons and herons. At times Lucrezia came to visit us, and we all admired her courageous calm, her flashing beauty, and her dress, not only appropriate but also very elegant, though with scant ornament. We knew that more clever than most, she had left in Milan, in a safe place, incalculable wealth.

AS IN A drama, one early winter day, that freezing December, we are all arranged in a space, like actors, in the great hall of the Mantegna "Trionfi." In one corner, the farthest from the windows, I have had a tent set up, of white and red stripes, lined with heavy crimson satin; thus I have isolated the cradle of Federico, happily asleep. There are the refugees from Milan, the ladies Crivelli and Pallavicino; the refugees from Rome, Count Caetani of Sermoneta with two nephews, darkly, stubbornly silent; there is the count of Pesaro, Giovanni Sforza, and Signor Gentile Varano of Camerino, who has also fled the Borgia troops.

The fireplace draws badly; but finally the flames defeat the ash, and Teodora, Francesco's little girl, his natural daughter, fills the braziers with embers veiled in gray, and she moves around, sweetly proffering them, as is the custom at my court. Francesco paces up and down in the room, rebelling against something he has not yet named. In this he would be right according to the situation. He is reading a letter just arrived in the chancellery. I know what is written in it; Pirro Donati brought me a copy. "Under pain of death and confiscation of all property no one must dare offer asylum to exiles and enemies." The signature is Cesare Borgia's, duke of Romagna. Francesco and I look at each other; we look at the refugees, unable to bring ourselves to speak. They are seated on benches and stools, on the cushions of a platform; the youngest is on the step of the hearth, following the movements of our Teodora.

"We receive nothing but injunctions," Francesco says. "Everyone thinks he can give us orders: the Venetians, the king of France, the pope, and this damned son of his."

I look at him, to soothe his complaints. At times my gaze calms him, but not today. It is futile to vex him; he stares into the void behind me, as he goes on, saying with weary anger: "We are like men being led to the gallows; they see one another hanged without being able to help themselves."

His words fall, lifeless. Each of those present is bowed over his own, most urgent thoughts. Count Giovanni Sforza, our brother-in-law as he first married Maddalena, Francesco's youngest sister, his noble face as if steeped in bitterness, comes forward to thank us for the fifty foot soldiers sent to protect his escape.

My husband bursts out: "Fifty foot soldiers! Nothing! We'd have needed at least a thousand to defend the city of Pesaro."

"Signor marchese"—Lucrezia Crivelli speaks up, with her soft Lombard cadence—"do not grieve. You have already done so much; these days people think only of saving their own lives. Sheltering us here is dangerous for you. No one knows the meaning of clemency any longer, and I do not fear so much for myself as for the children of the duke Ludovico. To whom can we turn for hope, we poor things, if not to you and your generosity?

She is humble, but with great dignity and extraordinarily beautiful in her woolen cloak with leafy green pattern, lined with lynx. The perhaps casual harmony between the deep green and the streaked paleness of the fur recalls my own latest creations.

Pallavicino dares express a hope: "For Ludovico it seems there is good news. They say King Louis will set him free, if the emperor—"

"The emperor has signed a truce with the French," Francesco blurts, "and without setting any conditions whatsoever. A dispatch arrived today in the chancellery confirming it. I have never trusted Maximilian. He even asked me to give the French Federico as hostage. All of you know my answer: I would rather die than behave with such cowardice. So let us forget the idea of help from the emperor. We can have no illusions: King Louis is bound to the Valentino; the Borgia will crush us all, one by one. To stop him, all of Italy would have to unite."

The Caetani men, puffed up with arrogance, declare they are ready and eager for an Italian league; they will be the first, and surely also the Orsinis and the Colonnas will join, provided the emperor allows it. They speak furiously, but without substance. I cannot remain silent; I exclaim, "Why don't you bestir yourselves? Look at the people of Faenza. They are few, but they are resisting. They burn the houses outside the walls of the cities and the trees and any kind of shelter. They are so loyal to their lord that by themselves, they restore the honor of Italy."

Francesco supports me. "We will send men and arms to the defense of Faenza; we will never abandon Astorre Manfredi."

But these words, too, are without weight. When winter ended, it would be impossible for Astorre Manfredi to resist further. But that eighteen-year-old, with the blazing heart of youth, showed how deeply he felt the union between the city and its lord, between the lord and the people. It was the idea I had seen in the flashing blue eyes of my father, Ercole, an idea that we of the Este house, reigning for centuries, had in our blood. I recalled that day in Ferrara, at the time of the war with Venice, when my father, destroyed by fatigue and gravely ill, lay in his bed, his wife and we children beside it, and allowed all the citizens who wished to see him come into the palace and pass before the bed; and he felt no shame to display himself so wasted, stripped of the armor that lay, bloated and empty, on the floor. He presented himself to them, for them to judge him and the war itself, considering him a man like themselves and, like them, exposed to the Venetian invader. The whole city sided with him, filing by with silent concentration. Even the most unruly came to touch his hand.

I feared for Francesco, so instinctively good but unstable; those ruinous days in store for us demanded unswerving conduct. What would it mean to resist enemies of a nature alien to ours? How could we say words and then forget them, without bearing them and their meaning carved in our hearts?

I AM surprised by a faint, soft sound, a cry from inside the tent and I rush beneath that sky of red and white stripes. Softly the little bells tinkle, hanging from the golden trellis of the crib, cadencing the baby's voice. I take Federico in my arms, shielding him; as I feel him grow calm, I determine to educate him as we were educated and better, far better, if possible.

"You will never be vanquished, Federico, my soul; you will never have to seek asylum," I say. "You will reign long in Mantua; you will be a perfect ruler. Your mother swears it."

When Federico falls asleep, I set him down on his little satin mattress and come out of the tent again, almost serene, strengthened by my vow. I realize I have discovered in myself a vein of infinite patience.

AS IT had echoed in my thoughts, so it echoed again when I resumed my place in the room: the name of Ferrara. Wrapped in their cloaks, the refugees were calculating the states that the Valentino could occupy, to extend the mosaic of his reign. And it seemed to them natural to name also the Este duchy, a land of papal investiture; it would take little for Alexander the Sixth to declare the Este line deposed because of some ancient, trifling oversight. They all knew what a great statesman Ercole d'Este was, but not how determined he was never to submit; the years only strengthened him. I decided to send him a dispatch, for a reply that would restore my spirit.

But old Caetani, directly facing me, smiling, turned to the lord of Pesaro and said to him in that mocking tone of his, a mixture of aristocratic, old-fashioned speech with the rough dialect of Rome: "Forgive me, dear Count, but you, as first husband of the signora Lucrezia Borgia, should have warned her second husband, that Aragonese, who had no idea how things are done in that family. Perhaps the poor youth might have avoided his ill fortune."

This ponderous joking on a tragic subject left me speechless. Through interwoven kinships Alfonso of Bisceglie was my cousin. I had seen him in Naples, a beautiful child, and now he lay in a grave, cruelly slain by order of Cesare Borgia. I was unable to speak. And Caetani, continuing his raillery, hinted at horrible rumors. I saw the count of Pesaro rise and draw his sword.

"One more word and I will kill you, you treacherous scoundrel," he said, in the frightened manner of weak men who have been insulted. "As if the stories of your house were not well known. The Borgias are ruthless murderers, but not she. The lady Lucrezia was a good wife to me. She is blameless; she was forced, sword held to her throat. Now you beware!" He was about to attack the other man but was restrained and disarmed by Francesco and his gentlemen.

Caetani wrapped himself in his cloak and retired a few steps, and finally from his mouth came the words that were to chill my blood: Wasn't it said in Rome that another Alfonso would soon take the Neapolitan's place, as third husband of the pope's daughter? The chosen man was Alfonso d'Este, heir of the duchy of Ferrara, my brother.

"My brother? Never, never!" I cried violently. "The Estes will never agree to such dishonor. And you, sir—for shame!"

Assuming an amazed expression, Caetani answered: "I am simply informing you, signora marchesana. Forgive me. I have said only what all Rome is saying."

"The Romans, in that case," I growled, "do not know what my father will answer if ever such a proposal is made to him."

My voice died in my throat. I, too, was lying. My father, the proud Ercole, the religious, indeed conventual man, the fearless warrior, whose sole delight was music, the inspired statesman, had only one failing: He was sick with greed. Gold dazzled him, though coldly. Attacked from that side, he might perhaps not resist. My hope lay in Alfonso; I remembered his first wife, Anna Sforza, sister of Gian Galeazzo, famous for her eyes, the most beautiful in Lombardy, capricious, a complete Visconti in her haughtiness and her extravagance, and at the same time happy and sweet. I had always thought that after his bereavement my brother would choose a woman like Anna, perhaps some great French lady among those King Louis was proposing to him.

Aching in my pride, thus assailed, I looked at the refugees. Humiliation and sorrow held them motionless, and no one knew what more to say. Even Caetani, with a shrug, repelled the attentions of his two saturnine nephews. I raised my thought to Federico, and that wretched group of the defeated inspired in me anger and pity.

T H E P A T H I S long that leads to the first letter with the jagged handwriting. I had suffered in those times, at the beginning of the century, for the public and the secret drama of our political fate, alleviated, even exalted by my happiness in having given life to Federico and having vowed for him a future that I, alone, would prepare. My raging blood flowed; I wished it could be changed into a clear, limpid stream, but never cold. My nature is such that I prefer hot anguish to icy peace.

On an afternoon of white sunlight I was in my Studiolo, crammed with letters, copies of documents, books, papers, and scrolls of poetry. I felt as if I were Saint Jerome in his study. My little puppy Aura also rummaged in the midst of that feverish disorder, occasionally digging out a place for herself and winking at me, one ear raised in a sly attitude. I was again examining the gold medallion crowned with bejeweled enamels that Gian Cristoforo Romano had devised for me. As a rule, medals have their own way of interpreting a face—they underline its bone structure at the expense of complexion, charm, expression—but this work of Gian Cristoforo was only a little unfaithful to me, and that little was to my advantage.

At the door Pirro Donati appeared, and I saw a discreet question in his face. I replaced the medal in a secret drawer where, far from all eyes, I kept some poems of mine that I occasionally enjoyed rereading, knowing it was a forbidden pleasure. Of all, I preferred the one that had been set to music for me by Tromboncino and approved by Tebaldeo, the only composition of mine that was heard sometimes in the concerts of our musicians, naturally without bearing my name. For that poem I had expounded a conceit contrary to my true nature; at least so I believed, directing the verse toward a total negation that does not resemble me. But verse leads to music perhaps out of a desire for absolute conjunction, and we cannot deny that the absolute is sad in tone.

Arboro son che li miei rami ho perso
lo tronco m'è seccato e la radice. . . .

I hummed very softly, to myself, slipping into the trunk of that poem's leafless tree.

Pirro Donati had stopped at some distance and waited, smiling, certain that he had been noticed. I left off my secret singing and motioned him to come forward. My head was brimming with sounds, and one intersected the other in a constant shift of harmonies, and I would gladly have picked up the lute resting on the dais. Instead, to the accompaniment of those harmonies, I learned of the existence of one Robert de la Pole, English by nationality, who had come to Italy with other envoys of King Henry the Seventh of England to report on a gathering of cardinals, met to discuss a hypothetical crusade against the Turks, an enterprise that Alexander the Sixth had been contemplating for some time. It never came to anything; perhaps the envoys had clearly understood that the money demanded would more quickly end up in the pope's private coffers than in the arming of a crusade against the infidel. Now the English ambassadors were returning to London, and one of them, the youngest, this Robert de la Pole, before leaving, wanted to visit our courts to see the beautiful treasures of Italy. He spoke, Pirro said, clear Italian as he had spent his youth in our most distinguished studia, such as Padua, Bologna, Florence, Rome; indeed, in Rome he had lived for several years, as his relatives wanted him to learn the art of composing political and diplomatic documents in the style of the Curia.

The familiar, complex emotion seized me, fleeting but always in ambush. The necessity of responding to a show of courtesy was sharpened by a curiosity to meet new people, but diminished by a kind of repugnance for a human interruption I had not sought. Every day, somehow, I risked flawing the course of my emotions, blocking my mental exercises. Today I had to sacrifice my music; there would be no time now to pick up the lute, summon the singers, and rehearse some compositions, new and old, or those Mantuan folk songs so rich in invention.

Pirro Donati was calmly waiting, studying me, and he begged me to make an effort and receive the visitor. The colloquy could be brief, if I chose. The Englishman had arrived from Florence, where he had been very well received and had been shown splendid works, drawings by Master Leonardo da Vinci and by that powerful young sculptor named Michelangiolo.

My life seems to me a series of performances that I must resume playing at every moment, and here I refer to my encounter with Robert de la Pole. I signaled for him to enter, and instinctively I twitched at my skirt and ran one finger over the neck of my dress, the actions of a woman who can reassure herself also with her clothing. That day I was wearing a gray-green dress, more gold than gray with little clusters of gold chain linked to one another and decorated with hanging pearl drops; around my neck I had a little ruche of white linen embroidered in threads of gold with the refinement that the nuns of Santa Paola bring to such work, a simple creation of mine, but quite new, though it would soon be imitated by many ladies. My hair had been brushed and coiffed with two braids coiled at the temples, knotted at the nape as in the medal by Gian Cristoforo. The awareness of dress is a habit of mine, and I do not believe it can be called vanity, at least not entirely. It is a science of appearing in harmony with the beauty of nature and the order of thought. And it may be that I express too much, or not enough.

I know, I am lingering over Robert de la Pole, but here he is, before me, with the usual courtier's bows, not deep in the Spanish style or light like the French, but gay and with something nonchalant about them. The Englishman's height was about that of Pirro Donati; he towered over me but was not excessively tall, like many of his countrymen. His cropped hair did not tend to the yellow hue of wheat but rather was the color of honey; he seemed quick and lively, though restrained in manner, and he turned on his interlocutor his frank black-enamel eyes, alien to his smooth, almost pink face. In speaking, he seemed to repress a vibrant emotion. He presented me with a book of verses translated into Latin and other Latin and Italian verses of his own composition; he paid me discreet compliments and mentioned the names of common friends, especially of the poet Vincenzo Calmeta, with whom he had conversed in Rome and who had instructed him in the courtliness customary in our palaces. I asked him if in his country it was customary to serve ladies.

"It is a custom we would gladly adopt," he replied, smiling. "But as a rule we are more austere," and he said the word "austere" with a vague merriment.

He spoke of Rome, of the memorable ruins that often, surrounded by trees and covered with green, suddenly loom up like fantastic visions of a still-present power. "Roma, Roma!" I said to myself, with the deep passion that sacred name always inspired in me. A turn in the conversation. Suddenly the visitor added that he had known me in Ferrara almost fifteen years before, and he had been wounded before my eyes in a students' riot outside the ducal palace. I returned to the memory of that day, and I seemed to glimpse a clue that I set aside for future investigation. With a smile I asked him about his king of England; in these visits it is an obligatory question. Henry the Seventh, de la Pole said, was a king who paid great attention to his duty as helmsman, and he was restoring peace to the country that had suffered from the long civil wars; it had to be said that Henry paid little heed to debates among people of culture and men of the Church, the disputes that divided clergy and populace. His only concern was the future of the Tudors. His firstborn son, Arthur, prince of Wales, was sickly, but luckily young Prince Henry was growing up well; at ten he was already strong and blazing with determination.

I said that I hoped a similar opinion would be expressed by our ambassadors to foreign countries of my son, Federico, still too young to be judged. And as a courtesy, I took from a shelf a handsome bronze seal with the Gonzaga and Este arms, the work of the Venetian smith Salomone. Its handle was in the rounded form of a nymph's body, and I gave it with a gesture that doubles the value of the gift. And after other formalities, as a curious twinkle persisted in his black eyes, the visitor went off with Pirro to see the chamber painted by Master Mantegna before darkness fell.

At evening the loss of music remained in me, and after a quick supper my girls, by torchlight, sang a four-part *strambotto* by Marchetto Cara, accompanied by three viols and a lute. It began: *"Aimè ch'io moro per te, donna crudele."* I thought no more of the English visitor, nor did it occur to me that I would be forced to think of him the following day. But so it happened, the very next day. I was leafing through the correspondence, the prompt messages of our envoys, the copies, official reports, and I happened upon a neatly folded letter, a different size from the others. The heading was written in jagged letters. I broke the seal and read the signature, amazed.

*To the Most Excellent and Magnificent Signora
Isabella, Marchesana of Mantua*

*P*ermit me to ask your pardon. I came yesterday to pay you
the homage that is owed you by anyone who has some
slight knowledge of illustrious and precious works, and I do
not know why I kept my identity hidden from you.

I am a priest. I have the title of monsignor and am attached
to the household of ambassadors and envoys of the king Henry
the Seventh of England, in the Vatican. Perhaps Your Ladyship
will find no great significance in my being a cleric rather than a
layman, but it is significant that I kept silent about my
condition, as if for some reason it displeased me, and such
displeasure can exist in these days of a worldly Church. I
cannot express my sorrow at having succumbed to such a
weakness, and to no effect, except for my having received from
you a seal with the figure of a nymph hardly suited to a
prelate. But the reason why I did not tell you, or your lord
secretary, of my condition is something I cannot explain, except
by recalling the vision I already knew in the past, before seeing
you yesterday in your splendor as a young princess, which
rightly dazzled me.

Instinctively I wanted to be what I was years ago, in Ferrara,
where for the first time I encountered your eyes, intent on
taking in everything visible beyond the lances of the
halberdiers, under the great entrance arch of the Este palace.
You wore the dress of a child, as you were, a pale blue dress,
edged in red and dark blue velvet, and a silver ribbon bound
your brow. There was a brawl among the scholars of the
studium, and I, who had come from Padua to hear the lessons
of Guarino, son and heir of the great Veronese, was caught in
the riot because of my ignorance of local customs. And I
confess I felt a delight in that violent outburst of student life
that is a comprehensible and perhaps just rebellion of youth. I
shouted with the others; but I quickly realized that the jest was

blazing into uncontrolled fury, and I turned toward my companions with my hands upraised in a gesture of peace. I was attacked by the hotter heads, flung to the ground, and blood flowing over my face, they carried me off. The last thing I was in time to see were your eyes, those eyes of a little sorceress-child, of an elf from our forests, which I rediscovered yesterday as I went through my clumsy courtier's maneuvers. And I must tell you that priest or not, I felt as young as I had been then: nothing but a cry of freedom in the face of a living apparition.

You would not believe it, and I myself cannot say how it happened, but that far-off day confirmed my determination to live in Italy. From Ferrara I went to the Studium of Bologna, then to the studia of Pisa and Rome. Afterward, when the vacillating political fortunes of my relatives the counts of Suffolk forced me to stay out of England, I traveled for my education in Germany, France, and the Low Countries, and I sought, ever eager, the rooms of the ambassadors of Italian language, for the opportunity of hearing your name mentioned.

With the assistance of these admirable informants of your courts I followed the little girl in Ferrara as she grew up: I learned of your marriage, of the courtly and poetic tourneys of the Sforza court, and I was unusually pleased to learn that you sided with Rinaldo rather than with Orlando, Rinaldo the man of feeling rather than Orlando the man of action. I learned how, a young bride in Mantua, you directed your court toward music and the reading of poems and Latin works; I knew of your studies and your bold, free speech. You were always a queen, whether you appeared to me as the warrior Bradamante, ancient progenitrix of the Este line, or as Boiardo's Angelica, creature of nature, all levity and enchanting caprice, divine freedom of invention.

As my family's affairs remained unsettled, I returned to live in Rome, and here the recommendations of my king and my kinsfolk opened the doors of the Curia to me. I was ordained, and a short time ago named Monsignor; I worked and still work with the prothonotary and secretary of His Holiness Adriano of Corneto, a man of stern doctrine and great fame, surely known to you.

Rome is the center of your praises; coming there, you could not save yourself from the chorus of gifted men who in the academies and studia speak of you. There is none who would not like to write of your feelings, but they seldom dare. And everyone praised you to the stars, and I, to begin with, when in March of the year 1499 all Italy read the words of veneration dedicated to you by the most illustrious poet of our time, Giovanni Pontano. In his academy in Naples, he was the first who spoke, in unforgettable words, of your intention of raising a statue in Mantua to honor Virgil, a statue designed by the divine Mantegna, to make up for the ill-judged act of the city's governor Carlo Malatesta, who many years ago had had an ancient statue of the poet thrown into the waters of the Mincio, meaning to cure the Mantuan people of their idolatrous worship of that deity. And Pontano never ceased praising your greatheartedness, a royal lady of such tender age, who would restore a supreme poet's glory.

Now I am about to return to the county of Suffolk, to reassert my fealty to King Henry the Seventh, and my kinsfolk will do the same. I leave this evening. Without knowing why, I lied to you, nor do I know if you will now forgive me. I realize that despite myself, I praise you distantly. The timidity of my boldness keeps me behind defenses, and I have also felt, I cannot say why, that it was my duty to give you some account of myself. I have written too many words, and yet I feel uneasy at these secrets I must confess. The first, which I curtly revealed to you at the beginning of the letter, is that of my habit, my condition as a priest; the second contradicts the first, because its nature is the opposite.

I swear that my desire to meet you was innocent. I wanted to see again the magic child of Ferrara to learn what sort of woman she had become, but as I came into your presence, I was gripped so violently by something that your image has overwhelmed me, provoking an incurable paralysis of thought. It is true, all too true, what they say about your person: From you a tempest of ideas explodes, and anyone who visits you heedlessly becomes the target of your infallible archery. How beautiful you were, how quick in your golden robe, almost dancing like the flickering pearls you wore at your ears. I have never seen a woman at once so simple and so insidious, and it was hard for me to tear myself away from your presence to visit the chamber painted by Master Mantegna and capture the sense of family glory, intense and pathetic, that gives life to those walls.

Before my eyes you had unfolded your magic cadence that lets you live at every moment in the center of your days and of the things that concern you. You received me with the greatest courtesy but did not fail to pierce me with your delicate arrows. And I believe I have discovered one of the secrets that make your power of seduction so rare: You are capable of placing your interlocutor, whoever he may be, in the most sensitive point of a world you do not merely inhabit but invent.

Ah, forgive me; I am led to speak, though I should not; I really should not. I could write about you a long ode, or rather a long elegy. A glimmer of prescience makes me suspect this letter is as futile as the words I uttered yesterday in your presence. You must forgive me twice over, for yesterday and for today, and yet I am and shall remain always

your slave
Robert de la Pole
native of England

Mantua, tenth day of August, 1501

I CLOSED THE letter, folding it with care, as if I could feel its language sizzling. I was surprised, irritated, and obscurely caught. I thought of showing the pages to Francesco so that we could then laugh together at the follies of those who came from beyond the mountains and beyond the seas, but I decided not to; it would be better to read them to Elisabetta in our hours of privacy. And first of all, it was clear that I would not answer; it would be impossible to answer. And answer what? I moved into my bedroom and opened a coffer where I kept my personal papers, and thoughtlessly I dropped the letter in a side compartment. After sending for Pirro, I began to dictate to him messages for the various courts, and I became absorbed in a difficult reply to the Valentino, who had suggested a nuptial contract between our Federico and his daughter Louise, born in France, where she was living with her mother, Charlotte d'Albret. These seemed distant matters, since the two were still infants. I evaded the question with vague politeness, but I was impatient and upset.

To escape from such thorny questions, I wrote to our envoy in Venice, Giorgio Brognolo, telling him to buy me twelve ermines for a mantle and crimson satin for the lining. One of the ermines should have the head intact, because I wanted to make a muff with it, which would arouse comment. I imagined the animal, rolled like a drum, its head resting beside the tail; the head would be encrusted with gold, and for the eyes I would seek two rubies, flawless, of a fiery red.

Toward evening, since we had staying with us a most excellent musician, Jacopo di San Secondo, formerly the boast of the Sforza court, there was a concert in my rooms with invitations to ladies and gentlemen, total pleasure for the whole company, and we wished those sounds, those almost divine songs, would never end. At a late hour I was with my women in my rooms again. Ever since the end of June, when the pope had formed a new league with the French, Spanish, and Venetians, Francesco had been restless. Often he would go off for undefined periods of time; he went to inspect the border with Cremona, near San Giovanni in Croce. He said that one of these days those damned Venetians would arrive with flags flying, to set up camp in Mantuan territory.

As I undressed, I was thinking of the thousand twists and turns of politics, ever changing, but then, resolutely, I dispelled all uneasiness. For some unknown reason I stopped at my coffer, with the intention, undeclared but precise, of rereading the unusual letter from the English Robert de la Pole. I restrained myself in time.

My women moved about the room, and I had to be careful; sudden impulses are forbidden us, surrounded as we are by people who can expose us to any suspicion. I reread it in my mind, and I could not tell if it was bold or not. It spoke of things that concerned him and me together, but I was not sure its audacity went beyond the confines of respect. I decided it did not, and reassured, I fell asleep.

THE DAYS that followed were thick with events, arrivals and departures, conjectures, breathtaking prophecies; there was no time for immediate things. I paled at every dispatch from Rome or from Ferrara. Almost gaily Gerolamo Stanga arrived, a gentleman of Francesco's court, with a Venetian paper that reported how the king of France, despite all his public favors shown the Valentino, had privately expressed his wonder that the Este family should be inclined to accept kinship with the Borgias. I observed that there was no great cause for rejoicing, but it was worth remarking how fickle was the protection of these French.

One morning toward the end of August I was in the villa at Porto, with its cool groves and gardens along the lake, and as I enjoyed the breeze in the high, delicate foliage of the woods, I was scolding my daughter Eleonora, who at all costs wanted to hold her little brother, Federico, in her arms, though he was too heavy for a frail girl of eight. She burst into one of her moaning, inconsolable fits of tears that made all of us feel guilty. Turning my head, I immediately saw Pirro Donati at the end of the avenue, coming forward, his expression heralding a secret.

In fact, it was a secret. My brother Alfonso had sent me a trusted messenger, telling me to come as soon as possible to the vicinity of Borgoforte, on the Po, where he would meet me. The curt, very guarded message worried me. With the roar of the wind in my ears, I rode, followed by Pirro and the lady Violante de' Preti, toward the appointed place; the messenger, at top speed, galloped ahead of us. Borgoforte was not far, and we soon sighted a barge, stopping close to the shore. I could make out Alfonso; his thick, youthful crop of brown hair with reddish glints covered his ears. He nodded toward a little boat that was heading in our direction. When we had stepped into it, we were rowed to the flat-bottomed river vessel. I alone was hoisted aboard. I embraced Alfonso, and we tried to joke about our clandestine encounter. I noticed how pale he was, trembling, and I asked him what was wrong.

"My marriage, Isabella," he said in a disheartened voice.

"What? From Rome Cattanei assured us only yesterday that the Borgias now have their eyes on one of the Orsini men."

"She has refused him. She has said that she will either marry me or enter a nunnery."

I was terrified, as one is when the misfortune you believe or want to believe you have eluded then suddenly happens. I could say only "Alfonso!" and I sank down on a pile of ropes.

My brother finally unburdened himself. "Our father has decided. He has always humiliated me. He enjoyed making me the laughingstock of my brothers and of all Ferrara. He has no hesitation in sacrificing me; he has never respected me, and now they have seduced him with the dowry. It's all the dowry, Isabella! The pope will give her a mountain of gold, a hundred thousand ducats, in gold pieces, and the castles of Cento and la Pieve, with their income, and jewels, dresses, chests of silver, carpets, tapestries, and an array of gifts to make a greedy man like our father die of joy. And further, the investiture of Ferrara, in solemn form, for all the descendants of the house of Este. Who could resist such offers? I could; I would not have sold myself. I would never have chosen this wife."

"Her! Her!" I burst out, forgetting all restraint. "With all the talk about her . . ."

Alfonso, distraught, looked at me, studying me from his great height, and he said in a steady, inexpressive voice: "Isabella, say no more. It's best. I would be obliged to defend her even to you. Yesterday, at Belfiore, I signed the contract of my marriage."

"My God!" I cried, wringing my hands. "Lucrezia Borgia will be my sister-in-law. And she will take the place of my mother, a king's daughter."

We felt far removed from the world, on the barge that advanced, driven by the current shuddering under a wind already autumnal.

* * *

FRANCESCO was absent, just when I needed him most. Perhaps it was all to the good, for he might have rejoiced at the humiliation of my brother, an Este. I could find no peace, and the gusts of rain heightened my agitation. All of a sudden a window flew open, and water poured into the room, making my women laugh, Lia and Colonna first of all; the two young girls enjoyed the delight of the unexpected. Summoned by the cries, my gentlemen rushed in, closed the windows, and the girls resumed their usual games. I was in no mood to put up with them and I closed myself in my Grotta, locking the door.

I have always loved living with myself in small, sometimes even minuscule rooms. The whole world knows, or has heard of, my little studies, more precious than those in the palaces of Urbino and Ferrara. The walls, so close that you can touch them by extending your arms, the scant space, the low ceiling seem to enfold one and, thanks to their balanced proportions, do not oppress. Such a room is easy to keep warm in winter, even with just a few braziers, and it is not possible for more than two people to be there; three are an excess. When the whim takes me, I like to stay there alone. The Grotta of Castello was a little room with a barrel vault of inlaid wood, with my emblem of musical rests, and my other emblems appeared on the floor of the room, with sweet gaiety of colors, blue and green on white. That motto *Nec spe nec metu* inspired endless poetical compositions.

At that time, in the Grotta and in the Studiolo above it, I was beginning to collect masterly paintings, antiquities, little marble busts and statues, tiny bronzes, manuscript books or printed volumes I sent to Venice for, ordering them from Aldo Manuzio. I had some beautiful musical instruments, among them the clavichord with silver strings given me by Master Leonardo da Vinci. In the Studiolo there was a world map that fascinated me, and I often examined it with some man of learning or with my women, in turn, ever since, shortly after my wedding, I had followed on that map the course of the Savona seaman who had landed in the West Indies, inhabited by handsome, naked people. At a certain moment I lost myself in the ocean and dreamed of seeing those new lands rise from the waters, impassioned, for I am much drawn to geographies.

They say the world is revealed only in momentary signs; thus in the late, calm hour after the storm, by the light of the torches, I was immersed in an intense meditation as I leaned against the embroidered satin back of my chair. And suddenly I saw before me the image of my English visitor, and I was sorry I had not shown him the Painted Chamber myself, the Hall of the "Trionfi," and my little rooms. To my own surprise, I asked myself, with unfamiliar meekness, who was Robert de la Pole? His family, the counts of Suffolk, were English grandees; his office, of mediocre importance; and that presence stirred something in my memory, something I had already perceived as a signal in his words, which took me back to Ferrara. I breathed deeply and realized that escaping the surveillance of a young governess, someone was running toward the great staircase of the Este palace.

T HE HOLY LITTLE girl descended the shining, snowy marble staircase, which ended in the lapping of shifting gold, the water's ripple. She was dressed in pure white and garlanded with a crown of tiny roses, white with a pink heart, and the air around her was gilded. From the gold of the miniature I saw myself advance with my solemn walk, defending myself against any bewilderment. I questioned myself. Was it right, could it be true, that Iphigenia was to be sacrificed by the decree of her father, Agamemnon, the king? And what did that single omnipotent syllable mean? I knew the answer, for a king's blood flowed in my veins. I repeated the words spoken to me by King Ferrante of Aragón in Naples: "Remember, woman's obedience is a royal virtue, and observe it in my daughter Eleonora." My reply burst out: "We are grateful to our mother, and to our father in his house." My grandfather's reply came then, fiercely joking: "Remember, Isabella, that you are allowed to answer me like that only because you are my granddaughter, the granddaughter of a king." His pallor, the cruel king's, looked yellow in that day of Neapolitan sunshine. But defying him, I had encouraged my grandfather's laughter, and I decided at that moment that I would be on the side of the mighty when they are capable of laughing; with them a woman, too, can combat.

Mentally I ratified that decision as I gradually left behind me the steps of the great staircase and between the slender columns of the balustrade observed the Court of Honor, connected to the tall Este palace. I heard the echo, now retreating, now close, of the young voice of Dionisia, who cried, "Isabella! Isabella, child, where are you?" I stood still. There was no longer any place for Iphigenia; the holy girl again sought refuge in the pages of the book of the Trojan War, the illustrations all with gold backgrounds, kept in my mother's room, where often I cautiously leafed through it.

It was an opaque time of day; people were bent on their private, everyday concerns, many in the kitchens of their houses. I re-

sumed descending the stairs, careful not to catch my long little
dress, and I almost sniffed the air to overhear some of the stories
that sprang up and spread between the courtyard and palace.
Soldiers and archers on guard were stationed at the different
entrances and outside the great arch that framed the cathedral
portal opposite, decorated with sculptures depicting the months,
so ancient and bizarre that they made me clap my hands in delight.
That morning, outside the arch, there was fog, thicker close to
the ground, and it seemed the people of Ferrara were walking
with a lunatic step, raised from the earth.

A sudden flash of that curiosity that I then knew only through
announcements of happiness calls me to new presences. Something has happened. Outside the arch a shouting comes forward,
clotted around shriller cries, the usual sound of young voices
gathered together. I rush forward; I am so eager to see that my
chest almost seems to ache. I grasp with my hand, one after the
other, the little marble columns, and looking around, I descend
farther, to the foot of the stairs; but I am forced to stop because
immediately, stepping forward from the walls, the ducal guards
occupy the entrance from left and right and cross their lances,
the tips pointed at the ground. Luckily the archers are impassive;
they pretend not to notice my presence; only the youngest glances
at me for an instant, with an absent smile of complicity. I stiffen,
without moving. Outside, the voices are near, and the archers
close their ranks defensively. In the triangles formed by the lances
and by the hems of their stiff capes, I frame the space between
the palace and cathedral.

I recognize them at once. The scholars of the studium pass in
slow procession, clashing with others coming from the opposite
direction, and brawling roughly, but in jest. All are making noise
in languages of different cadence: Italian tongue or foreign, gut-
tural German, crackling French, resonant Flemish. At one moment, in the rosy light, the form of a four-legged animal stands
out, its long, twitching ears awkwardly supporting a hat like the
rector of the studium's, a live ass, decked in red velvet, and before
him the students bow, now running forward, now popping from
the fog and going back into it a moment later. I am very alert.

"My lord Cipriotto!"

"Most Excellent Rector Cipriotto!"

Thus the scholars hail our new rector. The ass, inspired by
heaven knows what nervous impatience, brays loudly, and the
young men roll on the ground, in ridiculous somersaults, redoubling the confusion.

There has been talk at court of this public opposition to a certain Gasparino of Cyprus, elected rector by a majority, but much disliked by the minority, which supported a Bolognese, I have no idea why. But now the Cypriot's enemies chant clownish praises and declare that the venerated jackass has expressed his lofty opinion, brilliant in its intelligence and erudition. Softly, so the guards will not hear me, I laugh at the teetering, asinine trappings; but the cries change tone, and in the distance the hooves of the podestà's cavalry resound.

Intermittently I see the advance and retreat of the ass, jostled by blows and shoves. I am not afraid; it is a game, violent though it may be. But the clatter of arms is no longer a game. I draw back just a little, remaining alert. The soldiers arrive, and then the podestà in person; the curtain of shouts rises louder, veined with flashes of terror. At that moment I hear a name spread:

"Robert! Robert!"

"Robert is wounded!"

"The Englishman is hurt!"

"Help, help!"

There is a swaying of the ducal guards at the entrance arch, and then I discern him, I see him: a blond youth, his face bloodstained, carried aloft by his comrades. The student looks in my direction, with such intensity that I remain inert. His comrades drag him away.

Totally at a loss, I huddle close to the railing; a palace guard, appearing suddenly from nowhere, takes my hand with brusque kindness and says to me in an angry voice something I cannot grasp because in the meanwhile, outside, there is an intense clamor, and squads of armed soldiers rush into the courtyard, heading for the entrance. To my great annoyance the guard dares pick me up in his arms, but my protest goes unheard; it remains a whine. Kicking and yelping—I seem slight, but I am sturdy, as my mother says often with charming wonder—I free myself and am off, up the stair, though I stop at the first landing. I cling to a column of the railing and defy the guard with an imperative look. They leave me there, in a fury, warning me that they will go and inform people of the court. Alone against them all, I realize that for the first time I had seen blood spurt from a man's face because of another man's act. I am caught in the chill wonder of my discovery, and someone bends over me and calls me by name: "Lady Isabella. What are you doing here?"

"I saw, I saw," I stammer. "I saw everything."

"Why, this child is frightened! Lady Isabella, do you know me?"

I recover my princess's manners and smile at him. How could I have failed to recognize Pico della Mirandola, scholar of our studium and already so renowned?

I PUT my hand on his thin, bony wrist, defined by the blue linen sleeve of his pleated tunic. He lowered his arm to support me better. His every action was extraordinarily precise, and his every action seemed invented at that moment, as was his every thought, Battista Guarino would have said, his master and friend. Count Giovanni Pico della Mirandola was our pride, and long after his stay there, his memory lasted in the city of Ferrara during his peregrinations and his announcements of other peregrinations, broader in every sense. Respected by all as a miracle of learning, he had free entry at court, and even the least scholarly loved him, for he was the son of the signora Giulia, aunt of Matteo Maria Boiardo, our favorite gentleman as well as our first poet. In the young Pico there was, almost visible, the knowledge of every branch of learning, including religion and its mystery, and that knowledge was wed to an intellect splendidly restless in its goals and desires, as even I, a child of eight, could sense. With him a lucid world opened before me, where miracles were always about to happen. I listened to him, gaping, and even if I did not fully understand the things he was saying, it seemed to me unquestionable that he held the key to all knowledge. My mother and my master Jacopo Gallino tried to explain his words to me; in my memory Giovanni Pico occupies a place apart; he is an astral point.

With that flaunted escort, through passages and rooms crowded with handsome, sober people, I walked toward the great hall.

"I will accompany you to the duchess Eleonora," Pico said courteously. "Are you not afraid of a scolding? They will tell you that you were imprudent to remain there on the staircase of the Court of Honor. It is too close to the street, and the scholars sometimes brawl roughly. What made you venture that far?"

A face, white, streaked with blood, came back into my mind.

"I wanted to see," I replied.

Signor Pico stopped and, studying my face, added: "You have eyes made to see far; but you are a woman, and it may be hard for you."

"I want to see everything. And I will."

He was almost speechless. "I am not even sure I would wish that for you. Let us go now."

We had gone only a few steps when we encountered Dionisia,

my lady-in-waiting. As soon as she glimpsed my companion, she heaved a great sigh; she was a quick woman, aware of each person's moods. She asked me no questions, thanked Signor Pico, and led me to my room. In the taciturn presence of my sister Beatrice, curled up on the rug, she had me dressed and coiffed rapidly, and when I was ready, we went downstairs. On meeting my court friends, I pretended not to notice them, so as to avoid interrogation; I headed straight for my mother.

Courtiers of every rank, men at arms, councillors, officials of the chancellery, lecturers from the studium, noble ladies, and maids filled the rooms where I, alone among the children of the Este house, entered, aware of the general view of me as an uncommon individual, intelligent beyond my years. I had no doubt about this; advancing without any hesitation, I felt a confidence in my whole being, as if I were exercising a generally recognized right. I confess, I scorned my sister, Beatrice, one year my junior, who was not allowed at court because she would not have borne the constant coming and going of people and the talk of the wise or the indifferent, and she was defined as a little girl by the tears of boredom and of fear she could not repress when, on rare occasions, she appeared among the adults.

BEFORE me, immediately, some figures become distinct: Guarino, honored by all, surrounded by the studium masters, including Pellegrino Prisciano, astronomer-geographer and the court astrologer, devoted friend of all, pleased with himself. My mother, adorned with silver and pearls, gracious, yet always tinged by a hint of anxiety peculiar to her Neapolitan temperament, exceeds in beauty and dignity all the other women present, and her pathetic tone, which distinguishes her, inspires a strange tenderness in every heart. I, her favorite daughter, have made them dress me in my pink robe hemmed with gold-embroidered black velvet, with my hair undone according to the privilege granted women of royal blood. The ladies watch, seated on stools and benches with backs of dark velvet; the men are standing. For me the dais supporting the ducal seat is reserved, facing the men of letters and science. All are ready. My mother bends briefly to kiss my forehead, and I utter my little, lighthearted laugh that she likes so.

"I saw . . ." I begin to tell her, eagerly.

She motions me to be silent and turns to Signor Pico della Mirandola, standing before her with bared head, and in that accent of hers, half Ferrarese and half Neapolitan, which is music to my ears, she says: "Signor Pico, I suggest we take as the subject of our discussion something that happened today—just a little while ago, in fact. We have had a report on the exploits of our scholars: jests, rebellion, turmoil. You have been at the Studium of Padua, and you know what happens in the universities elsewhere, in Florence, Bologna, even Paris. I do not ask you to judge your companions, but to seek, with me, the reason for their intemperance. What do they want? In our studium are there not excellent lecturers for every branch of knowledge? The duke Ercole spares no expense to bring them from all of Italy, all of Europe. The fame of such masters has peopled Ferrara with young men who desire to learn. The new rector, Gasparino of Cyprus, elected by general assent, is a proper man, highly learned in jurisprudence. For what reason, then, is he opposed and even mocked in the ignoble guise of an ass?"

I am mortified for a moment because that very ass afforded me such amusement, and indeed, I had planned to tell my mother how comical it was and how its braying had inspired the scholars' jesting. But Signor Pico is preparing to speak.

"Your Ladyship," he says, "has come straight to the point, with her usual acumen. You are right—the Cypriot is not a cause, but rather a pretext. The true cause of these quarrels, which do not openly refer to matters of study, is always the same, not present in the mind of the young but at work in their spirit. Can you not perceive it, almost palpably? The young are driven by an anxiety of the soul, which they translate into their physical, mocking actions. But at heart they are discontent; they would like to think for themselves and for a different world. And to be sure, philosophy, poetry, and science open new ways to achieve the liberation of the spirit."

"For as long as I have lived"—Signor Ludovico Carbone, courtier and man of learning, speaks up in his smug and educated voice—"I have heard it said that the world is changing, and the causes and the effects are always the same. For centuries we have been living under the threat of the Turkish scimitar; various times the end of Christianity has been predicted, and here we are, discussing it. I suspect that the only thing conspiring against us is the fear of conspiracies."

Pellegrino Prisciano replies at length, expounding the meaning of his vague divinations, which have prophesied a great rotation of intersecting astral bodies. "The history of every man depends on fortune," he says, as he launches into one of his cloudy, flattering horoscopes, which have made him a favorite with women. Only

Master Battista Guarino succeeds in stopping him and giving the floor again to the young speaker who had been interrupted.

"To know Latin, to know Greek." Pico resumes in a tone both interrogatory and enlightened. "The supreme scholars of the past, men like Master Guarino Guarini, the great father of our Battista, both of them educators without peer, have brought the light of Greek knowledge into our understanding of the world and have changed the direction of the latest studies. But this is not enough; there is so much to be learned in books we do not read, in Hebrew, Arabic, Persian. The truth is hidden within many languages, and beyond languages, beyond symbols. The Bible itself, among the holy texts, contains all the mysteries of existence, but its authors wrote it in cipher. They offer veiled, dim images of all truths. We have had enough of those scholars who would count the hairs in Homer's beard; we want, and the young want—perhaps not clearly—to penetrate and discuss the most profound reasons of human and divine life."

I think, as this speech is repeated now in my mind, that unconsciously I am adding to it some detail read later in Pico's works, after this radiance of knowledge was suddenly extinguished. Its solar apparition had moved the world, and people attributed his death to the many lives that had consumed his brain. My image of Pico is a man of twenty, when the power of his genius did not threaten to overwhelm his existence.

With the greatest respect, after a pause, Pico asks permission to continue, and it is granted.

"Today," he says, "in the light of new meditations we must revise the method of gaining that knowledge from which new thought will be born. Study must be a common process between master and student, and not a collection of cold declarations to be handed down. Indeed, the good master must be alert and discover in which direction the young are directing their steps. We must never be afraid of the discoveries that await us. Man is all, because he can be all: animal, stone, and also angel. Everything has its center in him, and he animates and advances the history of creation."

AS PICO raised his head, shaking his brown hair, long over his slender nape, he seemed carried away by what he had been saying and as if stirred by an inner prophetic ardor I could not recapture. At that time the more hidden sense of his lesson escaped me, in its unequaled purity and vigor, but I felt myself in unison with him and as if invigorated. The future would allow me all discoveries; I did not distinguish the strength of physical life from the strength of the mind; if the two forces were to proceed equally, could not I, too, one day speak with the accents of a prophet? I looked at my mother, and she frowned; that thrilling speech gave her no joy; she had listened to it absently, as something prevented her from going beyond the words. Looking up from below, I saw her sigh, and I noticed her long, uneasy hand, covered with rings with red gems, corals, rubies, spinels, protective against evil influences.

At a sign of that hand glittering with fires, Matteo Maria Boiardo climbed onto the platform opposite us, to entertain us with the reading of some passages from his *Orlando Innamorato*. I have always been enchanted by French chivalric stories peopled with figures in enameled colors; many volumes of these tales were in the Este library, and others exist, also numerous and very beautiful, in the library of the Gonzagas, and there are some in my private collection in the Grotta, beginning with my *Amadís*, read and reread and the *Merlin* and on to the song of Fierabras. The news that Matteo Maria Boiardo was writing for our court an entirely new chivalric poem had made everyone rejoice; even my father, stern as he was, loved so greatly the poet that he had printed, at his own expense, the first cantos of the work, and there was no one who was not made ecstatic by the silvery tone of those verses. Tall and handsome, our poet began reciting in cadenced voice the octaves of the flowers of love:

> *Di rose e di viole e di ogni fiore*
> *costor ch'io dico, avean canestri in mano,*
> *e standosi con gioia e con amore,*
> *giunse tra loro il sir di Montalbano . . .*
> *Tutti a Rinaldo si aventarno addosso:*
> *chi getta rose, chi getta viole,*
> *chi gigli e chi giacinti a più non posso.*

Much of this poem I understood; at that age I had already seen paintings that depicted love; I was enchanted by the frescoes in the great room of Schifanoia, where Mars and Venus lay in a bed whose coverlets were carved in living marble. But in the *Orlando* of Count Boiardo there was such a burst of air that I was choosing Rinaldo as my champion, and for him the leaves and flowers thrown by the damsels turned to fire.

From the back of the room an eager voice was heard: "I would like to be in that meadow. . . ."

A discreet laughter, not too loud, ran beneath the vaulted ceiling. Even the lips of Pico della Mirandola curled in a smile. And why should he not smile, the friend closest to the dewy springtimes of Politian?

From the little Iphigenia and her vivid games inspired by the miniatures, I passed effortlessly to the concrete life of the adults, barely sensed. In the *Orlando Innamorato* there were living women, ardent, not resembling, as in French romances, the emblematic ladies of the knights. Most of all, I was drawn to Angelica, adventurous and without fear:

> . . . *dal vento è via portata*
> *sopra a un demonio che ha la faccia nera.*

She really resembled no one else, this Angelica, and I was pleased that Robert de la Pole, the bizarre Englishman, of the house of Suffolk, had placed her beside the Este heroine Bradamante in a comparison subtly hinting at an Isabella who, alone, in her Grotta, was now close to falling asleep.

BUT on the contrary, it is impossible to sleep, amid the din of Ferrara's ducal trumpets and bugles, which rattle the panes of the great windows in their leaden grilles. The father is announced, that Agamemnon who embodies every power: the duke Ercole of Este. It is another evening of joy in Ferrara; everyone speaks without restraint, in excited, festive voices. Dionisia has dressed me in white tabby edged in blue, and on my brow a diamond, set in gold, flashes when I shake my head. My sister Beatrice, holding the hand of the governess, is dressed in crimson satin with a bodice of black velvet. Her dress has been made, I believe, from an old one, and its color is too rich and gleaming for her olive skin. And again the silver trumpets and bugles, cadenced by the drums, and the shrilled skirl of pipers' notes make us start.

"Ercole! Ercole!"

"Diamante! Diamante!"

They applauded together—courtiers, ladies, pages, guards—some looking out of the windows over the narrow courtyard of the castle, some on the white staircase, stretching down toward the well. The biting air of a still-unsettled spring laves merry faces; the flames of the torches, stirred by the wind, writhe in a play of shadows and lights.

My father is returning from a visit to the fortifications along the Po. Fatigue, dust, mud, a constant tendency to foresee the worst for the hostile future, the best for the defense. He dismounts, limber but slow, supported by his squires. My mother, flouting the court rituals of welcome, runs down the steps and lightly goes to him, her fragile form almost linear; she falls on his breast, and they embrace. His embraces in armor seem guided by a slowed, clumsy rhythm; together they climb up to the great hall. Eleonora's beautiful, agitated face excludes anyone else, and the haggard face of the duke of Ferrara is bright with the joy of being home.

A stir of people moving in front of me hides the pair from my sight. I cannot glimpse them, and yet, holding myself erect, I reach the elbow of those surrounding me. With regal patience I restrain impetuosity; I wait. After a little while the people separate; my parents are near, nearer to me than I thought, and finally I reach them, without running. Eleonora is agitated. My father, at a long bench, assisted by his pages, is taking off the light cuirass; he breathes from the depth of his chest, throws his gauntlets aside, and stretches his legs one by one so that they can unbuckle his greaves. My mother again comes to embrace him and covers him with words of emotion, insistent, impassioned. Ercole looks at her; his face is kindly but sealed in a calm, impassive indifference. He is weary, that is it. She does not realize that he is weary and wants nothing; she does not understand that nothing on earth would induce him to accept her invitation to emerge from himself. She goes on pestering him. The war greatly frightens her; today she has had a warning, one of her chamber ladies, Caterina, has died, unable to bear the grief at the loss of her husband.

"How tender and vital," my mother says, "is the love we women feel for our husbands when they are far away, in danger; every horseman who gallops into the courtyard makes us tremble."

My father's voice, full and determined, interrupts her. "You are not a woman to tremble, Eleonora. King Ferrante schooled you too well."

But my mother does not take it all in. She weeps; my God, she is weeping. In fact, her husband politely thrusts her away, his arms extended, and he looks around the room. He sees me and calls me. I run to him, stopping a few paces from him, struck by an idea: What if he also rejected me, with extended arms? Instead, the duke laughs. He laughs, brightens (flattered by my respectful behavior? or pleased, and by what?); the furrows of his face relax, one by one.

"Isabella, come closer!"

I approach, and he takes me in his arms, lifts me from the ground, holding me to his face, and kisses me. I lack the courage to turn toward my mother, who has remained behind me. Then I am set down again; my father decides to speak to me.

"Rejoice, Isabella. Tomorrow you will make the acquaintance of your betrothed, the son of the marchese of Mantua, Francesco Gonzaga. This is a solemn visit, with an escort of gentlemen and an ambassador. We must prepare a fine hunting party. This is your first test as a woman, and I hardly need encourage you to behave as only you can."

I take a step backwards and make a stiff bow, overwhelmed with joy and with an indefinable anxiety. My mother is still to one side, as if neglected, with her domestic suffering and her conjugal passion unconsoled, incapable even of smiling at me. Nobody gives her any thought; the duke Ercole speaks with a court official; his hand is resting on my head and is heavy.

"VENICE the Magnificent!"

I cried out, and the cry was colored by tones of jest. And yet I did not mean to joke. Far from it. I turned to the other girls, my companions, who were catching their breath after all those stairs. "Thirty-six flights!" announced Emilia Pio, who had counted them, and behind her Margherita Cantelma, overconciliatory, remarked that it was not all that many after all. From beneath the low vault appeared the heads of Elisabetta and the prothonotary Sigismondo, who was about to say something but then looked around and kept his words to himself. Few things can be compared with that view, from a fixed spot as if from a focal center, of a breathing, grandly harmonious creation, self-aware to the point of folly: Venice. It seemed to me I was physically small, tiny; on the high loggia of the solitary campanile rising before the basilica, I observed how my companions constantly changed position to recognize or to discover, to feel the excitement of the painted palaces, the marble stairs, the churches huddled on the islands, the looming hauteur of the swollen domes, the jagged arcades of San Marco, and the incomparable water of the lagoon, with its shifting glints and sumptuous threats.

I recalled myself to my own presence. I, I alone could sustain such a wealth of inventions, and I alone could dare a rebellion.

The first time I had been here, nine years before, on a formal visit, Francesco then was Captain General of the Venetian troops, and I had had to submit to so many honors and celebrations that I was unbearably oppressed by them. Today I was here privately. For years a yearning for the city had remained in me, a desire to see it intimately, but up here, encased in the cold, thin air of March, I envied the joy of my companions absolutely unaware of my torment. It was an old torment, and I had no need to find it was contained in the very name of the Most Serene Republic of Venice. Time and again in the depths of my mind I had felt it nip at me. And since the same vaunted freedom that the republic bestowed even on fugitives should be extended also to me, a freedom tinged with provocation, I decided that I, too, would enjoy it. And so after my brother Alfonso's marriage to the Borgia woman, a little group of four noblewomen, friends, had set out from Ferrara for Venice; the only man was the prothonotary Sigismondo Gonzaga, my brother-in-law. At that challenge something in me rose up: challenge and admiration, both highly partisan. It was best that no one suspect them.

These Venetians had paid me some quite charming visits, and we had taken care to receive them, always prepared and dressed with studied simplicity, happily alert to every discourse. Emboldened by infinite compliments and by the prince's expressions of regret that I had come so informally, I had sent him word that I would like to go and pay him homage in his private chambers. But this Leonardo Loredan, only recently named Doge, a big old man, gaunt, touchy beyond words, sent me assurance that, no matter what, he would receive me with due pomp in the Council. I replied at once that I had not brought garments suitable for such a ceremony, and I sent promptly to the palace Alessandro and Benedetto Capilupi, our envoys, with a great load of compliments. I was tempted to be flattered by the Doge's insistence on honoring me in public, but something told me to distrust him. The fact was that the sly Doge had refused to meet me in private, having been duly informed that I was traveling incognita and without political powers. I even had the suspicion that he wanted to elicit from me in the presence of the whole Grand Council an act of submission to the republic that would have included Francesco and our government. It was no accident that this was the same Grand Council that a few years earlier had voted against Francesco, relieving him of his command as Captain General. Then, from the palace, I received gifts of candlesticks and candles, marzipan, sweets and syrups; the treasure of San Marco was opened for me, the ducal armory, the great audience hall. Flat two-oared boats were ready at our bidding at the door of Palazzo Trevisan. And so, through courtesy and attentions, the Doge Loredan kept himself to himself.

The gusts of air encouraged movement, up on that tower, so I also began to stir myself, moving from one arch to the next, so restless that Elisabetta asked me if I felt in a low mood. I had the strength to reply with a laugh that the height of the campanile would not have allowed it, and at that moment two Venetian gentlemen appeared from the stairs and came to kiss my hand. Delighted, my women friends rang peals of celebration; Venice was the first of cities. Sunday, the gentlemen said, was the day of Palms, and the prince would walk in solemn procession in Piazza San Marco. Elisabetta declared that at all costs she wanted to see the ceremony, and I was forced to agree, not without remarking that I would pay it no heed since I had already seen the procession on another occasion when the Doge was Agostino Barbarigo. No one remarked on my tone; I am accustomed to simulate when it is necessary, so as not to spoil the fun of the others and, above all, to salve my sense of decorum. But I could refuse Elisabetta nothing. It was cold, and we quickly went down the endless stairs.

We walked to the Columns, where our boat was awaiting us, and when we set our eyes on the white-and-pink ducal palace with its window tracery, I asked myself once again how it was possible with such colors and such an absurd design—the full surfaces above and the voids of the loggias below—to assert such proud, regal majesty. And in the basin of San Marco, after watching the traffic of every kind of ship, masts and sails and prows bedecked and gilded, we felt overpowered by the amazement inspired by things perfectly fashioned.

I had to reduce everything to reason, and in a tone of brilliant satiety I declared aloud: "Venice is a city without paragon, but for people like us it is enough to see such magnificence once. Twice is too much."

I RECOGNIZED no grace in the young novice at the clavichord, or in her companion standing beside her, waiting to sing, both dressed in gray habits, stiffly ironed, buttoned to the chin; and the white line edging the high collar hinted in vain at a liveliness more in keeping with their eighteen years. Their hair was drawn back so tightly and wound into thick braids tied with black strings that it did not even seem blond, and yet the girls were blond, of different coloring, and perhaps beautiful.

An irked compassion soured in me, and I was annoyed at having accepted the invitation of the nuns of the Convent of the Virgins, one of the most illustrious in Venice, celebrated for its female musicians. We had to break off our vague, unescorted wandering through the triumphant city, collecting surprises that, especially in the last part, after the Rialto and its docks thick with cries and goods, and the narrow streets of the Mercerie bright with odd, colorful crowds, had made us tense from almost too many emotions. The perfumes of the bazaars of the East mingling with the smell of the damp woolen cloth (it had rained in brief showers) of the seamen's heavy coats went strangely to my head; for the first time in my life I perceived the odor of strangers walking shoulder to shoulder with us, a singular irritation, mixed with a pungent headiness, as I thought of all the stories passing close to me, seeming to touch me, or rather jolt me, with successive swipes of their tails.

We had arrived at the proper time, a bit early, received with bows and every show of welcome from those poor good nuns; and we were awaiting the abbess, who had to conclude certain votive prayers of hers in the chapel. Seated near me, Elisabetta was savoring a cake encrusted with bits of pink sugar, the kind that is made, with the same recipe, in every convent in the world. Alert and amused, she examined those figures, indistinguishable, as they were all gray, and yet enlivened by a secret fire like the performers of a new drama. She would notice everything; she would save her story and then comment on it with me and enrich it with meaning, perhaps with imagined significance. How we liked this game! I, rational by nature, had never imagined what such a meeting of moods between two women could mean. My mother had been my mother, and that was all there was to it. My sister, Beatrice, first suspicious and mistrustful, later had been so busy proving herself capable of ruling everyone at every moment that she could never pause for talk. Who knows? If she had lived, if we had both continued growing, even at a distance . . .

As I rapidly linked thoughts together, I was grazed by different worries to be kept at bay. I continued looking at the serene Elisabetta, always ready to investigate with the same enigmatic dignity, resolute in her personal defenses. No matter how enigmatic she might choose to be, her secret was part of that beauty that all admired without deciphering.

I observed Emilia Pio, quick to reply in great outbursts, critical by habit and by habit curious, and Margherita Cantelma, marchesa of Cotrone, her small head covered with witty curls, and her merry temperament always devout, dedicated to me. In one voice we said that we had never enjoyed ourselves so much as in those March days spent in Venice, we four women on our own. And how easily we had shared the procurator Trevisan's hospitable little palace with its rooms of comfortable size, where the flickering glints of the intersecting canals were reflected on the ceilings whenever the sun struck the surface of the water. Nor had it been a trifling decision not to bring splendid dresses for appearance at festivities but to dress rapidly in fine wool or taffeta without flounces, without borders, without embroidery, adorned only with some jewel, delicately fashioned, though of no great value. We felt like girls again, almost children, except that our modesty had a sly quality and made us all the more enticing.

Elisabetta reminded me of Francesco, and at times I would start, catching her resemblance to her brother in a fleeting gesture, if it could be called a resemblance. Her long, dreaming face, just as in the Raffaello portrait, with no mobility to alter the set of the features, hardly echoed Francesco's face, aglow, radiant with manliness, constantly ready to change immediate expressions. In that hall with its high white ceiling the thought of Francesco entered the new geometry of space and expanded it, filled it with warmth. "Francesco," I repeated to myself, calling him as a shield, as a protection he gave me just with the magnetism of his name. Who was not aware of my love for him? And yet Elisabetta had never asked me those half questions that prompt secret confidences, nor had I asked her about her husband, Guidobaldo. But Francesco was one of those men who reveal themselves at first sight, and I accepted his virility as a homage due me, but with the clear knowledge that in husbands something very delicate exists and must be safeguarded, and only a wife can perform this office for him and for herself.

In a confused way I had sensed this even before my wedding, in my adolescence at the time of his visit to Ferrara, a year before we were married. I was in my bedchamber, ill from the cold, as we often are in our icy residences, especially during childhood. May that year proved very harsh, and I insisted on enfolding myself in a charming flutter of layered veils. Francesco appeared to me tawny and handsome, in his eighteenth year, and with an ineffably victorious authority. We played some games, I cannot remember which, perhaps *scartino*, with such gaiety that at a certain point I fell onto the bed, exhausted from laughing. And suddenly he was upon me as we joked together, not exactly childishly. He was happy; I, excited, and instinctively, on the defensive, until my mother, Eleonora, caught us and, with reproachful but indulgent tact, came to separate us. I did not even dare raise my eyes to her.

I could not explain to myself why Francesco no longer wanted to play but stood grimly looking out of the window or why his ill humor lasted until his departure. It is not that I knew then the rites and rules of amorous matters; I did not yet know what in the spirit corresponded to the prompting of the senses. Ten years of marriage have taught me no small amount on this subject, so decisive in conjugal life. And yet we have to bear it. The only thing I have learned is this: To say no or yes, when and how is something no one can teach; at times you err in one direction or the other; the reality, in this matter, is below or apart from reason.

Neither with Elisabetta, my elected sister, nor with other women companions or chambermaids did I ever discuss such things, which, in some people's opinion, are a part of female policy. Little by little, on my own, I determined that there is a total difference between the heavy, bold talk sometimes heard in court on questions of love and the way these affect ourselves. But how to curb the men who visit us, especially when they are our brothers, or famous poets, or men of great renown and high rank? And what can we do with our husbands, who at night enjoy murmuring to us words of extreme, lascivious intimacy about their own affairs and those of others? Many men believe that we women have only to marry and we lose any right to delicacy, and this loss coarsens us and makes us more like them. At the same time they deplore female boldness and indeed are outraged if some thoughtless woman assumes free manners and broaches licentious subjects. Truly we have to walk a taut rope like some acrobat.

In the white hall of the convent the girl musicians were aligned on either side of the little organ. Finally the abbess introduced herself, bowing, and the girls began to play and sing very diligently, but without personal expression, apparently forbidden by the German musician who was their instructor. Paying no heed to anyone, triumphantly, Francesco remained present in the hall with a vibration of such joyous ardor that it warmed me. The image came from afar, the echo of a sound of pipes and trumpets, a parade accompanied by the beat of drums. He was the victor of the Battle of the Taro at Fornovo, the great war exploit of our century, according to poets and astrologers. Captain General of the Venetians, summoned to battle, Francesco had defeated the king of France, the first foreign king who had ventured to cross the Alps in our time, Charles the Eighth, the repentant king. "Fornovo! Fornovo!"—that trumpet blast had also been my glorification as woman, as new wife, the new Gonzaga, the new marchesana. Even the duties, the so-called duties of a wife, so complex in their implications, became clear in the attentions necessary to mend a spirit lacerated by the cruelty necessary to war. At least this was my illusion.

Little time was granted me to enjoy that anthem of joy. Soon everything was tainted: The great victory that had driven the French back beyond the mountains had become suspect; Fornovo was deemed a half victory. As proof they said that Charles the Eighth of France felt so little defeated that he was preparing a new invasion. For their part, the Venetians, circumspect, indeed suspicious, investigated, distrusted Francesco; they looked with disapproval on the liberation without ransom of a great knight, the Bastard of Bourbon, our prisoner of war. It emerged that Francesco, in the field to stop the Slav mercenaries, looters of the royal treasury, had not troubled to pursue and capture the king; insistently the word "traitor" circulated. Francesco, furthermore, had not taken the accusations well; he could defend himself only by blurting out contumely and a swollen self-praise that did him no good; he chose the wrong language, dismissing my logic and mortifying my courage.

I NOTICE that the organ accompanied by the bass viol is intoning a laud, in strophes, with a beautiful opening tinged by sacred melancholy. The girl, standing, with a voice at once pure and carnal, of very rare quality, delivers the verse "*O Maria divina stella.*" And Elisabetta looks up into the air, her head bent slightly to her left shoulder, again reminding me of her resemblance to Francesco. This is how my husband used to look up at our initials, *F* and *IS*, running over the walls of our chamber. But that evening the light is faint, and I am alone in the silent, intense waiting. And someone knocks at my door and opens it.

"Finally you are here," I say. "Finally you have come back from Venice. Speak. Tell me."

I see Francesco stop in the deepest shadows of the room, avoiding the faint light of the lamps. He makes a gesture to keep me at a distance. He is dressed in black, a penitent's habit. My God, what is he playing at?

"Give me the volume of the *Lives of the Holy Fathers*," he says to me.

But what is going on? He answers me, maintaining his penitent's tone: "I have made a vow to the Madonna of Loreto to wear this sackcloth and this slave's collar until I am granted the grace of being recognized innocent."

He actually had on a slave collar, a circle of iron with a heavy ring where a chain could be attached. So the sentence had been decreed.

"The Venetians have obliterated my name; I am no longer Captain General of their army; they have erased the name of the victor of Fornovo, of the first warrior of Italy. The full Grand Council approved this infamy: two hundred votes against five. I have only five friends left in Venice."

I was felled. How had all this happened, from one moment to the next, when our ambassadors were still writing us words of confidence, insisting that Francesco should come to Venice and present himself in person? No one had foreseen this immediate and cruel conclusion, which seemed to allow no further hope.

"And what did you say in your defense? Did you rebel? Did you try to convince them?"

Francesco hung his head, humiliated.

"They did not even allow me to explain myself. They would not receive me in the Council. They left me in the antechamber," he said softly, without raising his eyes. "Give me the *Lives of the Holy Fathers*, please." He took the book and went out, not turning his head.

Thick gusts of thoughts stirred in my mind. With horror I saw the head of the count of Carmagnola roll over the platform of the executioner. The charge of treason seared me. And at that very moment from the next room the gurgle of an infant's voice was heard. I looked in at the door; Eleonora, my little girl of three, was sitting up in her crib. As soon as I approached, she turned to me and began one of those childish speeches without sense, or almost, mingled with calls, but she was not calling me, she was calling her father. My daughter and the other children that would surely be born to me, I thought bitterly, would have a declared traitor for a father, and not a great and upright warrior.

Though I was not her adored father, Eleonora was comforted by my presence, and she tried to pull herself up. I took her in my arms, then stopped at a mirror framed in silver, the most precious piece of all my furniture. I did not look at the silver leaves of the frame. I looked at that young woman reflected in the shining glass with her child in her arms, both woman and child weak but invested with sacred rights. Stiffening instinctively, I saw in the depths of that lucent slab the Grand Council of the Venetians, with the enthroned prince dressed in gold, the horned ducal hat on his head, and they were staring at me.

My voice rose, in a spirited and persuasive tone: "Most serene prince, most excellent senators, I am here to bear witness to the love and faith that we Gonzagas feel toward the Signoria of Venice. My husband is innocent of every charge; he is not guilty of even harboring thoughts hostile to the republic, and he would be here himself if he were not ill. To those of you who doubt this, I have come in person to offer myself and my daughter as hostages, thus to guarantee the devotion and fidelity of the marquis of Mantua. We entrust ourselves to you; we have the right not to be dishonored."

I hold out my arms, and then I come to, with a jerk; nuns and girls turn. My sister-in-law Elisabetta, Emilia Pio, and the marchesa of Cotrone observe me, without moving; they understand something, no matter what. I pretend to shift my position on the hard wooden seat, with no softening cushion, and I glide in the wake of the music. It is a noble motet of Loyset Compère; the supple soprano voices, interwoven, sing "Crux Triumphans."

WE WHO HOLD principalities have networks of kinship, and woe to him who has not. Sometimes the alliance among princes is more durable and binding than any signed treaty, since it is an expression of persons more than of peoples, who often betray. But they must act covertly. This has always been my way, and so it was with the Borgias and especially with the duke Valentino. What cold wrath seized me when some observers expressed surprise at our negotiations for the marriage of Federico with the daughter of the Borgia duke. The populace thinks little. We did not know where the might of that pope's son would strike next, and it seemed that everything had been promised him by Fortune. We knew all too well, however, the ferocity of his vengeance. The darkest suspicion was that the duke Valentino's offers were intended to allay our suspicions while he studied an invasion of our lands. But we had to play this game, perhaps with deceit, and keep our own counsel; this was the only way we could protect ourselves.

At the beginning of carnival I sent him the famous masks that became the talk of all Italy; in our city they invent very beautiful ones. I took care to have it said that this was a gesture of carnival courtesy and that I would send some to other people of rank if they were to ask me. But wait a moment. Carried away by my own words, I am saying things that distort the truth. Those masks, designed and painted one by one by most skilled craftsmen, witty and expressive: were they a common gift? I sent him masks to identify with a gift that had a thousand meanings for a man with evil intentions. When we arranged them in the chest that was to be sent off along the highroad to Ravenna, my girls played out a comedy, just for ourselves. Our Alda Boiarda covered her face first with one, then with another mask, improvising speeches in imitated voices, and asked us which of them was a worthy depiction of the duke of Romagna: not the mask of the pope, nor that of the king, nor yet that of the emperor, nor that of Jove, nor Mars, and not even that of the cook, the soldier, the monk, and the peasant. The devil's mask, perhaps? Loud cries of agreement were heard, as the girls and the pages clapped their hands.

It was, in fact, the devil, according to some informants, who got rid of him for us, freeing us all, the princes of Italy. From the treacherous marriage and from far more serious dangers we were saved, in August of 1503, by the poison he drank in the villa of Cardinal Adriano of Corneto, great enemy of the Borgia spirit and, in a general and more secret sense, opponent of the Roman Curia. Not he, an honest soul, but people circulating in that house almost certainly poisoned the pope and his son, even if there are those who deny the crime.

The letter Francesco wrote me, as he was away from home, but always informed by messengers, was so full of necromancy that I was startled. He said that Alexander the Sixth, taken ill, began to express himself in incomprehensible words, and he seemed to stagger. The words were: "I shall come, I shall come. You are right. Wait. Wait just a little longer," and they referred to the conclave held after the death of Innocent the Eighth, when Rodrigo Borgia had made a pact with the devil, paying for the papacy with his soul. Among the terms of the pact the duration of his reign was specified: eleven years. And so it was, with only four additional days. All of seven devils came out of his mouth at the moment of his decease, and afterward his body began to boil, losing its human shape, and it was so foul that only a porter would deign to drag it to the grave by one foot. That letter amused me, especially when I had it read in my chambers to ladies and courtiers and I watched them as they listened, pale and trembling as if at a tragedy. In reality we then received more precise and moderate letters, purged of any diabolical intervention.

More confused, more cruel but surely just was the fate of the duke Valentino, who fell from the heights of power to the earth; but we remembered one by one the stages of his dizzying rise, and especially we remembered the treacherous flash of his sword that had grazed us when he was buzzing threateningly, but with manners he proclaimed friendly, around our brother-in-law the duke of Urbino that summer of 1502. Guidobaldo received constant delegations from him and even a request for troops to be moved against Camerino and the rebel Pietro of Varano. His suspicions aroused, but not completely distrustful, Guidobaldo was slowly acting to satisfy him and day by day fell into the treacherous deceit. Elisabetta, after the carnival time, after our journey to Venice, had not returned to her handsome palace in Urbino but had stopped off in Mantua; together she and I enjoyed the burgeoning of the Mantuan spring and then the early summer, and as the days passed, we confirmed the delicate growth of our friendship.

We had shut ourselves away at Porto Mantovano in my favorite villa on the lake, favorite because it was still very close to the city, just beyond the Ponte San Giorgio, and yet, because of its rustic and charming design, its delightful woods and the lake, and its breezes in a fine and airy setting, it seemed to me far more comfortable than the halls of the castle. In that cool June, streaked with great white clouds, the distraught and dusty messenger who rose before our eyes, as if leaping from a nightmare, to repeat painful words suddenly robbed us of all peace with his announcement. He came from Urbino. The city had been taken in a flash by the Valentino, who had arrived by surprise at the head of an army; the duke Guidobaldo had fled, in his jerkin, with his adopted son, the little Francesco Maria della Rovere; no one had had news of them, and the Borgia had sent his henchmen to pursue them; he wanted to have them in his hands, alive, at all costs.

It was like a funeral drumbeat. Motionless on the bench beside the lake, we stared at the poor man, he as dazed as we were. I tried to make him say things he did not know. I was afraid to have Elisabetta speak. I sensed that an immense struggle was being fought inside her, and I followed the secret workings of her spirit to summon back useful thoughts, provident, truthful. Her face was drenched in tears as if they came from unknown springs; her eyes and her features were still; as I was beside her, she grasped my wrist; and from time to time she shivered.

How many secret agents we sent I cannot say. We never tired of hearing reports from any wayfarer who thought he might have glimpsed the fugitives, and when our men had spread out toward Rome, through Romagna and all of Italy with alert ears, Guidobaldo arrived alone, exhausted from fatigue and his long outrage. Elisabetta managed at once to smile at her husband, her eyes shining with happiness, and her grief was allayed in waves as she looked at him and spoke to him. That conjugal love was revealed as truly admirable; it was so real, so gently decorous in them both, though they had no illusions about their condition and their sad fate. It seemed to me even, as we returned to the castle, that Elisabetta looked around herself, as if she did not recognize the Gonzaga places of her childhood, where she had lived with her father and mother, and in fact, she did not recognize them: Every prospect was lost in distances beyond measure; here, now, she was only a refugee in a house that was no longer hers.

Italy was aghast at the infamous impertinence of the Borgia, who, without even the shadow of a pretext, had taken possession of a State, sacking the most beautiful palace of the peninsula. Messages of horror and deploration reached us from every side, but we were still counting the days after those deeds when even more horrifying news was added. It was not known which spies—according to some, a confessor, commanded by the pope, was responsible—had informed the Valentino that the marriage of Guidobaldo and Elisabetta had never been consummated and that the two of them slept together, tender and caressing, with no further consequence. Seizing on this information, the duke Valentino had been quick to give his orders: Guidobaldo should be made a cardinal, and Elisabetta should marry a great baron of France, while the state of Urbino would be ceded to the Borgias. Thus a badly patched-together life was planned for them.

That horrible dealing, with no thought of avoiding indelicacy, enraged us: Francesco, with that virile pride that so betrays men, and I, even more deeply distressed by the discovery of that completely unimagined quality of love. We had difficulty convincing ourselves. One day at the beginning of September Pirro Donati came into my chamber. He brought me copies of chancellery letters, but he was reluctant to give me one of them. It had been sent by an alert informant of ours, Ghivizzano, who from the Borgia's own mouth had been obliged to hear, after a little contemptuous laugh, the terrible rumor. Valentino declared it completely genuine and repeated that it was necessary for Guidobaldo to take orders: "If Montefeltro does not accept this condition, I will not grant him so much as a sigh."

The letter contained a peremptory warning for the rulers of Mantua. We, the close relatives, should send away the duke and duchess of Urbino, under pain of something fierce, which was allowed to hover menacingly in the air. It was hinted that Elisabetta could remain, and here lay the diabolical part of the plan: to separate Guidobaldo from Elisabetta, to plunge them into the mortal anguish of disjunction, in order to destroy them. Those impositions were too heavy to be borne. They, husband and wife, vouchsafed us no clarifications, but only a silence, a dumb apology. Francesco was outraged to the point of frenzy; he wanted to force me to question Elisabetta, but I felt she kept me at a distance; I sensed a private world that allowed no room for confidences.

Galloping off with two gentlemen of the court, Francesco went at once to our estate at Sacchetta, where the hapless exiles had taken refuge, to avoid the courtiers' falsely pitying eyes. Still not understanding, I wandered back and forth from Studiolo to Grotta, or I shut myself up in one of the tiny rooms with Leonardesque knots painted on the walls, and I looked down at the waters of the moat, shivering in the wind. My women saw that I was absent, lost in thought. Fifteen years of marriage lived without a moment of vacillation, a gesture, a glance that could arouse suspicion of what went on in that nuptial bed. What had the first days of their union been, when Elisabetta had changed the maiden's trepidation into the modest joy of the young bride? "Her face was radiant then," Francesco grumbled, angrily, considering himself tricked. What gave it radiance if not the possession of a secret, a secret worth as much as life? What hopes, what trials, what humiliations had they overcome between them, and how? That way of being together, with visible joy, of stroking each other's hands, with no horror of the physical, but rather seeking it, naturally, like married lovers: to what did it lead if not a more sublime condition of innocence, painful perhaps, wearing, but surely exciting? The happiness that emanated from them came from a delirium of pride and humility, or else it was the creation of an existence outside the ordinary rules in which reciprocal pity became boundless joy, miraculously distilled in a real philter.

Francesco returned to the castle before evening, even more furious than when he had set out. "I found them," he cried, "they told me, fearless both of them, that so it was, so it is, and so they wish to live. Guidobaldo declared himself ready for anything. Elisabetta can be free if she wishes. And she, my sweet sister, my mad sister, declared that she would prefer to live in a hospice with her husband than in a palace without him. It has never occurred to her that her behavior is an insult to me and that it would have been her duty to confess everything to her brother and not to make me go about with this stain on my brow, for all to laugh at, every court and the people as well."

"You dared say that to her? And what did she say?" I asked anxiously.

"She remained quite calm. She said she did not see what concern it was of others what happened between wife and husband. They owe nothing to anyone; they ask and will ask only justice.

And in the end she said: 'Send me no messengers, Francesco; we do not mean to offer explanations.' "

I measured Elisabetta's strength. I admired her with unconfined emotion, and that strong husband of mine who stood before me almost inspired pity; nothing was farther from him and his like than the idea that a woman can assert a choice of her own, not out of reprisal or ambitious affirmation but through a natural harmony of mind and heart.

They had to be allowed to leave; at this point it was they who were unwilling to remain, and Francesco looked at them severely, somehow offended by their inopportune chastity. They chose to take refuge in Venice, which, as the Doges kept repeating, was one of the most free of Italian states, where all could come and leave as they chose, for no gates or walls existed to seal off the city. Guidobaldo left us first, but Elisabetta decided to follow him at once. I accompanied her to her horse in the courtyard of the castle, where a small but stouthearted escort awaited her, and to cheer her, I reminded her of our Venetian excursions a few months before. I realized she was not listening to me. When she was about to leave, she recovered herself and even joked, with her inimitable grace: "Things will change. They will change, Isabella, and we will again make fun of you know whom, and perhaps someone will write it down. Do not think I am too stricken now. On the contrary, I feel very secure. I am Guidobaldo's shield; if he were alone, he would run the risk of being killed."

She lowered her voice. "You are wondering about things I cannot tell you; perhaps Guidobaldo and I demanded too much, inventing our own life, different from the lives of others; perhaps we committed the sin of pride."

There was a silence.

"And perhaps we committed other sins; we had discovered a way of assuming happiness in every sense, avoiding every suspicion; there was a paradise too many in our life. But I do not want to lose our secrets. Forgive me. I can say no more than that, not even to you."

Room of the clocks
the year 1533

M Y CLOCKS DISAGREE ; they sound or mark the passing of time at different moments, varying from minutes to hours. One, a golden egg of Nuremberg, blue-enameled, goes more slowly and is a good six hours behind the most exact; I know it is behind, for I have watched it slow down little by little. It is my favorite because each day it gives me a greater number of hours to be used as I please; in those hours, defeating time, I place everything that I will never do. For this reason I am reluctant to call engineers and jewelers to try to make the movements of all the works coincide. I confound dates, I muddle them, I draw out their hidden meaning; and the secret accord of inconceivable discoveries at times thrills me.

Before me is the little table of polished walnut, and around me, on brackets or hung against the walls, are the hundred clocks of my collection. When I am in here, I do not even know if this story unfolds in the course of one night, or two nights, or ten; only it is necessary for me to remain alert, at my sentry post. I have refolded the letter of Robert de la Pole, the sophistical and bizarre Englishman who thrust himself into my life with rare but even too self-assured signs. I have taken from a drawer a little coffer of papers, numbered in my own hand, that no one, save me, must ever read, and I am tempted to examine, and study, the letters in that jagged hand. I interrogate myself once again: Why did I not answer, either in person or dictating to Pirro Donati? I could compose cold letters, models of a higher friendship, even stern, with many reproaches. What a correspondence this could have been, in a tone never found elsewhere, and it would concentrate on the concrete human mysteries.

I cannot meditate on religion; I am unarmed in the face of the divinity; my nature knows no mystic impulses. I have always been precise and brisk in my devotions, but I have given to the Church two nuns and a cardinal, all three of great soul. If there is a lament in these words, at a wound of maternal sorrow, I erase even the scars. So I have always done, with that resolve that my poets call constancy of character.

II

Courageous Fears

To the most Illustrious Signora Isabella, Marchesana of Mantua

*M*y spirit trembles as the pen dips and bends over the paper, with the most reverent of bows. Five years have passed, five, counted day by day, since that first letter of mine, confused but truthful and a thousand times reread in my mind and blessed. Blessed because your image has lasted in me for a long time without fading. When my thoughts concentrate on you, I have peace and, at the same time, war; and I remember that I am a poet and regret that I am not enough of one. My courage fails if I tell myself that perhaps you will read these lines and, impatient, will raise your flashing eyes, asking yourself: "What does this man want?" Nothing, illustrious signora, indeed, less than nothing, for I know I cannot be forgiven my foolish deceit that for so long made me uncomfortable if I uttered your name, even to myself.

There can be no question of asking you the favor of allowing these pages to be received, and for my own amusement I would like to write in the style of your Signor Bibbiena, who has such a gift for composing those witty epistles that then circulate here in Rome, where their readers quote them with such light humor. This aspiration of mine will perhaps seem to you an attitude unsuited to a pensive spirit that should seek instead the serene aura of peace in these times of tumult. It is no accident that I am a friend and admirer of Erasmus of Rotterdam; nothing is so profoundly refreshing to the intellect as his ideal vision of mankind guided by justice, a moral Christianity ruling men. I refer to his idea of a *pax christiana*. I love Erasmus, and I love even more his fanaticism for freedom; but I cannot be his true follower as I lack that beautiful, shining steadfastness of his. I am too attracted by the variety of those who live around us. In this I resemble you.

I have no reason to talk to you about myself; I am not inspired by any vainglory, but only by the necessity of informing you that I am in the Curia, serving my distant king, Henry the Seventh of England. You certainly cannot imagine with what fear and joy I learned that His Holiness Julius the Second has assigned to you, as your residence during your stay in Rome, the delightful gardens of the late cardinal Ascanio Sforza. For me to imagine you in those gardens is an enchantment. But the thought of your coming here perturbs me; I do not know if I will ever be able to appear in your presence. But on to other matters; this is not why I am writing you.

Everything here in Rome is bustle and constant novelty and the protean energy of His Holiness, who demonstrates his activity at every instant of the day. The city is bristling with troops who daily go to exercise on horseback or on foot in the meadows of the castle; from the Vatican hill the squadrons of the militia can be easily discerned, beneath their banners lashed by the wind and by the sun. And surely you must have learned from one of your alert correspondents about the prodigious discovery made just recently: that statuary group of Laocoön described by the elder Pliny, a great marvel and festive presage that is already inspiring poetic outbursts in every place, including your own city, our Ferrara, where Tito Vespasiano Strozzi, light of the Italian language, is conceiving an epic to glorify this divine apparition.

And, yes, I can confirm it: The morning was divine, that eighth of March, when I found myself in a little group, its last member, behind the workmen, climbing the slopes of the Esquiline at a measured pace, in the area known as the Thermae of Titus, among those Roman ruins that inexplicably attract us with their ancient presence. At our head, rightfully in first place, strode Michelangiolo, the sculptor, with Giuliano da Sangallo, the architect, carrying on his back his delicate little son Francesco so that the boy would see great things to remember afterward. And behind them came the rest of us. In a place almost sealed off by walls, low and high, with brief, steep prospects and dusty mounds there were two armed guards, stationed there by the city's conservators after the first word of the discovery. Nearby was the hole, vast but irregular, and at the bottom of it there was a white arm bent upward, emerging from the dark earth as if beckoning. Orders were

given to dig; one spade followed another. As the heads and
arms came to the surface, and the smooth, swollen serpentine
coils, Giuliano da Sangallo said: "Yes, this is the 'Laocoön' that
the elder Pliny described, all carved from a single piece of
Parian marble."

"There are at least four pieces," Michelangiolo declared in a
stormy voice from the depth of the hole, where he had lowered
himself.

I cannot with justice describe the eager progress of the task
of excavation, the silence that accompanied the thuds of the
hefty spadefuls of earth, the tense patience of us all, and the
few words muttered amid private grumblings by Master
Michelangiolo: "Bound and confined, and yet free"; "the
movement proceeds like a chain"; "Flesh, the stone of the
human body." Things like these reveal their essence. The
gleaming emergence of the white marble was the terrestrial
proof of the eternal artist, and the names of the sculptors,
Agesander, Athenodorus, and Polydorus, mentioned by Pliny,
were passed from one to the other, and each of us enjoyed the
incomparable perfume of the Greek names of those ancient
masters. My lady, that morning appeared as the first dawn of
the resurrection of art, and it unfolded at a pace that seemed
slow to me then and now seems very rapid. The sun became
vertical and entered the hole as if with reverence, gliding over
the marble.

One of those present said: "Why does God send us gifts so
remote and precious? What is he telling us? Or how is he
testing us?"

I am excited by the example of His Holiness, completely
untroubled by such questions. He has brought to the Belvedere
the works that in these times have returned to the light of
Rome, and there, amid orange groves and jasmine hedges, he
is having them set in place. He seems to guarantee that God
does not exist only to strike us. These names and works of art
recall the story of the journey that brought to Mantua from
Rome the little marble cupid of Michelangiolo, formerly in the
house of the duke of Urbino. I saw that charming sculpture
that conveys to its viewer the power and grace of an infant god
in its innocent immortality, and I began to think how your soul

is possessed by a greed for beauty that drives you beyond the limits that others' will and your own would like to assign it.

I ask your forgiveness a thousand times if I am too bold. As I was born English, I express myself surely with less delicacy than your court sages, including the great singer of your praises, Signor Mario Equicola, but I have the presumption that I sense better than others your emotions. I may remind you of your inner conflict during those days when Cesare Borgia was carrying out his wicked depredation of Urbino. Amid all your great and generous feelings for your sister-in-law and her husband, you felt also a tempestuous, explosive, absolute desire: to gain possession of the Michelangiolo cupid that, among so many other perfect objects, was in the ducal palace. You could not resist that desire, and while those unfortunate relatives were your guests, you forwarded your anxious request, through the offices of your brother, Cardinal Ippolito d'Este. You told yourself that the duke Valentino does not appreciate works of genius, and someone else would in any case have got the cupid away from him. And in fact, Cesare Borgia passed it on to you heedlessly, adding a little ancient Venus. To salve your conscience, you spoke of it to the duchess Elisabetta, and she answered you with the exemplary words that so many have quoted, "I am very happy to see it in your hands rather than in anyone else's," and she added, "I'm sorry you didn't ask for it when it was still mine; it would have been a joy to give it to you."

Admirable reply, but I do not repeat it just to praise a great lady; I repeat it to praise you, who have such temperament, the wild Este marauding heart, that you can accept fearlessly any lesson and transform it into a kind of right. I mean that you love the cupid so much that you would kiss it as you do your son, as your husband secretly reproaches you, and not even your tender affection for your Elisabetta could deprive you of this supreme pleasure. A motive for life is asserted in your love of things that contain the movement of beauty, and this reveals your intellect, such that few could measure up to. I am sure these words will irritate you if you read them. I am saved by my initial lie, holding myself apart from your wrath as from your benevolence.

The pages are full of enigmas. Perhaps you have noticed that I have actually twice brought up the subject of your ardent curiosity, which solicits narration of events distant from Mantua. I know that you dispatch people daily and receive reports of every kind, from every land, and you insist that your agents follow the people who interest you "as the shadow follows the sun." I would like to add myself, last but not the least alert and willing, to your Gian Lucido Cattanei, your Antonio Costabili and Jacopo d'Atri, and all the others whom you often accuse of writing too little. I would be happy if such a reproach were to be my lot; you cannot imagine how happy. Was the tale of the rediscovered Laocoön too brief? Were you affected by my outburst of enthusiasm for your courageous conquest of the cupid?

To return to my duties as informant, I believe I can enhance the news that you already have with further information. I am sure that no one has written you about the letter the pope himself gave me a few days ago, to be sent to London personally to my king, in which Julius expounded his request for assistance from His Majesty and the bishops of England for the construction of the new Basilica of Saint Peter. And even more inflamed was his letter of April eighteenth; in it, also addressing my king, the pope, with thunderous rejoicing, announced that he had laid the first stone of the new foundations. At this event I myself was present. There were many of us, Italians and foreigners, on Low Sunday, at the pit of the foundations, seventy-five feet deep. You should have seen, my lady, the long, stupendous procession of prelates, and your great sculptor Caradosso, who presented the medals of solid gold with the portrait of Julius, and the pope himself, blessing them under an almost summery sun, as a gleaming air bore the tang of the sea. The inscription on the marble stone reads: "Pope Julius Second, of Liguria, in the year one thousand five hundred and six, third year of his pontificate, has had this crumbling basilica rebuilt." In a loud voice Bramante, tall and querulous, was directing the job under the eyes of the pope, who preceded him, taller than he and even more querulous.

I will not speak to you of politics because I know you are

informed daily. Accursed politics overwhelms this pope, who struggles without respite between French and Venetians, who say first one thing and then another, and he is always on the verge of breaking his bonds and setting off toward Perugia or Bologna without informing anyone, and I believe he will do this in any case. For the present in his rare hours, or I should say his minutes, of rest, he goes to enjoy the Belvedere, having placed there the "Apollo," which will soon be followed by the "Laocoön" and the other statues.

Most illustrious lady, perhaps you will have remarked that I let my writing run on, and I do this in the illusion that I am conversing with you. I fear my language is not very ornate. Though I have lived many years in Italy and I take infinite delight in the so-called vulgar Italian tongue, so filled with verbal confluences that it is open to any choice, I am always English at heart, and so I am also as a writer, I mean as nonwriter, an uninvited correspondent. I am impelled by a northern fire and a certain freedom that becomes invocation as I so thirst to see you. But is there no one in Rome who possesses a portrait of you? I ask myself this, of course, trusting that a reply from you will reach me on a current of the spirit. I ask your forgiveness, without any hope, as

your slave
Robert de la Pole

Rome, April thirtieth, 1506

A **PEACEFUL DAY** was beginning. As my astrological conjunction suggested, in May I was to enter into my new laboratory, the room with arched ceiling that I had prepared on the advice of Paride of Ceresara, the most trusted physician and astrologer there is in my court. The room is very large, on the ground floor near Francesco's apartments. Set on long shelves and step tables, vases and bowls are aligned, bottles and jars, wooden or alabaster boxes, large and very large trees of terracotta and of glass, marble, and bronze mortars, and scales with their weights; little kegs of distilled waters stand in a row along the left wall, and in the trays there are large and small scoops and paddles, an array of retorts and alembics. Two druggists, brother and sister, whom I unearthed in the province of Udine, sit at two desks and, with an absorbed manner, copy out and arrange recipes. I have chosen them as my assistants: young Giusto, with his long, keen face, and young Umbrasia, slender and pink. They greet me, rising and bowing, knowledgeable and serene, ready to carry out any idea of mine. They have examined and praised my unguents for the hands and my perfumed compounds that so please the queen of France and her ladies. We have decided to invent a face pomade to be kept a deep secret, which will lend a vital air to the complexion.

We have communicated to one another our pleasure in interrogating the secrets concealed in the volumes of nature, and I was gladdened by their simple readiness of intellect and their slow way of laughing while their eyes remain serious. I went back up to my lofty rooms accompanied by the conviction that I will work well in my laboratory, having in my hands formulas that would improve the health of all in my family and the court. And I found myself in my Studiolo, alone. As the evenly distributed light fell on my pictures, I observed the Perugino painting, which did not fraternize with the superb ones by Mantegna, of a spacious design, trees of delicate foliage and little figures of men and women abandoned in a kind of dance to tunes of musical breezes. My girls liked Perugino more than Mantegna, because they found the picture sweet and infinitely enjoyable to gaze upon, but it is certain that the forceful drawing power that moves our Mantegna's hand has no rival unless it is in the unparalleled Leonardo da Vinci, who surpasses all. In the diffuse glow a little picture by the Venetian Giovanni Bellini also shone, a Nativity that had made all experts of art exclaim. It is very beautiful, yes, in its bejeweled, serene color and in that distancing wonder at the divine mystery, but so tiny in size that it could not hang harmoniously in the Studiolo. Suddenly I saw its place: in the Grotta, in the position of honor on the right wall, directly facing with the white light from the north.

I was solaced by those thoughts of springtime lightness; I tried to dispel my uneasiness at the pope's planned enterprise against Perugia and against Bologna. Perugia did not alarm me greatly, but Bologna was truly too close to Ferrara. I was thinking of my Ferrara when Pirro Donati announced his approach with his measured step, coming toward me, his hands full of documents and letters, and among these I promptly recognized the jagged writing of Robert de la Pole, the Englishman.

I do not know what I felt: an irritation, it seemed to me, but shot through with rejoicing and a certain curiosity. In any case, a sense of being awake, while my reason, set in motion, advised me that the letter was to be rejected, without being read, indeed without even being opened, but that same advice stirred in me a flux of objections. Why not open it? Why not read it, when the author would never know whether or not I had opened it and read it? I was mistress of a private act, to be performed for myself alone. I set the letter aside, and Pirro followed my movement with his gaze; I felt his question so intensely that I was about to speak of it, but we talked of other matters.

As soon as he had gone away, I granted myself a time to deal with various papers, originals or copies, and once everything was in order and well pondered, I picked up again with cautious indifference the letter of the Englishman. It came from Rome, where he now lived at the Curia, as he himself informed me, and this source so cleared away my distrust that I found myself running over the lines naturally. His respectful presentation deceived me, and I read on, to the place where he spoke of the cupid of Michelangiolo. My cheeks flushed, I let the sheets of paper slip to the floor. Impossible to continue, to go on to the end. In what swamp would I fall, in what depth of indignity would I be lost? A hurricane of reproaches, secret but searing, assailed me; this thought jolted me with anger and without any check. It was an effort for me to pick up the papers, fold them, crush them tightly in a hard scroll.

My children arrived: Federico, proud of his little sword of gilded wood; Ercole, the *peteghin*, on the back of the jester Frittella, who pretended to be his horse; and their two sisters after them, little Ippolita and then Eleonora, who, as she was twelve, already wore a young maiden's dress, her long hair hanging loose, slightly waved. She appeared beautiful and transparent, a little sullen. For the first time I saw her as a woman, with still-fragile, womanly movements, already defined, and the familiar grief of living gripped my bosom. For her, too, fate was advancing, and there was no way to rescue her; already above her head wedding plans were being woven, to bring further honor and prestige to the Gonzaga name. She would obey our command, and someone would roughly fling her into the transformation of body and soul that conjugal life brings with it. Impelled by a yearning for compensation, I rose and rested one hand on Eleonora's shoulder as I conversed with her lady about a beautiful dress for my older daughter. I said they were to cut it out soon, at once; in the wardrobe there was a length of silver-and-white tabby, ready. Eleonora looked at me, amazed.

I waited all day before picking up again the tight roll of the pages of jagged writing that I had thrown into my coffer. I was like a sick person trying to reassure himself by studying his disease, and yet I felt unusually fortified and charged by a current of energy that made me free to confront anything. I readily found again the place that referred to the cupid, and I returned to it coldly. The story excited and grieved me at once; until then I had thought every episode belonged to me, to be debated only with myself, as no one else would dare utter a word. Now I was seized by the suspicion that I had been robbed, that someone had stolen inside the enclosure of Elisabetta's friendship with me, a barrier set up by our own wish, and was offending us.

I had already had to defend myself once, to Gian Lucido Cattanei, our expert ambassador, when the duke of Urbino had asked me, through him, for the Michelangiolo cupid, giving as his motive that if I were to return it, my gesture would persuade all those who possessed beautiful objects stolen from the palace or given away by the Borgias to make restitution, following my example. I answered Cattanei with the truth: Nothing gladdened me more than the recovery of the State by the duke and by the sister of my heart, Elisabetta; but the cupid was another matter:

It had been given me by the duke Valentino and, what meant more, with the affectionate consent of my brother- and sister-in-law. I conceded that Elisabetta had spoken the admirable words that were circulating among the courts, repeated by all as an example of noble generosity in misfortune. I even admitted that those words overwhelmed me, almost conquering me. But that was enough, my God. And now I was declared less great in generosity than my sister-in-law because I was won over by mad love for that little cherub sleeping in his polished marble.

What was this foreigner insinuating, and how dare he call me wild and greedy? And yet, read and reread, those words gradually illuminated my emotions; in their juxtaposition I discovered the outset of a free gallop toward a glittering destination, and I found myself, with a tug of the reins, in an outburst that surprised me, casting to the winds the conventions of the usual courtly bowing and scraping. The Englishman's words of aggressive praise rang in my ear, accustomed to other expressions and other weighing of conceits, with an unusual stimulation; pursued by the whirl of broad and insistent sounds, as in a pyrrhic dance I ran eastward, in the Ferrara forest, where the city ends amid the thick, hairy foliage of the woods, and everything became true. There existed in me something that no one had ever known except that foreigner in the ferment of his fancy; there existed, guessed at by Robert de la Pole, a space of my own, quite secret, alien to all my family, including Francesco, including Elisabetta, and there I entered, raising a banner of wild humors. So I was certain that the cupid belonged to me truly. The way I had desired it made it mine by right.

I laughed wholeheartedly, shaking my loose coppery hair that caressed my shoulders. I read the letter from the beginning, and I paused at the story of the rediscovered statue. "O Rome, O Rome," I said, "how you know the cadences of the spirit, you who can gleam in a sudden, glorious youth and open with your revelations the heart of an English barbarian." I would never forget that spring day, and the hole in the black earth at the Thermae of Titus, brightened by the smooth whiteness of the "Laocoön." Nor the medals of solid gold under the first stone of the new Saint Peter's, among those giants by the name of Michelangiolo, Bramante, Antonio da Sangallo, and Julius the Second, the masterful Ligurian. I had a destiny granted to few: a glimpsed moment of immortality.

I TURNED MY right shoulder, remembering with that movement my cloak of fine, tightly woven stuff; on the tower the wind blew even in June. I clung hard to the Ghibelline battlements as I asked, with a kind of hoarse gurgle, "Is she coming?" And what I meant was: Does she have the courage to come?

"They are on the road," Pirro Donati said, pretending to give me festive news. "I am about an hour ahead of them. I imagine they will soon be sighted from the guard tower. The signor marchese sent Amedeo Giglio ahead with me, ordering red carpets for the winding staircase, twelve grooms outside, pages with baskets of rose petals to fling in generous armfuls from the loggia when the duchessa enters the Court of Honor from the drawbridge. For you, my lady, his urgent entreaty is that you be properly in place with your children in a reception hall, whichever you wish. And I must inform the cardinal, your brother-in-law Sigismondo."

"Who is with them?" I managed to ask.

"The lame Strozzi, Ercole, the poet. The women and children of the duchessa, two knights of the marchese, and Tolomeo Spagnoli. The women are in a chariot draped with crimson, lent by the Anzilottis of Cremona. At Borgoforte they had a fine collation under the Oriental-style striped tent, hung among the trees on the meadow toward the dry bed of the Po. The whole company has always been in the open air: games and dances, decking the young girls with flowers, as is our custom here. The incessant talk of the duchessa, supported by Teodora and Polissena, filled the ears of the signor marchese with complaints about her brother imprisoned in the fortress of Medina. She greatly invoked his protection."

"And he?"

"My lord? All smiles, he promised her the Valentino's liberation from the Spanish prison, and his words seem to be so reassuring that she was induced to a more consoled mood. Her brow was serene as she listened to Strozzi's Latin verses, dedicated to certain red roses, verses quite beautiful according to what I heard; she even laughed, quite sweetly."

My cloak was flapping like a sail. Words, smiles, everything wounded me. I would not receive the stranger, the impudent woman, and she could be so foolish as to believe that Francesco had power over the king of Spain? And she could laugh with him "quite sweetly"!

"I will not receive her!" I cried. "I will be ill again; I will take advantage of my expectant condition. The children may go if their father wants to introduce them to his lady, but dressed as they are, in their everyday clothing, without display. No flowers, no red carpets. Four grooms will do, the number employed for the visits of ordinary gentle ladies. As for the cardinal, inform him. He will be happy to show himself in his newly gained purple, and she will be even happier to bow to that purple."

At times I fall into an odd humor. I seem divided in two: One speaks and acts; the other coldly watches and judges everything, myself included. Enraged, I told myself that anger does me no good, and I did not spare even my own Pirro Donati. I was walking on the brink of a probable defeat, and I could not dominate myself. June was more beautiful than May; from the lime trees a diluted languor rose all the way to the tower. This Mantua, which unfolded, flourishing, before my gaze, was my home, where I was entitled to live in my own way. What was irritating me? And yet I had to seek help from things, or rather from someone. In haste, but with effort, I arranged for the Painted Hall, the glory of Mantegna, to be made ready for the reception. I ordered a gilded stool for myself and stools for the children; for her, nothing. She could remain standing before us.

"I recognize the Isabellian virtue of obeying the laws of courtesy," Pirro Donati was saying meanwhile, in a whisper of approbation, turning his white face to the great light.

No, no! He had not understood. I was refusing to give way to the rational part of myself and was proceeding to a self-challenge. I was not evading but was determined to join battle. Or had he indeed understood, and was he privately measuring my strength?

We went down to my rooms. Over his arm Pirro was carrying that cloak that had accompanied my rebellion and had now been abandoned as something useless. "The Isabellian virtue," I said to myself, as my women dressed me in the light dress I had asked for, flesh-colored, with some glints of silver. I suddenly suspected that perhaps true virtue, for me, would have been acceptance of a defeat, but I promptly rebelled and prepared for the encounter.

The mirror reflected my image: The imminent maternity was all too visible; my face seemed a bit puffy, though the delicate-hued powder of Cyprus and the abundant red softened the damage. My God, was I really begging for the mirror's approval? And none of my girls bothered about that ribbon that had escaped from the lace arranged around the gorget. I stamped my foot, and in a swarm they were all by me, threading ribbons, discovering and mending an undone seam; they made me change my too-dark shoes. That considerate, external way of surrounding me, which should have allayed my anxiety, bored and irritated me. Now I was ready, but not pacified.

Through the half-opened door I saw two of the girls, Isabetta and Sabina, glued to the windows of the Hall of the "Trionfi"; the echoing vaults of the ceiling made their voices resound. The silly creatures were so busy commenting on what was happening in the courtyard that they had not heard my call, and they were laughing, absorbed in idle thoughts. I motioned the others beside me to be silent; channeled in the silence, the dialogue reached me distinctly.

"Wouldn't you like to be swaggering in the place of the duchess of Ferrara, Isabetta?" Sabina was saying.

Isabetta was not the least perturbed; laughing in a youthfully provoking way, she answered: "My hair is as blond as hers, and longer."

"And you are younger, and the signor marchese has a taste for blond girls."

They laughed again unbearably, as Isabetta smoothed her beautiful head with a proud hand; a light ribbon bound her forehead with a little golden heart pendant in the center. Anxiety stopped my breath.

"Let go of me!" I cried to my girls, who were still trying to restrain me, and they drew back, dismayed. I seized the scissors from the table and in a few long strides I was at the windows open on the Court of Honor. I wasted no time speaking. I grasped Isabetta's braid, felt it alive and heavy, and I dug the scissors into it with almost voluptuous force. I cut as close to the root as I could; the girl made a convulsive movement.

"Be still or I will cut your throat," I warned her. And at that moment the braid came away in my hand, a lifeless serpent that triumphantly horrified me. "Go, now." My tone was raised. "Go and play the nymph with the signor marchese."

The girl ran off weeping, and I resumed my calm. Sabina was paralyzed, not daring to move. The women and the pages were peering around the doors and shouting. At their shouts Pirro Donati appeared promptly. He looked at the braid on the floor.

"The family will make trouble," he said simply. He picked up the braid, silenced everyone, shook Sabina and said to her that after all it was only hair, and turning to me, impassive, he announced that Lucrezia Borgia was already on the drawbridge.

My children ran toward me in festive dress and adorned with jewels. And they were followed by their nurse, carrying the smallest little girl. I led them, in file, toward the Painted Hall. I reached the stool; from the frescoes on the walls something descended, like an approval. I could not see them, but I felt them inside me: Ludovico Gonzaga and his wife, Barbara, who, like two guardian saints, were surely on my side, they who for the family's sake had felt passions at times humiliated and tormented, but were never vanquished, never, not even by the physical condemnation of an evil blood that from the Malatestas had passed to the Gonzagas with that recurrent infirmity, that hump in the little bodies of so many of their children. So far I, with the vigor of my blood as the Este firstborn, had annulled every threat in my children, my Gonzagas, beautiful, erect, and healthy. The one I was carrying in my womb would be male, vigorous like Federico. A prophetic investiture ran through me. Interrogated various times secretly by Paride of Ceresara, the stars of maternity were rotating in my favor.

I leaned against the back of my seat. Every time I was in this hall I admitted to myself: Mantegna had painted a genuine family apotheosis with the mysterious sincerity of a man of reason. Against the massive northeastern tower of the castle, a military place of armed sentries, with the touch of his brush he had opened an eye of heaven at the peak of the vault, a transparent blue, enhanced by soft white clouds, and he had surrounded it with a balustrade where some women peered down, of snowy skin and black, with flowers and peacocks in secret symmetries and a little troop of shining babes. The investiture of the seigniory descended from that ceiling, where the painter had set monochrome medallions of the Roman emperors against the golden tesserae, and on the walls the sober invention unfolded, of changing backgrounds, frames, ribbons, classical landscapes restored, or rather renewed from ancient art.

Everything was addressed to the future in the family depiction: father, mother, children, grandchildren, fat and thin, affected by deformity or doomed to illness or splendidly healthy like the triumphant Barberina, a pale blue ribbon in her hair, who turned her goddess head on her proud young neck. From wall to wall a pact of patience unfolded that still did not prohibit a solemn happiness. Into that family pact I impulsively thrust myself, fervently determined. I arrived at the image of Francesco, so delightful to contemplate, on the wall by the window: an infant of a few years, with a rugged profile that sharply cut the air. But then I restrained myself. I did not want to wax tender over the child, now a man of foolish moods, and I directed my gaze straight ahead. I was just in time.

The door was flung wide, the pages flanked it, Lucrezia Borgia entered; soft and laughing, she seemed to glide. She came toward me, her hands outstretched, as I remained seated. It was my duty to kiss her. I made a move to rise, but she restrained me with a feminine, politely comprehensive gesture. Naturally in that movement she showed off her delicate beauty contrasted with my somewhat overripe shape. Behind her walked Francesco. What a smile he had.

"I have shown her everything," he said, with bright confidence, wanting to attract my attention. "The Studiolo, the Grotta, the cupid, the bronzes, the paintings, the books."

"I went from one wonder to another," Lucrezia said, and to me it seemed she was reciting a lesson. She clasped her slender hands to enforce her words.

"Our brother the cardinal is in the chapel, where he awaits us for vespers," Francesco informed me. "Naturally, in your condition, you are excused," he added considerately.

"He's afraid I'll ruin his little party," I said to myself. And at that moment Strozzi came forward, to the reiterated rhythm of his crutch.

"May a poet be allowed to say, illustrious marchesana, that your excellent works are all linked like beautiful words in a most elegant poem, which increases their beauty. I would like to tell in poetry everything that I have seen. But what can we deduce from such visions? Only this, perhaps: When the subject is too stirring, the poet's pen jams. What would even my supreme friend Pietro Bembo say? He came last year to pay you his homage and never ceases celebrating your person and your company."

I thanked him, immediately recalling the image of the Venetian poet, a rare visitor but an incomparable interlocutor. Strozzi emulated him well; his tone and his language were of great elegance. And both these poets belonged to her, to that Lucrezia, and Bembo had dedicated his *Asolani* to her. Still, I thanked the speaker with a nod and a smile.

Francesco, meanwhile, was pointing out to his guest the portrait of himself as a child and was exulting, with lively jest, in that childhood of his. Again she clasped her hands coyly. I introduced her to the family of Ludovico Gonzaga in its solidity, and I saw her eyes wander over the walls without pausing at any of the great figures. Faintly uneasy, she cast a glance around and saw the room devoid of stools and chairs. There was a moment's pause. I was about to say something when my children, at a sign from their father, ran toward him. The visitor's eyes shone. She began to wax ecstatic over Federico's face and his form, praising his childish elegance. Eleonora clung to Francesco's arm, and he introduced her.

"I know of you," Lucrezia said. "Rightly they call you La Bella; you are very beautiful."

I quivered at this foolishness, and I could not help protesting. Eleonora needed study; she, at twelve, already betrothed, could not remember the name of the river where the Battle of Fornovo was fought, her father's glory.

"I know it!" Federico cried. "It's the river Taro!"

Unexpectedly all laughed. Eleonora was not the least mortified, as usual, but insisted that she had known it all along, and she raised her face toward her father, who responded to her gaze, clasping her to him. Federico, meanwhile, gracefully carrying his little wooden sword at his side, was concerned with kneeling before the lady, who embraced him and spoke to him of a son of hers who lived far away; she could wish her boy had such good manners.

I was about to make a remark hinting at her sterility as an Este wife, but she, giving no evidence of realizing a seat had not been prepared for her, turned her back with a sliding movement and, holding her hand out to Francesco, started off toward the chapel. My Federico walked at her side full of decorum. I felt a long ache in my heart. Not that I highly valued the courtly manners I taught my son; I perceived the fascination that acted as a lure on the man and the boy.

"Signora, I imagine the barge is awaiting you at Borgoforte, to take you to Belriguardo. Your husband will be concerned for you."

Francesco intervened, considerately. "Have no fear, Isabella. Everything has already been arranged. I have sent word to the duke Alfonso that, to spare her excess fatigue, Signora Lucrezia and her court will stay in Mantua, in the house of Gerolamo Stanga, and will resume their journey tomorrow, early in the morning."

Lucrezia, gracefully throwing back her golden hair, assured me that Alfonso would not be at Belriguardo that evening; otherwise, she would not have delayed the resumption of her journey, even at the sacrifice of beautiful Mantua.

Francesco looked at me coldly. Court attendants arrived with refreshments and formalities; the Painted Hall was crowded with women and girls, knights, pages, my children. Even the little one moved around, clinging to her nurse's hand. Francesco had gone back to his childish portrait and was telling something; the sister-in-law laughed flatteringly, referring to unknown thoughts and emotions they shared. Daylight was failing, and the great figures on the walls withdrew into themselves. "Family," I said softly to myself, "it is really a power? Is it really proof against all enchantments?"

Lucrezia moved easily, but with a show of almost shyness, and she spoke of the beauty of the evening after the beauty of the full day, a day of festivity offered her and her ladies by the lord of Mantua. She discreetly recalled the visit to the chapel where Cardinal Sigismondo would be waiting; for vespers he had promised her a strophic laud sung by Tromboncino, that excellent musician. She enchanted my husband and my son; she shifted a white veil embroidered with tiny pearls and wrapped it around her throat and her head. She made an intimate sign of farewell to me, drawing the veil over her rounded shoulder. They went off, and behind them, protective and impudent, the crutch of Ercole Strozzi beat time. All of a sudden I realized how far that woman had cleverly kept herself from me and how she had responded to my determination to keep her standing, and she left without addressing a word to me of compliment. In my seat I remained speechless, bediamonded and adorned in vain; a subtle chill made my arms and shoulders ache.

IN THE morning, still early, I gathered my little court, giving all of them strict orders not to stray from the older part of Sacchetta; this was where we had taken refuge, fleeing the black plague that was devastating Mantua. "What a comfort Sacchetta would be if it were not for this day," I was thinking as I cast a sidelong glance over the countryside. The surrounding fields, planted in wheat, now in the yellow display before harvest, extending in the full summer, looked downright insolent in their lush gaiety. I had isolated myself on the highest tower, in a little room painted in rustic style, within sight of the Po, announced amid the thick clumps of trees.

Under the sun the white scree gleamed, accompanying the course of the waters with broad, majestic undulations, now and then patched in green. I felt I was a sentry up there, and it was true, I had escaped from the ground-floor rooms where Mantegna had set down his brush, open to the north, high-ceilinged, and only for brief periods illuminated by the cycle of the sun. The silence was heightened by some hazy summons of rural noises, and against that opaque background I perceived more clearly the tired footsteps climbing the stair. Though still distant, I recognized them as his, the tread of Giulio, my unfortunate brother. Nothing better than those exhausted steps could tell of a life on the brink of destruction. Now the steps slowed down, no longer distinct, confused with the shuffle of many other feet. Giulio must have stopped in one of the halls of the second floor or on the terrace between the two towers, overtaken by others, my secretary or his gentleman, Bartolomeo Pico, who were trying to persuade him by the power of words to face himself; but soon the silence absorbed every sound.

In whatever guise, painfully invented, Giulio sought a respite from his terrors; I stayed with mine in a total solitude. I stared at the sheets of paper on the table, the documents left the day before by Niccolò of Correggio, whom my brother Alfonso had sent in great haste to Sacchetta. I had read the memorial all night, feverishly, over and over, seeking some pretext that would enable me to rebut the ironclad demands, reason of state, peremptorily asserted by Ferrara. But the evidence was too copious and too clear, and I had known since birth how impossible it was to oppose that chill reason. There was no denying it: Giulio had really conspired, dragging after him the complicity of his brother Ferrante, the Saint George of the house of Este. The charge was lese majesty, for the duke Alfonso would have been trapped treacherously in the mortal noose, and the cardinal with him. My brothers had been poisoned by the hatred of Cain, the two younger against the two older. "Theban tragedies," a Florentine said later.

The intolerable thought made me spring to my feet. I opened the door to the stair. I was aghast at that emptiness that spread out like an invitation to peace, but what peace, good God? Since November of the previous year we had lived in an atmosphere of anguish. I could not erase the scene of that winter morning when Francesco read me the two letters from Alfonso with the horrid tale, in its different versions, the political story and the narration of the events, prologue to the more monstrous tragedy we were experiencing now: On the lawns of Belriguardo, Giulio had been pulled down from his horse and almost blinded by women's jealousy; his brother Cardinal Ippolito had signed the crime.

In that first year of Alfonso's reign after the death of our father, Ercole, days of unbearable tension had been Giulio's lot. A swarm of Ferrara physicians and our best from Mantua had cared for him day and night, restoring to him at least the gift of sight, but the handsome face of the old days was now horrible, distorted and bloated, and with one eye, the right, lacking its lid. For a question of state Alfonso wanted the wounded and the wounder to be reconciled, and he could not have made a greater error, drawing us into still worse errors. As the months passed, both the enemy brothers had come, at different times, to my Studiolo in Mantua to speak to me, the older sister for whom each of them professed veneration. In reality they heard me as it suited them; I suffered at their presence. Disconsolate, sealed in his horror of himself, Giulio sat down on the broad bench, facing me with the hesitant movement of one who, not seeing well, has to test the equilibrium of his body. Everything I could find to say to him encountered the barrier of his bitterness.

"Look at the way I am!" he repeated, to every word of true pacification. "When I appear, people either weep or flee."

He would spend hours doing nothing, drinking white Sirmione wine from a Murano glass. He wanted no music, no woman's company, no reading aloud. Once, when grief at those ceaseless groans seized my heart, I saw with a start the curve of his nose, too willful for him, sharply assume prominence and reject his other features; around that curve another face was composed, the face of someone else also seated on the bench opposite me. The Este nose of my father, Ercole, inherited by his legitimate sons, had been inherited by the illegitimate Giulio as well; it was the nose of our haughtiness and of very ancient origin, deriving perhaps from Ottone, the founder of our line, and it stood for excellence in military virtues or in the exercise of power or every other exercise, and was touched perhaps by the diabolical.

Now it was Ippolito whom I saw again on the bench. I heard again his speech that brought back to me the sweet tones of his singing; he told me without the slightest inflection of remorse about the blinding of his brother, and he explained it as something inevitable that had happened and that did not bear discussion. He shook his shining blond crop, took from a pocket one of his little ivory combs, and smoothed it.

I realized I was feeling an unusual excitement at the terrible story that he transformed from a criminal assault to a rational account beyond the snares of feeling. His rational tale had a quality of being reduced to an essentiality that enchanted me, and to prevent myself from being overcome by that unforeseen mental game, I rose in a fury and would have attacked him myself. My accusations, all too real, reassured me.

"How can a cardinal," I said to him, "in such great sin defend himself except through expiation and suffering? Your habit of peace and renunciation should hang on you like sackcloth."

He held me at a distance from himself.

"Isabella, this preaching is unworthy of you, you who can understand the truth of things and who never stop at mere catechism. Take care no one else hears you."

I had shouted.

"I am a sinner, as all of us are, and I need the catechism. But, Ippolito, if you consider me unsuited to speak of religion, let us speak of politics, of our brother Alfonso. You have undermined the calm of his reign. Young and still inexperienced as he is, he needed fraternal support and not fierce discord. In Rome you have unleashed the wrath of Pope Julius, who lacks any weakness and in the end will find the witnessed truth of this crime. He might decide upon any course, even deposing the Estes and banishing them from Ferrara forever. He can imprison you for unworthiness and put you on trial, and I cannot think who would save you. And as this ruin threatens us, the people of Ferrara are frightened, uncertain how to judge their rulers."

Ippolito sprang to his feet, beside me.

"Have no doubts, dear sister. Everything will become clear, and soon," he said, with such a cutting tone that my whole person shuddered. "The name of the man will be known to all, the traitor, and he who should be punished will be punished. And now, if it is of any use to you, I give you my blessing, and I leave you to your women."

Truly his blessing, which seemed to me blasphemous, was, I thought, of no use to me; but there were people at the end of the hall, and he was raising his hand in the gesture of benediction. I was forced to kneel and bow my head. I had not answered him.

Even now it would have been hard for me to answer him, as with a lump in my throat I unfolded on the table the papers brought by Niccolò of Correggio. Was it possible I had not guessed it before? In those papers there were only rare references to some intervention of the cardinal, but much of the multiplicity and iron logic of the events, the imprisonment of the conspirators, the grim, accelerating cadence of implications, suggested the presence of someone who had followed, step by step, the unfolding of the conspiracy itself. At the window open on the horizontal calm of the countryside, everything became obvious: Somewhere there had been spying, day after day, hour after hour, in every place; there had been no attempt to disarm Giulio's hatred, to forestall the irreparable, or to dismiss the long, drugged, and poisoned raving that would destroy Giulio and, with him, his brother Ferrante and the wretches who had listened to them. Always Ippolito had been spying; Ippolito had been acting; I was reluctant to think that Ippolito had perhaps also provoked.

Things had become clear, as he had foreseen in our meeting when secret threats seemed to be released. He had reacted at the word "people," I repeated to myself. And now, in those first, tragic July days, when the conspiracy had barely been discovered, all Ferrara gathered at court, around its duke; the churches were thick with incense and echoing with thanks. For Giulio there was only execration; from him every feeling of pity had receded.

The documents, swollen with mortal words, crackled beneath my fingers. Two of my brothers were ready for the scaffold. What could I do for them, exposed traitors, except make sure that they were allowed to live in decent conditions? I asked at least this, but someone could devise a way to elude the promise. And the moment had come to deliver Giulio to his judges, though he had taken refuge in Mantuan territory, where he felt safe under my protection.

The last act between Giulio and me was approaching its conclusion: He would climb the stairs, reaching this little room of mine, too sweetly grazed by vital currents, too elusive to house a tragedy. And how would I look at my brother, knowing I risked never seeing him again? What words would I find to offer him the germ of hope? Surely he would accuse me: He would refer to the ghastly blinding at Belriguardo; he would portray himself to me as one persecuted, provoked, and tricked; or worse, he would break down in a fit of guilt and would beg for pardon.

My pride was suffering. I was bound by all the torments of family love, but in that love I could discern a fraying of the will and the soul. Such rebellion assailed me that I could not prolong this waiting. My feelings were confounded; it was no longer an obligation for me to play this nightmare part.

Instinct was quicker than thought. I hid the papers brought from Ferrara. I went to the door in time to hear the animal cry of Giulio echoing up the stair, a desperate response to God knows

what exhortation. The cry was repeated. On the landing a little
stairway opened, a convenient passage I had had constructed in
order to reach the garden more rapidly. I slipped through it,
resolute, and flew down as far as the stables; my horse was sad-
dled for my daily morning ride. I left word with Teodora that I
was going to the rural convent of Suor Osanna and that she and
Margherita Cantelma should come and collect me before evening.
On his own initiative a groom, our old servant, followed me, and
I noticed his shadow behind me when the towers of Sacchetta
were out of sight.

     At the convent the nuns, speechless and concerned, came out
to receive me. I dismissed them; I had no wish for caresses and
compassion or anything else that might soothe my wounds. I had
betrayed one brother for another one, the weaker for the stronger.
True, the weaker was gravely guilty; but a ruthless hand had led
him to revolt, and I, without daring, without capacity for conflict,
for prescience or counsel, had weakly supported the cynical game.
Giulio had remained alone to face his guilt, as he was alone now
facing punishment and scorn. And yet I could still save him with
a determined, rebellious act, and even if I did not save him, I
should remain present, beside him, not refusing to hear his loud
cries.

     A flight· this had been my achievement. A loss: this was my
glory. I was so brimming with tears that I felt soaked; kneeling
at the little altar of Osanna, I deceived myself that exhaustion
meant peace.

I DISCOVER THAT the reasons of irritation, mixed with the reasons of attraction, somehow give the latter an unpredictable savor, as if the former stimulated the pleasantness of the other by the contrast of prickling and provocation. Delving more deeply, with clever mixtures, one could actually derive pleasure from annoyance. There, I am already laughing at these sparks struck from my special delight in antithesis. Enough of these counterfeits of thought.

Distant little voices, weak or shrill, cross in the apartment of the castle where the line of my rooms then unfolded. In those conjugal rooms I continually found myself pregnant with only moderate pleasure, though I welcomed without complaint these natural events as they occurred. At least so I believe now, but perhaps it was not exactly so. I was vexed and accepted reluctantly having to deny myself for repeated periods my rides in the open country, tasting the sun and the wind, shade and speed, and I grieved at putting my body to the test and combating those pains and the malaise that had stolen into my entrails. I did not rebel, but when I bore girls, I was disappointed, not because I loved them less, as Francesco charged, but because I was afraid and almost repelled when I considered the great suffering that lay in store for them unless they managed to rank among the leading women of the world. Those fragile creatures put my own privileges in doubt; I felt threatened by their future state and the unhappiness of submission that would befall them, as it did all other women. Though I had them educated as princesses, which they were—I could never have tolerated their being crude and ignorant—I did not foster their special talents to make them rise above a condition of cultivated, genteel innocence. Once when I thought I saw in Ippolita the genial gleam of an unusual idea, I trembled; luckily the convent gave her shelter in time, as it did her sister Livia. I loved them better as nuns, enhanced by their own dignity.

My male children have occupied great space in my life. When

I was young, the thought of them dominated me. When I came to more mature age and experience, each assumed a prominent but different position for me. I enthusiastically planned their actions, following them and shaping them in my fashion. My being a woman then became a virtue, an authority grasped and increased bit by bit within myself. I wanted all my children, male and female, to be beautiful and healthy, as any mother would wish. Some died in infancy because our inexplicable world is often hostile to an infant's fragility, and I duly mourned them; others followed, and I had to devote myself to them. Life does not grant pauses.

Once they were out of the cradle, I chose by myself a wise master for them, and I would allow no one else to appoint him. At times Francesco accused me of favoring some, in his opinion less worthy than others, like Vigilio, who had been my own master and whose cast of mind I knew. Though he was poor and always whining about the scant money he earned in the school he had opened for the children of the court gentlemen, Vigilio was to my liking. Already mature and eventually old, he was always impetuous and fresh in his way of teaching, and he taught not only grammar, philosophy, geometry, and Latin—Ovid was his favorite—but also the poets of vulgar Italian, such as our beloved Boiardo. He was well versed in Roman history, which Federico read like the Gospel itself, and especially he was skilled in having the children act in both prose and verse. Acting was my personal passion, which I had from my father, Ercole, the great restorer of the ancient theater.

At the Ferrara court they performed the greatest Latin plays translated by learned scholars, and as a child I was taught to distinguish the variations of tone that action imposes on the dialogue, the rhythm of development and contrast, and that sense of inner significance rising from the pauses that gives a work secret meanings of true allegory. I confess, I could have lived on plays in the theater. When Master Vigilio took up the papers and handed them out, assigning each of us a part, I was struck by a wind of expectation that lifted me off the ground. I was exalted by the idea that from every performance of a play it was possible to attain knowledge inaccessible to others even though they listened, and at each repeated performance of the same work to discover a new facet of the truth.

How I delighted in the gaiety of my little ones as they ardently repeated the few words that the master had written for them in tiny invented roles. Ah, that Christmas of 1506, when they were rehearsing *The Ant*, which Filippo Mantovano had adapted from the *Metamorphoses* of Apuleius. We spent day after day in a little room beyond the Painted Hall, where the fireplace consumed whole trunks, transformed as they burned, into white towers of ash brightened by red sparks. One afternoon of harshest cold, as Master Vigilio was correcting the tones and gestures of the players, Pirro Donati approached with his usual air of having matters of some importance to communicate to me; in the winter light his face blanched more than usual. The letters he handed me came from Rome and Bologna, and our informants sent us news writhing with ambiguity.

Two months had passed since Julius the Second entered Bologna, after driving out the Bentivoglios, abandoned by their French allies; thus that land, rich in material goods and strategically important, was restored to the Church. The enterprise had been achieved so suddenly that my Francesco, appointed with all magnificence lieutenant of the papal army, had rushed in vain to seize Bologna, because the Bentivoglios had fled without awaiting an armed confrontation. As often happens, the victory resolved nothing; the political tangle remained complex as ever. From France word came that Louis had determined to descend into Italy and take Genoa, on some dubious pretext of ancient concessions.

Disturbing reports were circulating in the Italian courts: It was said that the army readied by the French king was too powerful for a venture far from grandiose, and every day episodes took place, creating conflict between the Roman pontiff and King Louis, who had demanded the nomination of three French cardinals in compensation for the sacrifice of his Bentivoglio friends.

The meaning of all this intrigue, the extent to which the French could be trusted, I was unable to determine. And Francesco was about to go to Paris, summoned by the King, to receive another military investiture. But which? There was a plan behind it, but it was hard to deduce a truth that satisfied me. Pirro Donati and I exchanged long, puzzled glances, but he, ever tranquil, expressed no opinions. I returned the papers to him, to be replaced in my personal cupboard, and I tried to set aside my apprehensions.

As usual a terrible thunder of memory resounded within me; but I decided to concern myself with the plot of *The Ant*, and I relaxed in the flow of the speeches and the voice of Master Vigilio. I saw him bend forward, his hands expressively mobile or clenched in a gesture of strength, to remind the actors that they were reciting words from the first play written in the Italian language.

And inexorably, over these words, other speeches were super-imposed, from another play.

I closed my eyes, I returned to an earlier time. We were in the Hall of the "Trionfi," more than ten years before, during carnival of 1494. On the platform the players were rehearsing *The Prisoners of War* of Plautus, in the new translation that my father had sent me from Ferrara. The hall was cluttered with boxes, columns, whole or broken, capitals, and other architectonic elements in the Mantegna style. A wooden statue of Virgil, solemn in the verti-cally fluted drapery of the toga, stood in the background, almost filling the space. The "Trionfi" of Mantegna provided a noble setting, and on that platform the great painter moved about, keep-ing an eye on the men who were busily arranging the lights, candles, and lamps, according to his indications. He guarded the paintings, and from time to time he muttered a curse.

To one side the prisoners were lined up, chained and guarded by the Overseer and the Keeper of the prison. One moment of that wonderous dialogue is imprinted on my mind, when the keeper Hegio has the prisoners chained and urges them to be watched.

"The prisoner who tastes freedom is still like a wild bird; if he has an opportunity to escape, no one can catch him again."

The Overseer, philosophically, replies: "We all prefer to be free rather than slaves."

"Even you?" Hegio asks.

"I more than all," the other man replies. "Am I not the slave of my prisoners? If only I could escape!"

I was surprised and almost aghast at hearing a torturer's words echo the sorrow of his own condition, condemned to the impris-onment of others. The vigor of Plautus's discourse was revealed, with its hammered warnings. On the stage, against the base of the statue of Jove, someone had propped a marble slab with a gigantic 1494 carved on it in Roman numerals. Were the things they enacted of yesterday or today? Or perhaps tomorrow?

THE REHEARSAL continues; in the foreground are other char-acters, other symbols. From the left appears the chariot of the god Amor, and from the right the musicians enter briskly with their instruments, striking up a song. With cadenced steps toward cen-ter stage some girls advance, in Greek dress, crowned with roses, pretending to strew flowers. Impatiently I scold the beautiful Lia, one of my young maids.

"Lia, those are not rocks you are strewing before the god of love; they are rose petals."

The chariot proceeds, swaying on the stage. Our most radiant youths are on it, headed by my brother-in-law Giovanni, pretending, like the buffoon Metello, to be a prisoner of love. Amor is the handsome fifteen-year-old Baldesar Castiglione, the star of our court.

And again I speak up, exhorting: "Signor Baldesar, do you really think Love is an abstract god? Why are you looking around with such melancholy? Love conquers; Love shines; Love triumphs."

Then I address the musicians: "It's your fault. The music has no strength, no vitality. It puts us to sleep. Tibaldo, change key, change music. Invent something beautiful!"

And Tibaldo replies joyously: "We will change! Yes, I have everything that can serve, and it is all at your feet, signora marchesana. We will play a lively four-part frottola!"

The imperiousness of my willful twenty years inflames me. And how lightly I run! "Wait for me," I cry. I am in time to see Metello seize Cupid's bow, draw it, and shoot the arrow at the rotundities of a youth who has bent over. He starts and curses angrily, but his voice is drowned in the great laughter. I stand to one side in the background, by the statue of Virgil, to judge the effect of the entrance; there the players cannot spy me, but I hear a faint, silvery tinkle of bells coming from outside. The windows are opened; Metello cries, "The courtesans, the courtesans!" And all, including the melancholy Baldesar, crowd at the sills, brushing away the snow. I shake my head. Truly, men are ingenuous and laughable when they exult so coarsely at the sight of women of pleasure; they think such women are at their service, but they do not realize that they, the men, are more taunted by the women's intolerance along with a special kind of contempt. I wonder, then, if men really do love them. The youths hanging out of the windows call them, and unusual names fall on the snowy air: Stellata, Picinarda, Frontina, names that vaguely suggest those of the heifers in our barns. The women are going to the special Monday sermon devoted to them by our monks, who exhort them to redeem themselves. But those sermons are so irritating; poor girls, they are right to fall asleep in church.

I BELIEVE I must have had a reproachful look as I emerged from the shadow of Virgil's statue; I was amused to see Pirro Donati as catching sight of me, he moved quickly away from the windows and, with cautious steps, disappeared among the pieces of scenery. I pretended not to see him, but I was not expecting, as I turned my head, to see an apparition before me. The voices died, silence fell; in the center of the hall a colossal horse's skeleton rose, mounted by a giant skeleton, a scythe over its shoulder. I knew the drawing that had inspired it, by the hand of Master Leonardo da Vinci, but enlarged in this way, hoisted by the stage machinery, it was a specter of war and of death, the first of those that would mark that year of 1494.

Soon would come the time of the first invasion of the French, when they crossed the Alps and brought to us changes of realms, overturned thrones, fierce desolation of cities and country. Now, twelve years later, the army of King Louis was threatening us as the army of King Charles had threatened then. The army was arriving; was the moment of losing everything also here? I thought of our Bentivoglio kin, driven from their houses and their realm, and of the generous admonition of Francesco, who from afar had exorted me to help them; it seemed to him so unbearable and pathetic for them to be fugitives, roaming the world. And yet, at that very moment, Francesco was serving the pope, vanquisher of those same Bentivoglios, and in Mantua there had been great celebration of that expulsion. Everything seemed confused; our ideas wavered. I looked down at my children, seated with their little heads upraised, gaping, toward Master Vigilio, in that room gaily painted with astrological signs, flowers and fruit, and medallions of the great men of antiquity. The fireplace crackled as more faggots were added by the silent servants; everything was calm, peaceful, sheltered. But into my memory drifted the vision of the two skeletons, horse and horseman, who were directed, beyond anyone's power to stop them, toward our lands, immersed in their green peace.

THE STARS decided: My last male child would be born during carnival and would fear no one. But nature hesitated over that birth, my term passed, and nothing happened. My mood was saturnine; my body was heavy, shuddering. Every day I questioned the astrologer Paride of Ceresara, but his responses never clarified anything for me. I had learned that my chief druggist, Giusto of Udine, was a great scholar of astrological volumes, and I sent for him to come up to my chambers. His greatest masters were also mine—Abumashar, Pietro de Abano; and Giusto examined every paragraph of their works, discussing the arcana of Greek cosmology, and Egyptian, Indian, Arabic, handed down through Spanish codices to our own libraries. In part I knew his argumentation; I did not grow up for nothing in Ferrara, where I breathed the teachings of Pellegrino Prisciano, interpreter of every astral sign, who had prophesied for me, through endless twists and turns of words, a future crammed with greatness. My sign, in fact, is that of the Twins, as I was born on the fourteenth day of the month of May. But even Giusto's predictions were unreliable. As Pico rightly concluded, these astrologers are not secure in their science.

The first half of January was already gone, and after the great confusion of the court, busy with preparations for Pope Julius's war, now long silences followed. Francesco, with a part of his troops, was riding from Bologna toward Ferrara, and from there he would go on to France, to the court of the king. Unconsciously my distrust of the French was increasing: They were too haughty, impatient, contemptuously self-confident, and King Louis's head was too full of plans, which, being a king's plans, would perforce be carried out, to someone's harm. Francesco, on the contrary, with his natural tendency to trust the summons of good fortune, believed himself the object of every possibility and was of a spirit to hold his own with anyone. And further, he was distracted by thoughts of love. At Ferrara in the Este castle he would meet his duchess Lucrezia. I shrugged. Aching in every limb and rebelling against my dull condition, I told myself I had no time to give that senseless couple. It was not true. For her, Lucrezia, I imagined every sort of action to defeat her, to make her bow her head in humiliation, after which I would regain my husband and, with him, my lover.

I was shaken by a covert letter sent me from Ferrara by a secret informant of mine who described to me the merry carnival season at court and described a ball my brother Alfonso had given at Schifanoia. Amid the gold of the embroideries, the dresses, and the men's robes, the purple of six cardinals stood out, all of them young—Aragón, Cornaro, Volterra, Colonna, Cesarini, Medici— and all tireless in dancing with the most charming girls of the duchess. Francesco appeared all dressed in white, and she, Lucrezia, in silver, almost always paired, distracted and smiling. And I, here in my room, suffered the surging of my blood.

I dispelled those protagonists and dwelt on my Schifanoia's hall, and the first person I met there was Pellegrino Prisciano, who had devised for the painters that hall more dense with signs,

I believe, than any other ever conceived. The incredible concept of the astrologer, Latinist, Grecian, who derived his learning from the world's knowledge. It was a bold enterprise to read that story on the walls that our painters, Francesco del Cossa, Ercole de' Roberti, Cosmé Tura, and a host of lesser artists, had bejeweled with colors and inventions. The boldness lay in trying to understand them. I had grown up amid that painting and all my life had sensed the supreme rarity of the spare, incised drawing, at once archaic and germinal, bursting with opposed forces. The rational ordering of the great story was amazing, as it narrated the history of the months, the history of life, leaving its enigma unresolved.

He divided the four walls into twelve parts, according to the number of the year's months, and each part was then subdivided into three horizontal areas. In the lower section everyday life unfolded: the toil of the fields; the days of Duca Borso; the city's feasts. At the top the allegories of each month were connected with the myths of the ancient gods: Minerva, Apollo, Jove, Venus, Juno, Mercury. Between the two areas a mysterious astrological band, on dark blue ground, bore signs and figurations governed by fantasies distilled from Oriental influences, Arab legends, Egyptian, Hebrew, Greek, transfigurations of occult meaning.

Often I had fixed my gaze on the mystery of my month: Apollo dominant on his triumphant chariot in the upper area, among poets and the symbols of poetry and music, flanked by a group of naked twins delicately decorated with little necklaces and talismans. Below, Duca Borso smiles as a peasant offers him a basket of the first cherries. And in the middle band the facing twins balance a scene of solemn investiture, like the transmission of a sacred power. I had never managed to discover the secret meaning of the flute player before whom a symbolical man is kneeling, almost naked, his arms folded over his chest. Pellegrino had forecast for me the total meaning of my sign: a sovereignty in the world of harmony; a glorious fertility as a woman. Nothing so far had contradicted the prophecy, and my life seemed to evolve from a benignant allegory. But now? Was this the moment for the enigmatic figures painted by artists flirting with demonical powers to come forward, to extinguish the myths of the ancients and the solarity of terrestrial life? The troubled color of the central area, a mixture of shadows and blue, emanated a kind of horror from which I could not save myself.

I resumed reading the letter of the Ferrarese, and I found them there, those two—Francesco and Lucrezia still dancing—but they seemed caught in a sinister light, reflection of the shadowy blue band. The torch dance was announced, which the lady, as a privilege, could offer her gentleman, and he took the torch from her hands with a tender complicity. Behind them, measuring them and inciting, stood Ercole Strozzi with his forced smile, emanation of an astral demon. Alfonso and Ippolito entered, firm and distant figures, to be feared. My God, what flame burned within me, what presentiment of tragedy that I alone could grasp. The astrological symbols were menacing; the poetry of May was poisoned by the presence of a pander poet; against the troop of twins a Herod was sent; presages of death descended on the scene like a veil. I called Francesco with a sob, and at once Pirro Donati appeared beside my bed and spoke to me softly. A courier had arrived from Ferrara; soon the marchese would be home.

The door opened onto the adjoining room, and from time to time someone peered in. The jester Frittella, with my little Ercole like a monkey on his shoulder, stuck his head inside; I made a gesture to keep him away, but I was not understood. I remained motionless, my eyes half closed. Believing I had dozed off, they conferred in voices not too low, asking about me, about the child reluctant to be born. Ercole clapped his little hand on Frittella's head with a childish "ta-ta-ta." I caught the buffoon wiping his eyes; he was moved. Did he love me then? Beyond his condition, did he really feel something for his mistress? I would never have thought it; from now on he would have to be placed in a different position. A priest came; my clouded eyes prevented me from seeing him well. The nurse, Caterina, grieving, whispered to him: "She has no strength left, our lady; she can't go on."

I tugged and sat up against the pillows. I found again my clear and strong tone, and I ordered all to leave the room, save the nurse. They were to close the doors; no one should dare enter.

I had to be alone, to make my child come into the world. I had to rid myself of that dense clot that was oppressing me and give breath to a new existence. The first act of love toward him was this: to separate him from me, having now achieved him. Thrust, suffered, and incited, the hard knot dissolved, and when I emitted the last cry, the infant voice replied. Ferrante was born, the third of my sons, the last male, who would become a blond, curly-haired man of war.

IN DEEP winter a soft, heavy fog encircled trees and bushes, stiff, faded by the cold. Enfolded in a long overgarment lined with fur, cut sumptuously, of gold brocade with red flowers, I went through the slender, chilled stand of poplars, where in straight, precise rows the thin, lifeless trees were aligned. I observed the slender trunks.

"All of them have taken root, every one!" I said.

Outside the grove a young horseman was waiting for me, dressed in an elegant cloak of Alexandrine velvet, delicately beaded by the fog. He was a Ferrara gentleman, a man of letters, of my brother Ippolito's household, sent by him to congratulate me on the birth of Ferrante and to cheer me.

"Do you not find it a wise custom, the ancients' way of planting trees dedicated to the memory of people dear to us?" I asked him. "I have imitated them. And this poplar wood that rustles in my imagination will be the grove of Ercole, my dear father."

"We miss him in Ferrara," the gentleman murmured, and promptly added, "but we are growing accustomed to the rule of the duke Alfonso, who has displayed great prudence and firmness."

"And the cardinal?" I asked, laughing. "Does my brother continue inviting swarms of cardinals to his festivities?"

The gentleman replied, respectful and jovial: "I cannot say. I work with my pen."

I pulled the fur around my neck, and joyfully breathed the cold air and the fog.

"Let us go back inside now; a good fire will warm us."

How merry was that ground-floor room in the villa at Porto. A winding frieze of scrolls and escutcheons, volutes and colored geometries unfolded on the walls; besides the lighted fire, two great braziers warmed the air. At one of the two fires sat the young wet nurse, slender and pretty as the painters' view of spring. In her arms my son Ferrante, a few days old, grimaced, his eyes closed. I presented the infant to the guest, who uttered appropriate words; the baby, wrapped in his swaddling clothes, seemed to accept them loftily. I confessed that his calm detachment had cost me dearly; I could already joke freely about the pain he had given me.

Flashing, the green plumes of Frittella's cap swayed in the air, steamy from the smoke of the burning fires. Ercole, the *peteghin* of the family, was on his back. The gentleman inquired about Federico, and as always my thoughts flew to my firstborn son with a gratitude I felt only for him. Yes, Federico was at the castle with his master of arms, beginning his first exercises. I ordered Frittella to remove Ercole from his back; I did not want the child to have crooked legs from being carried around all day on the buffoon's shoulders.

"Never fear," he said gaily. "In any case my master Ercole is destined to become a cardinal, and that robe hides all defects."

I motioned the gentleman to sit down between fireplace and braziers, opposite me. I felt a vibration in his presence as if I were awaiting something from him alone, as my children, immersed in their heedless childhood, withdrew from me. We talked of plays, of those performed in Ferrara and of ours in Mantua. He confided in me that sometime ago he had begun writing an Italian play, and it was entitled *La Cassaria*; but it was not yet finished.

One of my chamber women entered with hot spiced wine and poured out a strong potion; we drank together. Curious about this visitor, I bent slightly toward him, and a question dangerous in conversation, but, in this case, direct, straightforward, escaped my bosom: What did he prefer doing above all else? He hesitated but replied frankly: He had a great idea in mind, surely far greater than he, he hastened to insist through some instinct of exorcism. He wanted to write a courtly epic; indeed, he had already written the first cantos. I knew that but did not say so; instead, I asked him if he planned to provide a sequel to the *Orlando Innamorato* of our beloved Boiardo.

"No, I do not think to continue it. My Orlando will be different, he will be furious, mad with love. The beautiful woman, Angelica, will cause him to lose his reason."

As a rule, poets carry in their pockets little pages with their verses and expect to be begged to read them. Signor Ludovico Ariosto had no pages with him, but very simply, from memory, he began to recite:

> *Dirò di Orlando in medesmo tratto*
> *cose non dette in prosa mai nè in rima*
> *che per amore venne in furore e matto*
> *d'uom che sì saggio era creduto prima.*

The flow of his words and then of images introduced a full-blooded tale; rhythm and melodious sound were expressed in those verses.

"Signora marchesana, I am happy that you are the first to know something of this work of mine. All of it is here, and here," he added, and raised his hand to touch his head and his heart; then he resumed:

Orlando che gran tempo innamorato
fu della bella Angelica e per lei
in India in Media in Tartaria lasciato
avea infiniti ed immortal trofei. . . .

"It will be a story of love, of all the loves that drive men mad. My Orlando, when he discovers Angelica's betrayal, is driven to black madness, and his comrade-at-arms, the paladin Astolfo, flies on the hippogriff and crosses the circle of fire around the earth, to land on the moon and seek his friend's reason."

"And what does Astolfo find on the moon? And what is this moon like?"

"An enormous glacial plain, blinding, steely. And there Astolfo will find everything that humans have misplaced and forgotten: the tears and sighs of lovers; the futile idleness of the ignorant; vain plans; vain yearnings; defeated hopes."

I thought of the rediscovery of beloved sufferings and the betrayed joys of men and by women. Crossed by the lonely astral rider, that immense plain of icy glints, where lost desires roamed like ghosts, announced a bold, new imagination that would affect us closely, encompassing all human feelings. I fixed my gaze on that face opposite me, so calm and polite; it did not seem the face of a great innovator, except for the brief spark that flashed from time to time in its features with an immediate warmth. Who was this Signor Ludovico degli Ariosti? The elegant and amiable and slightly lazy man who always followed my brother Ippolito, his master? Surely he considered the cardinal frantic, always ready to depart, return, bestir himself, give orders. And what was I for him? The marchesana of Mantua, a woman who could protect him amid the envy of courts, see that he was granted benefits. He would be grateful, perhaps, and surely proud, but I would never reach him because of that distance I felt existed between me and him like a space without bridges. I remained a powerful woman; he, a poet. The only thing I could do, I said to him with admiration and a touch of annoyance, was remain silent and listen further.

WHO IS at the organ? You do not know and do not ask. Excited laments rise up, to plunge headlong in an unfolding of mournful notes, accompanying your pain; your eyes are filled with tears. Not mine. I do not weep, I follow the sacred ceremony at the death of the friend dear to you, under the graceful vaulted ceiling of Sant'Andrea, I pray in fits and starts, and I hope God will be indulgent toward me. I must say it: I almost exult inwardly at the discovery of something I would have considered impossible an hour ago. I love you, Francesco; I love you still; this great emptiness that yawns in my breast as I see you fight against your tears has brought back to me the emotions of the far-off time when words and gestures were shared between us, confounded with our selves.

What have we made of life, Francesco? I speak to you, holding myself in a stiff silence, and you suffer elsewhere. The discovered delight of still loving you I must keep secret, so as not to lose it. You would never believe such a confession; you would think that this strange, fervid joy is actually the pleasure of attending a funeral service dedicated to a man I always regarded with suspicion. And—who knows?—you could even be right. No, I did not love your Ercole Strozzi, your great Latin poet, elegantly lame, the implacable judge of the Wise, the close friend and fearless courtier of the duchess of Ferrara, your Lucrezia.

I have always known everything about the two of you; I had my informants. I have gained the power to reconstruct the sequence of your passion's inner movements. He, Strozzi, helped you both: He sent messengers from Ferrara and received those that came from Mantua. At seven-towered Sermide, on the Po, your various agents met rapidly, fleetingly. I have never wanted to put my hands on your letters; proof is of no use to me, nor is imagining your words for her and hers for you.

How many tapers have been lighted for this mass of suffrage? The organ sings the pain of mortals. A heavy tear has slid down your cheek, pale today and prominent as in the Mantegna portrait in Santa Maria della Vittoria. You resolutely shake your cropped hair, angrily dry those tears with a gloved hand. But what a contradictory way you have of being resolute, Francesco.

This low year is passing, this June marred for me who would not accept the facts. For her, for your duchess, I care nothing, and I say it almost voluptuously. But you, my husband, the father of my children, the honored master of this Mantua great in enthusiasm as it is small in space, the city where I came at sixteen and that is now my country, you must be there for me. Feelings can waver, vanish, and rise again suddenly from their underground turmoil; but you must be there, and I say this to the man who is trying to evade me. You do not know it, but it is so: You praise me and bow to me, and neither praise nor bow is a com-

munication between us, but a way of closing yourself behind a
defense that holds you prisoner.

The chanting of the acolytes resumes, over a free rhythm. The
tenorish voice of Trombincino enters the musical pattern, as his
response rises: *"Circumderdeunt me gemitus mortis."*

You, torn between the solace of music and the vengeful intentions that make you frown, bow your head, your eyes full of
visions I will never know. And you do not know that this church
is also full of eyes that stare at you, harder, more disturbing, and
more dangerous. These are the eyes of Alfonso's informers and
those of the more detached Ippolito. Do you not know that Alfonso has had built a secret passage to reach the apartments of
his wife in the Este castle? And he has placed on guard there that
courtier of his, feigned or genuine eccentric, Barone, who spies
on her. And do you know what secret hypotheses, what suspicions are germinating in him, my brother? We write each other.
Carefully I try to peer beneath the lines, and I am certain that he
suspects you, a cold and cautious suspicion that will not blaze up
but seeks, rather, a confirmation, from your imprudence or her
vagueness, a foolish word of that fanatic of yours, who occupies
the place of our royal mother.

And do you really believe that the two of them, my brothers,
or at least one of them, did not covertly guide the hand, direct
the blow that killed him whose spirit we are recommending to
God, the victim of an assassination? Why do you refuse to see
what is hidden behind the air of performance that accompanied
the murder of Ercole Strozzi? Who knows the place where he was
stabbed nine times, to be carried, lifeless, to the Convent of San
Bernardino, and how was his corpse tidied, with all the clumps
of hair that had been torn from his head carefully placed beside
his body? Did you not suspect, in the horror of that theatricality,
the ironic satisfaction, the mocking admonition, the perfidious
laugh? The Estes, my brothers, forgive no one. In Ercole Strozzi
they perceived and judged the work of "most excellent pander"
(as he said, impudently, of himself); they provoked his enemies,
hinted that they would have a free hand, no one would hinder
them, no one would stop them.

You are defenseless, Francesco, exposed to the gravest danger,
and this thought does not make you blench. A great prey for you,
this Lucrezia, who closes her eyes against the menacing shadows
of her husband and her brother-in-law. Camillo and Tigrino: these
are the names the two of you have invented for Alfonso and
Ippolito, and Tigrino is surely an expressive name that well de-

notes its bearer's cruelty. Tigrino is the man who, after the tragedy of Don Giulio, my poor brother, still dying, half blind, in a prison of the castle of Ferrara, laughs at such suffering and its murky causes and goes about the city disguised in sumptuous masks.

This rite is long; the archpriest is enjoying the slow chant and the ritual gestures, the evocative music, the lights, the gold glints of the liturgical vessels. I wonder if any priest has confessed a voluptuousness in savoring the sacred, a voluptuousness which surely God disdains. And you, Francesco, have you ever thought to include your guilt in those confessions that you never neglect, in your mania for penance, perhaps to feel its sharp sense of stimulation? I wonder what God's role is in your life. And, I cannot say why, I refuse to ask myself what his role is in mine.

There you are, standing up; the service is about to end. We have already replied to the supreme invocation, *A porta inferis*. You motion me to rise as well; you are coming over, and you hold out your hand for our ceremonial exit. You are already here, Francesco. Gently I press your fingers, to communicate my warning: Beware of the Estes; beware of Alfonso and Ippolito; they would never forgive you the dishonor of their name, not even for my sake. Killed or crippled by a paid cutthroat, on a meadow like that of Belriguardo: this would be your lot.

We walk side by side. God! if only I could say to you, "Be on your guard, Francesco!" but I can prompt you only with a sidelong glance that becomes gradually more severe. I must take your life in hand and divert the mortal stream from you, and this I will do, at all costs. I feel again in my blood the icy impetus of my father, the west wind of my childhood. I will even sign a secret pact with your enemies that will transfix your passions, your prides, your very dignity. I will put the wall of a fortress between you and her, that dire Lucrezia, who never ceases crushing and destroying those who do not keep far enough away. But you will remain alive. And I? I will face the risk of no longer loving you.

To the Most Illustrious and Excellent Madama Isabella, Marchesana of Mantua and My Lady

*I*f I were not convinced, by the many legends surrounding your name, that you seek out and enjoy stories of things that happen in every land and stories gravid with the prescience of things still to happen, I would not dare write again after two years of silence, of which I hope you are to some small degree aware. Surely you have not counted them. And yet, in the proper abasement of my condition, this thread is also beautiful, suddenly binding your royalty and my subjection. The most obscure of your correspondents, I can look up at your serene eye, clear star in the stormy heavens.

Do not believe, illustrious and dear lady, that I would write you better and more often if there had come to my ear the slightest word of myself being somehow mentioned by you. I defend myself against the thought of you through prayer, and prayer sometimes fails me. The great silence that separates us is a kind of freedom in which I immerge myself with infinite ifs and infinite whens and hows.

I attach myself to your life, and I imagine it; but what is happening around us makes me uneasy about your existence (confined as you are in the narrow space of your State by the many ambitions of kings and potentates). I can even come to rejoice in the toilsome rule of my king, Henry the Seventh, sovereign of England, only to a slight degree involved in the events of Europe. And so we English, at present, are not responsible for any of the clamors and conspiracies that threaten you.

As a rule my residence is Rome (not today, but I will soon tell you of that), and I attend to questions of foreign policy that extend from the Vatican to our remote north, as assistant to our most worthy English ambassador and representative of the king. Here, in the Curia, we are witnesses to the new and

glorious progress begun in these first years of his papacy by
Julius the Second, and this would be a rare privilege were it
not for a deep shadow that is felt to fall over the excellence of
the arts and of letters. It is impossible not to sense that from
their geographical situations the various nations assert
unspeakably disturbing, incurable intolerance of their
neighbors. Everything can happen, and this everything
comprises the saddest possibilities. Men of destruction
dominate men of honor, interrupting great and wonderous
works that will cause our age to be eternally remembered. It is
truly terrible, this way we exist between superb spiritual
achievements and profound certitude of inconceivable sorrows,
pressing at our gates. Though the famous texts of antiquity that
have been recovered ennoble the world of modern study, the
spirit is afflicted by too many dire signs, and it is an effort not
to moan.

I do not want to becloud your lovely face, my lady, but you
will agree that it is unbearable not to be allowed to grasp
beauty and splendor when they are shown to us. When I say
Rome, I mean all Italy, and Europe. I have an example in this
triumphant city where I now am, far from my office in the
Curia. I am in Venice, in fact. Yes, I have come to Venice,
following one of the most illustrious scholars of our time, the
Dutchman Desiderius Erasmus of Rotterdam, of whom you
have surely heard. I will tell you something about him. Having
come to Italy to extend his already vast learning in the cities of
famous universities, he took his doctorate in Turin, got to
know Bologna, and is eager to visit Padua, planning to arrive
even as far as Rome. He is a supreme Latinist and Grecian,
author of already celebrated works, and he speaks only the
Latin language, amazed when some Italian cannot understand
him. His writings of genius, his infinitely subtle mind are for
those who surround him a constant source of admiration and
of blithe pleasure of the intellect.

I can say that in a certain sense Erasmus has become
attached to me, for he arrived from England accompanying
two sons of my king's preferred Genoese doctor, Signor
Boerio. Those promising young men stayed on in Bologna, to
undertake the study of jurisprudence. And as I had traveled

to meet Erasmus and pay him honor after his doctorate in
Turin, I came with him here to Venice, where he was led by
his desire to publish some of his works—a translation of
Euripides and a book, the *Adagia*, of proverbs and epigrams
taken from Latin texts—entrusting them to the finest printer
in the world, who is, as I know, also your correspondent:
Aldus Manutius.

You cannot imagine, my lady, how pleased I am at the
thought that you respect and love Aldus. It is right that you
can never have enough of his books, where words are set
precisely, with unparalleled clarity. I daydreamed of a colloquy
in that Latin, which you speak like a Roman Clelia, with
Erasmus himself. And I must tell you that he is inspired by
great admiration for women of true learning. Indeed, among
his notes he has shown me the draft of a work of his, in the
form of a dialogue between a certain clever Magdalia and an
ignorant abbot, who stubbornly denies that study befits
women. He has promised me, my friend Erasmus, to send me
a copy when he has finished it, and if you permit me, it shall
be yours. For you are Magdalia. A pity our fancy cannot dwell
at any length in a paradise on this earth, so shaken by fierce
trumpet blasts that seem to announce the horsemen of the
Apocalypse.

So then, I am in Venice, staying with Aldus Manutius, king
of printers. I am lodged in a little room of his house, near the
Rialto, and in these few rooms, kept in careful order, buzzes
the hive of the thickest honey of wisdom that has ever been
distilled. Erasmus himself has a room in the house, and all
during the day, amid the racket of the presses and the voices of
the other printers, we receive the men of greatest intellect and
knowledge in this proud city. We take delight in the work of
Aldus and his infallible discernment in choosing ancient and
modern texts. Erasmus oversees the printing, faultless, of his
works, listening to the advice of his keen and educated friend.
The idea of the *Adagia* had already come to him in London
sometime ago; I was informed of it by my English friends, four
polished scholars and Latinists trained in the most difficult
disciplines. If I may, I would like truly to introduce you to at
least their names, with the most respectful bow: Thomas

Linacre, William Croceyen, William Later, Cuthbert Dunstal.
You would surely like to discourse with them in Latin.

To return to Aldus: it is incredible how this simple house can
contain so much learning and industry, crowded with printers,
proofreaders, draftsmen, masters and professors of the
studium, who often come from Padua to restore their spirit
amid the great novelties of science and letters. Instruments tick
and click; the cries of the workmen overlap; snow-white paper
is unrolled, to be transformed into books of utter perfection.
Each man's work is very beautiful. Aldus's wife, an energetic
woman from Asolo, manages the entire household of thirty-
nine people, and among the benches and stools runs a little
boy, the Manuziolino of the house. Erasmus enters as if he
were followed by a swarm of students and masters, and often
he is. His person is never in the way; indeed, he is rather tiny;
he has a thin face that seems governed by the strength of his
thought, eyes of a shifting gray, a long, pointed nose which
lends irony and a supreme subtlety to his face; his refined voice
is strengthened by a clear resonance, at times gay, always
persuasive. In his expansive moods, Erasmus germinates ideas
in those who listen to him.

During the day we are in the company of men of science:
Giovanni Lascaris, Battista Egnazio, Marco Muscurus, Fra
Urbano Balzani. The talk begins when one of us improvises a
subject, and everything becomes material for reflections of
genius. It can be said, and has been said, that this simple Rialto
house in Venice is the center of the world. I assure you, we
are, we will be men of peace, and in our circle vehement
speeches and invectives are raised only against the folly of
arms and politics and against the dire ambitions that make both
peoples and potentates rapacious.

For truly in this Venice, city without walls, the danger
threatening us is felt more than elsewhere. I ponder the force
of the word "danger" and how it strikes us by menacing those
we venerate. Will you forgive me for having suffered great pain
without being authorized to do so? For some time I have
wanted to confess this abuse of feeling to you, but I did not
dare. Now, in these troubled and darkened times, I believe I
may. It was last year, in autumn, in Rome. I happened to see

in the Curia a letter sent from Mantua. As it was a copy, it bore no signature, but it was presumably sent to Pope Julius by the marquis of Mantua, your illustrious spouse. He accused the French of doubting his loyalty as an ally and of constantly taunting him about it. So he felt he had no other course than to send something of his as hostage to gray Paris, and as lesser evil, he was thinking of sending you, my lady, not wanting to deprive himself of his children or abandon his State himself.

I cannot tell you the chill I felt. To send you far away and alone with risk also to your life if the alliance went wrong or were revealed contrary to the aims of the French, robbed of your children in a foreign land and one not entirely to be trusted. Even to the marquis the idea seemed monstrous, and he begged His Holiness to provide him with a way of avoiding that "sinister step," and he concluded that if the pope were to succeed in mending things without his having to send a hostage, it would seem a paradise to him.

I quickly realized how desperate the poor lord must have been. Besieged by the emperor Maximilian, his feudal master; by the king of France, so invincibly attracted to conquests in Italy; by the pope, determined to take any course against the enemies of the Church; and by the Venetians, stubbornly bound to the idea of their own greatness and invincibility, a man could hardly keep from going mad, I thought, as he tried honorably to escape them all. My head hummed insistently with the thought of you, paragon of all women, forced into exile, scapegoat of errors, suspicions, enmities.

I was long uneasy, and only after having vainly used every sort of trick and meticulousness to learn something that would confirm or deny that autumn news, I was somewhat reassured. There was no more talk of hostages from Mantua, or at least I found no further trace among the Curia papers.

Nevertheless,

Much later

How appropriately that "nevertheless" appeared, to remain suspended, a few hours ago, when hearing noises in the house, I suddenly stopped writing, convinced I would soon return to my desk. But on the contrary, further news awaited me: To join our friends, Signor Marin Sanudo has arrived, historian of this republic; and he has informed us most precisely about the League formed at Cambrai between the most Christian king of France and the emperor, with the united aim of proceeding toward a so-called Peace of Europe. But what peace can it be if one of its declared purposes is to force Venice to make restitution of conquered lands, an imposition that can only mean war? Though we were expecting it, no one imagined this disaster would be sanctioned so quickly and actually proclaimed at Cambrai on the tenth of December this year of 1508. We were still speechless when the voice of Erasmus was raised, with supreme authority, sibilant with outrage, but calm in the vigor of argument.

"And they call themselves Christians!" he cried. "Envious one of the other, without faith, without any true wish for peace, these men, who, instead of rejoicing when a State is enjoying a moment of prosperity, think only of tearing one another to pieces. I am ashamed to recall the causes, frivolous or wicked, for which men drive the world to war. What fury could instill such poison in Christian souls? See how they prepare to assail their brothers with infernal weapons that will bring only massacre, blood, and death. Who would believe that the cannon is a human invention? To lacerate the flesh of their similars, to kill them, is the only purpose of these evil soldiers, who still raise the symbol of the cross and never wonder what the believers' cross has to do with their offensive arms. They invoke peace in loud voices, while they prepare instruments of death. Serpents, tigers, and wolves are better than these, who would call themselves men of Christ."

Majestic and sorrowing was the rage of this wise man, tortured by the mad inhumanity of rulers, of the mighty. We, as convinced and sorrowful as he, stood there listening to him. "Nevertheless" I had written you a moment before, and I meant to say that the announcements of war are gradually growing more frequent, disguised perhaps as a crusade against the Turks or behind political, quibbling disquisitions. We will pursue this maleficent adventure; the helpless and wretched will be slain by the thousands, victims of ferocious, arrogant men. And you? You are not a sheltered creature; your person can easily be commanded. And generous and strong as you are, if they were to send you as hostage to some foreign land, you would probably set out with head high, confident in meeting the challenge. This is why, rightly, I had a presentiment of danger with that suspended word, and this is why I was right to suffer so much because of that letter of a year ago. And now, as Erasmus's words strike me one by one like burning droplets, I do not want to go on writing you, for I fear more and more to provoke with these same words your most delicate frowns.

I will say only that at our urging, Erasmus has decided to journey to Rome, and I am going with him, having overcome the temptation to visit Mantua, incognito. I had a mad notion: to wait in the square for your coming out and then to swing my horse in tourney figures to attract your attention. I wonder if I might have discerned on your face an immediate expression of absolution, before the severity of your spirit turned alert. But I have no right to steal from you something to which I am not entitled. So our party will proceed by way of Ferrara, where a young English friend of mine, Robert Pace, resides in a palace at court, and perhaps someone will speak to me of you. Under the great arch of the ducal palace I will see you again, the slender little girl with a gaze as straight as a sword's blade, but this sweet recollection will not diminish my uneasiness, as everything proceeds to confirm possible disasters. The latest news is that the emperor Maximilian at Innsbruck is making such elaborate preparations that he seems determined to bring down not only Venice but the whole world.

What will happen? Where will you be? Do not leave Mantua; in your land, in your castle, in your house, surrounded by your children, you cannot be attacked. Do not agree to go as hostage anywhere. My God, why does this word "hostage" have such a sinister ring? I do not know if I will find the courage to write you again; it is a courage that needs, at least for a moment, to be comforted. I will pray devoutly and contritely that you may live through these times of fire like the mythical salamander, untouched.

I am your servant, asking your indulgence, and I do not know for what. Farewell, farewell. Your Excellency's

> *faithful slave*
> Robert de la Pole
> *born in England,*
> *if that can help me, in your eyes*

Venice, the twelfth of December, 1508

Room of the clocks
the year 1533

I AM NOT very successful in ordering my eyes not to turn toward the table inlaid with bits of mother-of-pearl where I have laid the pages of jagged handwriting, and even a mere attempt at such a command arouses in me a silent revolt. And still, though it is something different from a simple secret, it is true that at long and irregular intervals I have received letters from this distant relative of the duke of Suffolk, whom I saw only once, a visitor like so many others; yet he has dared write me without my assent or permission. Robert de la Pole: I pronounce this name always with amazement; it seems to ring false. Often I have questioned myself, to find out if some slight movement of mine during the visit he paid me had encouraged him, but I can find nothing. I have never answered his letters, never mentioned him, not even to my confessor. I know very well that sometimes a ruling family's secrets are too heavy for a man, a good friar, to bear them all his life, even if mine, at least so I believe, are not secrets but simply unrequested letters.

My Pirro Donati, the only one who knows vaguely of the existence of these papers, is of a fidelity so tried and true that he would never allow himself to utter a word, and he surely thinks these are letters of philosophical thought, of the sort that many ecclesiastics or poets write to ladies. I am trying to persuade myself that the name of Robert de la Pole signifies something innocent, but I cannot. Perhaps there is innocence on his part, but on mine there might not be; the lines between virtue and guilt are so faint.

This Englishman's sincerity, his realism so intermingled with his idealism always impress me. They belong to a man intolerant of patient endurance, and yet, with me, extremely patient, curious about everything, easily aroused to enthusiasms that would seem more suited to a southerner than to one born among the brumes of the north. But perhaps ardor is all the stronger when it springs from the deep chill of the climate. I have also forbidden myself to seek, in our Gonzaga library, books that describe the island of Albion; it would be like seeking him. And further, I am amazed at his open concern, as if he had some right not over me perhaps but to move about in a circle in which I stand as center.

The only real thing, I have often repeated to myself, is that he trusts my silence, and indeed, if Francesco had read these papers, there would have been a real explosion of protests, and he might even have taken steps to have the Englishman sent away from Rome, from Italy, and would have added to his own wrath that of his bishop. Imagine this letter of 1508: "You are not defended"; "Refuse to go as hostage"; "Watch your words with those closest to you." Like a madman, he ran the risk of provoking my husband. Reading this, Francesco would have believed in an offensive hallucination, not out of love for me but for himself.

I sigh, but what could he have reproached me with? By dint of staying with my enemies, Francesco has learned to see me as the woman they saw. Once again I ask myself what the foreigner's words have aroused in me: an ardent curiosity, penetrating, almost an anxiety; an impression of closeness; a freshness of emotions and the possibility of harboring them, eluding everything. Yes, I found myself again a very young woman, intact, her life barely begun.

He was right, the Englishman: I am not "sheltered," but who is ever sheltered from everything? And what if I were, in reality, the least rooted creature on earth? Though I have always been alert to real things, metaphysical things have also seduced me infinitely; I have felt all affects and known all the most secret traps of feelings. At any moment a new idea can come to me and change everything.

How thoughts unfold at the ticking of clocks and especially when the hours strike. The clock that has the most liquid sound, the first, the one that surprises me still, is facing me, a little gold aedicula framing the painted dial, a German jewel that Francesco's mother, the pearl of Bavaria, Margaret von Wittelsbach, brought with her when she came to Mantua as a bride. In this sound I hear her and her love of her land and her family; I taste the flavor of the extreme obedience that led her here, to die young, most lovable but not happy wife of Federico, an unheeding humpback. The sound of those hours is the sound of the sadness that nourished the princess come from too far into a land of limited domains with limited riches, of private lords. An empress can be consumed in the blaze of empire and exalt her life as she accepts herself as symbol, but she, the blond Margaret, had nothing left but children, beloved but of scant future. My story has been different: I have loved Francesco from the age of eight, from the moment that my father, pulling off his iron gauntlet, announced the first visit and said it was my task to make myself loved. And this I have done. For the males I have aimed high. The children have always been mine, more than my husband's; even Eleonora, mad for her father, depended only on my shifts of mood.

Has it been a trap, this seeing everything clearly? Margaret's clock ends its subdued protest, and now the others will echo it, almost superimposed one upon the other in the counterpoint of the mechanical sounds. And as usual, I will start as I hear the bronze tone of the great Nuremberg clock, its strokes echoing as if to announce what can happen, strokes of fortune or decrees I choose not to imagine.

III

Armed Only with a Shield

I T F A L L S O N us, too: the shadow of the two giants who loom over Europe, the emperor Maximilian and the king of France, who have openly revealed their desire of conquest in the states of Italy, while deceiving us with false and constantly shifting alliances. And as always with the most fatal deceits, at the beginning they seem to garner every favor of fortune.

The League of Cambrai is a reality. French, Ferrarese, imperial, and papal troops are moving toward the Venetian boundaries. Bergamo, Cremona, Crema, Brescia have fallen; and now the great Venetian defeat at Agnadello. At this point there can be no doubt: The emperor and Louis the Twelfth have decided to divide up the lands of the Serenissima and perhaps of all Italy. Their great ally Pope Julius publicly rejoices at every victory over scornful Venice, but his intimates already see a frown on his countenance.

WE THEN were on the victors' side. Francesco had the titles of captain of the pontifical troops and lieutenant of the king of France. And yet the Venetians never ceased sending us ambassadors, among them Carlo Valerio, a gentleman and friend of ours, to offer us, in imploring and tearful tones, a hundred thousand gold ducats if Francesco would take command of their army; all their generals would obey him like babes. They did not remember, those Venetians, how they had once rejected us. Francesco and I sent a haughty answer, and we were not tempted for a moment to accept. To humiliate those arrogant Venetians was too great a gift, and it repaid us for the humiliations received for so many years.

But the taunts did not end. At Agnadello Francesco could not be present to harvest his meed of laurels; he was kept in bed by his nasty French disease, covered with sores, bemoaning his malevolent stars. And he had to read the letter from the king of France, who, pretending to jest, called him a poltroon. The mockery was beginning again. But Francesco was truly ill. The physician had communicated his results, and I knew how the disease was proceeding. The truth was this: At his still-vigorous age the attacks that had tormented him for some time were becoming more frequent and serious. With my druggist, Giusto of Udine, I prepared unguents and mixed waters, after the teachings of Fracastoro, modified by our own discoveries. The medical art gave me a calm sense of mending; I was alert, and I studied most patiently the various recipes of Italian and non-Italian physicians, ancient and modern. Like my mother and all the Este women, I had the healer's touch.

When I came out of my laboratory, I attended to the government of our land, and I realized with renewed amazement that the acts of governing held no secrets for me. My habit of doing things properly made chancellery matters seem easy to deal with. After all, the State was a great family, to be run judiciously, best when its governor was purged of all passion. The July heat came. Francesco was better and could finally take the field, determined to show his prowess as captain. We entered August. Though the victory of Agnadello was several months old, we were enjoying the wake of glory; by our order the escutcheons of San Marco were chipped off our palaces, and in the square the populace burned effigies of Venetian captains, swaying in their makeshift gondolas. The shadows of the giants, Louis the Twelfth and Maximilian, seemed to menace no more but rather to protect us. I imagined Francesco in Verona, where the king had sent him to garrison the city against possible attacks. I could see him moving among his soldiers, invigorated by those military surroundings, filled with mettlesome intentions. And I prayed God that the clouds of fantasy would not trouble his mind.

ON THE eighth of August, all unawares, I am in the palace, occupied with the usual concerns of court. Count Ludovico della Mirandola, loyal officer of Francesco's, is announced, and I prepare to hear him with joyous spirit; no presage disturbs me. And here he is, he presents himself, and immediately my throat is gripped by the remembered sensation of another appearance: Giovanni Gonzaga, when he came to announce the rout of the Milanese. The face of defeat has the same grayness. And so I learn the truth: While I was making every effort to maintain balance, perfect peace in our city, Francesco transgressed the command of the king of France. Sallying forth from Verona, he went toward Isola della Scala to attack Legnago, the aim of ancient Mantuan ambitions, once subject to the Gonzagas, then retaken by the Venetians. Here there is a pause in the narrative. Surprised by nightfall, Francesco took shelter in a peasant house, in his jacket, unarmed, and thus he was taken prisoner as he was hiding in a field of millet, after escaping through a window. In chains he was dragged to Venice, where riotous in vindictive joy, the populace awaited him.

This humiliating report unfolds before me, and I am unwilling to grasp its meaning. "This is a dream, a fierce jest," I say to myself, and already I am beginning to credit it. All is interrogative, dismay, raving, supreme despair, rebellion. Francesco a prisoner? Prisoner of those hated Venetians? Why did he leave Verona; why did he embark on the mad risk of Legnago? To defy fortune, so unprepared, is typical of him, typical of him to stay a few paces from the enemy sentries without the vigilance of his own sentries. And once surrounded, why did he not rebel? Yes, I know, they found him without his sword, in a thoughtless moment. Oh, why did I fail to realize it before? He was with a woman. But to run off like a thief! My God! I feel myself plummeting into an abyss, and yet my mind remains totally clear, my feet are firmly on the ground, as Ludovico della Mirandola adds that all our wealth has been seized: horses, silver, arms, cannons, jewels, all the accoutrements of a leader, of the lieutenant of the pope and the king of France.

Reality cannot be argued with. If my wrath blinded me, it would only increase our dishonor. I will pretend it has not happened to me, and I am struggling among the hypotheses and the images that assail us in a night of bad dreams. First of all, we must defend ourselves, defend our children, defend the people. Gather the prominent men of the city, here in the great hall. What will I say? Will I beg in tears; will I play the heartbroken wife? A surge of revolt presses me on; I would almost ask for an Amazon's sword. I must tell them a story. I will say that three thousand foot soldiers attacked the marquis by surprise, and we still do not know whether or not he was wounded in the fighting. I will invent a massacre, sentries treacherously slain, swarms of soldiers attacking. I will change the cowardly tale into an ill-fated event of battle. No more bitter misfortune could befall me.

Courage. First I will have the mayors of our towns speak, especially those from the border. Woe to us if the panic were to spread. And Federico? The children are so little that the very sight of them arouses compassion. I send for Federico. He will again put on his flesh-colored habit; he will be with me; I will place my hand on his shoulder. No sooner said than done. I do not waste a minute. A resolute fire animates my actions and my words. I spend the night, wakeful, pursuing the hours, dictating letter after letter to Pirro Donati, who is calm and aghast. A letter to the king of France, desperate; a letter to the queen of France, dramatic; a letter to the emperor, imploring. An injunction to my brother-in-law Cardinal Sigismondo: He must immediately leave Macerata, where he is in the pope's service; he must come to me, to protect me with his purple.

In the morning I examine myself in the mirror; I am not the least haggard; I am sustained by the fever to take action. How many orders have I given, all without hesitation? I have carefully chosen my dress, simple but nobly cut. A light, pale gray taffeta, it somehow suggests a riding costume, and a light plume in my hair gives me the appearance of being prepared for anything demanded of me. My youngest sons are with their nurses; my daughters, behind them; and I, with Federico, in the front row. We enter the great hall. All the mayors are assembled, in a dejected atmosphere of bewilderment and dispersal; our entrance is the first signal of cohesion. I repeat, now convinced, the story of Francesco taken prisoner with his sword in hand. I am outraged and moving, and I am also moved by the truth lying beneath my tale, more pitiful than the invention.

"You must not believe I have lost heart," I declare. "I promise you the marchese will soon be free."

Where I find this certitude I could not say, but my tone is vibrant, affirmative. The mayor of Sermide, the one who seems most aghast, steps forward. His people are collecting their possessions, to flee to safety; the Venetians could arrive at any moment. The mayor of Revere brings similar news, and the mayor of Borgofranco says the peasants there are burning the oats in the field rather than leave fodder for the enemy.

I dominate them with my authority. They must convince all their people to return to their homes; we will transfer soldiers of our guard and those guarding the castle; we will dispatch them to defend the borders. The plan develops before my eyes sharply, so clear that it is almost simple: Strip the fortresses of the south, toward Bologna, and pour arms and soldiers eastward into the forts most exposed to the Venetians. Gather provisions, so as to have reserves in whatever circumstances. There will be no lack of money; all my jewels are in order, gleaming in their strongboxes, ready to be pawned.

"Remain calm. Believe me," I insist warmly. "Yesterday our

ambassadors were already sent on journeys in every direction. King Louis cannot deny us aid—we are allies—and the same is true of the emperor. We will throw ourselves at the feet of His Holiness; we will move the whole world if necessary."

The mayor of Mantua takes the floor. What can he want? I know him as a man who casts doubt, who will stir up muddled ideas in every situation. He says smugly that he must guarantee peace in our city, that the populace is greatly agitated, that a rumor has been spread affirming that I and the children will leave for Ferrara. He casts a rapid glance at my hat; he pauses. Luckily he thinks he is very clever, asking that Federico ride alone through Mantua; the people would feel more secure, more certain they were not being abandoned.

After a moment's suspense I breathe again; you never know what fog the irresolute may plunge you into. I consent at once (such a ride was already part of my plans). I look at Federico. He is radiant, demure, childish for his nine years, but afraid of nothing. How remote in my mind is the miserable image of Francesco, humiliated prisoner, compared with this magnificent boy, who, by his mere appearance, inspires the trust and assent of his subjects. I am grateful to him for being my son. With a sign, I entrust him to Rozone, his tutor; Federico salutes me, irresistibly, with just a hint of gravity, but also slightly laughing in the depths of his eyes as if in his spirit, no matter what, there were a lingering sense of play. This instant thrills me; I hear the people gathered in the square, shouting his name. They have understood: Whatever may be about to happen, the marchese of Mantua is in Mantua.

IN THOSE first days of conflict, I was divided between alternating hope and despair. In an uninterrupted ferment, ambassadors and envoys brought missives, which I studied and answered in the early morning, when my spirit was fresh. Of a single letter I would have twenty copies made, each adapted to the addressee. I wrote each of the cardinals, of whatever political faction; I wrote to Florence, Naples, Spain, England, even to the Turk. To each potentate there was something to say and something not to say; I had to decide without error. There could be not the slightest sign of pride in addressing King Louis, who was prompt to remind me, from the loftiness of his consolatory letter, that the deplorable imprisonment of Francesco would never have occurred if the captain had not disobeyed the king's order to remain inside Verona. A truth, cruel to hear repeated. With the emperor Maximilian the cruelty came not only from opinions and mortifications. He seized on every pretext, as German emperors have done for centuries in our lands, to demand money and provisions for his army in Italy, which, in his view, was defending us. And this tribute, the imperial chancellery underlined, was something we allies were duty-bound to pay. I had little money, and the stores were needed for our own people. So I had to reply evasively, with difficulty granting the twentieth part of what was asked.

The war against Venice allowed glimpses of hope for a truce. The pope, at the first news of Francesco's capture, had flung his biretta on the floor, cursing Saint Peter; but now his fury had abated, and he was already receiving Venetian ambassadors, who begged him to lift his excommunication from the city. And from time to time he sent me words of praise, especially for the deployment of troops in the border fortresses. The moment I thought I had parried one blow, another arrived; new suffering was added to old. The king of France confided to some gentlemen of ours, as Alberto Pio da Carpi asserted, that the valor of the marchese of Mantua was unreliable and that easily undermined by prison, he would be capable of betrayal, of coming to terms with the Venetians. My pride was truly wounded. But it was worse when the French king informed me that he wanted to send to Mantua some troops under the command of Monseigneur d'Allègre to defend our land. I drew myself up and immediately replied that we had no need of soldiers; the populace was tranquil and industrious; all we needed was to have Francesco home again. Meanwhile, I was sending the queen a beautiful painting, one of the best I had by Costa, a painter she admired supremely, and among our master hatmakers I was looking for some handsome caps for King Louis, who, I had been told, went around wearing a head covering of crumpled plush. I laughed without merriment, thinking that beneath that worn felt there was a crowned head, capable of commanding.

From Rome the pope kept repeating only that irritating praise of his, while the emperor announced the arrival of a trusted agent, who would help me govern. I sent him a gentle but absolute no: From him, the emperor, we expected all good, but not people to meddle in the government, for which, with my brother-in-law Cardinal Sigismondo, I sufficed. And so when autumn gave way to winter, I decided that I had at least to obligate Pope Julius, and I had the way to do it. Luckily for us, sometime before, a wedding contract had been prepared between my firstborn daughter, Eleonora, and the pope's nephew Francesco Maria della Rovere, now duke of Urbino after the death of Guidobaldo, that leader of bold men, valorous in battle as he was privately sick and tormented.

My Elisabetta, the sister-in-law I called sister, had suffered with great dignity her husband's premature death at thirty-five, close to her heart as no other, in their most singular love. I have never tired of directing my thoughts to Elisabetta. With her I tasted the sweetness of a dear and beloved companionship; she could face my occasional boisterousness with a demeanor I have never since found in anyone else, a light smile that came from her soul, gently teasing and quietly resigned and, at the same time, beyond resignation. Her limpid spirit never failed her; she was always ready to share the feelings of others and set aside her own sufferings. And she had made even Francesco accept that chaste marriage of hers—though he always shook his head when he referred to it —as something that, for her alone, could be right and sacred. With her great soul she bore with detachment the insistent praises of the poets and courtiers who exalted her legendary purity.

She had been the one who desired that wedding contract between the nephew she had adopted as a son and my oldest daughter: she had been partial to Eleonora since the child's birth and loved her more than she loved Federico. I can see before me the delicate movement of Elisabetta's hands, followed by Guidobaldo's shy gaze, when, in my bedroom, she lifted the baby from the cradle to carry her to the baptism. Little by little, an affinity of melancholy grew up between them, that tender melancholy of the Gonzagas when they are named Cecilia, Paolina, Dorotea, Ludovico, and Federico, Francesco's father.

I must say that I, young and dazzling, did not appreciate Eleonora's tendency to sadness, which in Elisabetta seemed to me quite lovable, perhaps because I felt myself obscurely judged by my daughter from the time she was a baby. The grave face, the modulated voice that could suddenly harden, her taciturn detachment created in her a strangeness that dissolved only when music was played. She would burst into tears at the slightest reproach, or worse, she would shut herself up in a hostile obedience. And yet she concealed secret impulses of joyous vitality. I had watched her when there was dancing at rustic feasts, especially at Cavriana, ladies and peasant girls together, and I could see her lose all restraint, an ingenuous glow in her face, which soon frowned if she encountered my gaze. Blossoming with grace, she grew up well; when she was barely adolescent, the report of her beauty circulated among the courts, but I did not consider it so extraordinary, and it did not seem to me right that a description superior to her merit should be heard abroad; I feared it might harm her. So I was obliged to request the queen of France, who, having heard such praises, had asked for a portrait, to forgive us but our young girl's beauty was not such that her portraits should make the rounds of the world.

I am not mistaken, Eleonora adored her father and assumed an expression of appeased passion every time she saw him; he returned her love with the sweetest enthusiasm. She was never on my side, never, not even in my finest moments; I have never understood what she was reproaching me for. But if Elisabetta loved her, there was surely in her something to love, and out of love for my sister-in-law, I mentioned her in my will, leaving her a precious bequest.

THE MARRIAGE contract with the pope's nephew, which Francesco had affectionately championed for Eleonora, when she was still only twelve, was very hard to respect in every detail. The pope demanded a dowry greater than the one I had brought to Mantua, thirty thousand ducats, to be divided thus: twenty thousand at the moment of the nuptial ceremony—fifteen thousand in cash and five in clothes and jewels—the other ten thousand paid subsequently, the dates to be established by Elisabetta. It was really a bad moment for wedding expenditures, but I decided to make them, even though the men who had come from Urbino to receive the dowry, the clothing and the furnishings according to the contract, pursed their lips and murmured that those lengths of precious fabric, gold stuffs, brocades, cloth of gold and of silver, made up a trousseau that, to put it mildly, was slight for a princess. I allowed her to take all the dresses she possessed, some of them extremely rich, which should have been taken into account, but this was not enough. Eleonora's humor, then, when she heard that she was to be wed immediately, turned grim. No festive word escaped her lips, she constantly wore a kerchief over her eyes, and in addition, she let it be understood that we were trying to send her off as a bride cheaply.

Finally Elisabetta arrived with an ample retinue; dressed and bejeweled, to honor the bride, she had put off her widow's mourning. I could no longer bear my daughter's sullen face; it was impossible to remain calm in the presence of those tears and those complaints. Eleonora wanted her father, to bless her, reassure her, and warm her with his presence. I understood her. But she did not understand how beset I was by so many different concerns, how I had at all costs to save money for the family, for the court, for our people. One winter morning, when the castle was immersed in a shifting curtain of fog, she repeated yet again her whining about her unhappiness.

"No, I don't want to be married without my father's kiss."

I tried to be patient, remarking that this was not a time for kisses, and she cried out: "No, I will not marry until my beloved father has returned, free, from Venice. I have made up my mind."

"You will do what I have arranged," I said peremptorily. "The husband is the one we have long since chosen for you; he is handsome, he is very young, and you like him. At least so you have always said."

"I said that out of obedience," she grumbled in a low voice. "And besides, that has nothing to do with it. I do not want to be married without my father."

I lost my temper.

"Silly child!" I cried. "Thrice silly! You do nothing but whine. You still refuse to understand the lesson I have explained to you so often. Your husband is the son of the pope's brother, and we need the pope because only he can make the Venetians set your father free. They will agree to anything in order to have their excommunication lifted. If we beseech him in the right tone, Pope Julius can have your father home at once."

"But I will not be here when he returns."

"No, not you. But all the rest of us will be: your brothers; the people."

"But not I."

"You will be in Urbino, revered and worshiped, with a young husband, with our dearest Elisabetta, who loves you tenderly, and in the most handsome palace in Italy. Indeed, a sad fate."

I noticed that one of the women was carrying in her arms a length of gold cloth worked with pearls, about to put it in the dowry chest. I muttered an order to her: "No, not that one, Venanzia. That is mine."

Eleonora's sobs redoubled. "Of course, I deserve nothing; everything must be denied me."

At that moment Elisabetta appeared. She looked at me, at her niece, and did not stop smiling. She had Venanzia give her the piece of gold cloth, and with that enfolding manner of hers, she said: "Isabella, dear sister, isn't this the stuff you promised to the pope's envoy when he came to conclude the contract? Gold cloth with pearl embroidery, this must be the very one. And how can Eleonora present herself at the court of Rome, the first in the world, if she lacks suitable dresses? You would not want people to think you have had so little influence on her. We will take this cloth, won't we, Eleonora? You will leave the whole Vatican speechless. And I will also give you a cloth of brocade with pendant pearls and rubies, a gift of my Guidobaldo. There was no time for me to make a dress from it. It will be for the new duchess of Urbino."

Then, turning to me, still smiling: "Isabella, our secretary has been waiting since yesterday for the first payment of five thousand ducats toward the dowry."

"We will pay! We will pay," I replied, my teeth clenched slightly. "Your wardrobe gentlemen, your secretaries are constantly nagging. They always behave like this."

"Isabella," Elisabetta said sweetly, "you must not dwell on these trivialities. Eleonora and I will be your envoys in Rome; we will give the pope no respite; he will perforce make the Venetians free Francesco." She put her hand on Eleonora's shoulder and led her out of the room, and I heard her say with calm fervor: "You will be the one, my child, who strikes the chains from your father's wrists."

My sister-in-law acted with such happy charm that after a few days of alternate weeping and serenity (and after a considerable number of sacrifices on my part), the nuptial retinue was ready to leave. All the children shed rivers of tears, and so did the court, when Eleonora went off one morning of dense fog. On the castle bridge the people seeing off the bride emerged one by one from the thick curtain, like players when they introduce themselves on the stage. Soon the party was swallowed up in the grayness, and we saw nothing more.

Days of festivity and balls were already prepared for the bride in Bologna, Imola, Faenza, Rimini, and finally Urbino. On Christmas night, at the proper astrological moment, the couple was united, and the next morning Elisabetta entered their room, jokingly pretending to reproach Eleonora, who answered her with some grumpiness that she had done what had been commanded of her. I wondered if the wedding night had gone smoothly; I thought of my own distant night, inflamed by Francesco's assaults, too many, searing.

*   *   *

THOUGH every situation requires time to be resolved, I was hoping that this marriage, at the price of so much renunciation, would achieve all its aims, and quickly. The pope summoned the young couple to Rome, with Elisabetta and Emilia Pio and a great entourage. The ceremony of confirmation of the sacrament was celebrated with great pomp, followed by balls, performances of plays, concerts, buffalo races in the squares. Faithful to our plans, Eleonora began to implore Pope Julius on her father's behalf, supported by her aunt; but he replied vaguely, vaguely reassuring.

We were still far from Francesco's liberation, and his letters, more and more complaining, grew frequent. I declared in good faith that I was disheartened and tortured by the Venetians' wicked treatment of the prisoner shut up in the Torresella: I was not even allowed to send him his physician. For Christmas I had sent him his favorite singer, Marchetto Cara, who was allowed to go only three times to cheer his lord's sadness. A strange thing happened to me: I was almost disappointed to learn from Marchetto that Francesco was well and lacked for nothing. Obviously there was truth both in his comfort and in his bemoaned hardships; the guards teased him, to dishearten him further.

One day I had to shrug my shoulders indignantly. Before the full Council the Doge said that I had come to enjoy governing, and therefore, I was not concerned for my husband's fate. I wept real tears, angry more than insulted. My brother Ippolito, when he came to Mantua to assess my behavior, observing me directly, remarked that the Venetians are torturers one moment and generous hosts the next, to offer a glimmer first of hope and then of suffering; thus, with frequent alternation, they keep their enemies in suspense.

Ferrara, more than ever loyal ally of the French, was keeping the forces of the Serenissima engaged along its borders. Alfonso had made his choice, joining the League of Cambrai; he counted on regaining the lands our father lost in the war against Venice, that beautiful delta of Rovigo, object of burning regret in the Este family. When Ippolito arrived at the castle to inspect me, there was no trace of cardinallike virtue in him; he had buckled on his cuirass and was armed with his sword. "These are not times when praying is enough," he said to me sharply, shaking his head, his locks neatly trimmed as always. In the lining of his biretta he had had a mirror sewn, and so he kept his hair always neat. In contrast, his military bearing seemed incredible: curt, charged with energy. He revealed to me that in those days a great army would move, in boats, along the Po to Ferrara, and he, the cardinal, would command the operations of defense. He displayed that ferocious determination that foreboded the disastrous rout of the Venetian fleet and the great hunt along the river that occupied the Ferrara men, unleashing them after the fugitives in the violent shattering of Venetian pride.

In the blanched light of a full moon, Alfonso's artillery thundered throughout the night, striking the armada of San Marco that moved up the broad river. And throughout the night Ippolito, in that whiteness, remained mounted, prompt to direct the movements of the defenders. The Ferrarese apotheosis, my two brothers' triumph, the blow inflicted on our enemies gave me a thrill of joy and of fear.

How would this defeat affect the Venetians, who held the hapless Francesco in their hands? Would they take revenge on the poor prisoner? Their possible vengeance wrung my heart, oppressed it, and kindled again in me my old scorn of the republic's power, too absolute in the equilibrium of our little states. But I seemed to breathe again when I thought that a hostage of Francesco's stature—sufficient almost to decide the fate of the League—was too valuable to be eliminated with a dose of poison. As my thoughts followed a lesson of practical politics, I imagined the behavior of great captains when they mentally foresee the enemy's attack on their own strongholds, and so I behaved, arranging for one of our people, admitted to the prison, to provoke in Francesco one of his generous impulses. In fact, he issued an order to return all the Venetian prisoners we held in Mantua. The gesture pleased Doge Loredan, but it failed to cause a new turn of events.

Christmas passed, the months of the new year were already numbered, and Francesco remained shut up behind the ironclad gate of the Torresella. At a given moment there was talk of an exchange of prisoners, as the French held the Serenissima's great captain Bartolomeo d'Alviano, taken at Agnadello, but, to this proposal, King Louis reacted so violently, so contemptuously toward Francesco, considered of scant significance compared with the highly esteemed general, that scorching tears of humiliation streaked my face. Drying them, I returned for the hundredth time to the idea that help could come only from the pope, and at whatever price, I would gain it.

With the gnawing thought of the prisoner always consuming me, I devoured even the most trivial news of our Roman informants, to deduce the vacillation of Julius, gradually moving away from the League, toward a different idea: toward ridding Italy of the foreigners. And there was clear evidence that the pope was inclined to lift the Venetians' excommunication, a first step toward an agreement. But we had to wait.

IN THOSE TIMES I began to divide up my days again as I had done in my first youth, when it seemed to me the hours would never suffice to contain my exuberant greed for life. I had to prevent our waiting from depressing the spirit of the court, and it would surely not be depressed while I showed a serene countenance. Help now had to come to me from my friends, and among them I chose the most congenial, assigning them roles to play according to their temperament. In my heart I called them the Delighters. Of different rank and quality, they included, most prominent, Bernardo Bibbiena, not yet cardinal; he wrote to console me when Eleonora had left and her empty form still wandered through the rooms. My friend was at the court of Urbino, and from there he sent me words so gay and sapid that he lifted our mood. It was a tonic, his witty narration, his joyous invention, as he accused Elisabetta, for example, of stern retaliations. She never ceased scolding him for not having been a member of the nuptial party when he, poor man, was actually lying in bed, stricken with gout. And he went on, with many sparkling fancies, imitating himself with his quick Tuscan language, all prickles and without affectation. I read the letter. Then I reread it, aloud, to my women and girls, including Alda Boiarda, his chosen favorite; too soon we came to the private signature, "your Moccicone," the word in our part of the country for "fool." After an hour of reading and comment, we went to bed in a better humor to confront the ghosts of the night, and after that day Moccicone's letters were events in my rooms in the castle.

I assembled my musicians, and we learned new *strambotti*. Marchetto worked miracles, and his most renowned song, "Forse che si forse che no," opened every concert and was the beginning of our harmonic exercises. The frottola that starts *"Rotta è l'aspra mia catena/ ch'io son fora de prison,"* among all our songs, seemed to us a good omen, and we sang it in four parts, a sprightly rhythm, accompanied by viols.

I also took to riding out in the morning with some of the castle's officers to inspect the banks of the Mincio and the Po. I had invented a tightly cut riding dress of dark blue wool trimmed with silver braid, and over it I wore a blue, French-embroidered scarf across my shoulder; if it had not been for my full skirt, I would have felt like a captain of the guard. As I devised that style, I had to think how today's fashion was more suited to men than to women, for men, in their way, could be elegant but still trim, compared with our elaborate dress, at times so thickened with stuffs that the garment seemed a heavy weight even for one who only looked at it. I admit that our dresses at times also have a noble and considerable grace, but they must be very carefully studied, especially in the relation between the body's volume and the quality and cut of the cloth.

One morning we rode all the way to the lock gate at Govérnolo. My blood froze! On the opposite shore, following the Mincio, French and German patrols were going by, dragging their cannons. Farther off, on a rise in the terrain, a camp could be discerned, soldiers resting around their fires, the gold lilies of France gleaming on the tents. Poor peasants with long faces were reluctantly handing over sausages, ducks, chickens, sacks of grain; the soldiers, laughing, seized everything. So they were close, at a very short distance; the siege was visible. Preceded by our herald carrying the Gonzaga standard, we reached the lock and were received by the engineer in charge, an open-faced Mantuan, with small, quick blue eyes. He showed me the machinery and operated it easily. The engineer had a reassuring voice.

"Never fear, signora marchesana," he said to me, "Mantua cannot be taken. At your command it will be surrounded by water, and no one will be able to offer insult to the city."

I smiled in agreement, but I returned to the castle sadly. And here I found waiting for me Tolomeo Spagnoli, Francesco's favorite councillor. His vulpine face, always set in a mask of fixed deference, allowed no presage to be read. He had returned from Venice, where they had allowed him to enter the Torresella and speak with his lord.

I went to him, exclaiming: "And what news of Francesco? How is my husband? What did he say?"

"He is not well," Spagnoli answered me, "but he is beginning to breathe easier." Then, displaying a sudden gaiety, he continued: "Great news, signora marchesana, great news!"

I asked if there was hope.

"Hope, indeed! The Venetians want to appoint our marchese

Captain General of the Serenissima with the highest honor. He will be free and reverenced by all."

Rapidly in my mind those tents appeared, the camp with the lilies of the king of France, so close to us, and I could see the line of imperial cannons.

"Free?" I cried. "Free from what?"

"He will be able to return to Mantua and defend his city," the Spagnoli replied pompously.

"This is madness," I exclaimed, with an immediate grasp of the real situation. "It spells ruin! The French, the imperials cannot wait to occupy Mantua, and it would be an easy move for the emperor to declare us traitors and thus deposed from our feudal investiture."

"I thought to give you happy news. I realize that seeing my lord marquis free means nothing to you."

"Can you not imagine anything? The Venetians will want to keep their Captain General under observation, and he will be a prisoner still, only in a different way from now. And we will be exposed to every kind of reprisal."

Spagnoli stiffened before me; the mask of respect fell from his face, and he spoke to me with impudence: "Signora, be careful. For some time the Venetians have been saying that you want to keep your husband far from home because you wish to rule. The signor marchese also says this."

"That cannot be!" I exclaimed. "And in any case, I do not care. Let Francesco accuse me, let him insult me, deprive me of his love, but he must not accept such a shameful offer. I will resist him, I will preserve his State for him at all costs. He cannot betray the League, deny his pledges, become the paid servant of our enemies. And you be careful, Signor Tolomeo. Make sure not a word of this insane proposal escapes you. The people must be certain that their lord is a man of trust."

In those days, coming and going among talks with the captains of the fortresses to the east, I had an almost fierce energy, and I issued the order that then went the rounds of Italy and Europe. To our captains I said to hold out, with all their strength, against the troops of the Serenissima. And they were to pay careful attention: If the Venetians were to bring the marchese of Mantua beneath their walls, threatening to kill him if the fortress was not surrendered to them, they were not to let themselves be moved, and they were not to open their gates. When my words were reported to the king of France, he had tears in his eyes, whether of admiration or of pity, I cannot say, as he saw me driven to such excess. Some judged me cruel-spirited; others called me a shrew. I paid no heed.

THE SPRING brought more serious woes. The Doge Loredan protested because in Mantuan territory the rebel city, Verona, was garnering provisions; Julius the Second delayed lifting the excommunication in Venice; and the emperor Maximilian used the word "hostage" for the first time, referring to my Federico. Maximilian asked for him, with a shattering tone of imperial authority, and I replied that nothing in the world would make me send away from his home a delicate boy just reaching the age of ten. The pope encouraged me to resist, saying I would be mad to deprive myself of my firstborn son, and I naturally agreed.

A month later the king of France made the same demand of me, with a peremptory letter. I raised my arms, as if to shelter myself against a weight about to plunge down on me, but my Pirro Donati, in a grave and mournful voice, read me the royal letter, translating from the French. I had only words to use against the will of such a powerful king. Alfonso, my brother, exhorted me to hand over Federico; Giangiacomo Trivulzio wrote, to persuade me to obey, as the supreme power of the French now dominated Europe. And all this, as I had foreseen, was due to the Venetians and their foolish idea of appointing Francesco their captain. No one trusted the marquis of Mantua any longer.

Immediately I sent one of our best diplomats, the clever Soardino, to France, with eight pages of instructions, prompting him, sentence by sentence, to repeat my speech of refusal. Confining in words the violent turmoil of my spirit, I assured, swore, protested my unyielding loyalty; I declared, against all truth, how I had realized that only the king of France could give me back Francesco since the pope had not listed his liberation among the conditions set the Venetians for the lifting of the excommunication. Thus I recognized all power in King Louis, but I denied him my son, a delicate child, still tended by women; I would never consent to giving him up. To make him change climate, food, habits would amount to killing him, and if he died, I would follow him.

This was in March; in May the invisible archer aiming at Federico fired another arrow. My son was now demanded as hostage by Venice, and the one who asked me to deliver him to the Serenissima was his father. Pirro Donati, who brought me Francesco's letter, was himself aghast, seeing me laugh nervously as I read it. To me, it was like being at a play when for every scene the players change, all fascinated by a single object that each believes himself entitled to possess. I was beside myself; I wavered. One night I woke with a start, and I seemed to hear a heartrending moan. I had the impression my husband was in the room, and I began speaking to him, aloud: "Francesco, have you forgotten who you are? Who we are? Has prison, isolation from the life of others, so altered you? You trust your enemies, and you order me to deliver our son to you, not thinking that they will then hold both of you, leaving me alone with our daughters and babies. What will our people say? They will consider a falsehood the festivities we held to celebrate the defeats of the Republic of Saint Mark's. If you declare yourself the Venetians' ally, we will be invaded by French and imperials. Be patient. Bear it all a little longer. I am struggling against enormous enemies, and you know it, and you know that my reasoning is right. I love you more than you love yourself, and be sure that if I could trust the Venetians, I would give you Federico, Ercole, Ferrante, all our children; but I know the unreliability of your jailers, their fatal tricks."

It seemed to me that he was close, and I could make him hear my words. I came to; I was shivering, all alone, and the cool, scented May night was suddenly brimming with wrath. I refused to accept the idea that Francesco did not understand the things that I so clearly expounded in their every political correlation, and I was filled only with furious pity of his blind desire to get out of the Torresella, that stagnant imprisonment. My words became a letter to the Doge.

When it reached Venice, the lords of the Senate, early one morning, sent their armigers to the tower for Francesco, abruptly waked, to learn what his wife had decided. He read and cursed, wept and pitied himself aloud, called me whore, said I would be responsible for his death. If I did not give him Federico, he threatened, he would cut my throat; how unfortunate he was, to have a wife who wanted everything her own way. Without raising his eyes, Pirro Donati, his voice chilling in private scorn, leafed through the pages, delivered in person by Tolomeo Spagnoli. And my thoughts took another path.

I sat, immobile, grasping the arm of my chair; I can still feel that rounded wooden form, smooth as satin, beneath my fingers. My nature, always ready for a change of interpretation, bade me make a bold leap. What if this reaction of Francesco's were a pretense? If that excessive exasperation were a means to say to me, "I understand you, I am playing a role to deceive our enemies, I am exaggerating so that you will understand me, but you, be faithful to your role"? On other occasions such things had happened, and we had harmonized our different courses of action toward a same end. Now I regretted that we had not devised between us a secret code for reassuring each other. I felt the danger of falling into a vortex, and I ardently grasped at all possible signs, even the most remote, that might sustain me. I seized on the thought that Francesco, perhaps himself unaware, was communicating to me an uncertain inner truth of his, nebulous also for him but a true expression of himself. He was still my husband, my spouse, a different person from the man who insulted me and repudiated my actions. I did not want to lose him, and at the same time the idea of giving in horrified me.

Snatches of a brief conversation returned to me, from the time before Eleonora went off as a bride, on one of the many uneasy days when her stubborn refusal to marry was tormenting me. One morning, when I had just dressed, impelled by my daily torment, I had started, without any companion, toward the chancellery. At their desks there were my private secretaries, Benedetto Capilupi and Pirro Donati. Benedetto was speaking with a foreign gentleman, a university man or secretary, dressed in simply cut pink cloth. He was not notable of stature or person: a small head; narrow face; slightly receding chin. His eye was dark and piercing. He and Capilupi were counting out ducats on the table and stacking them in equal piles. The two men looked at me, pausing. The strange gentleman came from Florence and was bringing to us the sum of forty thousand gold ducats, which, in the name of his republic, we were to pass on to the emperor; Florence was paying tribute so the imperials would stay out of Tuscany. I told Signor Niccolò Machiavelli how lucky the Florentines were, to have reached an agreement, keeping the war at a distance. We, on the contrary, not only paid tribute but also had to supply the German Army, which then, like the French, like all armies, looted and raided throughout our countryside.

Meanwhile, Capilupi had shown me a dispatch warning us that Vicenza had rebelled against the French and had gone over to the Venetians, not good news. Were we to consider this an isolated episode or would other cities spontaneously return to Venice? I asked.

"Sometimes people obey a whim without thinking of the consequences," the Florentine replied slowly, as if he were reading a book. His eyes looked hard into mine but did not in the least upset me.

"It does not seem to me that the emperor and the French are making any great effort," I went on, "to guarantee that the Venetians keep losing steadily."

"Perhaps not. But the Serenissima's power on the mainland has crumbled by now. And as for the allies, they are merely holding one another at bay. Your Ladyship can see how things stand: The king of France could wage a great war but does not want to; the emperor wants to but cannot."

"Signor Machiavelli," I cried spontaneously, "if the king and emperor will not help me free my husband, who can? I trust in the pope. Do you believe other obstacles will arise?"

"No one can say. You have only this card, signora marchesana; do not waste it. Pope Julius fears King Louis wants to dominate Italy and dominate also the Papal States, but remember Venice is a great bulwark against the Muslim East. The pope will come to terms with the Venetians, rest assured."

"I hope you are right." I sighed, and—this was singular—to that man I had never seen before, I confided: "I ordered my daughter to marry against her will and to go to Rome and plead for her father's cause. To force the will of a daughter of sixteen was hard."

"To command strong things, one must be strong. And you are that. Humanity can be used only in private life. And one who lacks loftiness of spirit cannot command a State."

I do not remember our whole conversation, though it was brief. That Florentine had offered me then an indirect reply, and now his words, not gentle but clear, answered my wish. I was no longer lured by weakness, tempted by wifely obedience. I was in the right, consoled by reason. I knew now how to answer Francesco and how to deny him my son as hostage. I would dispose, not plead. My prayers should rise only to God.

AN INTERVAL of apparently calm days was followed by an unexpected (but not entirely) outburst that threw my expectations into upheaval. Ludovico of Canossa, our ambassador, arrived from Rome, and as if he were asking something trivial, he told me why Pope Julius had sent him: He had orders to take Federico to Rome, hostage of His Holiness, who had given such assurance to the Venetians.

"Federico, my son, you are the target of the whole world," I said with impassioned sympathy and not without a sorrowful pride. The pontiff was the only card I could play, as that enigmatic Florentine secretary had hinted. And I was not making light of him; his lesson was taking effect.

Federico in Rome, guest of his sister Eleonora, wife of the pope's nephew, and of his aunt Elisabetta, in that grand court, under the world's highest moral authority: This was less upsetting than the thought of Federico in Germany or in France or Venice. Still, he would be very far away; I would no longer be watching over him minute by minute. In Rome I had many, many friends who declared themselves totally devoted to my cause, but the authority of the Vatican could crush them all. Rome was an undisciplined city; poison circulated there easily; from every alley swift cut-throats could appear, quick to murder. Could I trust Rome, and how far? And yet I knew refusal was no longer possible. Francesco was cursing me and my stubbornness from the dungeon of the Torresella; Venice was rife with insistent, inhuman slanders about my cold desire to reign; even Julius the Second cried that my husband was the prisoner not of the Venetians but of a villainous whore. The epithet by now was old; it no longer upset me.

THE SUMMER heat presses on the walls and vaulted ceilings, wafts along the ramparts of the castle. We spend all our time on the towers, among pots of greenery and blossoms, under awnings stretched on ropes to shield us against the sun, and we breathe in gusts the very faint breezes of the lake. There, gasping, my informants and envoys arrive, the incomparable Ludovico of Canossa, quick to smooth in kindly tones my thorny requests, Ludovico Brognolo, Jacopo d'Atri from Paris, Capilupi more or less from everywhere, Folenghino with the difficult missives, at times a feigned madman, but the most alert and shrewd of all, and for this very reason to be used sparingly. On my final condition I will not be budged: I agree that Federico shall go to Rome, but I decide he will not move until his father has returned to Mantua. Since I, a woman, have set this condition, of such elementary security for our State and the serenity of the people, it seems disrespectful, mistrustful, provocatory. But I will not give in.

It is a day of bells, that ninth of July, when Pirro brings me the dispatch from Brognolo: I have won unconditionally; I have really won. Though reluctantly, Venice will give back Francesco, free of any pledge, and hand him over to the papal power. Federico will go not to Venice but to Rome. He will live at the Belvedere, the prettiest spot on the Vatican hill; Eleonora and Elisabetta, sister and aunt, will visit him and take him to their houses as they please. The moment my son has set out for Bologna, where Pope Julius is awaiting him, Francesco will also leave Venice for home. There was another thing I wanted, and I have achieved that also: The pope has declared that never, for any reason, will he hand Federico over to the Venetians. All has been pondered, signed, sealed.

I gather the people at Broletto, and I am applauded unanimously, almost tempestuously by our subjects. I look at that crowd, compact, hot, their eyes glued to the window of the *arengo*; they stare at me in a pure transport of affection. Smiling, I draw myself up to my full height. I have defied half the world, emperor, king of France, Venice, pope, and without neglecting the most trivial duties of chancellery and town hall. I have allowed myself the satisfaction of writing Ludovico Brognolo a letter both humble and haughty. Informed that the pope would intercede on my behalf with my husband, I have asked that Julius be begged not to take such trouble. My actions were public; I have always done what was right. In all conscience I know I acted for the good of the State and my family, and no one more than the pope, that reader of the human heart, could judge me. And so I am alone before Francesco, and I wait for him serenely.

*To the Most Illustrious and Excellent Signora
Isabella, Marchesana of Mantua, My Lady*

*M*y lady, I come to you full of confusion and enthusiasm.
I had privately vowed to send you no more of these
letters, considering them vain effusions. Then I revoked my
own veto, gaily plunging into a merriment crammed with
words, images, and stories. My punishment is ready: When I
stop writing, the fires will die down and go out, and then
spiritual debate will begin about what someone in my condition
may suitably do or not do. But it is asking too much of
ourselves to live only by reason.

All of us here in Rome followed your vicissitudes during the
imprisonment of your illustrious spouse in Venice, and we
admired your stance, a new heroine, defending him and the
State of Mantua. The form of your talent was revealed as, at the
magic hand of Raffaello of Urbino, the life of his figures is
revealed when they emerge to people the world with immortal
emblems. Beneath your fingers events were shaped. In the
Curia there are many who do not love our pontiff, as he makes
life very uncomfortable for the corrupt and the idle, and some of
them were tallying with satisfaction your defensive reactions, as
if they were keeping score in a game of cards. I felt nothing of
that sort. You were so firmly in your right as wife and ruler that
you could not be judged simply an enemy, one to inflict defeats
on the allies. It was like reading a tale, an open book; those
episodes linked one to another, so it was evident how sincere
feelings can reinforce skillful plans. In a little notebook I copied
—and it pleases me to quote here—the words you wrote to the
king of France when he asked for your son as hostage, to
guarantee the loyalty of the house of Gonzaga: "In the wretched
situation of our lord and husband, the presence of this dear son
is an ineffable solace, and it brings great refreshment and hope
to the people and the subjects. Anyone who deprived me of

him would deprive me of my soul; taking my life and State or taking Federico from me is the same thing."

Ah, my lady, not only most dear but also most excellent, what subtle pleasure I derive from the choice of words, for in them lies the certainty that there is no man so rough that he cannot be shamed and struck by them. And finally, it is only right to have led our pontiff to a just solution: to restore your husband to you and to keep, with his own full authority, your son with him at the court of Rome, more an ornament of his palace than a hostage.

Evoked as you are by my seamless devotion (and I would be tempted to call it an Oriental carpet spread beneath your foot), I wish to tell you, my lady, how like an apparition, for all these Roman gentlemen, the arrival of your Federico was. It is not surprising that he is your living portrait, but it is surprising how he seems to reason with your own keen wisdom, though not yet knowing all the words and all the argumentation. His gaze tells what he sees, and in him a lively, personal critical sense shines already. His small person, clothed and adorned in the most charming garb, is its own master, and he displays, even to the point of total disobedience, his full dignity. This disobedience possesses, in flashes, your own awesomeness in moments of decision. His tutor, Matteo Ippoliti, is well aware of this, and at times, in his duties as instructor, he has to raise his voice and perhaps threaten the boy with a slap or two, rebuking him.

I know your just deploration of the acts of violence some educators consider necessary, especially since your son is too immature to accept and then forget them. And God save us from those childish grudges that we can bear with us all our lives. For that matter, his rebellions are rare; indeed, most of the time he behaves splendidly, often joyous, as is proper at his age, and sweetly greeting others with that laughter of his so fresh that you would think it newly born. I have come upon him in the Belvedere several times or in secluded places where he is always the flower of the company, and truly his fearless circulation among men already frayed by daily life is a miracle of nature and of your education.

You will be pleased to know that your Federico gets along

very well with the pope; they joke and play cards together
amid cries from Julius echoed by the boy's laughter. The
educational walks are magnificent, taken almost every day in
the company of learned men. He has been to the Capitoline,
the Baths of Titus, and a villa of Agostino Chigi's in the
country not far from the pope's alum mines ten miles from
Civitavecchia, amid thick woods and green meadows. An air of
fond curiosity surrounds him, and it is singular, as I have
already indicated, that his name rarely suggests the attribute of
hostage since he seems a little king, playing at prisoner.

I understand how Your Ladyship must suffer, dwelling on
the word "play," which includes also a possibility of losing. I
wrote it deliberately so as to add at once my exhortation to
serenity: There are no conspiracies or dangers for Federico; he
is safer here than in his room in Mantua. The pope has come to
love him exceedingly (and you must pay no heed to the
slanders of the envious) and wants Raffaello of Urbino to
portray him in the rooms where that prodigy of nature is
leaving the seal of his divine brush. Depending on the various
messages, the pope roars that he will send the boy to take his
father's place in the Torresella in Venice, but he does this when
your illustrious consort, his gonfalonier, seems to show little
will to combat the French, now that those former allies of the
Church have become her enemy. But for no reason, I assure
you, would Julius send the boy away.

I know that even the most detailed information about your
son is never enough for you, and so that you will read my
pages more willingly, I will say further that I have visited the
Belvedere rooms where he is lodged, and they are among the
most charming of the apostolic palace. He eats in a lovely
loggia that overlooks the moist, rolling meadows of Castello,
dotted with groves. Here gather your friends of the Roman
Academy, members of great families, illustrious ambassadors,
poets, distinguished Latin scholars. The most refined singers of
the Vatican Chapel also participate, and mad characters like
Frate Mariano, with that delightful wit that you know.
Important men go there, including Bernardo Bibbiena, your
great friend, and Bernardo Accolti, who improvises
compositions with rather pedantic skill and has an irritating

habit of seeking applause. And the most charming thing is the way your son mentions you constantly; a few days ago, as we were looking at the Laocoön statue, he said seriously that he wanted it for his mother and would ask the pope for it.

Rome is always Rome, even in its violent contrasts, and at this moment it is a river into which all the world's wealth and grandeur are poured, in contrast with the unspeakable wretchedness of the populace. Courtesans are much admired; they go about dressed in gold, and with heads high, they ride prized mules and horses; and often these women are of radiant beauty. There were many of them at San Sebastiano, with great, sumptuous pomp, some in male garb, for such is the fashion. At a splendid supper, a few evenings ago, a cardinal, whom I will not name, was present with a very young blond courtesan, haughty and ill humored, by the name of Albina, and with Frate Mariano, the king of lunatics, she performed a play, full of quips and many sweet untruths that made everyone laugh. And your young lord Federico also laughed, without understanding, thus redoubling the amusement of the others. Do not charge me with excessive severity, my lady, but on this occasion things seemed to me to go too far, and perhaps there should have been more concern for a youth. Perhaps, I say, because someone I reproached on this matter replied that the lord Federico has a life of pleasure and grandeur ahead of him and it is good for him to learn its rules early.

Plays, my lady! We are beset with plays, new ones or ancient newly translated by the most refined Latinists. In the Capitol the Roman officials allowed us to hear *The Menaechmi* of Plautus, an elegant enactment by players trained in exemplary diction. At Agostino Chigi's villa on the Tiber a company from Siena gave a charming performance in the most perfect language. Rome itself is a constant performance, revealed in the impalpable reflection of its purple light. The pope displays to us the beautiful things he has bought: statues; excavated objects. Yesterday he showed us two new triple crowns, one by Caradosso, absolutely magnificent, garnished with gems and gold worth two hundred thousand ducats, and another of the most elaborate design, covered with pearls and wrought gold, worth a hundred thousand. Our Julius said, displaying these pieces, that they were symbols of the Church triumphant, for which he would give the last drop of his blood. And there can be no doubting that.

Now I am before you with the timid concern that made me consider it opportune to revoke my own prohibition to write you and confess myself to you as in the past. I have said all these things about your son not only for the delight the boy, in his charming form, communicates to those who admire him but also to prepare you, with this sincere report, for the uneasiness that troubles me when I think of the clarity of your gaze, a clarity that often derives from the free conflict with yourself. You, you, my lady, what are you thinking now? How will your spirit, combative in its farsightedness, but also peaceful, react to the events that have convinced our pontiff suddenly to alter his policy and have made him cry against the French the words "Barbarians, get out"? What will you do when Julius goes to Bologna, to be closer to the enterprise against your—our—Ferrara?

I say Ferrara, and there is no need to explain further; I am borne by a current of gratitude, contradicted. There, at that school, the doors of reason were opened to me; there I faced your constant enigma for the first time. It is awkward to tune this gratitude to our English diplomacy, which supports our pope in war against the French ensconced in Ferrara, because he would not have them dominators in Italy, nor would we— who for centuries have been France's rival—want them. I can justify the determination of your brother Alfonso and, a bit less (for religious reasons), that of your brother Cardinal Ippolito. They are loyal to their alliance, but they do not know how untrustworthy French friendship is. Certainly, if Venetians and the Papal State were to be defeated, the French would not spare the Este family in building their dominion over Italy. Ferrara, of such robust imagination, depository of every sort of learning for the soul's enrichment, city of rare achievements in painting and architecture and of decorous ease in living, a recognized center of Europe's culture, is quite right to wish to retain its independence as the capital of a state independent for centuries. But how can this be done?

Your brothers have already answered, or rather two of them
have answered that question, while the other two are kept alive
but silenced in a prison of the castle. Forgive me, we must
speak openly. To recall them is a sorrow for you, but it is
nevertheless true that they exist, carved in an ideal medallion
that bears Triumph on its recto and Grief and Humiliation on
the verso. More than once our pope has demanded their
liberation, but there has been not a hint of it. I know you have
called this demand insincere; for you, proud as you are, it was
an assault on the power of rulers. For me, it will be difficult to
keep my bearings if the war grows worse. In a future could I
rebel against reason? Personally, my lady, as you know, if I
were to find myself chained at your feet, if I simply looked at
you, I would be on your side.

Your chiming voice asks me: "What does being on my side
matter to you?" And in fact, it should not matter to me, but I
see you moving toward ruinous times; I do not know how your
alliance with these Estes, of whom you are, alas, the flower,
will proceed against Julius, who at all costs wants Ferrara for
the Church after the proud disobedience of Duke Alfonso. Your
consort gonfalonier will not be ill forever; they will force him to
set out on his way. I understand, you, a woman, cannot avoid
the disasters caused by men. And so? So what policy can you
put together and carry out, my venerated lady? It will be my
lot to be torn to pieces, and above all, I will risk seeing you
lacerated and in danger in your admirable little State. But what
a heavy burden life is when loyalty becomes a sentence for one
who lives life to the full. Because of this loyalty, I will follow
the immense Julius on his desperate but self-willed venture,
but I cannot renounce being your subject.

For some time I have seen a dazzling image. There is one
who is your ally in spirit, a wise man I love, after you, with all
my faculties. You know him, I have already told you about
Erasmus of Rotterdam. He has recently written a book of
genius, which is circulating through the world amid
enthusiasm and deploration. I do not know if some echo of this
Praise of Folly has reached you. In it, realistic humor and the
most fearless morality, crackling caustic wit and smiling irony
denounce man's follies. In this work and in his other

discourses, my master hurls splendid invectives against the pope, who "puts his helmet on over his white hair, and respects the sword more than the shepherd's crook, and wants war rather than peace." I, who bask in Erasmus's glory, cannot separate myself from the real greatness of Julius and the unparalleled generosity of his vocation. His is not the mere vanity of the conqueror but the concept of a spiritual authority, the Church, ruling over a pacified world.

I will stop now. All that is uncertain, divided, unshared, painful indecision: this is my fate. Perhaps I will soon return to my homeland, to distant England, where I am called to the court of the new king. For you have surely been informed that Henry the Eighth last year ascended the throne, bringing with him all the old passions against the French that have long nourished our embitterment. My nineteen-year-old king has every gift—looks, intelligence, refinement, audacity—and history will surely speak of him. Julius has addressed him, inviting him to join the league against France, a welcome invitation, as if to a wedding feast. But Henry's recent wedding, in fact, to Catherine of Aragón, has arrested his enthusiasm; there are bonds of kinship and prohibitions still too new for his scant experience. So our brilliant young king listens to the pope's voice with an interested ear but proceeds cautiously. I can tell you something quite secret that perhaps your informers do not know but we in the Curia know well: The abrogation of the excommunication which Julius granted Venice last February was much supported by us English and is partly considered a personal success of my king. It is no accident that the papal delegation seemed smug and merry when it set out from Rome last month with the golden rose for His Majesty Henry the Eighth.

The time has come for me to return to the shadows. Can you guess what I most envied your charming son? The cap you sent, of white velvet with a gold plate adorned with gems forming the letters *ACTV*, and according to the interpretation of some, these would stand for: *Amore caro torna vivo*, "My love, come back alive," which would contain also a grim warning. My dream is an illusion, for I would not be allowed to wear it, being what I am, but if I had it, even without such a rich ornament but simply with the letters engraved on a metal band, I would interpret it to mean *Andate contro tutto voi*, "Go alone against all," an effective exhortation or stern counsel.

And through my inner severity, as I write, my bosom is drained, and I have sunk into a sadness beyond consolation. I wanted the mention of the cap to seem playful, and instead, my spirit has grown ever gloomier. I make an effort to be different from myself, so that nothing, not even irony, may be lacking in my behavior, which, before you, I wish to be perfect; but there are moments that defeat such effort. At such moments I lose the desire to live and even the desire to recommend myself to God, and I await only for your name to attach me, mercifully, to the necessity of existing.

From this desert I ask to be allowed to think of you, though repenting and accusing myself, before the aridness that does not even make me feel a sinner. Then, if the devil were to strike me with a fiery spear, I would be grateful to him for drawing from me the most violent cry. But not even the devil heeds our requests.

Head bowed, my lady, I salute you.

Robert de la Pole
forever slave
of your silences

Rome, the twentieth of October, 1510

Room of the clocks
the year 1533

I **HAVE NEVER** seen Julius the Second; I have never measured myself against his gigantic physical presence. Thirty-one years younger than he, I have always considered him a fierce, indestructible old man, but when he was on the scene, I began clashing with him, again and again, in magnificent combat. For years and years he shouted, at first covertly, then releasing his temper without restraint; he towered over the politics of Italy and of Europe, pressing the enemy of the moment hard, facing all.

Nor did I ever hear his voice; I will never know if I might have moved him to some denial of himself, which is the highest point of one spirit's victory over another. He was the only adversary who dared call me whore, and he called me that to my own husband. I think that if he had said it to my face, I would have felt a flush of happiness as I could reply to him with some sharp syllables. Or would I have had recourse to his pardon, crushed by the supreme authority of God's vicar on earth, the only one who can call the divine thunderbolt down upon us?

I fought with Julius because I had to fight. I called upon a legion of potentates and friends, soliciting them in different ways, and I sought help even in the science of astrology. And here I suffered a moment of terror. The astrologer Paride of Ceresara, who constantly came to the castle for my sometimes fevered consultations, questioned on various occasions as to how long Julius would remain on the throne of Saint Peter, revealed his dismay; his calculations of the celestial revolutions gave a contradictory answer. There was a whole cluster of stars over the pontiff's head; it seemed that through some awful prodigy, he was to die and rise again. The heavens clearly indicated that they wished to remain silent; woe to him who assayed them.

Woe? Why? For some time astrologers had been announcing great conjunctions that were to provoke overwhelming events, clamorous changes. I was only a little girl when our Ferrarese

prophet Gerolamo Savonarola predicted the proximity of the
Apocalypse, making even my impassive father black at these incendiary visions, and the most desolate of them was the one in
which herds of wild horses returned to graze among the ruins of
the Vatican hill. It is possible, however, that prophets see through
millennia.

I have chosen to postpone fear, and I prefer to recite the prayer
of the legendary Arab Abumashar, in which a maiden full of grace,
honesty, and purity rises into the constellation of the Virgin. If
anything, I entrust myself to the moon, the white star that returns
always with its changes, connected with the fecundity of women,
in whom it marks the passage of the twelve lunar times. Here,
in the striking of these clocks, perfect or imperfect, I perceive the
rhythm of the universe as an uninterrupted flow; I have the proof
that I can trust the unchanging constellations, drawing from them
direction and movement.

IN THE MORNING lamps are lighted, and candles in the candelabra; the sun is scant on these days of November fog, a cold fog that cloaks our shoulders, unexpected. Already at dawn, in every room and hall, great fires burn in the fireplaces, tended by hosts of servants. I have instructed my steward to double the supply of wood in the room where Francesco is to be examined by the doctor sent by the pope, who wants to verify the condition of his gonfalonier's health. Julius is increasingly impatient to send him into battle.

One by one, we have used up all the excuses for not taking the field. The best, recurring to the imperial authority that enjoined us against undertaking action hostile to Ferrara, was eked out with endless expedients. Then the Vatican chancellery intervened, the emperor added new ideas to old, and yet again things changed. Now Venice also insists, prodding the pontiff. To test our position, we have asked for the restitution of Asola, Lonato, Peschiera, and Sirmione, which, according to the agreement with the League of Cambrai, were to be handed over to us. The Venetians have refused to listen to us. They merely suggested a condottiere's fee so small as to be almost offensive. A good pretext for us to reply that the marchese would not deign to hear such proposals, which he would not have accepted even as a boy. Tireless, the Venetians still send us those ceremonious gentlemen with their singsong voices, to celebrate the glories of Francesco's military prowess, going on and on in rhetorical orations in honor of the man who restored Italy's ancient freedom.

I was determined to sate them all with words, not an easy task, as Julius the Second is firmly established in Bologna, ready to direct his ferocity at us, while my brothers are secretly urging me to act on their behalf. And so we have reached this November day, and everyone in the castle is holding his breath, awaiting the arrival of the papal physician. He is known to be Bolognese, and his name is Maestro Zannettino. Early this morning I went down to Francesco's rooms, which are under mine, and I set the scene. In the middle of the room a kind of curtain, stretched between two vertical poles, allows the outlines of figures to be glimpsed. Beyond it the form of a reclining man can be discerned: Francesco. On this side are Tolomeo Spagnoli, weasellike in his haughtiness, and the archdeacon of Gabbioneta, ever jolly at all costs. Before the physician arrives, I raise the curtain and bend toward Francesco, lying on his camp bed. To flatter and cheer him, I pretend to worry because he doesn't look the least bit sick; I enact wonder; I express doubt that we will bring off the deceit successfully. Then I change the subject. I tell him that this Maestro Zannettino seems a proper person and costs little; the archdeacon of Gabbioneta will pay him twenty gold ducats for his report.

Francesco signals me to lower my voice. It is not prudent to be overheard, but this is not the only thing that troubles him. I see he is restless and ill at ease. I circle him, toy with his shirt, unbuttoned at the throat; I pick up a comb and carefully tidy his cropped hair, faintly streaked with gray. I realize I am moving with feminine grace.

"Francesco," I say to him, and my voice is made captious by a tinge of hesitation, "Francesco, will you come up to my apartment this evening? I will expect you."

"With your army of handmaidens?" he says, surprised. "Don't oblige me to encounter those silly creatures, or I will run off. Boiarda, your favorite, has set such a fire in my house that I'm not sure I'll be able to put it out."

"Alda Boiarda is out of it all; she has gone back to her relatives at Scandiano. I'm sorry for Bibbiena, who loved her," and I add, in a light voice, "when he comes to Mantua, he won't find her anymore." And I immediately resume my coaxing. "Never fear. No one else will be there this evening."

Francesco sits up, looking at me, circumspect and interrogative at the same time, as if he were afraid of being mistaken.

"We will be alone," I say a bit superficially, like any mindless female. "It's been such a long time since we were alone together, don't you think?"

This time he understands and laughs, uncertain, but already with complicity. He reaches to grasp me; but I wriggle free, and murmuring, "Until this evening," I escape by the little stairway set in the walls, leading up to my apartments. I climb a few steps; I creep down stealthily and stand motionless to listen to the diverse sounds from the room; after all, it is licit for a wife to spy when her husband's health is being discussed. Maestro Zannettino has arrived. I press my ear against the little door. I can distinguish his Bolognese voice among the other voices and the customary formalities and welcomes.

Then, in his jovial tone, the archdeacon exclaims: "Why, look at the condition of these sores. No, Captain, I wasn't speaking to you, but to Maestro Zannettino."

It is obvious, the archdeacon is trying to avoid an overthorough examination and is keeping at a distance the Venetian captain who is escorting the papal physician.

A moment later there is another outburst of voices and, over all of them, most clear, that of our Gabbioneta: "I wish the whole Council of the republic could see these sores. I'm amazed His Lordship the marchese can stand up at all."

More bustle; a softer questioning and answering; the voices move off. Water is poured into a basin; the doctor washes his hands. There is intense conferral between the archdeacon and the captain; they walk in the direction of my little door. Another brief pause.

"My Lord," the doctor decrees, "the French sickness is far advanced; these sores must be treated. First of all, no more salves. Wash them. Wash them often with distilled water, which you must have prepared for you."

Now the archdeacon speaks up: "His Holiness also says that salves only make the disease worse. What are we to report to the Holy Father and the Signoria of Venice?"

I am holding my breath.

"It's my opinion," Maestro Zannettino states, "that in this condition it is impossible for the marchese to mount a horse and ride in the Ferrara war. I personally will tell His Holiness the result of the consultation."

"Signor marchese," the cadenced voice of the Venetian captain says, "all are waiting for you to take the field."

There is a moment of silence. Then the archdeacon protests. "Didn't you hear the report, Captain?"

"This little phial of mercury solution will take the place of the salves, and it will work miracles," the Bolognese voice announces, not the least perturbed. "And wash! Wash often. Remember that!"

The captain's voice again: "And yet, to look at you, signor marchese, you don't seem all that sick."

"This sickness," the physician condescends to explain, "does not always correspond to external signs. The sores exist, but if the marchese treats himself carefully, he can fight all the wars he wants to."

* * *

I HAD heard enough; flying up the high, narrow steps, I was soon in my bedroom. My women were rather listlessly embroidering linens and brocades; out of discretion, they asked me nothing. The day went by slowly. In all the castle the news had spread that for the moment Francesco would not go to war. I assumed a stony mask when anyone started to say a word to me, even Pirro Donati. I ate in my room alone; at dusk I dismissed the girls, who did not venture to broach my detached mood, and I chose a Moorish shift and a robe of white velvet with an ermine border. I began to comb my hair, and led by the slow movement of the comb, I questioned myself about the morning's events. I should have been content, but instead, I was full of uncertainty, I felt an inexplicable, inner gnawing, almost like remorse. Francesco had never spoken during the medical examination, and surely he did not like being considered an impostor, even by people like the archdeacon of Gabbioneta and Tolomeo Spagnoli. That silence of his had been gloomy. And I, too, had spoken deceitfully, on an impulse that drove me to exploit any means to safeguard our aims and my brother's lands in Ferrara. Had I somehow betrayed him?

I continued combing my hair at the mirror, as my thoughts returned to his arrival, four months earlier. He had arrived from Venice pale, stooped, visibly bitter toward everyone, especially toward us who had remained in Mantua, free, though we had grieved for his fate; but our grief at his imprisonment did not count. He embraced me, sobbing, and was ashamed of his tears. At a rural celebration in his honor, the sort of festivity where as a rule he enjoyed being protagonist, he stayed always off to one side, bemoaning his sad fate. In these four months he had never climbed the little stairway of our conjugal meetings, nor had he received any hint of invitation from me. This is why my words had surprised him.

At that moment I heard the sound of a footstep on the stairs and then the light, decisive rap that was my husband's usual signal. Rapidly I finished smoothing my hair, and at the same time in the double mirrors I studied the effect, carefully flattering myself. He entered. I welcomed him gaily and showed him the shining new mirrors of purest steel, the frames worked in silver; I had received them from Master Angelone, an excellent craftsman of such objects. Francesco examined them with an expert's attention, found them beautiful, and as he handed them back to me, he called me enchantress and sorceress, two of the oldest words in our intimacy. He told me of his day, made a sharp comment on the report of the papal physician, and fell silent, his face dark. The discontent weighing on his shoulders bowed him; he moved in jerks; his face was marked by deep furrows. I had to raise the tone of our discourse. I reminded him of that time when, coming back from Sirmione and recklessly sliding off my horse, I had run up the steps, shouting, "Beautiful fields! Beautiful air! Beautiful vineyards," and adding, in a whisper, "beautiful husband!" He laughed, and finally he was mine. He came forward slowly, cast a rapid glance at the mirror that reflected him; surely he was wondering with his whole self if he was still handsome, if I loved him, if I would feel happy with him in the great bed as in a nameless country where the roses bloomed on the silver curtains. Then everything caught fire; my will prompted heartrending urges in me that became demand. We had a fanciful, blazing conjugal night.

AFTER that night I was victor. Now it was easy for me to talk with Francesco, who was on my side; we both felt unusually swept away by the reburgeoning of our passion. As he dressed in the morning, Francesco sang, and before going down the steps, he would kiss me several times; he no longer seemed downcast, no longer talked of his imprisonment in Venice. We ate together, to ourselves, often and well; my girls were dumbstruck by these suppers apart from the court and always prepared with greedy choices, for I have always had the appetite of a "little glutton," as Bernardo Bibbiena used to say, my dear old Moccicone. And I was enjoying my just revenge on Tolomeo Spagnoli and the other councillors, who found themselves set aside with brisk vigor by their master.

We listened to music together, and I played popular songs for him on a violone. Francesco would join me in singing "*E la bella Franceschina, che la piange e la sospira.*" From time to time a yearning for poetry would seize us. He would share with me his impressions of Equicola, our learned secretary and Latin scholar, who seemed to him too exclamatory, and we discussed the well-turned sonnets of Antonio Tebaldeo. Once he wanted to know what I thought of the poem being written by that gentleman in the service of my cardinal brother, that Signor Ludovico Ariosto. To tell the truth, I had read little of his *Orlando* since the work was still unfinished; I retained only the memory of a dancing light, the fugitive Angelica, insolent and mocking with men, great paladins or powerful Saracens, all of them banned from the hut where she clasped Medoro, laughing and young, as her hair became entangled with her lover's blond curls. I won a voluptuous kiss that isolated us again.

Afterward, when we were tranquil, we talked about our children, especially Federico, who was growing up well but so far from us; we talked about our household people, about relatives arrogant or disloyal, and also about our whims. We spent hours, lying close and calm, within the glitter of the curtains and the silver canopy. There is nothing like conjugal trust, when you can relax freely and love flows into a lake of peace. On certain days his sickness flared up and weakened him; then, with no false shame, we would talk about remedies and treatments, I would call on my herbalist and alchemist, Giusto of Udine, with his unguents; he had prepared for me a supreme one, which made me immune to any contagion of the French disease. I could not, however, avoid contracting a slight gonorrhea. I bore it well. I even had the courage to joke about ailments caused by love, asking myself if we had to pay also a physical price for pleasure.

"By the dragon of Saint George!" Francesco exploded when I murmured those words to him. "You are really the bravest woman and the boldest wife in this world!"

The two of us were defying Julius, and circumstances carried us so far that our plotting became visible, bringing the risk of falling into disgrace with everyone, emperor, pope, Venetians. And yet, for my brothers, our warnings, accords, aid were never enough. Alfonso never stopped complaining if papal troops built a bridge of boats at Sermide on the Po. And how could I prevent it when we were so closely watched by Julius's agents? Even at home we had to be alert to the sidelong glances that studied our changes of mood. Vigo of Camposampiero, belonging to the faction of Tolomeo Spagnoli, my dire enemy who posed as a devoted partisan of the pope and Francesco, spied whenever he could and tried to do me all possible harm and to damage my reputation at every opportunity.

My alliance with Francesco won me the freedom to maintain constant contact, through special outriders, with my brother Ippolito, and from him I received the confirmation that the emperor, our lord and master, among his many harebrained projects, seemed to favor that of selling Mantua and Verona to the king of France. I determined that we had to seek support from one of the great powers, and I chose the French. Maximilian, enemy of Venice, still had not decided between France and Julius, and we could ignore him, at least as long as the Ferrara war was raging. As the good feudal lords of Mantua, we had only to fob him off with words of loyalty and obedience, timeworn words that still allowed us to unravel the complex designs that became daily more tangled.

I was forced to even greater daring. Boldly we reached a secret agreement with the French: They would come to our borders, giving the impression that they wanted to wreak havoc and destroy—in other words, simulate hostility toward us—so the marquis of Mantua would have a pretext to remain and defend his state. Ceaselessly the swarm of Venetian and papal spies increased, slipping into our lands in various guises. Ours was a life filled with anxiety, warnings, and counterwarnings, and every day some new alarm was announced. The French, arrogant, as soldiers always are when far from home, exploited our agreement, sacking and looting our villages with no restraint, and Francesco cried that he wanted immediate compensation for all damage. To my impetuous husband I kept repeating patiently: "Wait and see, the more we can publicly complain of damage and violations, the longer you will be able to stay at home and live with me through our war and our peace." At night violent tenderness and sweetly suffered exhaustion separated us from the world.

NOVEMBER was ending, and the pope seemed miraculously recovered from a nasty illness that had led us to imagine a different conclusion of the war. Now he was fine; indeed, he swore that if his gonfalonier continued to be ill, he himself, though almost seventy, would set off on the Ferrara enterprise. Alone at the head of his troops he would attack the well-supplied fortress of Mirandola, that "gem set in gold." And meanwhile, inspired by the report of my connivances, many Este captains sent messages, pleading with me to use every means to keep my husband here in Mantua while they would defend Ferrara. I did not show such letters to Francesco; they might shame his pride and his ancient passion as a soldier.

Julius the Second entered Mirandola in January, through wind and snow, perched on a ladder, and to many cardinals this seemed the worst possible demeanor, while to the pope's admirers it was a demonstration of fiery valor. These admirers never ceased celebrating the courage of the old Ligurian, who, like a cabin boy clinging to the rigging of a ship, flew onto the high ladder and climbed into the conquered fortress.

A ray of hope appeared two months later, the hint of a possible truce. The envoys of France, Spain, and England met in Mantua, along with the fearsome bishop of Gurk, Matthäus Lang, the emperor's confidant, imperious and haughty, who demanded to keep his head covered in the presence of the pope and treated everyone with flaunted insolence. I moved the pawns on my chessboard, alert to the most difficult piece, this Gurk bishop. It was hard to catch him out and direct him toward profitable discussion, but I succeeded, setting my host of women in motion. Truly I was aided by their regal, burgeoning beauty and their way of using it, under my influence, with that bold air on a foundation of purity that excited men. I maneuvered to direct to our advantage the arid play of that gathering, called in the name of the European peace that so many of us wanted and so many others pretended to want. Then I received word that Julius had asked Camposampiero if my husband allowed me to deceive him in matters of government and if he acted according to my designs. Camposampiero could hardly believe his luck. He assured the pope that in the Gonzaga house it was the marchese who wore the trousers, and the marchesana was, to be sure, revered as a queen but concerned only with the usual petty female matters, and he added that Francesco disliked women's counsel, as did His Holiness, for that matter. I am not vindictive by nature, but I made a note of these denigrations, adding them to the score that I would settle at the opportune moment.

The congress decided that the bishop of Gurk was to go with imperial credentials from nation to nation and sue for peace, and he would be supported also by warm missives from the ambassadors of Spain, France, and England. At one point it was said that the pope would be satisfied to abandon his war in exchange for one hundred thousand gold ducats toward the new fabric of Saint Peter's, but then that absurd hypothesis was forgotten, like so many others. Peace, battered and betrayed, recurred in every speech, but always in vain.

The Mantua meeting ended without any resolution. It secretly allowed the French passage over our lands, as a secure base for their military movements, and in time this discouraged Julius from pursuing the attack on Ferrara. And when Trivulzio, the chief French general, with a rapid move laid siege to Bologna and recaptured it, the pope moved to the safer base of Ravenna. For me, this was a great moment; the storm cloud over Ferrara had moved off, perhaps dissolved.

We had been exulting in the victory for two days, when Francesco Maria della Rovere, my dull and ill-tempered son-in-law,

in a Ravenna street confronted Cardinal Aldolisi, the pope's favorite, and plunged a sword into his chest, shouting, "Traitor!
Receive your pay!" Truly a singular way to get the better of that
furious prelate. Della Rovere said that Aldolisi had accused him
of not defending Bologna, whereas Aldolisi himself had been the
one to withdraw from the city with his troops. Meanwhile, all
Italy applauded the fierce act since Aldolisi was hated as an unrestrained profiteer, ambitious, vice-ridden, and bloodthirsty, and
many thanked God for having armed Francesco Maria's hand. I
was thinking of the dismay of my daughter Eleonora, who was
so religious and now saw her husband struck by papal excommunication.

That May I had to test my strength against my brother cardinal
d'Este, who with his innate cold impudence ordered me to post
on the doors of Mantua's Duomo the manifestos of the Council
of Pisa, signed by a handful of schismatic cardinals who had met
at the prompting of the king of France to depose the pope. Ippolito
not only wanted to force this manifesto on me but also demanded
it be posted at night, in the presence of a notary and witnesses.
I asked myself if the terrible times he was living through had
made him insane. With Federico hostage in Rome and Francesco
the pope's gonfalonier, how could we openly set ourselves against
the Roman Church without exposing my poor child to terrible
risks and being excommunicated, along with our subjects? I am
a woman who is not afraid of words because I can perceive their
strength and weakness, but I was born Catholic. I feel the nature
of this religion of ours, prompt to offer comfort and hope beyond
recited prayers. The very thought of being outside the Church,
excommunicated, filled me with desolation. At what altars would
I kneel; to whom would I pray; what priest would give me his
blessing? No schismatic manifesto was posted in Mantua. At the
end of July, in Rome, Julius the Second proclaimed that the Church,
sanctified by the blood of the martyrs, without error, and first
among all churches, had to oppose any schism; and he announced, for April of the year 1512, an ecumenical council to
combat heresy, promote the reform of morals, and fight for the
peace of Christendom. So he said.

FROM England, that place of forbidden thoughts for me, a new
enemy arose, distant but menacing. This king, Henry the Eighth,
whom my English correspondent brought to vivid life in his lines,
after the conquest of Bologna sided with the pope and was out-

raged against the French, who tore the robe of Christ with such impiety. My memory, terribly subtle when it so chooses, unfolded before my eyes the letter of Robert de la Pole, and I was finally flattered by the choice he declared himself ready to make between an Italian marchesana and his own king. Before me I could see this man who had abruptly dropped into my life with his clear skin, his northerner's fair, smooth hair falling over his ears, framing a handsome, cold face. Cold, indeed! Those few letters were written on pages of fire, and I could never recall myself to prudence sufficiently. I had dreamed of him one night as I lay next to Francesco within the silver curtains of our bed, and I had waked in horror as if I had committed a sin of black infidelity. It was an ingenuous dream, a meeting in a nonexistent place, where we ran, one toward the other, to communicate some discovery of that moment. My face was inflamed with fear, but a strange emotion prompted a rejoicing cry in me: "I saw him! I saw him!" Francesco woke with a start; thinking I was in the grip of a nightmare, he embraced me, and feeling me tremble, he clasped me to his heart. I became calm again, but it seemed to me I was doubly a traitor, while at the same time I was intoxicated with innocence.

Unexpectedly, in full summer, the pope was struck down; it was the so-called August illness. The dispatches from Rome declared him in grave danger; at the castle everyone heaved a sigh of relief except Francesco, shrouded in somber thoughts, and me, uncertain whether or not to accept the fortune I had so long invoked. I did not know how to discipline my emotions; I felt disgust and triumph for having prayed for his death. I wandered around, uneasy, and I uneasily perused the reports from our envoys. This was the news: On the sixteenth of August Julius had gone to Castel Sant'Angelo, where he kept his treasure, to take there a sum of thirty thousand gold ducats to add to the five hundred thousand he already possessed. In the evening he invited to supper my Federico, his usual guest, and having played cards with the boy, he fell asleep in his chair. The next day he was pronounced seriously ill; he refused to eat, cursed and raged, and sank into sudden fits of drowsiness. His della Rovere relations watched over his waking hours and insisted he revoke Francesco Maria's excommunication; he signed the act when he was almost at the end. Rome stirred in disorder, riots broke out, the cardinals were already preparing for the imminent conclave when, surprisingly, Julius, after eating an abundance of peaches and plums, sank into deep sleep and then was cured. Federico, with his engaging grace, had been constantly at his side; in the great bedchamber the boy had remained with Julius when the kinsfolk had left him alone. And the stewards, all around them, on the pretext of making an inventory of the important objects, were stealing as much as they could.

On October fourth Julius, radiant with leonine vigor, presented himself in Santa Maria del Popolo, and publicly solemnized the Holy League uniting the pope, Venice, and Spain against Ferrara and the French, the rebels against the Church; and he cast his excommunication on the schismatic cardinals of the Council of Pisa. I hoped only that my brother Ippolito was not among them. News now was pressing: Ferdinand, king of Spain, proud of nothing so much as the title Protector of the Church, was quick to suspend the war in Africa against the Moors in order to redirect his troops to Italy. He named as his general in chief the viceroy of Sicily, Raimundo of Cardona, who with a great, beplumed army was ready to come up from the south and move against the French encamped in Ferrara. My brother Alfonso sent me word not to worry. Those troops had no artillery, and in his forges he was casting very powerful cannons of iron and bronze; he denied, however, that two bombards had been cast from the bronze of Julius's statue, the work of Michelangiolo, pulled down in Bologna by the fury of the populace.

Another woman would have been flattered by the life I was leading, courted, you could say, by all Europe. The emperor, a recent widower, told me he was in love with me, and empowered an envoy of ours, Gerolamo Cassola, to act as his pander. This envoy proved quite bold, as some men are; in a whisper he told me how he had promised Maximilian to make me more pliant to the imperial desires, and he allowed me to glimpse an empress's throne if Francesco were to succumb to his illness. From France, Louis, who considered himself a chivalrous king, sent messages to the pope enjoining him to return Federico to me at once, and he declared he was making this request to please a lady he greatly admired. But the king's letters were often unpleasant, not to say insolent, when he wrote me from Paris, calling my husband rogue; Louis knew my husband well, he added, and if I knew him equally well, I would not love him the way I apparently did. Such jests did not make me laugh. Francesco was irritated by them; he could not bear being called rogue even if the barb came from His Most Christian Majesty. I truly did not let myself be deceived by an emperor or by a king; but their letters provoked my replies, and in my fashion, and to my own ends, I could keep them both discreetly at bay.

DURING THOSE MONTHS, the stormiest of my life and in the life of our people, whom Francesco and I guarded carefully to prevent their being sacrificed, I had to give up one of my daughters, Ippolita, hardly more than a child. She was good-natured and resembled her father, though with more delicate features, and she was beautiful, more beautiful than her much praised sister Eleonora. I have never been very close to my daughters. The cares of state, the infinite world to be understood through reflection, the necessity of pondering the rules of government and the needs of the people, the correspondence with men and women of rank and with our envoys, and finally the duties of court consumed every minute of my day, and I must admit that only the thought of Federico could steal my heart away. Examining myself now, I realize I loved my daughters with a love overwhelmed by the impossibility, or near impossibility of helping them, but it is also true that the smooth, cool little arms of her tiny girls are the tender delight of a mother.

Ippolita's rebellion lasted almost six months, during which she was confined, of her own will, in the Convent of San Vincenzo, where her cousins Isabella and Eleonora Bentivoglio had been educated. On the eve of the Feast of Saint Francis, all of a sudden, her father consented to her assuming the Dominican habit. Feverish and trembling, the three adolescent girls were dressed as brides of Christ. At the ceremony Francesco's irrepressible affectionate nature made him weep, and I would also have been in tears if I had not been thinking of the humiliating news reaching me at that time about our son-in-law Francesco Maria della Rovere, murderer of cardinals and man of scant wisdom. I said as much openly, and a quip of mine circulated through the castle: "At least my new son-in-law will cause me no suffering."

The ceremony in the Church of San Vincenzo brought my attention back to the life of my family and to my own. I looked around, exploiting the intervals of silence granted me from time to time. Francesco and I went out riding. Once we ventured as

far as Lake Garda to taste the garlic sauce of the archpriest of
Toscolano. I listened to the new songs of a young musician from
Flanders, and I followed with curiosity the story of the portrait
that Francia was doing of me in Bologna from memory. I took
ardent interest in a curious little house being constructed by Biagio
Rossetti, the great Ferrara engineer patronized by my father. With
him I visited the elegant building that rose with its facade toward
the lake near the Palace of Porto. Amid flowers, groves, and
shrubs, open to the currents of light and air, this palace would
refresh me after those years spent almost constantly immured in
the castle tallying favorable advents and misfortunes. I wished
the little palace could be finished at once, and the flowers and
trees grow immediately, so I would find myself in a place of new
fantasies where the echo of distant battles was heard only faintly,
as if perhaps transferred to other nations, while our life would
be once more serene.

War blazed up as soon as Gaston de Foix, King Louis's chief
general, arrived from France. This warrior, handsome and brave
as a paladin, was incomparably skilled in strategy. He sent messages to Francesco and to me, curt but vigorous, wanting to es-
tablish the base of his military operations on our lands, so we
granted him free passage of the Po at Sermide and we informed
him of the Venetians' movements. The general occupied Brescia,
then abandoned it to the sack, to admonish the arrogance of the
Serenissima, as he said. I could not rejoice. Thousands of citizens
died from the soldiers' ferocity, and the whole city was stained
with blood. "We are murdered by the marquis of Mantua," the
Venetians cried in the field, and at night, beside me, Francesco
was unable to sleep. I held myself immobile, pretended to be
calm, and I repeated silently: It's for Ferrara; it's to save Ferrara.

In a flash Gaston de Foix, renewing the surprise tactics of Cesare
Borgia, came down toward Romagna and clashed with the Span-
ish-papal army a mile from Ravenna, near a little stream. There
Raimundo of Cardona had positioned himself, also a good strat-
egist, to prevent the taking of that city where the Spaniards had
assembled impressive amounts of provisions and arms. Gascons
and Picards began the heavy attack. The great battle joined by
the young French general at eight in the morning lasted until four
in the afternoon. The Spaniards were defeated, and Alfonso's
artillery reaped infinite victims: More than ten thousand soldiers
died, and many captains. Gaston de Foix himself died.

The way that a victory led to the collapse of the victorious army
amazed everyone. We realized that for the French the Italian ad-

included when the army of the new
...se, daily dwindling, left Milan. And
... in bound to the fealty of an alliance?
...: Alfonso, besieged within the walls
...d, was alone and excommunicated.
...iant turned to me. With great ra-
...is asked me to act as go-between
... make his peace with the Church.
...ner course. We had to aim at peace,
... depths of my spirit I had always strongly
... except, it is true, during the brief apparition of Gaston
de Foix, who, as with all creatures of genius, summed up personally the moral nature of events, altering that nature in his own
likeness. Now the word "pardon" was also prickly. What would
be the conditions set by Julius, who dominated Rome, confident
that he had been called by the voice of God? Against the failure
of the schismatic cardinals, mocked in Pisa even by children and
forced to flee Italy, the majesty of the Council rose in the Lateran;
the figure of that pope, triumphant in all his pontifical authority,
haunted me.

Federico, too, my dearest son still held in Rome, was a pawn
in the chess game of the wily Julius, who truly loved the boy,
however, and showered favors on him, though this did not prevent him from having the boy write, addressed to me, a charmingly composed little missive to urge me to serve the pope. I sent
my son a tender letter and quoted a saying, "A running horse
needs no spur," which went down very well in the Curia. I was
moved, thinking of that youth, barely twelve, caught in our plots,
and with some truth I signed my reply "Your mother who loves
you as her own soul."

It was actually Federico who let me share in some of the secret
moments of the pope with information in his own hand or from
his household. One morning the boy was in the company of Stazio
Gladio, our excellent envoy, who was delivering to the Vatican
some letters from Francesco about the taking of Cremona, wrested
from the French. The two entered the chamber of His Holiness,
who ordered the windows opened wide and then, barefoot, in
his nightshirt, in the presence of everyone, flung himself out of
bed and rapidly read Francesco's dispatches. As soon as he had
glanced at the lines, he exploded in irrepressible jubilation, shouting, "Church! Church! Julius! Julius!" and, having said that the
most beautiful thing in the world was to see the French driven
from Italy, he burst out singing.

Federico laughed all that day with the pope, w
clowned as if he had taken leave of his senses. As fo
tians, Julius said he could tolerate for the present the
conquered Cremona should be in their hands, but he
mean to leave the city in their domain or to let them expa
that they could raise their horns and frighten the rest of the I
ians. And other lively tales followed; in my son's words the pope
firm determination was constantly evident: Julius wanted to see
Alfonso before him, contrite, asking forgiveness.

I tried to be hopeful, and I moved with extreme caution. In
mid-June I left for Ferrara with Mario Equicola, who had just
arrived from Rome with the papal safe-conduct. I met my brother
in the country, at La Stellata. He was quite ready to fling himself
at the feet of His Holiness; he would immediately release the
prisoners taken at Ravenna, and first among them Lord Fabrizio
Colonna, though in Ferrara this prisoner was enjoying his own
private carnival, ardently courting all the duchess's ladies. I did
not see her, the duchess; at that moment she was in bed, ill with
some distemper of the body. I handed my brother the safe-conduct so that he could go to Rome, and we read it over severa!
times to make sure it guaranteed his life and liberty; but the
magnanimity of that pardon was heavy.

In my rooms I pictured in my mind the Roman encounter between my brother and my son, the penitent and the hostage; I
lingered on Federico's gentle speech to which Julius entrusted a
message of reception and an assurance as to the papal good intentions. Colonnas and Orsinis escorted the man and the boy
dear to me from Porta del Popolo to the Vatican and saw to it
that Alfonso's entrance seemed a victor's. I must say that my will
was insufficient to sustain my hope, and it was quickly evident
that my doubts had been justified, for after the cordial reception
ceremonies, it became clear that the pope would never renounce
his longed-for Ferrara. It was not at all sure that after the renunciation demanded of Alfonso, Julius would then confirm his
investiture of the dukedom. At this point my brother could not
bear such pressure, and he fled Rome, taking refuge at Marino
with the Colonnas.

What did Alfonso fear if not the predictable, boundless determination of the pope to wreak vengeance on his disobedient vassal? And what could Julius fear, or make a show of fearing, from
an Alfonso, resolute and frightful, as if he were standing by his
cannons at Ravenna? Perhaps a surprise move, surely a total rebellion. Both knew they were enemies to the depths of their souls,

and forever. And I, who had thought to fight and defeat the pope, by myself, without arms, in a kind of secret challenge, I had to admit it: I had come to the confrontation without a grain of humility, nor did I wish to find any in myself.

THE INTRIGUES swelling from day to day brought the congress of confederates to converge on Mantua, gathering to set Italy's affairs in order; or so it seemed. I was to have within reach the protagonists of the gathering: Raimundo of Cardona, Spain's viceroy in Sicily and commander of the Spanish Army; and Matthäus Lang, bishop of Gurk, the emperor's much-listened-to envoy, whom I had already met, a handsome blond man of about forty, at times crudely vulgar, one of those Germans convinced that the freedom of speech we permit at our courts justifies an intemperate freedom of manner and action. Raimundo of Cardona, on the other hand, was of fine and reserved demeanor, a bit pompous, but also a man of sensuality behind his seductive words.

To represent the pope, Bibbiena, my witty Moccicone, came to the Diet, and Venetians and Florentines came. It was a question of restoring the Medicis to the rule of Florence to punish the republic for its vaunted French sympathies, and similarly, but more triumphantly, after thirteen years of exile spent at the emperor's court, Massimiliano Sforza, son of my sister, Beatrice, and the Moro, was to return to the duchy of Milan. With him the past would become the present.

This restoration was marked further by an eagerness to form new alliances to save Alfonso, then a fugitive through Italy after he had left Rome on a rebellious impulse. I was working on his behalf, not the least dismayed, but rather determined to see his dukedom remain intact, without mutilation; this enterprise demanded patience at every turn and bright smiles as of one with no thought of defeat, who solicits not the charity of others but their affection. Every weapon would be of use in my battle.

I began by decking the castle as if for a celebration; at the same time I assembled the leading Mantuan families, and to each I assigned the guests they were to receive in the palaces. Only Matthäus Lang would live at court, in the so-called white chambers, splendidly redone, under my supervision as always. I got out my dresses, my richest and most exquisite inventions, I added ornaments, I had jewels cleaned and polished, I smeared myself with pomades, and for a whole day Umbrasia, my herbalist, worked to lighten my hair; and meanwhile, I gave my girls instructions and trained them with suitable speeches. I told them that we lacked men's weapons to defend our states, but we still had the spirit to find ways of doing just that. They were all to show themselves my allies and should keep in readiness for our guests their gaiety, their jesting wit, and all the charms that rob men of their wisdom, without going beyond the boundaries I always preached to them.

In those times I had at court a host of truly remarkable girls, already expert in amorous sallies but aware of the limits. With them, the year before at court, during a memorable evening we had gone quite far with verbal jests, laughing till our stomachs ached; we sang a song whose refrain went *"Tolle in mano,"* and the bishop of Gurk had invited me to do what the song said. Now I warned them to remember how difficult it had been then to switch from obscene proposals to pleasant and amusing topics. Outstanding among my pupils were Isabella Lavagnola, known as the ballerina for her elegance as a dancer, and the youngest, Eleonora Brognina, whose nickname recalled the agile Brogna and the delicate Catalina, who had died young. But all the others, all those names and faces, were beautiful for one feature or another. I do not agree with those ladies who are content to have only one or two girls charming for their youth, employing older women in other offices, no matter what they look like. No, mine was to be an army that dazzled and put men in the mood for concessions. If they were not beautiful, let them become beautiful, or let them be clever like my friend Emilia Pio, who charms anyone who converses with her. Nothing, not pages, not gentlemen, not liveried grooms, not jesters or musicians, gives more prestige to a court than a band of maidens who know the so-called art of being a woman.

Those days of the Mantuan Diet, when I was bent on winning over the bishop of Gurk and the viceroy, Spain, and empire in favor of Ferrara, proved fruitful. The climax came with the supper I offered the guests in the Porto villa, at the peak of an August that was not actually too warm. Without interruption, at the table arrived pheasants, fat partridges, hare, every sort of dish, salt or sweet, and a flood of other creations of my master cooks, under the command of Mantellina, the laurel-crowned cook of the marchese himself. On the pretext of a slight indisposition, Francesco had withdrawn to his rooms to rest; the next day he was to give a great banquet in his palace near the grove of limes.

The evening was mild and calm, and from the lake came a light breeze that bore the music with it; flutes and viols were being played, accompanying the passage of the moon in the sky and all our lunatic gaiety. Among the young maids who made a good showing Brognina was awarded the crown of beauty; that man was happy who could steal one of her gloves or her fan. Two Spanish gentlemen, overflowing with compliments for me, were quick to detach from my satin dress seven little candlesticks of finely worked gold. Gaily I asked what time it was, and they answered, "Three in the morning."

"That's odd," I replied, "I thought the hour of the sack had struck."

Nobody could refrain from laughing, and the imperials laughed as well. If I close my eyes, I can recompose the scene in the garden of Porto under the shadows of my newly built little pavilion starred with jasmine. The girls are eating melon and teasing the men. All the ambassadors are there, except the Florentines and Venetians, kept apart by their punctilio. Mario Equicola, opposite me, pays his absurd court to Lavagnola, swearing that the more she hates him, the more he loves her, and the words fly. My beloved lunatic Bernardo Bibbiena tries to convince Brognina that youth desires love and wants her to tell him what she desires.

"I desire the mouth of one of you, more than all of you put together," the clever girl replies enigmatically.

Not bad, her reply. Equicola decrees that love is like the fire that destroys and reanimates man, and Bibbiena echoes him: "Love raises the dead! Ah, my Brognina, I love you even if loving you means embracing a shadow and trapping the wind with nets."

Raimundo of Cardona greedily kisses the girl's hand, and again my Moccicone speaks up: "My lord viceroy, do you know how to drink a woman?"

The viceroy is dumbfounded for a moment.

Bibbiena continues. "What? The viceroy of Sicily doesn't know that? When a man kisses a woman, doesn't he suck her lips? And when you drink wine, don't you suck it as well? And don't you know that some of your Spaniards kiss women's hands to suck the rings they wear on their fingers?"

"Fever take you, old Moccicone!" I cry gaily. "But now be silent and drink!"

Even if I am not too pleased to see my dress shorn of the golden candlesticks, I remain patient. Bibbiena looks at me; his facetious manner fades, and in another tone he whispers to me that I laugh like little Federico. For two years that son has been far from me. Who knows how he has grown? At his age boys shoot up quickly. I ask Moccicone to describe him to me.

"He is handsome, tall, fair," Bibbiena says. "Your Federichino is a perfect horesman, can dance in the French style, sings in the Mantuan style, rides Spanish fashion, and speaks Latin like his mother. The pope cannot do without him; when Raffaello was portraying Julius in the room of the School of Athens, by the window, the pope insisted that his gaze, directed toward the great fresco, should seem to rest on the head of little Federico, as he peers out between Epicurus and Averroës."

"It is hard," I murmur, "to think of that son of mine, in others' hands, down there."

The bishop of Gurk answers me, pretending to joke, but with fairly crude realism: "Your son in Rome is guarding your back. He is Mantua's best ambassador."

"Do you believe the emperor will agree to what we have decided?" I ask him in a low voice.

"Never fear, Spaniards and imperials for the present will not join in the Ferrara expedition."

"And the pope?"

"He will shout and shout! And it will pass!"

We hear the shot of a pistolone, and we all fall silent immediately. Pirro Donati, who has been keeping a discreet eye on the party, informs me that the Spaniards are shooting at the silver plates on the credenza in a marksmanship competition. Lips clenched, I tell him to let them have their way. The viceroy's expression turns grim.

I WAS seized by a sudden melancholy, as so often happens during a feast where there is much laughter. Rising, I moved onto the terrace, gliding and rustling over the pavement of white marble squares, and I headed toward a solitary guest seated on a marble bench, leaning against a low wall of patterned black-and-white slabs. Under the moon the design had a geometrical prominence. With his small, thin body, his sharp head nobly bald, the man emanated a creative strength that set him apart from the others. He stared at the sky dotted with stars and did not notice me until I was close to him.

"Signor Pomponazzi," I said to the master, and my voice was unusually respectful, "do you read the stars to forget mankind? To be sure, our girls do not trouble the thoughts of a master of philosophy like you. Perhaps you are simply repeating to yourself how silly women are."

"I could never say that in your presence, signora marchesana," he answered with his Mantuan accent, smiling. "For that matter, what I said was that women—apart from rare exceptions, of which you are an eminent example—are not truly wise, and cannot be so, by nature. But I also said that men are more animals than human, and those who seem rational are so only by comparison with the others, supremely animal. But these are trivial philosophical divagations, my lady, and have no place in a night like this, when all of us should be on our feet to search the sky for the mysteries of life."

I heard his rich voice, deep and natural; it was easy for him to achieve speech denied others.

"You have little esteem for mankind, Maestro Perottino, is that true? You do not agree with Giovanni Pico della Mirandola that man is the image and symbol of God and can be degraded, true, but can also become an angel or a god according to his choice."

He looked at me, limpid and pensive. The spark of future learning brightened his face. "For me," he said, calm and bold, "man can understand only if he sets out from feeling, even though it is possible to posit an independence of the mind from the body. The soul then can be mortal; morality, absolute virtue consist of spiritual harmony, and the essential prize of virtue is virtue itself, which makes man happy."

"But the soul is immortal; so our faith assures us."

"He who has faith is faithful and saved," the philosopher said softly. "Man can believe in what he cannot demonstrate. There is a desire in him, a yearning, a kind of perfume of immortality."

His voice became bodiless. We stood immobile on the squares of white marble bathed by the lunar light.

ALFONSO'S return to Ferrara, after infinite peregrinations through the mountains, woods, and countryside between Rome and the Romagna seemed a miracle, and the excitement was shared by all the citizens. I sent my tried-and-true Capilupi to inform my brother fully about what I had done for him, and that duke of cast iron, at the end, was in tears. I had undertaken offices that put my own life at risk, my secretary reported to him, but without winning the battle. Far from it. We would have faced an infernal time if Julius had lasted on the throne of Peter.

In November Massimiliano Sforza, my very young nephew, turned up on the drawbridge of the castle; he had stopped to greet me with every show of homage before proceeding with his rich retinue to take possession of the duchy of Milan. What a wondrous dream, to hear again the triumphal cry from the guard turret, the cry that had hailed the Moro: "Sforza! Sforza!" All our display of gaiety seemed inadequate to celebrate him; Francesco prepared a splendid reception and a very merry banquet in his palace near San Sebastiano, where I could glimpse the new rooms, delightful in their lighthearted, fresh elegance, prepared for the duchess my sister-in-law, in the deplorable eventuality of the fall of Ferrara. I could not refrain from touching an amulet I had on my wrist.

My nephew was dressed in German style and spoke a bastard language, but his happiness at ruling Milan and his emotion in thanking me for all I had done for him added great charm to his youthful presence; at times, glimpsing some movement that recalled his mother, I summoned to my heart my sister, Beatrice. In the whirling of clowns and dancers, at the height of the festivity, my brother Ippolito was announced, all decked out in his usual haughty fashion. Irritated by this impudence, Francesco angrily abandoned the banquet he had ordered for Massimiliano; that ostentatious presence of a schismatic cardinal in his house might arouse Julius's suspicions. I learned later that my nephew apologized, in writing, to the pope for having tolerated this intrusion; being in the house of others, he could not deny entrance to cardinal d'Este, though he had not spoken to him.

And at this point I lost all concrete, private support. Francesco became alien to me beyond any possible doubt and reported to the pope my renewed correspondence with my brothers about things hidden even from him. Julius reproached Francesco for indulging the wiles of a wife who showed no respect for him, and Francesco, in turn, reproached me. I defended myself vigorously, unable to suppress tones of grief; when I saw that he did not admit them, even in order to reject them, I sadly concluded that nothing I did could please him anymore.

At this point our love was wearing out, and a rekindling was virtually beyond hope. At ever briefer intervals, and increasingly terrible, the attacks of his illness recurred. My husband no longer came up to my rooms, and his face, on all occasions, was an outraged mask; nor did I have the heart to invite him to any conjugal play, as I saw him detaching himself from everything that concerned me. I pitied him for the illness that fiercely separated him from the present; still of virile age, Francesco could not assimilate the new times. He often uttered invectives against the war of cannons, brute instruments of destruction that undermined the soldier's courage. And he bawled these views openly against my brother Alfonso, inventor of artillery warfare in Italy.

He also separated his conduct as chief of state from mine. Toward December the pope sent Folenghino to us with explicit messages threatening to rain spiritual and temporal thunderbolts on Mantua, as he was weary of our taunting. And things grew worse when the emperor Maximilian, who had never joined the Holy League, clamorously entered it, and Francesco decided this was the right moment for us to show we were loyal vassals. Now my husband every day really did side more and more with the pope, constantly accusing me. The discovery that I was fighting alone exasperated me. I even forgot my patron goddess of prudence, and I hurled an invective against Julius, praying God would make him die, and, I hoped, soon.

Having preserved the gift of reason was no help, as I soon realized when my nephew Massimiliano Sforza invited me with my court to the imminent carnival in Milan, which he wanted to be memorable in its dazzling festivities, its ornament of beautiful women. I spoke of it with Francesco, convinced he would deny me the Milanese celebrations; he listened to me, frowning, controlling himself in a cold attitude. Then he said it would be good for me to spend some time away from Mantua, where, he explained, I had become a stain on his honor. I, daughter of Ercole of Este and Eleonora of Aragón, a stain on my husband's honor! I, the stellar paragon among women according to the poets and scholars of my time; I, revered by princes and kings; I—and at this point I moaned—the wife of Francesco Gonzaga, with whom I had lived a life of fiery instinct, such as to flatter any virile pride, I saw myself not only refused but humiliated and insulted.

I questioned myself. Where was sorrow? It was dumb. Only wrath and pity fed me, my every fiber. Would I live then on wrath and pity? I was drowning. But catching my breath, I assumed a still-stronger eagerness to act, as if every barb stimulated, incited me. Drop by drop, I regained possession of myself; it was as if someone were drawing for me a secret map of my strategy. And I knew my target. In Milan there was a man to be conquered, the official who at that moment possessed power beyond reckoning, the viceroy Raimundo of Cardona, more and more entrapped in his love for my Brognina and so chivalrous as to place his feelings above his actions. He commanded the army that was to attack Ferrara, so he was the man to be subjugated; if the venture were to succeed, Eros would defeat Mars.

Reacting, with revived spirits, in moments of wrath I outdid myself in preparations. The rooms were transformed into palettes of colors, glossed by gilded and silvered trimmings and enhanced by laces and embroideries. My jewels, cleaned and polished, shone in their little caskets. I went down often to the herbarium, and I was endlessly patient in mixing pomades and preparing little boxes of rouge in different tints to compose the glory of the face. I ordered new dresses and cloaks trimmed and lined with fur, I renewed the cut of a green cloak lined with snowy-white Russian fox, and I was content because even this whim looked good on me. Swarms of women, among the most expert seamstresses of Mantua, were at work in the wardrobe rooms.

We set out on January eighth in three coaches decked in crimson satin, with embroidered curtains, doubled to protect us against drafts. Dressed in wools and velvets, we provided ourselves with muffs containing little jars of hot water to keep our hands warm. The more delicate of our party sported satin masks with eye slits, meant to keep the nose from reddening and the eyes from watering. Those masks transfigured the girls' faces; they looked like fantastic birds of prey. Our departure was a great confusion of dresses, shawls, and cloaks, a stamping of horses and mules made nervous by the endless running to and fro of excited jesters and servants and outriders obeying often contradictory orders. The wagons with our packed hampers had preceded us the day before, and we would find them in Milan. Up to the last moment I was pursued by the fulminations of Julius, who disapproved of this journey, suspecting me of new plots. Francesco announced this to me, coming to bid me a hasty good-bye. He added a few words about the excessive expenditures; then we embraced for show, displaying gaiety in front of the court.

Our party set off on the icy road in high spirits. The young girls in their coaches behind mine conversed in low voices and laughed. Little by little, the silence expanded as the plain opened out, the laughter diminished, and in the end they fell silent. Something resounded in me, in the suspended immobility of the winter, among the stiffened trees and the embroidery of the leafless boughs. I saw myself twenty years younger, a happy bride, next to my royal mother, with my only sister, Beatrice, and our Ferrara girls in the great gondola conducting me by water toward Pavia, where Beatrice was to marry Ludovico, the Moro. She brooded on her enormous adventure, shut up in herself, her tiny, huddled body a clot of stubborn, sorrowing strength. Because of that stubbornness and that sorrow, my mother looked at her shyly, heart-rent. Around us our women groaned, complaining of the snow, the cold, the craft that advanced slowly, between the deserted white shores, and also lamenting their hunger, for we had lost sight of the boat with our provisions and there was no telling where it had got stuck. I felt myself growing and flourishing; the complaints seemed to me incitements; nothing could weaken me, not even the thought of Francesco, who had remained in Mantua. He warmed my blood, even from the distance, with the vehemence of his living; when we separated, he suffered my leaving as an injustice or, rather, as a sin against life's just rights. And now? I refused to give any answer, I kept for myself the warmth evoked by those old apparitions, and greeting the dear images, I heard again past voices, my own among them, sharp as a diamond. I fell asleep to the cadenced sway of the coach, teetering under the rain.

IN FEBRUARY, in Milan, it was the twenty-second of the month, a Spanish messenger brought the news of the sudden death of Julius the Second. I was thunderstruck. Even though I had hoped for it, I could not believe that the heavy oak would give way, that that spirit driven by inflexible enthusiasms would vanish from the world, that the head which tenaciously conceived boundless action would sink back and lie still. And it happened in the very week he had chosen to order the sending of the Spanish Army against Ferrara, while we women, in regal dress, were desperately trying to capture in our nets the commanding general of that expedition, Raimundo of Cardona, to divert him from the war. An immense physical relief made me draw a deep breath; we were all saved. I mean, Ferrara, the Este family, I myself, and— who knows?—also Francesco, no longer oppressed by that unsuitable fealty, hostile to me. I clasped the hands of my women, who allowed themselves some joyous whispering and exclamations. I could find no way to make them keep still.

I thought immediately of Federico. He would come home immediately; the cardinals surely would not hold him in Rome. All the knots were unraveling; I need not fear every day the news of the morrow. My steps flew, and at the same time I had no idea what to do with myself; the tone, the key of my incredibly empty day, eluded me. At night I lay awake, repeating to myself that fears no longer existed, but not even Nurse Caterina's potions brought me sleep. I could think of everything that gave me pleasure, and I thought of Julius. The dead pontiff obsessed me in my brief dreams; he accused me without rancor but sternly of having called for his death, wished him in hell, cursed him. I was unable to ask his forgiveness. But when I let myself go, collected my thoughts, and took the measure of my imminent antagonists, I saw before me men of scant substance, shadow men. I had lost my great adversary, worthy of defeating me or of defeat at my hands.

Finally I was caught up by the wave of living that struck me from every side, and I became impassioned over the fate of my nephew Massimiliano and the restored dukedom of Milan. Carnival blazed, vast amusements and gilded banquets; but now that Julius was dead, the most conflicting events ensued. Piacenza declared itself free, chose the duke of Milan as its lord, and summoned him there, to acclaim him. I seemed to be summoned as well. When I consider my frank decision of March second, I cannot give a reason for the impulse that drove me to that bizarre resolve: to order our carriages, assign my women their traveling places, and, with our little escort, fall in behind the ranks of the duke's troops and of Raimundo of Cardona's Spaniards. Our sharing in the army's march flattered and troubled our friends, who rode alongside us, excited at living in the verses of an epic poem. I circulated an order among my girls: to show themselves not just valorous but laughing, as if they were in a decked hall or a green garden.

I do not know the reason for the impulse that made me accept (and perhaps had provoked) Massimiliano's invitation to enter the festive city with him. I accepted, in any case, and dressed sumptuously; led by a kind of secret yearning, I found myself at the entrance of Piacenza, at my nephew's right, under the ducal canopy. I tried to clarify my own feelings, and the yearning became all the more voracious. Strange, instinctive joy burst out in me without any rational nature, until Francesco roughly called me back, informing me that Federico had set out from Rome and was on his way to Mantua. Calculating the days, I decided my son's arrival would not be immediate.

I had expected Francesco to let me decide my return—now he had nothing more to fear from the pope because of my abhorred intrigues with Ferrara—but on the contrary, he began to torment me with acid, irritating commands. In vain I told him how many friends I had won for our State, how many favors I had obtained, how useful the eternal gratitude of our nephew would be, for he felt protected by our family and, because of his youth, was in need of counsel. I was not enjoying myself; my husband could be certain of that. In that war campaign I was really expending my life. Without the least respect, he reminded me that my mature age did not allow me whims and caprices, and he told me it was necessary to silence the gossip circulating among the populace and at court. In the end he said it even more explicitly: He demanded of me a wife's proper regard for her husband. Perhaps because I am not accustomed to disapproval, I took these impositions as an insult; the very thought of my enemies' sly laughter as they pricked Francesco's pride and the sardonic pursing of the clerks' lips as they made copies of their lord's letters made my flesh crawl.

I composed an answer, aggressive and cold, without any weakness of sentiment, though I reminded him of my long years of obedience and service and of my enduring love. Yes, love. To underline this word, I did not spare him lashes. "My lord," I said, thrusting him from me, "Your Lordship owes me all duty that ever a husband owed a wife, and if even you honored me and loved me as much as possible, you could never sufficiently repay my loyalty." When I had sealed the paper, I felt a liberation, a warm desire for peace, and that night, in my cramped lodging, as the rain drummed on the roof, I fell asleep with no need of potions, all passions sated at last.

Having recalled my rights and reaffirmed my wifely fidelity made me more relieved and circumspect the next day. At all costs I decided to delay my return. I had to get used to the idea of meeting my husband and to the idea of shutting myself up within those walls, so stony in their verticality. The castle where my first girlhood had passed would not, I was determined, be changed into an emblem of spent love: my apartments, my Studiolo, my Grotta, my Leonardesque rooms, and my Painted Halls must receive me as always, stimulating my tendency to use my reason and my fancy. I wrote, therefore, a second letter in which I asked, almost politely, three days' extension of my return, and only to satisfy the desire of the viceroy and the duke my nephew. "Would God that Your Lordship could see into my inmost spirit!" my message concluded. And it was not hypocrisy. I may be a woman who always wants to have her own way and think with her own mind, as Francesco's accusation says, but as I act always for the common good, I demand to be thanked.

At this point the situation was stagnant. The Spanish troops had rebelled because they had not been paid, and the army made camp near Parma. I delayed far more than three days, and these were days different from those spent till then. I came to know the strange all-male land of an army camp, the arid and barren existence of soldiers passed only in the physical life of eating, drinking, sleeping, exercising with their weapons, always in conflict with matter, and I thought of another world, illuminated by benevolent apparitions, the world of Venus and Mars, of Guinevere and Launcelot, of Isolde and Tristan. We reached Mantua by way of Cremona one windy morning, sunny and crisp, that made the castle's red walls vibrant. The paintings of the Studiolo were like a discovery, new, especially the enameled perspectives, sharply outlined, in my Mantegnas. Francesco sent the whole court out to meet me, but he remained shut up in his chambers because of the recurrent attacks of his sickness. Later, when we were together at dinner, he mentioned our letters; he seemed absent, somehow intimidated at seeing me calm and lighthearted. Out of curiosity, toward evening, I went down the little stairway to his apartments; the little door was barred.

MY EXISTENCE, however, did not recover a character apt to dispel my sufferings. Removed from the hampers and cases, the dresses and ornaments that had shone in Milan were now all put away properly; I found myself with my chambers in order, but I was inwardly restless. I almost turned nasty; my famous benevolent manner that acted like a philter on those who came to speak to me was losing its powers. To the viceroy Raimundo of Cardona I sent a "discipline" of the kind sinners use in doing penance, striking themselves. With this symbolic gift I was ironically urging chastity on that overpassionate lover; at that moment I enjoyed making this Spaniard, master of half of Italy, pay for the ostentation of his frenzy for Brognina. His scrawled letters pursued us, sent first of all to me, considered the "intermediary" of his suit, though he wrote in the most devoted tone. Having established with him a language of rather urgent amatory skirmish, I had no right to forbid him certain dubious expressions such as the plea to intercede, as a haloed saint, with his beloved. He moved with supple agility, parrying blows with an air of accepting them as favors, and I, even if somehow offended, could not directly make an enemy of this powerful arbiter of events, and I unburdened myself by asking him favors, large and small.

The more I teased him, the more the Spanish viceroy became obsessed with Brognina, and crowned by such love, she felt its allure without, however, boasting of it. I studied her. She was truly beautiful, though too tall and slender: white skin, creamy and unblemished; blue eyes with hints of green and gold, very big, shining, a bit dazzled in her grave face that, when she smiled, became irresistible. In Milan, after an evening of festivity, the viceroy had given her jewels of refined craftsmanship and two lengths of velvet, one crimson and one black, to signify joy of a kiss received and mourning for a kiss denied, and she covered her face with her little hands, overcome with modesty. I began to keep my distance from Brognina, to protect the reputation of my maids, and the viceroy must somehow have learned of it as he begged me to treat his lady well; with inconceivable clumsiness, thinking to flatter me, he wrote that Brognina loved me very much, and serving me, she regarded me with veneration and love. Coldly, in the presence of all my other women, I had Tortorina read those sentences aloud so the girl's delicacy would be stricken and she would take care not to involve me in her tales.

Pirro Donati, always dedicated to me, seemed visibly troubled after my return. He did not like my maids' adventures or my heroic system of training them, and he could not bear to see me so trapped. Benedetto Capilupi, my other secretary, was, on the contrary, so happy to see me back in my place in the castle that he made constant references to my position as wife. He told me that while I was in Milan, Francesco had shown him the sores of his French sickness, all closed and healed, and had assured him he was ready to consummate matrimony. I pretended to laugh, but I told him nothing of the little barred door. Pirro Donati disapproved of the liberty taken by my good gentleman, considering me a goddess, and I was amused by his excessive modesty. I appreciated, however, his ever-alert concern for respect, and I was pleased that he considered me too elevated to hear confidences and conceits of dubious taste. At that moment being involved in the agreements and disagreements of my court put me out of patience.

THE PERSON who saved me from sinking into a swamp of malign humors, who restored to me all my talents for constructing the future in the present was my son Federico. He had returned from Rome tired, and since the physician declared that he found the boy exhausted, Federico spent several days in his bed resting. But the moment he got up he appeared as I had always dreamed and wished: no longer a boy but the promise of an enchanting man, his thirteen years radiant, transparent, roseate. Not only was his person sweetly formed, but, what is more rare, he had

an easy, lordly way of moving, a turn of the head at once exclamatory and vocative; his shaking of his coppery chestnut hair,
the color of Francesco's short crop, announced in him a youth in
many ways alert. I was surprised to rediscover his resemblances
to me as he measured his gestures and held his left hand up in
assurance; he walked like a courtier, perfectly poised, bent just
slightly to the left with an elegant indolence all his own. He sang
every day in his room, sometimes with our musicians and sometimes alone in a clear and sweet voice; he practiced the use of
arms seriously, rode like a Saint George, and spoke well. In more
than two years' absence he had lost much of the Mantuan accent
that still inflected, however, the cadence of his sentences, and he
took care to observe the proper pronunciation learned from the
masters of the Roman Academy. Everything interested him; instinctively he knew the art of the courtier as well as it was described to us by Count Baldesar Castiglione, perhaps even better.
With me he behaved in a way he had not learned from anyone:
He knelt before my chair to kiss my hand, and often he remained
seated for a long time at my feet on the edge of the dais. Our
conversations soon acquired a tone of open confidentiality that
allowed real accord. The women, my girls, did not intimidate
him; he joked boldly with them, and he never lacked the appropriate word.

A wondrous appropriation took place within me. Only now I
understood that such a son was entirely different from his younger
brothers, Ercole and Ferrante, absorbed in rough games and physical competitions. Federico would make himself loved and willingly put himself to any test. I had always been mad for him,
ever since he was born, coming after the two girls, saving me
from the humiliating suspicion of being a mother only of females.
But now I saw in him the docility of a perfect pupil, promising
the possibility of times strengthened, indeed redoubled. It was
understood, secretly, that I would be at his side. He would have
everything: talent for enlarging the State; ability in handling political negotiations; great and tempered skill in choosing among
the rarest pleasures of the spirit and the heart. I would foster in
him the prince, the exemplary man of his time, a happy human
model.

Though all Gonzagas shared it, I considered Federico's predi-
lection for our lakes eccentric. The favorite pastime of this true
Mantuan was to climb into a boat and proceed along the narrow,
shaded channels among the sandbars covered with the fringed

green of the canebrakes, and he was drawn to navigating on the broad mirror of the upper lake, populated with aquatic birds uttering elegiac strains or pathetic shrill cries. For me those places concealed a strange magic that could reassure or disturb, but above all, they recalled the legend of the white statue of Virgil drowned in the lake by a bigot governor who suspected the Mantuan populace of idolatry. For Federico the lakes were the splendid preserves of hunting for coots and wild ducks and sometimes fine fishing for pike and carp. And so, every now and then, in two or three boats with several rowers, we spent hours on those pools of shifting color. We took musicians with us and singers and some of my son's companions, sly little cockerels that my girls disdained, referring them to the chambermaids. After the songs and the fishing (I would not follow the hunting of coot with guns, which for some time had been the custom, noisy and cruel), I would arrange to be isolated at length with Federico, to talk of many things that could spur his curiosity or provoke his pleasure, an art I know. We came to talk of my brother Alfonso, and I told summarily of the valor, courage, and constancy of spirit that this uncle had shown in defending his title of duke of Ferrara.

"*Olim*," he interrupted. "Alfonso d'Este *olim* duke of Ferrara, as His Holiness always said. Ferrara is Church territory, and it must return to the Church."

I explained to him about our Este family, feudal lords for many centuries, about the dukedom and our constant glory that has made our name one with the name of the city. He listened carefully, but unconvinced. And stimulated by my eagerness to delve into his soul, I asked him, in a conversational tone, how he had got along in Rome with the pope. Federico held his little body erect and studied me with glistening eyes.

"Oh, Mother dear, do you really want to know? You really wish that? I will tell you everything about Rome if you like. It is a magnificent city, great, almost hidden by foliage, because there are so many villas with gardens full of trees, woods, and statues. Even many of the churches are on knolls surrounded by groves; the center of the city is full of ancient Roman monuments, and the river flows through it and divides it. Gold is poured out in palaces, clothes, the trappings of horses, on the banquet tables; the Vatican is an endless palace; the villa where I lived, very close to the pope's houses, is on a hill covered with umbrella pines. Do you want to know about His Holiness? He was a great friend to me. He made me laugh with his violent words when he lost at games and flew into a temper; then he would laugh, too, and call me his handsome Federichino. Eleonora's husband was jealous. Really!"

He sighed, a grown-up's sigh, then went on. "If you want to know, Mother dear, His Holiness was a good man. He always had a present for me; he sent me wines and dishes from his table. He would fly into a fury, true, but he calmed down at once and asked everyone's forgiveness. When he discussed the Church, he would become heated and would make us who listened to him grow heated as well. I see him always, Mother, even now; at evening I pray for him, and he seems to be near me, to greet me and raise his hand to bless me."

He had spoken in haste, a bit breathless as if he had freed himself from a weight. I did not reply. I could see clearly that my adversary was winning, crouched in the heart of my adolescent. Federico's brief, ingenuous story suggested a daily history of confidences and simple revelations, an atmosphere of curmudgeonly tenderness beyond which the young sense deep, true feelings. And he summoned up this figure in the evening at the moment of prayer; only by him did Federico wish to be protected, not by me, not by his father. This aggressive image had to be erased, but through gradual fading, without imposition or argument.

Soon, at once, I would order Rozone, Federico's tutor, to write, if possible in the style of Plutarch, a good history of the Este family, very clearly expounded. Julius the Second would play his actual role, and the shrewdness of reason would prevail. Still, it was bitter to leave all to the future and, after having struggled so much with that man, to find myself facing his living ghost. To conceal the searing pain of my heart, I turned my head away and bent over the water as if I wished to discover something on the lake bed, beyond the scattered flight of the tiny black minnows.

"Mother, dear Mother," Federico cried, "what are you looking at? Have you spied the statue of Virgil? Tell me! Tell! I want to see it, too!"

IV

Flee
in Order
to Return

Room of the clocks
the year 1533

IN THE WAY of nature discordant spirits contradict one another, but not in this room of clocks, where they seem to seek out one another to create a universal truce in measuring time. An eagerness for concord enters amid the lights and the shadow; in solitude, I am summoning up the full, even frenzied years that were my lot. I could say that the moment, as it proffers itself, allows a glimpse of some throb of happiness, a word too often used to assert a right we are convinced we acquired with birth. Happiness, on the contrary, is properly an instant, a flash that calls physical heat from every part of our body, and as it rises to the brain, it vanishes. Unhappiness, on the other hand, has a more obstinate radiation in attacking us and enduring, and it is revealed in more ways, even analogous. For me one of its usual ways is this: I lower my gaze to the wooden surface where I rest my hand; terrified, I discern a slow wave that engulfs objects one by one, and at the moment it floods, to erase the world, it stops with a deckled foam at the edges of the table, and thence it withdraws, dissolving. Happiness and unhappiness, unfathomable and curious and indocile, I confront them, like every being confronting itself.

Within reach, on a yellow marble shelf, is the separate coffer where I keep the papers in the jagged writing of Robert de la Pole, less suspect today than they were in the past. I do not like, or at least I should not like to dwell on, this secret of mine but I am so involved in it that I cannot dispel its reality. In my ear some words are repeated, a conversation I had a few years ago with Emilia Pio. We were sympathizing with a woman, our friend, who had had too melancholy a life, and Emilia came out with one of her reflective barbs, observing that since our friend was an intelligent woman, we could presume she had thoughts all her own hidden in some niche or refuge from which she drew courage, for only a stay in that inner place, our inviolate realm, has the power to renew our strength. And even my unique Elisabetta gravely agreed with these words of two initiates. The Englishman's letters, which at stunned intervals come to speak to me, are rare; they allow me pause to become accustomed to their stings. If, for the hundredth time, I ask myself what sense the appearance, completely unexpected, of this foreigner has for me, I cannot answer. I believe he is not a person necessary to my life, but as I say this, I retard the syllables because they have a doubtful ring.

There is a way to rebel and to resign oneself to his arguments. I follow him easily when he comments on events unknown to me, perhaps because his field of vision has a different angle from mine and illuminates things that without him I would be hard put to know, and he has a way of interesting me in his pages and perhaps even making me enjoy some compliment more imaginative than the preciosities of Bembo. But the morality of such letters—I mean, the morality of receiving them—remains an enigma. Should I have torn up the pages the moment I glimpsed them? I suspect that Robert de la Pole, innocent though he may seem, is vaguely diabolical. He presented himself, beyond grasping, with his sins that are not sins, isolating himself in his priestly station, not revealed at first. And I did not immediately realize that his isolation was a strength; I deluded myself that I was free in all conscience, free to read letters to which I would never reply, and meanwhile, they penetrated the texture of my existence. I granted him the possibility of waxing fanciful over my unwritten replies, and naturally he can have imagined an answer from me, not scornful even though severe about his confidences. And yet, if I must tell the truth, it is his confidence that I like, when it does not send me into a rage. If I were to see him appear again—and random events, combustive imagination, encounters of studious devotion, as in the return of his friend Erasmus to Italy, could bring him back in our midst—if I were to see him, with those deep black, judging eyes in his pale face, would I feel like combating or would I hold out my hand to him? Ah, what am I saying?

T HE BLACK SATIN dress with the bodice of alternating silver and crimson stripes is bold, but with the tempered boldness that wins universal approval as a rule: set off with delicate jewels, little double chains of gold subtly wrought in the French fashion, and a necklace of medium-sized pearls, very white, with a ruby clasp. This dress clothes me without making me heavy. And so in the swelling corolla of satin I am at ease and steadily amused in private audience before the throne of the new pope, Leo the Tenth, of the house of Medici, son of Lorenzo the Magnificent. I have knelt at his feet with deference and grace, and with respectful rejoicing I have kissed the holy ring. In the face of my easy performance he seems a bit awkward, but then he stands up and, holding out his hand, leads me with great courtesy to a gold-studded seat of red leather, seating himself in a similar chair. Without smiling, except for a very slight suggestion of reverent joy, I speak to him of my infinite devotion, which he receives well, as he expresses his satisfaction that my husband has granted me permission to remain in Rome until Christmas.

"I shall expect you at my mass in Saint Peter's, signora marchesana," he says in an amiably imperative tone.

"Your Holiness," I reply, "I can answer you with heartfelt, humble happiness. It is true, the lord marchese my husband has permitted me to spend Christmas in Rome and to go now to Naples, where the queens of the house of Aragón, my kinswomen, have invited me. But above all, my extreme contentment comes from knowing that he is on the road back to full health, for which I constantly pray, lighting candles in all the churches of this city. Now I ask Your Holiness to grant me leave for my journey to Naples, while you may rest assured that I will be back in Rome and will attend the holy midnight mass at Christmas; nothing could be more welcome to me."

Leo, the Tuscan, paying careful attention to my words, nods benevolently. The archdeacon of Gabbioneta, who has accom-

panied me with two of my women, remaining with them respectfully at the end of the hall, preens himself and speaks up, to sing
the praises of Francesco, his clemency, his sweet nature displayed
also on this occasion, indulging his most amiable spouse—namely,
me. Behind the pope's chair the Magnifico Giuliano de' Medici
stands, his brother, a bit absent, with his cousin the Medici cardinal, Giulio, a handsome man, but cold.

I am in one of my laughing, capricious moods. This new audience, which I requested, is unfolding in a mendacious key;
everyone seems agreed to honor with incense an image of Francesco, magnanimous in granting me what I would have taken in
any case: my stay in Rome and Naples. The false and ceremonious
game even involves a pope, too keen a mind not to weigh the
hidden meaning of our talk. Truth is swathed in vestments.

I KNEW what Francesco was really thinking. I cannot say why
this seemed to him the right moment to seek, among the many
intrigues that were being minutely interwoven in the Vatican, the
definitive assignment of the lands the house of Gonzaga so desired: Asola, Lonato, Peschiera. With that inner levity that comes
over us when our plans work out and we care little for those of
others, I asked Leo for the allotment of those lands; after having
thought a good while, as he always did, he answered me, de-
ploring with pontifical gravity the fact that peace between the
Venetians and the emperor was still so distant; only when it came,
in fact, could he decide about those places. But if God were to
grant him the blessing of peace, he would remember Mantua as
he remembered the Holy See, for he loved our city well. Never,
he added, never would he fail to protect the Gonzagas. Everything
was said well, with little bombast and with persuasiveness.

"Only this hope allows me to live in happiness, for I can imagine
the happiness of my lord," I concluded, sighing, and I administered my dose of benevolent meekness, dedicating praises to all,
to His Holiness, for whom I would offer my life if necessary, to
my husband, to my blood kin of Aragón, and I indicated my
happiness in seeing myself on the eve of Christmas in Rome, in
Saint Peter's.

And I said all this with conviction because in part it was true;
Christmas celebrated in Saint Peter's did affectionately warm the
religious area of my heart. Religion aside, I could not suppress
my joy in the prospect of a whole month of freedom before me,

when I would be caressed and feted by the two Aragón queens in that royal city of Naples, still vivid in my distant childhood visions that carried me back to my mother, Eleonora. The pope was now conversing with the archdeacon of Gabbioneta. And the Magnifico Giuliano, stirring from his torpor, paid me the homage of reading me some of his Petrarchesque sonnets; he declaimed them, pouring into the hendecasyllables all the lovely harmony of Tuscan speech. I seized on one verse—"If my step were so swift"—and composed an appreciative turn of phrase, keeping one eye, obliquely, on Leo, who listened ecstatically to his brother. This Giovanni de' Medici, having attained the supreme power, so gifted at seeming another person, constantly creating himself anew, remained impenetrable to all influence, not to maintain his own self-confidence but to catch in others the essence of their acts and somehow appropriate them. I sensed under that constant affability an incurable aridity of spirit and an innate indifference that made him study every opportunity to perceive a moment of passion in the person who came to speak to him. He was young, not yet forty, temperate in his behavior, a scholar of Latin and Greek, splendid in his donations, a sound Christian. But in him was there really that icy current that had touched me?

I was seduced by the supple coils of the Magnifico Giuliano's sonnets; the hall shone, in its marble whiteness, hung with brocade, sumptuous and chilling. I sat there, my head full of cadences, and I felt a mounting sympathy for the unaware Francesco, who now dreamed of his lands transferred, through me, from the pontiff's hands to his own. Francesco did not understand how difficult it was, in those upset times, to claim a city, a town, a fortress. Everything now whetted everyone's appetite; ambition now knew no shame. This same pope, who appeared so scrupulous, was proving, from what I had gleaned from direct witnesses in the Curia, a determined nepotist, and he spent whole days weighing cases and persons, planning kingdoms and principalities for his brother and for his nephew Lorenzo. We feudal lords were beginning to fear the twists of his hypotheses: First Naples, actually a kingdom, had attracted them; then Modena, purchased for forty thousand ducats from the emperor, and Reggio, and perhaps Lucca with other lands, for a moment also Ferrara and Urbino; now one city, now another were the object of the Medici greed. This gave the pope a vital surge: designating places of power and command to his family. I wondered where it would end.

* * *

DRAWN by four horses, the carriage of the cardinal of Aragón, followed at a distance by those of my court, men and women, proceeds at a good pace on this November morning. Before I am aware of it, I recognize that I am on the Appian Way, flanked by pines and cypresses, capitals and architraves fallen to the ground and framed by waving grass. It is as if the road had been hurled forward, following the trajectory of a javelin in the open countryside, shrouded in wintry tones, intense ochers and faint purples; in the brume made pink by the dawn rotund monuments are immersed and columns are isolated like cries. Rome becomes great just here, where it is desolate and uninhabited, and the white ruins are shattered in sublime mutilations. "A countryside to be painted," I say to myself, and immediately I recall a book on Rome, with drawn maps, that I leafed through many times during my childhood in Ferrara, pausing at every page to ask for more particulars, more discoveries, more aspects of the city. In Mantua in the Painted Hall I loved especially the detail by the window where, on an ideal hill, our Mantegna had arranged, according to his fancy, the symbols by which Rome is recognized in any portrayal: the Colosseum, the Arch of Titus inserted into the walls of the city, the great statue of the Vatican Hercules towering on a high pedestal, the red Nomentana Bridge, and the sharp pyramid of Caius Cestius in pale triangles.

With me in the carriage smelling of new leather are a few girls, their knees protected by a soft blanket of Persian cats, gift of the cardinal of Aragón, who has a special affection for me as a close relative. The jolting of the wheels over the Roman slabs inspires in me an extraordinary emotion; on those smooth stones rode Nero, ever a fugitive from himself, and Tiberius, as he rushed for Capri in search of a convincing reason to live. Memories of my studies accompany me for a while until they are gradually blurred.

A few hours earlier we waked in the heart of the night, in order to be ready, and a fog of sleep still presses on my eyes, lulling me into a warm doze. After an hour I wake again; my women are sleeping. The Appian Way stretches out in a total silence, penetrated only by the cadence of the trotting horses, adorned with rattles. The monuments have grown thicker at the sides of the road, each with its story of concluded life. Gleaming white or graying, they arouse no sadness; they live in that silence, distanced in an almost mythical solitude. The ancient scenery delineated on the horizon by the outline of the Alban Hills exalts me to an intense peace long unfamiliar; all of a sudden in this peace of centuries the events surface that carry me far from my city, toward my Aragonese kinsfolk.

Such a controversial year, this 1514, so evil in its moments. It began its conniving on the first day of January, predicting to me the arrival of May, when I would reach the age of forty. After that the days sped. I looked at myself in the mirror, and I did not see evidence of age: My hair shone with its gilded glints; my well-tended skin was white and unblemished; a bit of rouge helped, as it had always soberly helped me even at twenty; and that slight rotundity of my limbs was balanced by a bright step that the girls of my court imitated in vain. No, I was not suffering any loss of energy.

The seventeenth of May came, and it was a speechless day. I noticed everything. My women, including the elderly Jacopa, pre-tended to forget the date. Francesco really did forget it, Equicola, always alert to any literary opportunity, filled my drawer with anthems, amatory decalogues, extended poems in the orotund style that was congenial to him. I held no audience or festivity; a concert I postponed to the following day; only from Pirro Donati I accepted the charming gift of a Petrarch printed on airy pages by Aldo Manuzio, and I welcomed a simple compliment that came to him spontaneously as if in reply to my unspoken question as I studied myself once again in the mirror: "Signora, you do well to look at yourself; you are more beautiful than ever."

And yet that tolling of the number forty persecuted me with lugubrious, almost mortal insistence. I tried to discipline myself with severity; picking up the Greek grammar, I forced myself to look into it, to study the language of our gods. I, who have never felt fear, trembled at the stroke of that round number. I went to vespers, and finally, toward evening, there arrived the blessed rebellion of thought that reminded me of the great examples of virtue and energy of strong spirits in the face of grave turmoil of the soul. I was ashamed of myself, and I decided that my fortieth year would resemble none other. I would enter it bravely, pluck-ing away thorns, laughing at specters. Having regained dominion of myself, I was ready to bear with untroubled spirit all the an-niversaries that God might grant me.

That was a May of battle. My existence had always been reg-ulated by the changes in Francesco's health; now it suffered the renewed aggression of his sullen disease, which weakened him to such a degree that I was charged with every act of government and the State correspondence was placed in my hands. I pondered those papers throughout the day; I drew up answers, compared, reread. I was almost separated from court life, from amusements; I set my girls to embroidery work which had become discipline; and I went every day to Francesco, even when he was at Marmirolo, reporting to him the most urgent news, always finding at his side Tolomeo Spagnoli, his beloved counselor, who, at my appearance, fled, making his master also smile. And he, Francesco, made admirable efforts to answer me appropriately; he frowned to concentrate but then let his head sink back exhausted on the pillow, and with a cramped smile he praised me, kissing my hands. I felt compassion, more tender than I would have believed; I felt an affection growing in me, very different from the impetuous love that had bound me to him. I defined areas of clearsighted work; it was my precise way of judging, foreseeing, and providing what they call policy. I no longer thought of my forty years. I was only faintly aware of Spagnoli's irksome shadow and of how that lost soul who went by the name of Vigo di Camposampiero roamed the corridors.

That life lasted little more than a month. A good monk and an instinctive physician turned up at court. I never learned who had sent him, Serafino da Ostuni, an Apulian who seemed anything but a southerner, with a Norman pirate's blue eyes. The monk, a devout and worthy man, brought with him unique remedies for the French disease, and those medicines of his, whose composition he would never allow me to know, worked admirably. Francesco really was cured; he gained strength, jollity, and interest in the whole world. One morning Pirro Donati did not find the usual dispatches in the chancellery. Tolomeo Spagnoli had taken them away on orders from the signor marchese, who, we were told, wanted to read them at once, and thus, without any forewarning, the door was slammed in my face. I was informed that my husband was well and I was to return to my role of woman.

I LEAN back against the padding of the carriage. I breathe in deeply the view of the majestic aqueducts with their flight of broad arches, broken here and there to suggest itineraries lost in the broad Roman plain. My eyes light on the muff that gives some warmth to my hands chilled by anguish, the real anguish of finding myself completely deprived of the office that gave meaning to the hours of my life. But what else could I have wanted? Surely not for Francesco to worsen, not that; far from me such a thought, but stubborn and ingenuous as I am, I hoped that between us a higher bond would be forged, an alliance in governing that would keep us together in the name of that great third party the State. My hands writhe in the muff as I recall the decision I came to that morning. I had sprung up, gone down our secret stairway, and pushed at the door, which opened with a creak. Francesco was on his feet, in a good humor, and I gathered my wits to devote myself to him, speaking to him of his health, an inexhaustible source of questions and answers, hints and congratulations. Needless to say, Tolomeo Spagnoli was listening in a corner of the room. I turned my back on him, and he made some signal because Francesco hastily searched among the papers on his table, chose some, and handed them to me.

"These letters are yours, Isabella, and you must forgive me for opening them, as I found them together with mine. But mine or yours are the same between us."

I leafed through the papers without answering. My letters: a confidential note from the marchesa of Cotrone, two reports from the courts of Naples and Urbino, a missive from my nephew Massimiliano Sforza, personal things, delicate private news or information addressed to me alone. Papers in hand, I moved to the window; I pretended to read them, to give myself time to repress my trembling, as I felt hurt and outraged. That scoundrel Spagnoli could hardly conceal his sneer. Everything had failed me, and losing all authority and consideration, I had lost also respect. "Francesco!" I would have liked to cry out. "Francesco, what are you doing to me, your wife? Can't you see I am fighting back my tears?" At this point, through the stifled tears I discerned some lines of my nephew on the page before my eyes. "Signora marchesana, Aunt, and also Mother," he wrote to me, "I am truly in Milan with much expectation of you, more than you can even imagine. My enemies oppress me, and I am much afraid of a new visit, announced on all sides, from the king of France. If I do not have your help in finding my way through this maze, I risk being lost." Calmly I turned my head with a haughty movement and, with the hint of a very distant smile, moved, then stopped in such a way as to block the presence of Spagnoli.

"My lord," I said in a tone of light contempt, "now that you are better, God be thanked, the moment has come for me to go to Milan to see how things are proceeding for the duke my nephew. For some time you and I have agreed that it is best to know promptly and at close hand the situation in which he finds himself, to advise him and attend to our defenses, which must be planned as quickly as possible. More than once you have urged my departure, but till now your illness would not allow it. So I shall leave very soon; this letter, which you have surely read, urges me to go. I will take an escort suited to my rank, but not festive, not a carnival retinue."

Francesco was silent, peering past me to catch Spagnoli's eye.

"I will come this evening to confer with you," I said, "before you take your potion, and I want to speak once again with Friar Serafino." With steady step I advanced toward his chair. I kissed his brow and smiled, as we always do, my face close to his. Again with steady step I began climbing the stairs, keeping the papers in my hand, my left arm bent to my waist, with all the majesty I could summon.

THAT same left hand is clenched convulsively inside the muff, as if it still held those papers. I lean out of the carriage a little. The sky is covered with a mass of low clouds, moving down from the Alban Hills, but the Roman cold does not resemble our inexorable cold in the north; here it wafts and barely rests on our shoulders covered by fur-lined cloaks. I shake my head, dismissing the phantoms of unconquered sorrow; I concentrate my gaze on the sable muff, round and good-sized, but not cumbersome, enriched and prettified by the cordons of a dark tawny color and the golden studs arranged around the brocaded velvet.

> La devota amicizia il suo tepore
> alle candide mani consacrato

So Pietro Bembo wrote in the dedicatory verses on the scroll that accompanied this precious object before, as the great secretary of Leo the Tenth, he set out on his mission to Venice. With a quality of brilliance and discretion, men of such refinement are rare ornaments of a court, favorite friends of women from whom they derive infinite, delicate pleasures that other men scarcely know and perhaps do not even imagine. Their loves, however, at times approach a sluggishness generated by excessive equilibrium of feeling, and this is something the duchess of Ferrara must know well, adored as she is by her Venetian poet. This thought suddenly stings me: Who knows if those two still write each other? But a devoted friendship better resists the passage of the years. Bembo's muff will accompany me all winter, in this eccentric journey of mine; I will happily enjoy the warmth of its nearness, imagining with an entirely feminine pleasure the jealousy that the duchess my sister-in-law might feel.

My women wake up, one after the other, and talk only of our imminent arrival at Velletri, where the pope has ordered a welcome for us and a dinner. Meanwhile, we have a collation of grapes and cheese and drink a light white wine; then Tortorina, our turtledove, picks up the lute and sings a song newly learned in Milan, composed by a student of the famous Franchino Gaffurio.

We did not make much music during that Milanese summer, my nephew the duke and I. I was in an exile's mood. That was a season, our summer, of enormous white clouds in the heavens and subtle black clouds on earth, where a thousand reports intersected and caused complications, even anxieties. I was infected by a mounting, heartsick disappointment in Massimiliano. The young man, burdened by the rank of duke, revealed a sweet nature, but he no longer had the heedlessness and boldness of his first appearance and no quality of his suggested a chief of state. His agile mind took an interest in everything, but in reality he wasted his energy on futile things, slept little, and ate as the whim took him. He paid no attention to the advice of his ministers, still hesitant and unaccustomed to him, and among all the speeches he heard, he could not discern which were to his advantage. I was fond of him because of his uneasy goodness and his devoted love of me. He believed in me as if I were the first person in the world, and still bleeding from the wounds suffered in Mantua, I welcomed his affection like a medicine, and I was consoled by his calling me Mother. I decided to stay in Milan for some time because I saw him more and more frightened and alone in a city that seemed not to belong to him. The duchy of Milan, in my memory a place of unparalleled splendors, was deteriorating; that city of wondrous craftsmen, of flourishing trade, of ingenious workers was wearing out, and I could foresee, almost ineluctable, its ruin under the foreign dominations that would strip it of all wealth and all hope. French, imperials, Spaniards would take turns claiming it, and the benevolence of the emperor, now that his wife, Bianca Maria Sforza, was dead, vacillated from moment to moment.

I advised Massimiliano to marry a woman whose relations could enforce his destiny as a prince, and in my mind I searched for the name of the bride, without finding any suitable; but I vowed not to abandon the idea. In Milan, then, the only way I could help my nephew was by inventing unadventurous pleasures, and I was restrained even in that. A disagreeable taste came to me, remembering the great festivities held the year before, the devilish enthusiasm I myself had unleashed in my ladies and my girls, among whom Brognina had been outstanding, the most insidious pupil I had ever had at my court, the only one who, in her excess of temperament, had exceeded my plans, designed to quell the political resistances so inherent in the stony male nature. My suite today did not permit risks of any kind; still, the presence of the girls, beautiful all the same, helped me: Livia, first of all, and then the dancer Lavagnola, Lucia, Delia, and Teodorina Pedoca. I had not trained them in that art that unites the charms of Bembo's platonism with the boldness of the language used in our country; I had realized what a dangerous weapon this was. Francesco would have no occasion to protest about this journey.

He soon began, my husband, summoning me back to Mantua in a master's tone. But I would not go back, not for the present at least. I was overcome by the sensual pleasure of disobeying him. I questioned myself at length in the sultry nights of the Lombard summer, when I remained alone, in introspection. I could not forgive; indeed, I could not even think how to utter the word "forgiveness." I was truly wounded. No treatment could heal me except time, which in successive waves would erode also this boulder of grief. My rebellion was a repulse, a denial, no longer confused but precise as a command, for I no longer wanted anything from Francesco; also, his disease, which I had treated and even loved with true woman's heroism, now revolted me. I had fled, I was fleeing, and my flight should lead me on until I could discern a new acceptance of my life along other lines of thought. Surely from Milan I would not return to Mantua, though the thought of Federico and my other children made me grieve. I had been moved by a quip of Ercole, who, with the ingenuousness of his nine years, had remarked that for his mother the words "I will be home soon" meant "I will be home late."

Deep sighs accompanied my awareness of my flight. Coming down to practical matters, I counted my dresses and those of the people of my court, and I calculated that our wardrobe was sufficient. I did not have much money, but I would ask loans of friends. I remembered the invitation of Monsignor Fregoso and I said I was curious to see the great lighthouse of the harbor of Genoa before it was demolished. I was at once happy and sorrowful to be so desired by the Genoese, who were already involved in the preparation of sumptuous receptions and banquets for me. I refused them; I would travel privately and virtually by surprise so as not to be stopped by official vetos. Thus I found myself in Genoa almost without realizing that I had set out. The great sea of that city made me aware of the necessity of space. I wanted to plunge into the void with the wings of Icarus; I imagined valleys, plains, rivers, castles, the map of Italy over which, in my Studiolo, I had so often dreamed, my finger tracing precise itineraries. In Genoa I would only make a start; I would husband my strength; I would listen to the countless friends who called me to Rome, first among them Bernardo Bibbiena, now cardinal and treasurer and adviser of the new pope. I stirred up the desire in my mind by recalling the bright words of Guido Postumo, who had written me the year before, "Come to Rome, where the golden century has begun." From Liguria I would descend toward the gentle and severe Tuscan countryside, stopping one night at Pisa, and from there, like an arrow hungering for its target, I would aim at the great city. I guessed that my old Moccicone and his friends like the Magnifico Giuliano dei Medici were burning with curiosity about this sudden journey of which Francesco would disapprove. It was up to me to maintain the mysterious suspense that excited them all.

OUR CARRIAGES keeping close together, our guards protecting us against bandits' attack, we plunge with some difficulty into the bowl of the hills, thick with brush. Winding constantly through the valleys, we approach the steep slope leading up to Velletri, a place that promises to be strange and kindly, where we will sleep tonight after celebrating at the sumptuous dinner ordered by the pope. We climb the hill along an oblique track, and Tortorina complains of the jolting. I cannot understand how anyone can relish the little complaints of discomfort when thoughts, lively and intense, pulse in the mind. I review the receptions, the honors, the festivities that have been given me in Rome in less than a month; I am stimulated by this enigmatic pope Leo, who every day erases a stroke of his portrait finished the day before and prompts a new one. When I arrived in Rome in November, I was not thinking of a Neapolitan interlude, or I was thinking of it only vaguely. But now that the carriage ventures southward and in the fading afternoon I see the shapes and colors of nature gradually alter, I concentrate and feel within myself a shudder of gaiety. I pronounce the word "Naples"; something blue and gold spreads out, supported by two elements of light: the sea light, tender and vivid as the day enfolds the lovely, hilly shore, the palaces and the white houses built on high, squared outlines with arched windows, separated by steep churches and slim spires; and the soft, thick light of the torches and candelabra that suggest nocturnal apparitions.

Our entrance is memorable, at the enormous Aragonese palace near Porta Capuana, where the two queens and their courts await us. A majestic figure advances toward us, the dowager queen Giovanna, widowed second wife of King Ferrante; she takes me into her arms, clasping me, amid the joyous shouts of all present. The young queen Giovanna, widow of King Ferrandino, repeats the same embrace. In Mantua Tromboncino has sung for us several times "Tristi Regine," the tearful but popular song of the two sad queens, deprived, both mother and daughter, of the Neapolitan kingdom. In reality, the two queens do not seem so sad, or at least they have learned to turn their sadness into a claim of glory. The older Giovanna is hieratic; the younger, just over thirty, delightfully ready to explode beneath her apparent composure; both are very rich and of grand demeanor. Nobles swirl around them, ladies and knights, great Italian and Spanish names, and their sole occupation all day long is encountering one another in some elegant game of love or courtliness. How wonderful, in all its contrasts, is the pace of this court. The long and gloomy religious ceremonies, alleviated only by the music, are followed by stormy jousts, bull hunts, dances, receptions, and banquets overflowing with excellent and refined dishes, ending with overhoneyed sweets and whipped cream flavored with roses and vanilla, in the Oriental fashion.

On the day of our arrival, after a good hour of formalities, I am shown to my rooms. There are four of them, quite vast, and neither walls nor floors are visible, as everything is covered with drapery, gilded leather, carpets. The beds have canopies and curtains of precious stuffs, nor is any useful thing lacking. We discover exquisite little private gifts that amuse and flatter us, like young girls. When Tortorina discovers a box of needles, thread and spools of gold, silver and silk and a little sack filled with brand-new nightcaps, my girls' awed gaiety abruptly dispels their weariness. I look at them spinning around me, as I sit on my stuffed chair, my hands lying on its arms; those attentions rest me.

I recall then certain irrepressible joys as little girls, I and my sister, Beatrice, when, having come to Naples with our mother, we tirelessly ran through the Castel Nuovo to explore the marvelous places where the people of royal rank lived. I, too, was royal; I had known that since my birth, but as I grew up, knowing it or not knowing it made no difference in my way of living. In the regal performance that was played out at court incessantly for a fortnight, I experienced the responsibility that royal power imposes. I did not lose my head for the thaumaturge king or for the king master of a people of slaves. We northerners are alien equally to Hispanic hyperbole and to Neapolitan exaggeration; but I was filled with that dynastic, magnanimous sense inspired by ceremonies whose tone was at once heroic and celebratory, and I managed to ward off my ceaseless rages, always on the verge of assailing me.

The Neapolitan days fly past. I am always out on horseback, and I observe everything. Afterward I climb up to my rooms crammed with ladies and gentlemen who have come to honor me, and the oldest recognize in me the daughter of Eleonora of Aragón. With the countess of Venafro I go to witness a miracle of San Gennaro especially arranged for me, even if out of season, not something I would want to miss. I genuflect to the saint, I see the blood bubble, and I take this as a presage to be revered; a court poet composes a sonnet announcing to the world my power to move saints in heaven. One morning the young queen Giovanna takes me, in a comfortable carriage, to the Church of San Pietro Martire; in that holy place, she whispers, there is a surprise in store for me.

In fact, when I enter the Chapel of San Vincenzo Ferrer, she points out an ancient panel with some figures painted in the old Flemish style, especially a lady in the foreground. This is Isabella of Chiaromonte, mother of my mother, the most beautiful queen the world has ever had. Tall and slim, white and pink, with pale eyes, blond hair, the descendant of three great French families, Brienne, del Balzo, and Chiaromonte. I knew everything about her; my mother had told me often of how Isabella had had to live amid the furious fighting with the Angevins, who would not hear of leaving the kingdom in the hands of the Aragonese. Her husband in the field, she ruled over Naples. She gathered the populace in this church of San Pietro Martire and spoke to the crowd. She showed them her children and declared them Neapolitan from head to foot and swore they would never impose foreign customs; rather, they would share the ordinary life of the poor, dividing their wealth among all, not imitating Angevin greed and insolence.

One part of the story of Isabella of Chiaromonte particularly attracted me, concrete and yet also a fairy tale. One day, as she was alone and poor, she disguised herself and begged for alms at the church door. She was recognized, and the whole city was moved; nobles, merchants, and populace came to give her their tribute, and so it was possible to fit out a new army and send it against the Angevins. Her regency lasted six years, while King Ferrante fought until he won his victory. Chroniclers and poets praised not only her modesty and self-restraint, virtues glowing in the white heat of her pride, but also her skill in governing.

The slim form dressed in black velvet housed enough energy to overcome anybody. Only one thing I could not trace in that story whose every word I recalled, a secret thing, that only now I sensed was missing. After six years of good government Queen Isabella handed the city, more vigorous, flourishing, and at peace, back to her husband, but in what spirit had she been rewarded? Thanks, homage must have been strewn at her feet, but in what tone? How had Ferrante, cruel and overweening man, monarch of black blood, received her achievement? Isabella of Chiaromonte died the year after the triumph of Aragón and her husband's return to power. Was this pure chance, or was it a clue? Trapped by these questions and by the ghosts evoked, I am here in the Chapel of San Vincenzo Ferrer, unable to move, plunged into a vortex from which voices rise. I control myself, I smile at Queen Giovanna, intent on her prayers, and I look again at the painted panel where my ancestress Isabella holds her head erect, decorated with white, shifting veils as she reads a prayer book. We do not know the stifled words of her other prayers.

I continue staring at the scene. At some distance from the protagonist, to the right, I discern her son, the future King Alfonso, also with an open book, and behind, the little figure of the child Eleonora is visible, a bit frightened but standing firmly in her place under the white wing of her headdress. All three, in prayer, are imploring the Spanish saint, immersed in that rarefaction of lines converging upward, acutely, while, his head protruding from some drapery, a steward intently observes the queen. A scene of severe peace: I felt warned to respect it, not to tempt the dead by inserting my afflictions to mirror ancient afflictions. I was to remain silent. But how could I help wondering? In six years of governing, a woman born to be queen had suffered the strain of risky decisions and had experienced the triumphal thrill of power, and after sufferings, challenges, victories, what was left to Isabella of Chiaromonte? She could even have died of a passion for government denied and extinguished, and I could have followed her in her advance toward the end, minute by minute. Yes, I could have, but she rejects me, seals herself off in prayer and in the distance of silence.

In unison with Queen Giovanna, kneeling beside me on the icy floor, I make the sign of the cross and stand up. Coming out of the chapel, my kinswoman is pleased with the surprise she has chosen to give me, and she promises me a copy of the picture. I am struck by the innocent kindness of those immense, sweet eyes that seem somehow expectant. Can it be true that she does not spurn the idea of remarrying, for all her thirty-six years surrendered to the demands of life? At once an idea comes to me that gradually improves and becomes complete when I share it with the old queen Giovanna. The idea is that the young queen should marry my nephew Massimiliano Sforza and so become duchess of Milan. She would bring her husband a considerable dowry and, above all, the protection of the Spanish, strengthening that of the emperor, also her relative.

THE YOUNG queen Giovanna did not reject the idea, and immediately the news stole from mouth to mouth with merry excitement; if doubts were expressed, they were resolved without hesitation, and everyone seemed stimulated by the word "marriage" that heralded boundless nuptial festivities at court. I noticed that no one paid any heed to the one real obstacle: that of age, for my nephew was twenty-three and the presumptive bride, thirteen years older. But Massimiliano did not look so young, and on the contrary, Giovanna was of charming aspect and radiant face. I enjoyed maneuvering this wedding between my kin, a queen for him, a duke for her, and for both, the state of Milan invigorated. But my own imagination made me uneasy, and I was in conflict with myself, pondering the unfathomable enigma of the conjugal condition. Who would prevail in this marriage I was fostering? Who would be unhappy? They were two meek creatures, I reassured myself, but cannot meekness also be corrupted by lack of love?

NAPLES gave me a gift. One Saturday morning I was invited by Signor Fabrizio Colonna, the stern warrior and fanciful lover I had met in Ferrara as Alfonso's prisoner after the Battle of Ravenna. We rode out early in a small party and just in a mood to visit the villa that the Colonnas maintain two miles from the city, toward the Certosa. We miscalculated the time and arrived an hour early. Seeing an unplanned space open before me, I decided not to linger and wait but to go up the mountain to San Martino, to see the friars of the Certosa. I had been told that it is a very pretty site, and so I found it, for from up there I contemplated the most beautiful view in the world, with the blue sea and the white city below us in an air sweet and fine such as I have never breathed elsewhere. I dismounted and abandoned myself to the attraction of that place with a delight of body and spirit that I cannot narrate. Like an amnesiac, I absorbed the sweet breath with eyes closed, fearing the vision might vanish, erased by my gaze. Breathing seemed the only way to testify that I was alive and deemed worthy of that paradise.

It was a day of grace. After the banquet and a play enlivened with rustic songs and dances, as it was growing late we returned home. I realized that to a great extent the perfect joy lasting through that day was due to that hour of freedom, pure to the point of abstraction, spent at the Certosa of Monte San Martino. I did not fail to describe it to Francesco, hoping he would receive my hints openheartedly or at least would sigh with a desire to be with me in those divine places. And to make sure that Francesco would also know it, I wrote to my Capilupi that everyone worshiped me like an oracle. My every outing seemed a spectacle, bombards fired rounds of blanks when, mounted or in my carriage, I appeared at the entrance of the palace toward Porta Capuana, and the Neapolitan populace shouted with joy. I could even distinguish the Saracen cheers, harsh in those yelling throats.

One feeling that men seldom know profoundly is the absence of children, the lack of their presence, within reach. I knew this maternal affliction that has an anxious base and presses deep into the soul. I pictured my children, one after the other: Ercole, Ferrante, little Livia, the sweet nun Ippolita, and, especially, Federico. I could almost see him in the young prince of Chiaromonte, bound to me by distant kinship, who insisted on entertaining me in his palace. Of an age somewhere between twelve and thirteen, he came to meet me, unaffected, serious but smiling, like a grown man doing the honors as host, and it must be said that he gave new life to those duties, his behavior was so charming and easy. Mature in spirit, he revealed a physical vigor equal to the liveliness of his mind; I could not stop looking at him, unusually attracted to such precocity. He was my partner during the sumptuous feast; with pretty words he offered me a miniature galleon laden with Egyptian perfumes; we danced together, and the dancing was beautiful. Together we followed a very daring Spanish farce, and he laughed with me at the right moments. Leaving him, I kissed him on the brow as I would the child he was, in age, but I had the impression of having committed a pleasant indiscretion.

I wrote immediately, in my own hand, to Federico about the young Chiaromonte, and I dwelt on the description of his courtly way of attending women. I have to say that compared with the little Neapolitan, Federico appeared to me still hampered by childish awkwardness, handsome and intelligent but of scant manly confidence for his full fourteen years. "He must wake up," I thought as I extolled the prince of Chiaromonte in his every act and described the exercises of skill with staves that I had seen him perform in my honor. In the end I discreetly advised my son to practice merriment a little. He answered a few days later. He proposed to follow the young prince's example, and as a start he had given a supper for my women and girls left behind in Mantua, Laura, Innocenza, and Isabetta, diverting them until late at night with music, dancing, singing, and other delights. In Federico's words there was an air of gaiety, carefree and slightly swaggering, and it reassured me; his nature would not lead him to moodiness. Names and new plans were forming in me. Naples had given me a stimulus; some response would arrive.

To the Most Illustrious and Excellent Signora Isabella, Marchesana of Mantua and My Sovereign

*H*ave the patience, my lady, to examine these pages that with an act of proud humility I meant to form the last of my ill-fated letters. I wish I could tell myself that from now on I need not always be on the lookout for the occasion of a trustworthy horseman I can then accompany with my thoughts, in secret alarm, all the way to Mantua as he carries an envelope of mine for you in his saddlebag. And to believe that I will sacrifice the Isabellian hours, those hours of the day and of the evening dedicated to the meditation of matters prompted by you, but truly I lack the strength to abandon my delirium, as you will surely call this adventure that has been experienced only by one of its characters, and hopelessly at that. I must ask of you the familiar and, this time, painful balm of forgiveness.

I believe but do not hope that you have already received a letter written at the end of December, as I was about to leave London for Paris, where I now reside in the household of Count Ludovico of Canossa, the papal nuncio and your devoted servant. I must repeat that I will never sufficiently repent having written you and, more, having even thought of writing. I appealed then to your clemency, and I make that same appeal now, because I would tremble if I were to examine the follies that escaped me in a kind of fiery jet the moment Count Ludovico told me that you were in Rome, honored and beloved by all, beginning with His Holiness. I saw you as a white dove, its wings spread to defy the wrath of Mantua, and a strange, harsh joy in me applauded what seemed a wondrous flight of liberty. Then my joy knew no bounds when I learned that in Rome you were lodged in the upper rooms of the palace belonging to the cardinal of Aragón. I imagined you at those lancet windows looking down at the lines of litany-chanting pilgrims on their way to Saint Peter's, and in my imagination I was there in my study in the palace opposite, fourth floor, fifth window. For, my lady, that handsome palace designed in imitation of the architecture of our chamberlain's vast building and constructed for Cardinal Adriano Castellesi, apostolic collector in England, is the place where we English live, ambassadors and envoys with offices in the Curia. Go to your window, look out at the place I describe, and have pity, for this imaginary nearness is what so overwhelmed me and caused me to write that letter, and the words I used gnaw at my heart, especially those of the "magnificent suspicion" in the central sentences. A dazed man's suppositions, a lunatic's dreams, foolish conjectures spilled onto that paper, and a secret thought that, luckily for me, I only hinted at, and now it makes me ache because it went unpunished.

I beg you to be patient; your absolving strength must bear also the plea I am about to make to you. My letter of that last day of December was sent from London by a long route, and it may not have reached you yet. By the faith in God, my lady, I beg you: If it were to reach you after this one, do not read it. Do me the favor of burning it unopened, for murky and confused as it is, it deserves nothing else. What I wrote from London I deny today from Paris, not because of change of thought but because I was wrong to release that flood of feelings. Truly I let my fancy soar as in a courtly novel with the dreams, forbidden to me, of an Amadís or a Tristan. And for all, once again, I ask forgiveness.

I cannot take leave of this paper, which wafts a scent of hope. Do not fold the page. I will change the subject at once; I will make some mention for you of events taking place around me. Their description might appease you. I am in Paris, as I said, dispatched by my king to support the work of Count Ludovico of Canossa, who, in his turn, is observer in the name of the pope, and I believe that you, such an avid follower of events, will read what I tell you with pleasure at least as great as your displeasure in reading the first part of my missive. You must surely know that the death of the king of France, Louis the Twelfth, has changed overnight the face of Europe. On two great thrones now two very young kings are seated: in

England, my Henry the Eighth, and Francis, first of his name, in France. Both are handsome, enterprising, brilliant, with a vast desire to reign over their nations that for centuries have been rivals. Secretly, some months ago, I arrived here in the suite of the papal nuncio so that I could give aid and counsel to a courageous plan: an alliance between France and England to turn away from Italy those Spanish ambitions that increasingly occupy the peninsula from the south northward. Our task was to undo the already arranged marriage between Prince Charles, grandson of Ferdinand of Spain, with Renée, the daughter of Louis, to whom was proposed the condition that he renounce forever his claims to the kingdom of Naples; and it was then that our Henry promptly married off his sister Mary Tudor to the same Louis, who perhaps took such pleasure in his young wife that he hastened his death, or so they say.

In these early days of his reign the new king is already raising his head defiantly. Francis the First is a young man who renounces nothing, not the ancient claims on Milan or, still less, on Naples, but rather he resumes, in fierce outbursts, with the boldness of his character, the plan to descend soon into Lombardy. The French nobility supports him, and Pope Leo is not entirely opposed to him because the pontiff also has greater fear of being caught in the Spanish trap. We are here to restrain, if not prevent, these hot-blooded plans, but our task is difficult. This is our mission's situation, which will force me to stay in Paris for an indefinite time, according to the orders I receive from London.

Are you appeased by this long tale I have undertaken only to be more agreeable to you? I, on the contrary, loathe the political interweavings that keep me in the north. A stern punishment looms over me, though I deserve it for the excessive boldness of the thoughts combating in my spirit, intense and desolate thoughts. And you, my revered lady, are in Rome. I see you emerge from the white portal with your escort, amid the admiration of the populace, who in the Borgo come to gawk at their illustrious guests and observe you as you proceed, ardent and laughing, to the so-called holy places of ancient Rome. I do not ask myself if I also will be free, as an ordinary wayfarer, to observe you, if you are still the guest of the cardinal of Aragón when I return. But as you see, temptations assail me, and it is likely that they make me unworthy of your indulgence. Nevertheless, I ask it of you, as a poor solitary who detaches himself from the tumult of life in impossible dreams. Commending you to God, I am

> *your slave*
> Robert de la Pole

Paris, the nineteenth of January, 1515

DO NOT forget to burn the letter of the thirty-first of December. By the grace of God, do not read it.

I WAS ALONE in my Porto villa, gazing at the mirror of the lake. Instinctively I leaped up from the bench of gray and white marble squares, amazed to catch some words among the sound of the trees and the bushes, shaken by the bold May wind. No one was in sight as far as my eyes could see; no human being moved nearby, under the play of conflicting gusts that drove huge, transparent clouds of a white splendor through the heavens. The words were distinct and improper, "a dove with spread wings," the "magnificent suspicion," and others, murmured in a lower voice. Beyond any possible doubt, someone was warning me; it was useless to reject the warning. I had to clarify, prohibit.

The letter of the Englishman Robert de la Pole, written in Paris, which I had received in Rome, was still in my mind, imploring and wily, and more than the pleas for forgiveness, it was the political events that upset me, the actions mentioned on those pages of jagged handwriting. But where was the other letter, the one sent from London on December thirty-first? I had not received it, in Rome or in Mantua; now the months were tolling. I counted almost five. The pages sent the "long way" had taken a tortuous path, indeed, unless they had been lost like so many packets sent from far off. I was left with the obscurity of the contents, the uneasiness, and the rational fear of scandals that could also involve me even though I had never made the slightest gesture toward that man of England and could barely remember his fleeting visit a few years ago under a false identity, later denied.

Here lies the evil of life. I am utterly innocent of any guilt, but tomorrow, if this Robert de la Pole's letter were to circulate among the courts, what would become of me? What would Francesco say? What would be the impression on my children, on all my friends in every part of Italy? And on my enemies? That extra freedom that we of princely rank enjoy derives from our authority, and it is yet subject to the whim of courtiers of every faction, skilled at inventing perfidy and calumny. Two, in particular, are the mysterious words that sting me: "magnificent suspicion." My God! "magnificent suspicion"! How dare he have any suspicion of me and make me his accomplice, calling it magnificent? It is possible that the man is a reckless fool, an inventor of deceits, and that the December thirty-first letter was never written. I feel a sort of flush come over me. I am almost reassured that this must be the case. And if he had wagered with himself (I refuse to imagine a wager with another) that this time he will succeed in wresting some sign from me? A sign would mean consent. Indignant, I might send him some scourging lines. They would still be a sign, and the wager would be won.

But what am I talking about? Are my fingers already seeking the pen, and will the sly Englishman finally win? No, the tone of his letters seems to me true, if unruly; certain excesses come perhaps from an imperfect knowledge of our language, in which he is also capable of using choice, weighty expressions. Thinking again of the letter's delay, I reflect for a moment. It sometimes happens that we have no news of many lost missives, and we hear of others delivered after many years, long forgotten in some corner of the world. And there is another possibility: After being brought from Rome to Mantua, the letter may have been engulfed by the papers of our own chancellery. True, no one should take the liberty of opening it, since it is addressed to me. But if it fell into the hands of my enemies, of Tolomeo Spagnoli, or Camposampiero, or their evil henchmen, who would stop them from violating its seal?

A dreadful vision, this idea. I cannot bear it. I must take steps. I realize immediately that I need the protection of someone who will never betray me, whatever may befall. There was a time when I would have gone straight to Francesco, telling him the whole story. But what am I saying? What distorted idol have I made, unaware, of my husband? I attribute to him even that impartiality he has never possessed, mentally adding, "In the past, when we loved each other." But on the contrary, in the past he was much as he is now; even if he loved me, he would be my friend only in spells, having safeguarded first every male susceptibility and every privilege of chief of state afterward. No, we can dismiss the idea of Francesco; there is no place for him in these thoughts.

Rapidly I evoke and measure women and men, of the court and outside it, all the many people who declare themselves devoted to me, all the people I have helped, on impulse, without reservations. Not one would place himself at risk to lend me a hand. An immense desert spreads out around me, and in the gray void a thought suddenly rises: I am alone. I have not yet uttered these words when I see the face of Pirro Donati, my private secretary. Why had I failed to think of him at once? Pirro, my dear Pirro Donati, who wordlessly dispels every fear, who can move freely in our palaces and in the neighboring houses, and knows all but says little, who loves me like an intelligent page, to put it youthfully, and also as a grown man, wise in his discernment. Let him come; let him come; I will speak to him immediately.

I wave to a cloud, collect my women, and on horses and in carriages we rush to the castle. As if summoned, Pirro himself comes to meet me, calm, wearing a tunic of soft brown color, severely cut, edged in satin; he has his usual smile, protective and interrogative. I would never have believed it. A cloak of shyness falls over me; I shrink from the idea of giving him ambiguous instructions; I am intimidated by his judgment; I must master a genuine attack of cowardice. I would have liked to say to him, "Pirro, I need your help; without you, circumstances could destroy me," and instead, I say, "Pirro, are there any letters from Rome?"

There are, and from his hands they pass to mine: one from Cardinal Petrucci, one from the cardinal of Aragón, one from the cardinal of Santa Maria in Portico, my Bibbiena, the companions of my Roman season. I break the seals with a light hand, and meanwhile, in my mind I see the letter of Robert de la Pole unsealed by hostile hands, and I hear the echo of mockery and laughter.

Finally I say: "Pirro, a letter should come to me from Rome, addressed there and sent, I believe from London in my name. It is a letter that could cause me countless troubles, a letter I have reason to suspect might endanger my life. For five months or so the packet has been roaming the routes of the world; I do not know in whose hands it is, nor do I want any investigation to be made. I entrust myself to you, Pirro. Keep your eyes open and make sure my enemies never gain possession of this dangerous document."

"Is the name known of the messenger to whom the packet was given?"

"Nothing is known," I say sharply, raising my chin to give myself courage, "and nothing must be asked; our only action is defense."

On this occasion or never I must be what a poet of ours discovered in me, defining me as the Amazon armed only with her shield. Pirro meanwhile supports me in my attempt to joke. He smiles; he makes a brief gesture with his open hand and says: "He will not elude me, my lady. I know how to lay my nets. No rider will be able to get past me."

As if someone had relieved me of a physical burden, I feel restored, whole again. I head for my *casinetto*, sending the women to their work. The younger ones play in the garden. Isabella Lavagnola chases Bonatta and cries: "It's no good trying to act superior with me; I went to Rome, and you didn't!" Rome! Once again I can turn to those peerless images, in a space crammed with echoes. I read the letters of my friends that Pirro has left with me. I feel I am with them, in the daze of having lived in a season of unique privilege, even menacing since it was so free, merry, naturally stimulated by the exercise of the intellect. And the Roman carnival: that dizzying creation can be called a Saturnalia, a boundless cry of joy, an invention without bounds that has come to us from the most remote times.

I cannot say why the pope was so determined that I should remain throughout carnival, but truly he found no peace until Francesco gave me permission to stay. Then I, more capricious, set a condition: I agreed to stay, provided that I could fix the date of departure, precisely the twenty-eighth of February. I gave myself therefore more than a month to discover, with my eager, lively girls, the color of Roman joy. It was as if a highly imaginative master of the stage guided our days. Our party always included cardinals, gentlemen, poets, scholars, and was enlivened by comical Latinists like Fra Mariano. In the morning we went out riding on classical pilgrimages. When we first arrived at the Colosseum, I almost fainted when I saw it rise, high and massive, from the ground. In that immense construction, which I had so often visited in drawings or in paintings, it is not the memory of emperors or gladiators or martyrs that overwhelms us, but the beauty of the architectonic form that asserts in its powerful construction the bold life of the populace. At the Pantheon we breathed an Augustan severity, dumb and echoless, cleanly expressive, in numbers of harmony. Arches, columns, porticoes, temples, towers, palaces in a millennial space posed for our inspection, isolated from the context of the little ocher-colored houses and the churches, in a single vibration. The names of the characters in Roman history and in sacred legend rose within us; our contemporaries seemed Servius Tullius, Hadrian, Nero, Constantine, and the apostle Peter, the apostle Paul. Spontaneously, at every church I came to, I dismounted and approached the altar to light votive tapers to our God and our patron saints.

The cardinal of Aragón writes me that since our departure his day is empty; he regrets he can no longer accompany us to banquets, concerts, to the play, and he complains that conversations and feasts have become tedious. And yet nothing is comparable to the Roman court, where in a hall of noble dimensions young cardinals in sumptuous purple dance in figured steps to cadenced music with ladies and maids dressed in brocade and satin with fine patterns in stripes, circles, fanciful geometries of gold and silver. Dresses and cloaks sway with an almost sacred majesty in the slow movements, and even if they are a bit faster, they are strictly checked by the confines of the tempo.

The hunt at La Magliana, horse races and the procession of triumphant chariots in Agone, boats competing on the Tiber, bull hunts at Testaccio: The bold Cardinal Petrucci overlooks nothing in his reminiscences to me. But none of my friends, not even my Moccicone, can report to me now the quips that the Roman populace, lively and independent as they are, and accustomed to their Pasquino, dared to make about my girls, so nonchalant with the young cardinals. The time has past when the archdeacon of Gabbioneta, our escort, had to defend himself to Francesco, replying to his lord: "It may be true that Rome is not a seemly or suitable place for women, but then the spotless life of our Madama appears all the more exceptional, annulling any other consideration." Everything in that city was so easygoing that it was natural for me to borrow sums from Agostino Chigi and from Caetani of Sermoneta, though His Holiness took care of the necessary expenses of my household with two large gifts of ducats. Who knows when I will be able to repay those debts?

There is also a letter from my dear Baldesar Castiglione; he also takes me back to that generous Roman festiveness. He announces that Raffaello will paint the picture I personally asked of him. I saw this god of art there in the Vatican rooms. Sweet and gentle he seemed; truth to tell, his serene countenance is also remote, consumed by incommunicable visions. In the places where he lives, he wants to be alone, or such is the impression he gives, unconsciously eluding everything that does not lead him to his search for perfection. At times I pursued him with my gaze from my window as he passed through the square, below the palace where I was living, or in the company of people of art or people of renown who were content simply to gaze on him. He seemed disarmed, fragile in his dark, short mantle, usually of finest velvet. The crowd parted at his passage and hailed him.

From my window, I said. I did not add that it was difficult to forbid myself a glance at the palace opposite, fourth floor, fifth window, indicated in the Englishman's letter from Paris. It is a window designed with a curve at the top, so small that I have to smile at my fear of glancing at it. I must confess to myself, after I happened to raise my eyes, I left the sill with a feeling of lightness that refreshed my mind the whole day. Good Lord! I must immediately answer Signor Castiglione about the Raffaello painting; the painter wants to know only the dimensions and from what direction the light will strike the canvas. If I could propose a subject, I would like one like the artist's small, earlier pictures, with one of those Madonnas of his that give a sense of the ineffable and perhaps with some other figure, like the divine infant and a little Saint John or a Saint Anna. I see them in an open place with the ruins of Rome as a background, in a faint luminescent mist, the Pantheon recognizable with its powerful colonnade, or the gigantic arched walls of the Baths of Diocletian or the Corinthian columns of the Temple of Vespasian. I would like the ghost of Rome inscribed in the background and the figuration of our religion in the foreground, in the majestic harmony of a time without sunsets.

FOR MORE than a month I had been suspecting that our sarcastic contempt for the whims of the new French king was a mistake, but it was an unexpressed suspicion that I tried to dispel. The adventurous Francis the First showed up at the border so suddenly that his enterprise seemed hasty, bound to collapse. But gradually more disturbing news followed: There was talk of thirty-five thousand well-trained men, sixty cannons, a hundred culverins. Naturally the Venetians were allies of the French, and what did that mean? They were opposed, not by us Mantuans, forced into inaction as Francesco became more and more exhausted, but rather by the armies of the Holy League that united the king of Spain, the emperor, and the pope, in perfect battle array, commanded by the viceroy of Sicily, Raimundo of Cardona, and by Prospero Colonna, the illustrious captain. And there were the Swiss, well paid and well established on the Alpine passes.

The vigilance of the Swiss proved futile, as the French king blew up cliffs, flung bold bridges over chasms, and descended into the valley of the Stura, briskly advancing toward Milan. Prospero Colonna was taken prisoner, and the Swiss were forced to defend the city, sealing themselves up in the Sforza castle. And yet to us it still seemed impossible that there would be any real upheavals. We deluded ourselves reciprocally; I tried to reassure Massimiliano, who with the prescience of the weak saw the death throes of his Milanese adventure and was too young and inexperienced to oppose his enemies seriously. I grew sadder daily. All my constructions were in ruins, including the latest, the marriage of my nephew to the young queen of Naples, Giovanna of Aragón. The king of France was pressing us so hard that we had no time to think.

On that day, the thirteenth of September, early in the morning, harried by anxiety and suspense, we went up to the rooms of the chancellery, to receive the messengers' information as promptly as possible. This was the previous night's news: The French were moving forward, and their advance seemed irresistible. It was late summer; the tawny sun enfolded the castle in cloaks of light and intensified the green of the Lombard countryside. Francesco, Cardinal Sigismondo, and two of our most expert counselors sat with me around a great table covered with maps, dispatches, papers. Francesco, his illness momentarily alleviated, conceived plans of attack and plans of defense and even new ways of proposing universal peace to the disputants. Distracted by our impatience, we barely answered him. I was tormented by something insidious that had been reported to me in those days: In Venice it was said of my husband that at this point his good was no help, and his evil no harm. I knew this, but on hearing it repeated, I shook my head violently.

HOUR by hour dispatches arrive; they come from a locality near Milan where the soldiers of the League are encamped. At noon the sound of bells announces the breaking of the truce, and rapid troop movements can be discerned. The armies move toward a violent clash. Swiss and Landsknechts get the upper hand, and it seems the French are defeated, routed. Bonaventura Pistofilo, our agent in the field, sends us military messages at top speed. The triumph that had made us vibrant with hope immediately loses its force. The night passes; the morning is well advanced when a final messenger arrives with a final message: The king of France, with his cavalry, has flung himself frontally against the enemy, and from the Lodi road, all of a sudden, commanded by Alviano, the fresh forces of the Venetians have appeared to succor them. It is the end of a battle between giants: Marignano is a glorious name in the story of Francis the First.

These days are endless, punctuated by the constant appearance of messengers with announcements and details, all disastrous for us. Once again I admire the human heart, strong enough to support such misfortunes. I fear for Massimiliano Sforza, surely in flight from Milan, perhaps toward the Tyrol, protected by the emperor's Swiss mercenaries. For our immediate future we must fear everything. Nor would it be hard for a drunken army in victory to seize the lucky moment and head for Mantua. Would the prophecy of that Veronese astrologer come true, the prediction that the Gonzaga breed would go wandering outside of their lands?

Now that I have formulated this question, my will regains vigor; I am convinced that any horoscope can be reversed if reason is applied. I examine my playing cards, to choose carefully those that are most reliable. One is Alfonso, my brother, with the strength of his faithful friendship toward the French, who now perorates, with authority, our cause with King Francis. Another is a nephew, son of Chiara Gonzaga of Montpensier, sister of my husband. He is the constable of Bourbon, a young captain but one of undisputed authority. Yet another is the pope. Leo seems to be moved by our troubles, all too clearly displayed by Francesco, who allows himself wild outbursts and lamentations, as he is roughly pressed by the Spaniards and by the king of France, both demanding passage on the Po. Alfonso deplores this whining, but Francesco only increases his moans. "If that brother of yours were in our situation here," he protests, with tears in his eyes, "if he were ill, in bed, as we are, without soldiers, with garrisons exposed to any sort of attack, what would he do?"

FRANCIS the First, who had entered Milan with his overwhelming gray army, listened to his faithful Ferrarese ally, and with his curiosity about the Italian courts, he lent an ear also to the talk of others, among them his beloved squire Galeazzo of San Severino, who told him tales about me, even describing my dresses. The king, very courtly in the French way, invited me to Milan, prepared to entertain me with every kind of festivity, ready to call his mother and sister from Paris, to present them to the great ladies of Italy, and in particular, to the marchesana of Mantua.

I refused to budge. I lived with my life, as every aware person does, and something of the events we have lived through always rises from our thought. Milan meant encountering my Sforzas again. It meant the irreparable fall of those Titans of our land, the beginning of the fear of foreign invaders, the constant thought of being sacked, expelled, deprived of every right; it meant having suffered the terrible grief of the Sforza collapse, which changed the very tone of our existence. More recently Milan had given me an illusion, with the reappearance of the Sforzas in the person of Massimiliano, who loved me dearly "as a mother" and who always wanted me at his side, as on that day under the ducal canopy after the ephemeral surrender of Piacenza. I was reminded how I had been present at the festivities of Louis, the other conqueror king of France, but no one knew how much that presence had cost me and how I had had to summon my strength then to bear the terror I felt on seeing those new faces, those men who were bringing ruin to each of our states. Enough of all that. Unfortunately I had lost all curiosity; I did not consider myself an object to be displayed in order to win vital sympathy; my celebrated wisdom did not resemble one of Fra Mariano's spectacles. No, I would not go to entertain the king of France, though he was handsome and courtly, everyone said.

All my people tried to convince me, but I insisted that I could not leave my husband, who was so ill, almost in danger of his life, and to one of our envoys I also revealed that I lacked the three or four thousand ducats to dress myself in a style equal to my reputation. For us, finding such a loan would have been as difficult as flying, but after this confidence I forbade the man to mention it to the king, who should not believe I was seeking money from him. In short, I stayed in Mantua. Francis the First muttered a word or two of disappointment and showed displeasure at my refusal. I wonder if we are foolish or wise, we human beings, to rejoice in a little victory when great disasters are in the offing.

From the dispatches of our envoys and our agents it was clear that we had to resign ourselves to sending Federico as a guest, or, to put it bluntly, as hostage, to the French court. His Most Christian Majesty wanted him, with all honors and also with a bold show of affection and in a benevolent and loyal condition, and Francis was not a man to contradict himself. But it was evident that in addition to ensuring himself against us, he wanted to have in his household a pupil to rear as his own creature, a faithful servant in his future dominion over Italy. My son was attracted by the prospect of living in France, at the side of that young demigod; before seeing him leave, I had encouraged his spirit in our conversations, reminding him of his boyhood exile in Rome, as the pledge of his imprisoned father's liberation. I told him how he had then seemed to me an ancient Roman and how today I imagined him far away on French soil, acting as safeguard of his State. He was to go with calm and intrepid spirit. I promised him that as a grown man he would take incomparable pride in that memory and great solace.

"Mother dear," he answered, always with his slightly childish manner, "I will do everything you wish, and you will be pleased with me."

And he kept asking me how he should behave toward the ladies, especially the king's mother, and the queen, and the maids of the court. This monarch intimidated him a little, but not too much, accustomed as he was to being in Rome with a pope, and he liked the show of handsome jackets, tight-waisted, of cut and colors never seen, thanks to which Francis the First stood out among his suite of nobles with glorious names, all dressed in tan fustian. And so from Milan Federico accompanied the king to Bologna, where the pope was lodged, with his court, for the great congress for universal peace. But more than anything else this was the exhibition of a rising star, the chivalrous and victorious sovereign, who held aloft a banner of peace. I cannot say how holy this banner seemed to me, but at this point I could tell deception by its smell. Behind the speeches repeated to the four winds by the two protagonists, I could sniff subtle dealings in power, plans for dominion, indications of areas to be subjugated; chiefs of state prefer division to union in the interest of stable peace.

December was ending, the last days of that year begun with the glittering discoveries of the many secret freedoms Naples and Rome had allowed me. The time of farewells tolled inexorably. Federico was about to follow King Francis to his own land, to those cold cities, the cathedrals bristling with sharp points. We had to face the last visit he would pay us now, shortly; his king granted him permission to come and say good-bye to us.

Permission. I could not bear the word applied to my son and to us. Something new was happening. I called Soardino, and I spoke to him clearly and sharply. I did not want to see Federico again. I did not want to take upon myself, upon us the suffering of resignation. Already Federico had left Mantua to join the court in Milan; at that time I had rationally mastered my rebellion. What was the sense of this return for a few days, perhaps only hours? Francesco, undermined by his disease, would weep, and in the wave of that emotion, everyone would weep, my sons, daughters, my ladies, the girls who adored him, perhaps even the men of the palace and I myself, because the act of separation dissolves all courage. And why sap also his strength, Federico's? "You went off gaily," I wrote him in a letter full of incitements, in the style of our conversations on the subject of Roman manliness; I transferred myself into the joyousness of his sixteen years, and from there I directed him to look ahead. I gave Francesco the letter to read. He nodded and, as I had feared, wept with tenderness and pride, but there were no other corroding tears at court. It took great strength to reject my son.

"THE POPE nodded his head slightly and murmured, 'That rogue!' After a moment's reflection, he added, more sharply: 'That traitorous rogue.' " I reread the whole letter. My Bibbiena no longer reassured me. Francesco Maria, my son-in-law, was doomed. There was no hope: Leo the Tenth masked his tone, arrived even at wrath, but then relaxed in a conditioned good humor, but he never swerved from his intention of punishing my daughter's husband. I know, Francesco Maria is an unreliable man: He is never to be found where there is fighting; he rebels against the generals' plans; he will not be commanded by anyone. But he is young, he can change yet, and his faults, however grave, are not a good reason for taking Urbino from him and transferring its seigniory from the Montefeltro family to the Medici. Now the Magnifico Giuliano is on his deathbed in Florence, slowly removing himself from the plans, the realms invented for him by his brother the pope. His illness has alarmed everyone; he is much loved, so charming with women, a respected man of letters, a good poet, elegantly Tuscan, friend of subtle wits like Signor Niccolò Machiavelli and Pietro Bembo, the great patron of the "vulgar tongue," and quite bold in supporting a plan for drying up the malarial Pontine Marshes, following the advice of Master Leonardo da Vinci. He never forgot his long exile in Urbino, and he would have no part in the Medici usurpation of that duchy, never accepting it for himself. But he is dying, and his nephew Lorenzo is stepping onto the stage, handsome and arrogant, casual to the point of cynicism. This young Medici holds sway in the Vatican, is always present at the ambassadors' visits, and while they are heard in audience, he does not refrain from murmuring into the ear of His Holiness. Unsuited to govern, he has some of the inertia of his father, Piero the Unlucky, who had himself expelled from Florence. And yet Pope Leo favors him and has destined Urbino to him; Lorenzo will appropriate this land if the Medicis find a way of getting their hands on it.

Necessity of State and family affection both require me to choose my side. I try to dismiss all partisan passion, and I help my son-in-law coldly, having his cause recommended by my brother Alfonso to the king of France. I advise him to make acts of submission to the pope, but he refuses to present himself in Rome. He claims to know all too well what would be in store for him, and perhaps he is right. He frowns, uses futile words, and unburdens himself to my daughter, who is wasting away in the constant exercise of prayer, without sinew. But what could she do, against the pope?

February days are short. At this hour my Elisabetta, my only real sister, at our Bibbiena's suggestion, is traveling toward Rome. She will be our final defender, she whom Leo the Tenth claims to honor, remembering Urbino's generous hospitality when he was roaming Italy, an exile from republican Florence. I cannot sit still. I wander aimlessly through the rooms of the castle. I shut myself up in the little chambers with the Leonardesque knots, overlooking the green moat where chilly white swans drift. Madama Laura comes to tell me that the girls are grumpy; they feel neglected and saddened. It is raining; there is a storm; thunder and lightning chase each other over the lake. This is a good moment to think of life as a burden to be lightened by some intervention. But what? I cannot get Elisabetta out of my mind. She has borne too great a share of others' ills, as Castiglione says. Her serenity, wed to a natural and happy spirit, is vulnerable, as only I know. What will happen in Rome? Leo disconcerts me with his postponing and suspense, considering himself secretive so as not to admit being irresolute. Such characters, as everyone knows, when they decide something cling to their decision as the only one that exists absolutely.

I was cold, and from those now-darkening rooms I returned to the chamber with the initials, passing through the Hall of the "Trionfi." The "Trionfi" of Mantegna are not there any longer; Francesco wanted them for his San Sebastiano palace, so the hall has been sheathed in red leather with gold background that runs over the walls with warm, colorful grace.

From the snail-shaped staircase Pirro Donati emerged and rapidly entered the room. He glanced around, saw me. He was animated, almost red in the face, and he moved with cautious agitation. He closed the door after him, as is our custom during the cold seasons so the drafts will not whistle through the halls. I stood unmoving by the fireplace, the name of Elisabetta still on my tongue.

"Signora," my secretary said, "the groom of Signor Castiglione has arrived, and his mother has sent this letter addressed to you."

He held out the envelope, and I recognized the jagged handwriting. God, how far was I from the thought of the Englishman at that moment, and yet I was almost grateful to the circumstances that tore me from my meditations on undeserved misfortunes.

"That letter . . ." I began hesitantly.

"It comes from Rome. Signor Castiglione had it from one of Cardinal Castellesi's household, where it had been lying among the cardinal's papers for some months. The cardinal is a bit feebleminded now; he didn't recall having put it in his cupboard. I hope its rediscovery does not displease you. . . ."

His last words were faint. He was still gasping for breath; he must have run up the steps. He observed me, mute. Surely he had in his ears my anxious urgings, but now he was amazed; a vague frown made his face grave. Yes, that was the letter sent from London on December thirty-first, an annotation under the address said that; yes, this was the mislaid letter, the letter denied, dangerous, full of guilty secrets, the letter which, by my faith in God, I was not to read. Everything became clear, and I was assailed by a kind of frenzy. Now I will know the sin of that man; I will discover the meaning of the words that have tormented me to the point of exasperation. Now I will drag him to be burned in the volcano of my haughtiness; that "magnificent suspicion" and the other expressions will vanish forever.

In my eagerness to know, I looked for the seals; they were big and intact. I stopped, amazed, glancing at Pirro Donati. He was something to be seen, that face suddenly blanched and at the same time flushed with red patches. What was he expecting from me? My God, what had I told him that morning when I ordered him to be vigilant? I could hear again my voice saying "an evil letter that can be dangerous for me, not to be read. . . ." I was gripped in a vise: I wanted with all my strength to know, and I did not dare break the seals. My old friend would judge me; I must not appear a liar to him or, worse, an accomplice. Suddenly all the wrath fell from my heart, and everything in me was clear, in a precise thought that surpassed all emotion.

"Let us thank God, Pirro," I said in a resolute voice, "let us thank God, who has chosen to console me and save me from a treacherous risk. Has anyone seen this envelope?"

Too moved to speak, Pirro made a negative gesture.

"And no one will ever see it," I declared, inspired by my clear wish to resolve things, the will that sometimes decides for us almost without our knowledge.

I went to the fireplace, I threw the envelope among the embers; flames rose, eager and strong in their capacity for transformation. With a little shovel I bent, to break up the singed papers among the ashes. I thought I could discern the jagged letters, and I read in my mind, very rapidly, the words "for the love of God, signora, do not read it!" and within me something replied, "I have not read it." Pirro stood there, his face relaxed, barely pink. He had faith in me, and perhaps it was not entirely justified.

"I WENT to Rome," Elisabetta is saying, with her slightly tremulous, musical voice, "I followed your advice. The day I arrived the papal monitory was published: Leo ordered Francesco Maria to appear in person before the pope. I immediately said this was an act of hostility aimed at me so that I would expect the worst. And the whole sequel was cruel. It was cruel to have to go to the chambers of the pope, who came toward me with a friendly expression, embraced me, and kept me there briefly, postponing our talks until the next day. The next day came, and the comedy of deceits began. My anguished torment wakes with me in the morning, and I ask first of all the real reason why he is thinking of taking our State from us. Has he, now he is pope, forgotten the kindnesses the Medicis received from us when they were in exile and persecuted? Has he forgotten how the Magnifico Giuliano was loved and welcomed with honor in Urbino in rooms of our palace that to this day are called the apartment of the Magnifico? Has he forgotten how we prayed for his safe return to Florence? 'Oh, Holy Father,' I implored, 'why does Your Holiness wish us to be driven out, to go about the world as beggars?' Through my tears I beseeched him."

"And what did he say?" Francesco asks faintly.

"He was silent. He held up his eyeglass, to look at me. Then he trained it on the court. All were frozen, turned toward him in supplication. And seeing such expressions all around him, he looked away. One courtier who seemed about to speak was nailed fast by that penetrating beam. And I continued my pleas. I asked, I begged the Medicis not to repeat the blows of the Borgias. Blameless, we could not lose our land, which had come to us through rightful inheritance. When I finished speaking, there was no one in the room who was not in tears, except the pope himself; from time to time he shrugged and glared at me, silent and indifferent."

As she tells this, Elisabetta is no longer weeping, but still a sob shakes her. I touch her lightly on the shoulder, to keep from being overcome by compassion. She is seated next to me on my favorite marble bench, of black-and-white squares, on the terrace of the Porto villa, overlooking the lake. On a camp bed under an awning Francesco is lying, racked by illness and pain; nearby, my daughter Eleonora and her little son Guidobaldo are seated on stools; my son-in-law stands, wearing his mud-stained boots, dusty with defeat.

Stirred by an access of his old energy, Francesco rebels: "Why didn't you defend Urbino? The city is in a good position to resist. You should have fought."

"Your captain, Alessio Beccaguto, here present, can answer that," Francesco Maria answers readily. "Everyone abandoned us, our own people first of all. The enemy army was enormous. Whole columns of wagons and cannons were climbing up the hill, and ranks of soldiers that seemed to stretch to infinity. The populace could already be heard shouting, 'Sanctuary! sanctuary!' before the attackers had set foot in the city. We fled barely in time. The harbingers of misfortune had been too numerous; already the day before, we had stripped the palace of all valuables and sent everything to Pesaro with the caravan of the women and children. I joined them quickly. In Pesaro we took ship, but a sudden hurricane struck us and drove the ship almost within sight of Schiavonia. Only after much suffering were we able to come back toward Italy safe and sound, arriving at Pietole, where you lodged us so well and comforted us. Now we are here to thank you and to ask you the charity of allowing us to stay with you."

I WOULD never have thought to regret the Borgias, least of all because of the wise and much-acclaimed Medicis. The inexorable Leo the Tenth, with his golden eyeglass, stood before me, called up by Elisabetta's words. A kind of unbearable rigidity kept me motionless on the stone seat. Francesco talked to himself aloud, softly complaining, stroking his daughter Eleonora's head, resting near him on the cot.

"My daughter, do not torment yourself. Both of you will soon come to Mantua, and live with us. Meanwhile, the Pietole palace is not a bad lodging after all: so vast, with its bright facade. You and your people will live there comfortably. The pope will not deny me the right to give refuge to my daughter and my sister."

"The pope will deny anything if it is to his advantage," Elisabetta said. "No pity can have any hold of him. The worst of it is that we have no money; we will be forced to break up our most beautiful silver objects, which we have saved. In Rome they even have the audacity to refuse to return my dowry to me."

"What? Break up your silver?" I said, almost incredulous.

The Urbino credenza was renowned for the supreme elegance of its fittings; famous silversmiths had signed it. And we ourselves had so little money that we could make no offer.

With an effort Francesco raised himself slightly in the cot, to address his beloved sister. "We will be able to help you very little, sister dear. Everyone is forcing us to spend money; wars and invasions have impoverished us; the spring floods have destroyed the crops. But still, you will lack for nothing. Never fear, your brother will not abandon you."

At that moment Tolomeo Spagnoli appeared at the far end of the terrace; no one else could have flaunted that facetiously concerned smile of his. He greeted us briefly. Francesco asked him if he had drawn up the letter for the pope; the marchese was asking permission for the della Rovere family, refugees from Urbino, to be granted asylum in Mantua. Tolomeo handed him a paper.

"Sign here, my lord. And if you please, sign here also. The city Council is awaiting a decree to announce the new tax on salt."

I sprang to my feet and took the two papers from Francesco's hand. One of them was blank.

"A blank paper. Look!"

Without moving a muscle of his face, Spagnoli answered: "A blank paper, of course. My lord is ill; his heart must not be troubled at every moment. And the formula of the decree is the same as usual; I will write it out."

I turned toward Francesco. "Think this matter over carefully, husband. The people are tired, bled white; serious protests are circulating in the city. A new tax will be intolerable. Instead, we should urge the repeal of the salt tax that we owe to the Papal States. At this point we have lost Asola and Lonato, so if we demonstrate there are many fewer mouths in our State, we will gain a reduction of the tax and not have to make our poor citizens pay an additional one."

"What do you say, Signor Tolomeo?" Francesco asked, uncertain.

Ignoring all those present, including me, Spagnoli looked straight at his master and said: "The treasury is empty. We need money at once; we must pay our annual tribute to the emperor. I beg you, my lord, sign."

Francesco took the papers from his hands.

"I do it reluctantly; my long-suffering people are close to my heart, but there is no way out. And as for appealing to the papal Curia, I can imagine the reply they would send us."

He signed, his hand weak and unsteady. A surge of indignation ran through my whole body. Spagnoli left in haste. As I took Elisabetta's hand to feel her loyal clasp, Eleonora let out a little cry.

"Father! Father! He is ill!"

Francesco had turned pale. I tried to support his head, so that he could breathe more easily. Little by little he regained color; he was immediately given something to drink.

"It's nothing," he said, trying to smile. "The heat is too much for me."

"Go back into your rooms," I advised him softly. "You must rest. I will come soon with the doctor."

Francesco managed to stand up, supported by his sister and his daughter. The group of Gonzagas, followed by Francesco Maria with his head bowed, went off, pathetically united. Life's inclemency was weighing upon them, and at the same time instinct drove them to collect, to suffer together in that secret place of melancholy that lay in the depths of their breed. And I had seen more: My Elisabetta's caressing gaze touched my daughter Eleonora, that same gaze that used to enfold me, calming my wrath and my outrage. They were going away, forgetting me, as if they had no need of me, and the truth was that I alone could find the way to help them all, I alone was strong and knew the passage from thought to action. The beneficent warmth of the call to action ran through me. I made my decisions. "First of all," I said to myself, "I will pawn my jewels, the faceted ruby, the largest diamond jewel, the great pearls, the dress all glittering with beads of gold interspersed with pearl clusters. Not the emerald. For that, we will wait."

Room of the clocks
the year 1533

MEMORY DISSOLVES THE words that had remained clotted in a space of time and makes them come flowing down, rustling like snow in May. I listen to them. I am here, at my nighttime tryst with myself, in the room of the clocks. At the flicker of the little flames atop the candles, my largest casket, wide open, gives off delicate glints, signals in the night. Do these signals ask to be understood, in their prismatic radiance? I still have not moved my hand over the velvet shelves, drawn forward one by one, but I know the form of the jewels that I have at different times worn around my neck, on my bosom and on my forehead, creating at the great court gatherings that fairy tale suspense that accompanies our appearance as rulers.

These have made, they make a history of me; they have expressed something of the inventive fever that stirs in me when I enter a decked and decorated hall. "If you wish to see something matchless, you must see our lady Beatrice at a festivity," the people of Ferrara used to say, and the words still are remembered. That Beatrice d'Este, my ancestress, lived more than a hundred years ago, and surely her secret has descended to me at least in part; it is a fire, courtliness, that urges people on, as if to battle, arousing unknown strength that can cause turmoil within us. Gems exalt such dizziness, for they are insignia of security. Never does a man feel so vigorous, Francesco has often confided in me, as when the clank of the medal or the jewel that attaches to his jerkin a chain designed by Caradosso or by a similar master. And if this were not so, why would kings and princes and the pope himself load themselves with gold and gems? These symbols of rank will never cease to act.

I have always passionately followed astrologers' studies of the powers of precious stones. The most astute of all my astrologers is Paride of Ceresara, a master of the correlations between stars and objects, a man who can derive useful thoughts from everything. He taught me that red stones stimulate even the most recalcitrant vitality in November and March, that blue stones promise spiritual victories, that green stones prompt bold plans, and that white diamonds, haughty in their radiance, foretell all sorts of triumph, while milky opals are to be interrogated with caution. What influence do they have on us? We pass through the vicissitudes of our days, stars or no, in generous or inglorious combat with things and with passions. I could say, on the contrary, that alert as they are to such games, astrologers ignore the real power of jewels; you must possess them to realize that. When I touch them, my jewels, one by one, on the shelves where they lie, inexorably beautiful, I perceive in the depths of their glistening waters almost superhuman deeds. From the rubies I see long ranks of armed men emerge, infantry and horse, and weapons and bombards, deployed for our difficult defensive wars. How many times have rubies, emeralds, and sapphires paid for costly equipment or served as guaranty, locked in the iron chests of the Jew Salomone or other rich Venetian jewelers, always ready to evaluate well the most sumptuous pledges? And weapons are not all I see: From the depths of the diamonds come wagons of grain and provisions that have succored our people in the hard times of famine and flood.

In this sense, my most trusted jewel is my emerald, which astounded even people of the most refined taste, like Bembo. Mounted in gold, it is of a green so intense that it has the diamond's brilliance, which as a rule green gems lack, and the pope's goldsmith, that Benvenuto Cellini, unrivaled in creating precious things, actually called it a green diamond. Unique jewel, it alone would suffice to buy a throne. And how the silky pearls release their singing glow, some of them an incredible white, others a pale gray or faded pink; and the jewels of rubies, pearls, and sapphires that I have so often worn at feasts, blazing crimson, white, or pale blue, depending on how I moved my head; and all the others of select stones that Cesare Borgia so coveted but was never able even to touch.

On all occasions I have used them gladly. I believe gems do not suffer from being worn; on the contrary, they renew their essence, assimilating the passions of the blood. They have energy. Here is a condensed word that always stirs me. Two energies rise from my casket: one mineral, intrinsic in each gem, and the other infused by the goldsmith's hand, or the chaser's, the engraver's, the cutter's, capable of catching the remote, arcane language of the stones. To my hand comes, as if offering itself as an example, a "Deposition of Christ" engraved in an unparalleled way, so that the stone, a green jasper dotted with red patches, seems to bleed from the body of the Redeemer. This kind of energy is shared also by necklaces without gems, long or short, so covered with enamel that the gold vanishes beneath the perfect work, and there are also the carved turquoises that relieve a necklace of pearls carved in arabesques, chasing one another in the dizzying whirl of the pattern.

I know what my strongest thrill is, perhaps a sin or a vice, which I approach with measured gestures. The shelves slip back into the cabinet, and below I expose a silver cup that stands in a low space, held fast by a curl of black velvet. I observe its delicate oval form closed by a fastened lid. I shift it just slightly; I listen to a remote tinkle of astral crystals. I open it with all the old emotion of youthful passion. Loose gems glow and radiate in all their colors, not all large, but of pure Orient, which I have gradually collected for myself and which only I know I own: the red stones, the balas rubies, garnets, spinels, the milky opals, disturbing in their rainbow glints, the sublime diamonds, stones of metaphysical aura, the dizzying blue sapphires, and the green stones, the emeralds or beryls, and the aquamarines, the topazes of very pale yellow or very dark, agates, carnelians, graceful in their pensive hue. The light plays on them as in Aladdin's cavern, and if from one hand I pass them to the other, allowing them to fall like a little cascade, blazes flare. I plunge my fingers into the cup till I touch the smooth bottom. I communicate with the creative force of the world, with the first formation of petrified matter, and I perceive a tactile tremor like a mineral voluptuousness of nature.

I **PULLED MY HOOD** over my face as I en-
tered San Francesco, nor did I turn to see with whom Pirro
Donati was speaking, even though I had noticed the movement
of a guard, who seemed to want to prevent me from proceeding
farther. "Not even God would stop me," I said to myself as I
walked forward with my usual briskness. But I had to stop. Darkness was hovering on all sides. Black drapery around the doors,
black curtains at the windows turned that beautiful church, with
its pointed arches, so protective, into a kind of antechamber of
purgatory. Overtaken by my secretary's footsteps, I slowly resumed advancing. I recognized at once the stairs of wood and
plaster that I had ordered designed and built for the funeral service
of my husband, Francesco. It was a well-proportioned little temple
with six columns, Corinthian capitals of curled leaves; on the
pediment, as if struck by a storm, the coat of arms was askew,
the four black eagles of the Gonzagas. Inside the temple stood a
truncated pyramid, its six steps covered with gray-green cloth; at
the sides statues of hooded warriors held banners. On the short
stairway the coats of arms of Milan, Saint Mark's, the emperor,
the pope, the king of France were placed at intervals. Above, on
the level top lay the sarcophagus and, on it, reclining, the symbolic
figure of a captain in armor, his visor lowered.

Seven days had gone by since his death, and the day of the
great funeral was beginning. Already the first torches were being
lit, and that darkened space, which rejected the light of the rainy
day, dotted by the flames, became a cavern, and its depths sank
into blackness. The torches would outline the sharp arches, flank-
ing the altars; they would climb up on the truncated pyramid,
run along the pediment of the temple, where the date could be
read: nineteenth March, 1519.

I approached the little Roman temple, so slender and yet majestic in its simple geometric form; Francesco would have liked it.
Lines of young monks were approaching silently. Some, quick
and precise, carried newly lighted torches; others hung from the

columns dense panoplies of weapons and flags held together by the shield of the Gonzagas with Francesco's emblems painted on it. I could not bear the dismay in my heart. This was the last celebration totally dedicated to him. His body had been buried under the floor of the church by his wish; he had been dressed in the Franciscan habit he had chosen, indeed, imposed as his last garment on the morning of his death.

"The light is dim," I said in a whisper to Pirro Donati, who was behind me.

He led me to a pew and seated me as if we were in our audience chamber. Then he ran to inquire. The minutes surrendered slowly to the gloom. Pirro soon returned to tell me there were five hundred thirty-one torches, all of white wax, each weighing three pounds. Not even a third part of them had yet been set in place. My eye penetrated sharply among spaces and forms, as if seeking mistakes to rectify. I managed to see an ill-fastened shield and a banner at the wrong angle, and I sent Pirro to the decorators. One of them, the head, came to bow before me. His voice was unsteady as he spoke: "Your Excellency, Your Ladyship, here! Not a thread will be out of place, signora, I swear. I was also at Fornovo. No one who was not at our marchese's side on that day of battle can know the meaning of valor in war." He bent his gray head, took my hand with the composure of a gentleman, and kissed it, barely grazing it; then he vanished into the shadows. "Fornovo!" The name still echoed. That glory of his still shone.

"Let us go," I said with a great sigh. "Everything is as I wished. Everything is in order, and our people commemorate their lord in the proper fashion."

An impossible desire tormented my breast: that you, Francesco, could come back. That last day of yours had been filled with lessons. Your voice was bodiless in its depth, the voice of one dying, who knew it; your courage was not the ferine impulse of the young warrior but a suffered courage whose like I had never seen in anyone. I admired you sorrowfully.

I knelt in the center of the church, where I seemed to be closer to him. I prayed very little. It was as if my limbs and my spirit, separated from me, were praying on their own account. I went straight to the main door. Once again I drew my hood down over my face, I put my hand on the arm of my escort, I went out, and having climbed in my carriage, I went back to the castle, entering by a side gate. Closed in the solitude of the Painted Chamber, before the portrait of Francesco as a boy on the left wall, I sank into a dazed peace. The secret visit to San Francesco had been the last act of affection between us, an act of recognition of ours, or, indeed, of mine toward him; in the familiar task of arranging things, the deep, strong grief that had surrounded me all night was placated.

I looked at that boy with his little, flattened nose, his suit, and his two-toned stockings, caught by the painter in the instinctive gravity that makes childhood venerable. I caught myself smiling at him. It seems to me that yesterday it was the voice of this aged child that, clear and aware, dictated, bit by bit, his testament. He remembered every friend, courtier, or servant. But first of all, he named me Federico's regent until our son completed his twenty-first year. And so, with that act he recognized me, loyally and publicly, as chief of state capable of guaranteeing the future seigniory of the Gonzagas. All dispatches, every law, every decision would pass through my hands; Francesco summoned me to responsibility of offices that would have been excessive if I had not had the spirit to assume it. I could share with my son every experience and perception and transmit that impalpable talent in foreseeing the possible development of others' actions at every stage. I would be a woman reigning, beyond any further risks of humiliations, with no need to hide behind a man to prompt his speeches, his political moves. My son would read my ideas in my eyes, and I would grasp in his ideas those born from mine. This last possibility of giving him life, in constant motivation, and receiving it back from him, making me almost the offspring of my son, was the discovery of a sole fate. It was only a consideration of modesty that made me strenuously force back my tears of gratitude and humility.

NOW IT is up to me. The last years of Francesco's life had virtually crushed me, with the risk of overpowering my faith in my own judgment. I resisted with redoubled vigor, I would say, the perversity of others, which aroused me, provoking storm clouds of rebellion, which multiplies life into the future. I had noted everything: Vigo of Camposampiero's slanders of me as a woman, of my spirit of government. I kept well in mind the murmured accusation, the doubts concerning my friendship with General Lautrec, a French gentleman of great courtesy and loyalty, devoted to his king and country. Nor did I forget how that Vigo had called me a woman of petty female concerns, as he used that diabolical perfidy that teaches how to wound someone in the very spot where that person is worth most. For Camposampiero we decreed banishment from Mantua and the court, and so I was freed of his presence. I acted with justice: I looked after his wife, otherwise deprived of all support. She was a woman like many others, pretty, unlettered, good.

It was another story with that weasel-faced bear Tolomeo Spagnoli, who had exploited Francesco's favor in order to fabricate measures against the unprotected weak, poor gentlemen, widows without relatives, hapless merchants, rural folk, priests. The podestà of Mantua, a man with an open face, distinguished by his very summary activity, presented me with the documents cleverly collected. We summoned Spagnoli to trial, and facing the official of the tribunal, he did not bat an eye. But on the day of the hearing he defied us with his absence. Cardinal Sigismondo and I took our places in the rulers' seats in the great audience chamber in the Castello. I wanted the trial to be impeccable and thus more severe. As the hour came and went and the accused did not appear, we sent people to his house and discovered that he had fled. The podestà, who held the acts of accusation, was outraged.

"So it is! Tolomeo Spagnoli has fled. He pretended to agree in order to gain time."

"Signor podestà," Sigismondo asked, "are you absolutely sure of his flight?"

"Yes. He was seen riding toward Verona. The Council of Justice could, if authorized, proceed against Spagnoli in contumacy."

Sigismondo, pensive, murmured: "Sister-in-law, we must be careful. A commission had just arrived from Rome with a brief of His Holiness Leo the Tenth. It says that Spagnoli is being unjustly persecuted and his trial should be suspended."

"Or perhaps annulled!" the podestà cried. "Signora marchesana, the people have a right to investigate the activities of government officials."

Like a gust of wind the canon Alessandro Spagnoli entered, Tolomeo's brother and business associate. He looked around with furious eyes. In a calm and, I believe, ironic voice, I allowed myself the pleasure of inviting him to speak. "Monsignor Alessandro, give us news of your brother Tolomeo."

"My brother has fled, and rightly. A knight of his rank should not be forced to defend himself."

"He should have defended himself," the podestà replied curtly. "The people have called him to justice."

"Tolomeo Spagnoli is the victim of conspiracies, I proclaim that by my faith in God."

"Here are proofs of his misdeeds," the podestà rebutted, waving his papers. "They are eyewitness depositions, signed before notaries. The accusation is of falsifying documents, abuse of trust, harassment, unlawful appropriation. It is all proven."

"Lies, base calumny!"

"Have you forgotten, Monsignor, when your brother had the feet of the priest of Asola held in a fire?" the podestà insisted. "And plunged his arms in boiling water?"

"That man was a lunatic!"

"And was it because of his madness that the poor man was forced to cede the income of his church to you? Is that true?"

Spagnoli writhed. But there was no way out for him. I could rely on the podestà; we had conferred at length, and the documents left no room for doubt. The Dominican complained that everyone was envious of the many kindnesses their family had received from the late marchese Francesco, rest his soul. I felt myself turn pale.

"Signora marchesana," the podestà said, "may I proceed with this trial, in the name of the citizens of Mantua?"

I addressed Spagnoli icily: "Monsignor Spagnoli, tell us your arguments in favor of stopping the course of justice."

He rebelled, as if bitten by an asp. "Signora," he shouted, "you are a vindictive woman. For years you have harbored rancor against my poor brother. Now you want to ruin him, trample him, crush him."

I heaved a great sigh. My moment had come. "It is not I who ask justice. You have heard the podestà. It is the people of Mantua. If I had wished to punish your brother for his insults to me, I would have taken other steps. But Tolomeo Spagnoli betrayed the trust of his master in order to oppress the people; it is right that he be judged by the citizens and that his crimes be publicly revealed."

"We will not allow ourselves to be intimidated by contemptible plots," Spagnoli replied venomously. "I will go to Rome. There I will find justice, and the punishment of His Holiness will strike all." And he went on threatening.

"Signor podestà," I said in a very clear voice, "begin the trial and let the examination of the proofs be entrusted to three professors. Inform us the day of the sentence."

THAT day came quickly; the podestà acted with irked speed. I suspected his wrath had a personal reason, but I was unable to find it. So I had to conclude that his was a public wrath and thus more direct and violent, without passion. One morning the cardinal and I were summoned to the tribunal.

That September morning, still warm and bright, I put on a silk dress, almost black, lightly embroidered in silver, with a bodice of black-and-white stripes and a gorget, also white and simply embroidered; no jewels, except for a chain of finest gold wound about my neck, the ends falling on my bosom; in my hand a white veil, for my shoulders. The mirror reflected a young face, somehow glowing. We rode in a brief procession, the cardinal, I, my women, Pirro Donati, and Mario Equicola. Our own guards, dressed in yellow, on black horses, followed us. We got down at the tribunal, protected by the city guards, and we began to climb the steep stairway. The immense hall was deserted. As is my habit, I had arrived too early. I was goaded by my impatience for action, and perhaps instinctively I remembered my father, Ercole, who deliberately, regularly arrived early for meetings, public gatherings, and even the play. "Those few minutes are always an advantage, to learn something further," he used to say.

The podestà was advised, and I entered the hall, an almost endless rectangular space, illuminated by big triple-arched windows. Some attendants moved rapidly between light and shadow, setting things in order. This hall of justice had its own majesty, this place where the people of Mantua dealt with their public questions with such easy freedom. On occasion I had attended ceremonies here, and debates concerning our people. In the same hall, completely frescoed with ancient scenes, faded but still legible, there were counters set up in various points: the stand of the gold merchant and money changer; the stand of tradesmen; the great table of the weavers and the capmakers. In front of the wall at the end, justice was administered. A tall bench with a polished wooden back, with seats for the judges, was flanked by stools and by two smaller benches; over the right-hand one were the gilded words *Porta Paradisi*, and over its twin on the left, the gilded words *Porta Inferi*. According to the verdict, the sentence would be pronounced from one bench or the other.

"This," Equicola said, "is an important day. Everyone is awaiting the conclusion of Spagnoli's trial, and as long as the reading of the papers and the sentence lasts, trading will be suspended."

We advanced with measured steps, conversing. The day with

its blue sky, the warm murmur of the crowd that rose from the market square, the flying shadows of doves that dipped and darted festively at the windows did not help me. Into my mind came a Latin phrase preserved in my memory, and I wondered if it was some remote schoolroom reading, a Ciceronian exercise. It expounded this notion: When a man is sentenced to death, even if the sentence is just, the air itself grieves.

Perhaps Pirro Donati realized that I was bowing my head without complaining, but as if complaining; he turned toward me and, with smiling eyes, pointed out the empty place of the legumes vendor; at that very spot, during Francesco's imprisonment in Venice, there had been those memorable sales of the grain of my lands. Pirro in a whisper imitated the cries of the buyers and the sellers: "Twenty-five pence! Twenty-five, twenty-eight! Twenty-five! Thirty!" And he continued the tale: "The price of the grain was rising, and the shadow of scarcity, perhaps famine becoming evident, and then I cried, 'Ten pence the bushel, the grain of the marchesana! She wants prices to remain low!' " He mimed the amazement of the merchants and the traders and the joy of the buyers. That day I was acclaimed savior of the people.

We took our seats on the bench with the high back, near the chair of the podestà, and in the meanwhile, the three famous jurists who had conducted the investigation made their entrance. On the stools perpendicular to the great bench were seated Equicola, Pirro Donati, my women; opposite us the officers of justice were aligned. Gradually the people, in little curious groups, filled the enormous empty space of the hall. When everything was ready, the podestà initiated the reading of the trial documentation. One by one, Tolomeo Spagnoli's misdeeds filed past as laborers carried, stuck into a square base, a wooden outline crudely painted to represent him; this is the custom in our city when the accused is contumacious. At the end of the reading the chief judge stood up and went to the bench of the *Porta Inferi*. Over the agitated, swelling murmur in the room the podestà's voice rose, as he read the sentence.

It had not been possible also to try Alessandro Spagnoli, Tolomeo's brother and accomplice. On his side the canon had the pope himself, who demanded an ecclesiastical court to judge Monsignor Alessandro.

"Let the Dominican go for now; we'll deal with him later," I murmured to myself, alert to every word, which I drank in with punitive impatience. Only this mattered: Tolomeo Spagnoli, guilty of proven crimes, had been sentenced in contumacy by the Council of Justice, condemned to the pain of death and the confiscation of his property except his children's legitimate share. The sentence would be promulgated in all the squares of Mantua and through the countryside.

Cries of assent rose from all sides, mixed with disparaging epithets and raucous insults; they grew louder, became yells. As our guards lined up on either side to make way for us, the wooden shape representing Tolomeo swayed under the blows of rotten fruit and vegetables, amid curses and jeers. The people's wrath caressed my ear; their contempt and derision were finally applied to that hated name. The wooden shape fell down, to bloodthirsty curses. I would have stayed to watch the spectacle if the podestà, grave and stately, had not offered me his hand, to escort me. At the door we came face-to-face with our people; the wrathful cries were drowned out by the cheers of my Mantuans. Some of the women touched my dress furtively. On my face I felt the warm September sun, we went toward our horses, the guards hastily formed ranks, the procession was recomposed, and the whole market was now calling me by name in the old way of the people, "Isabella-bella," "Isabella-bella."

After passing through the court of the castle, I arrived at my room with the initials, a bit breathless because I had rushed up the stairs, flying. My women came to me, happily congratulating, and to be even more festive, they insisted on changing my dress. But, then, what was the harsh taste that embittered my breath? "Tolomeo," I said softly. The name is made of ashes.

THAT time, which was preparing the upheaval of the world, proved ineffably ripe and hale for me. I spent many hours of the day in the chancellery. I saw and foresaw from every angle. Beyond any doubt, a rivalry was forming between the new king of Spain, Charles the Fifth, born the same year as Federico, and Francis the First, young men both and full of an ambition that might rush them into dangerous decisions. They seemed always on the point of coming to threaten each other on the hapless terrain of Italy. Seeing them in perspective, truly shrewd and foresighted people remained in suspense; all prognostication was dubious.

From Alemagna came bad news. Alert minds were perturbed by the religious revolt of the monk Martin Luther, but we were still far from the conflagration of that reform. In the midst of these storm clouds, Mantua maintained its reputation as one of the liveliest cities of Europe, where feasts, music, tournaments displayed a refinement still unknown at most courts. An unwelcome primacy was given to the city by the number of its duels, which we Gonzagas abhorred. Men have a consuming desire to measure themselves with blows of the sword, and the more they are civilly educated, the more they are attracted by the desire to kill one one another.

To Mantua came whole companies of gentlemen escorting duelists such as that Camillo Gozadino, publicly challenged by Emilio Marescotti. And many people, summoned by those mortal games, swarmed in from places in the vicinity, to witness the fighting on the field that we had been obliged to grant. This particular case drove His Holiness to send us a brief of solemn censure. Federico and I, to satisfy the pope, following also our own wishes, so exerted ourselves that we convinced Marescotti to withdraw the challenge and declare the falsity of the accusation: that Gozadino had witnessed without intervening the murder of Ercole Marescotti, Emilio's father. And in the end there was general peace.

It is impossible to describe the foreigners' fascination with us, with our knowledge of life and the fine living at court. I opened my halls of the castle every day after dinner to ladies, gentlemen, prelates, and noblemen, and I received them in my usual familiar style. My women and girls were always busy, taking care about their dress, the arrangement of their hair, inventing pranks and jokes, and, above all, learning new songs. The festivities became more frequent in early July, when the news came from Frankfurt that Charles the Fifth had been elected emperor, as Maximilian of Hapsburg had died a year before. Francis the First had set in motion great maneuvers to gain the title of Caesar, king of the Romans, but the electors finally preferred Charles, arousing the spiteful anger of the French. Since our fiefdom is imperial, we had to celebrate, and we did so in the merriest of fashions, calling pages and youths to perform plays, and singers—we gathered more than sixty in one evening—and ladies and good dancers. And for the banquets, too, we did not fail in our duty.

But I grew sad, more than slightly sad, when I looked at our delightfully bedecked rooms, crowded with festive people, and thought of the tormented time that my brother Alfonso was undergoing. In June he had lost his wife, Lucrezia Borgia, and had mourned her with a grief I would never have thought credible. I was even more stunned, toward the end of the year, by a letter from him with some singular news. To the queen of France, who was proposing to him a new marriage with a French noblewoman, Alfonso had sent word that he would never marry again, he, a man of forty-five, with the responsibility of five small children. In this letter there were clear signs of something radiant, shining, and truthful. For no reason would he have his wife's place taken by another. "I could never force my spirit," Alfonso said to me, among other things, warning me absolutely not to fall in with that idea, a sharp admonition, revealing true repugnance. So he had loved her, and she, him, in a mysterious way. But what sort of feeling had bound Lucrezia, then, to Francesco? This question prompted contradictory answers.

The attracting affection of youth had certainly influenced both brother-in-law and sister-in-law, as they found themselves in a tide of passion. But after the death of Ercole Strozzi, their go-between, something occurred, thanks to an unspoken accord between me and Alfonso, that kept the two of them separated. They never saw, never met each other again, and often I laughed to myself at the plots they hatched and we foiled, one after the other. And passion had been forced to transform itself into a friendship with an underlying devotion that made them feel innocent in their constant search for each other. And while she held her husband in fiery love, she refreshed her spirit with Francesco and enjoyed with him an ambiguous tenderness.

A truth was burning inside me. I had never been told anything by Alfonso—there are no confidences between us—but I had been informed by Lorenzo Strozzi that the two in-laws, remaining separated, wrote each other in amorous, though not unchaste, spirit. And I had been the one to give all of them their own love stories: conjugal harmony to Lucrezia and Alfonso and ardent and yet very sweet separations to the two lovers. What delight Francesco must have felt in preparing for Lucrezia the handsome palace toward San Sebastiano, where he would have lived near her if Pope Julius, conquering Ferrara, had forced her to go into exile. Julius had died, events had taken a different course, but the secret affection, creator of that hope, had gone on. I had acted, sure of making them suffer, and they had fulfilled themselves in cautious, grand tenderness. My brother, not in the least disarmed by doubts, wanted only to have his wife all for himself carnally. I thought I had won, and I had been defeated forever.

I no longer wanted to hear the prompting of other visions,

but I was surprised, the moment I perceived it, by the absence
of the Englishman Robert de la Pole. It was now five years
since he had last written, and I should think of him as a closed
episode. And yet that unusual story of his, which left me intact,
sealed in my integrity, had powers of its own, nevertheless.

V

Federico, My Soul

O N M Y H E A D I wear the crown, a queen's crown, concrete sign of power. My bearing assumes a regality that, from above, descends along my person, falling like a cloak. Perhaps the coiffure I am inventing is an allusion to that imaginary crown, a hairstyle that will circulate through the world, imitated by all women. The first times I display it at my receptions as chief of state, it provokes some hesitation; we are too accustomed to hair being combed flat or gathered, with hair loose, or braided and coiled in a knot, or in a half braid falling down the back. I set a new style, appearing with this arrangement that suggests a turban or a diadem. Colored, of starched tulle, decorated soberly, but with glints, embroidery, and ribbon, or reinforced with light fabrics, the headdress submits freely to any whim. I now wear it adorned with strands of small or medium-sized pearls, often twisted into a spiral. My maids are keen to try it, but I will not allow them. For them I will find some style that does not suggest such authority.

In that year, 1519, a great knight appeared as protagonist on the Mantuan scene, an emblem of our time, universally hailed as champion of faith and virtue and confirmed as such on all sides: Count Baldesar Castiglione, our beloved fellow citizen, first counselor at Urbino at the time of the duke Guidobaldo and my Elisabetta, and always faithful to us even when sent away from court after a disagreement with Francesco. But at the fall of the della Rovere family, crushed by the bitter greed of Leo the Tenth, he returned to us, reconciled, and was immediately placed in charge of our transactions, versed as he was in every political argument and in all other possible arguments.

Baldesar was a man quick to anger, unreasonable. His eyes would blaze before he gave consent—a handsome gentleman somewhat severe in appearance, at times witty and smiling, and then irresistible. Four years my junior, now and then he seemed to me older. His wisdom had ripened in the Milanese schools of the Sforzas' universities with the Greek masters Calcondila and

Giorgio Marullo, and in Milan I also met him, at the wedding of Beatrice to the Moro, in that period illuminated by every glory of letters and the arts. He shone supremely in his talent for writing, displayed with his unique *Book of the Courtier*, a very bible of the society of our courts, a work somewhat rigid with moral pretensions. For me this great knight always seemed to lack suppleness, but his fidelity and affection were to be prized above all, and also his patience, that of a man who took others' problems to heart and could assume their burden even when he did not approve of them.

Now he was in Rome, our ambassador to Leo the Tenth, who esteemed him highly for his alert mind, and from that city Baldesar sent us letters, precise and very sharp comments on Vatican life. Reading those detailed dispatches, I learned lessons of the most advanced political practice, even if at times their excessive impartiality made them almost abstract. His mother, Aloisia, of the house of Gonzaga, resembled her son in that sort of inflexible wisdom and lightness of mind; she used to tell me how, at her request, he had sent her some of that "red cloth" that we moisten and rub on the face to give it color. He actually procured for her a whole little sheet of it, and then, not entirely convinced of his purchase, he decided to try it out on the cheeks of a workman with very pale complexion. The result was excellent, but Aloisia and I could not stop laughing at the thought of the made-up servant moving through the embassy's rooms under our envoy's critical eye.

It is not easy to know how to read dispatches, not so much Castiglione's always clear, beautiful ones as the infinite others that perhaps announce tales of deception impossible to prove. When my brother Alfonso was seriously ill, I went mad reading through all those papers; it seemed at every moment that whole armies threatened the city of Ferrara. Profoundly uneasy, I warned him, reporting the plots and the messages that told of soldiers poised for the conquest in the name of the pope, with the consent of the king of France and the emperor. Alfonso thanked me, underwent his convalescence, continued to proclaim himself free of matrimonial plans, and remained calm. Once and for all, he said to me, let anyone come who wishes, he will taste my artillery; it takes more than shadows to frighten me. I learned painfully, but I did learn to distinguish which news had some probability of being true or at least half true. As for Castiglione, his unswerving loyalty occasionally misled him. Though he duly recorded the duplicity of Pope Leo, he did not doubt the pontiff's assertion that he had nothing to do with the plots against Ferrara. I had irrefutable proof to the contrary, however.

We also made use of expert informers and were warned that in Mantua there were some false friars going about, papal spies, who had come to make sure of our loyalty. Further, Leo more and more preferred Tolomeo Spagnoli, now installed at his court, and called him a "rare man," though I could not say where his rarity lay if not in his rascality. Had not his own brother, Canon Alessandro, said that if the ducats in Tolomeo's purse were chopped in half, the blood of the poor would gush out? This man incited the pope and the French to move their troops against Ferrara and against Mantua; he had even prepared a division of our lands: Ferrara to the French; Mantua divided between the pope and the Venetians. A correspondent of ours in Rome, Feltrio, criticized us for having let Camposampiero and Spagnoli leave. "They should have met the end of Rozone," he added, "for in all Italy there are no worse traitors than they."

More and more I realize that to reign means to live in a tight spiral of words from which we try to free ourselves, to find again the straight line of true discernment. But are these words right either? Does true discernment really move in a straight line or does it exploit serpentine coils, sly, even painful? And yet the flash of good perception is like an acrobat's leap: He does not sway in the air; he springs and arrives. So I would like to arrive, in thinking and judging. The crown is on my head, and I turn my neck slowly in a majestic movement that corresponds to my thoughts. And yet I feel always drawn to the capacity for enjoying the charm of life, the sublime grace of music, the splendor of nature and the arts. I am drawn also to play: chess, charades, riddles. I have an old passion, often denied, for theater and for poetry, and I enjoy knowing many things, in order to be more entertained by all the riches that exist in the world.

I have almost inexhaustible springs of the strength that especially acts on Federico. My soul, my son, is now a young man, tall, slim, with dark eyes, my eyes, absolutely mine. He already holds the title of Marchese of Mantua, and soon he will be its absolute lord. My regent's crown will fly away from my head, losing one by one its fragile plumes. I regret nothing. I know that for me the crown is only a test, and the true crown will be set only on the head of my son. But he will never do without me. He becomes radiant when I explain something to him, as if I were revealing secrets of genius or the working of the mental machines that stir men. He has a great desire to enjoy himself and great ease of manner, a regal grace in giving and receiving flattery and compliments, but in his depths I alone can suspect a shadow of awkwardness, an inner check not yet dissolved even by his familiarity with those exquisite ladies of France and by the boldness I allow in my maidens. I must give my teachings a practical solidity, an awareness of that rarefied hauteur that his future destiny as a prince demands.

AMONG Mantua's convents this one has always been my favorite. It belongs to Dominican nuns, active in their work and in their studies, as in their prayers. It houses a nun-mathematician, short and dark-skinned, who combines the mysticism of a religious with that of a scientist; two nun-theologians, furious rivals as theologians always are; a Latinist, scholar of Titus Livy; and a Greek specialist in Plutarch. There are other nuns less gifted for scholarship, some excellent cooks of foods, humble but accented in their homely goodness with a touch of originality. The church is simple and airy, a single nave, and the cloister is airy, too, with its little Lombard columns and fine-ribbed arches. All is painted a milky color in the room where they dine, a vast ground-floor hall with caplike vaults, little columns pursuing one another all around, in a light race, and their shaded tone joined with the pearliness of the walls suggests an interplay of clarities, like a song. The room can be entered directly from the church or from the cloister, though then you must first pass through the larder and the kitchen.

AUTUMN was about to end. Fireplaces and braziers emitted hot gusts, and as the cold was not yet piercing, we savored the pleasures of winter without suffering from it. Naturally I entered by way of the cloister, through the larder and kitchen. With the ever keen instinct of the mistress of a house, I unobtrusively examined the rooms and the things prepared for the meal. I cannot remember why, but that was a day of abstinence. Such meals put cooks to the test, and in fact, I was reassured to see, already prepared on the tables in the larder, pike in jelly, roast sturgeon, stewed eels, stuffed eggs. Rice cakes, not yet dropped into the boiling oil, would open the dinner along with the spicy or sweet appetizers. I advanced and discovered hot vegetable pies, marzipan, cream tubes, fruit jellies, milk and honey puddings with cakes. The troops were in order. In that stark atmosphere the nuns traced gestures inscribed in a conventual geometry. Against the walls the pure, starched whites of their aprons and hoods stood out, and the creamy whites of the Dominican habits. Hands with slender or stumpy fingers, chapped and very clean, aligned the plates on a long table; from the chapel next door came the choir of novices.

FROM the Convent of San Vincenzo my daughter Ippolita, eight years a nun, has now arrived; she is barely twenty. Every time I see her again my heart makes a leap, too much, almost excessively, and more and more as time passes, does she resemble her father. She exchanges greetings with Livia, whom I have brought with me from the castle. Livia is already a novice, but her age, eleven years, still cannot dampen her innate gaiety, as she announces to her sister the arrival of their brother Ercole, the prothonotary, and Ferrante, with his short sword on his hip. Here they are; the four of them form a group, still so close to their childhood that they immediately lapse into their playful family language. And from the church our guests enter: Matteo Bandello, the monk and poet and storyteller; Baldesar Castiglione, just back from Rome, having taken his leave of the pope; and Mario Equicola, my chief secretary and teacher. I enjoy the presence of my children. Federico is absent, off with his gentlemen on a hunt, but the four young ones, without their tutors, lighthearted and free, warm my soul. Meanwhile, the nuns in the kitchen have knelt before Ercole, who blesses them. Livia, a born wit, points at her brother Ercole and protests: "Brother dear, how awkwardly you give your blessing! You look like the archdeacon of Gabbioneta."

Ercole, his back stiff, assumes an ecclesiastical gravity, singularly expressive for a youth of fourteen, but he blushes as Ippolita gently reproaches Livia.

Instinctively the novice insists: "Go on, brother, try again!"

Patiently Ercole essays another benediction.

"That's better," Ippolita says. "When you are a prince of the Church, you will bless very well."

Ferrante interrupts in a loud voice: "I will defend the Church with my sword."

"My dear Ferrante," Ippolita says, "surely you will not defend this pope, who is such an enemy of our house?"

Livia, as could be expected, seizes the occasion to reply. "Leave the pope alone, Ferrante's godfather. You know he is the godson of Pope Leo? He even wears the pope's arms over his shoulder!"

Ferrante, irked, rips off the sash, draws his little sword, and cuts away the Medici arms. Then he tramples on it, nervously tearing it again, and shouts, "You see? You see whether or not I am one of his men!"

I try to calm my children. Ferrante, with his head of tight blond curls, looks like a sulky shepherd. It is time to go to the table; in the hall there is also Pirro Donati, and he jokes happily with my daughters. He has a young granddaughter who is a novice, and he displays a discreet affection toward the nuns. Madama Laura, my kinswoman and companion, sits next to Bandello, followed by Ercole, and after Ercole come Ippolita and Pirro Donati. On the other side, Mario Equicola and Castiglione; the children at the end of the table, at left and right. A prayer is chanted. They begin by passing rose water, warmed, for our hands. Then the dishes come around, one after the other. Sister Taddea approaches to apologize for her meatless meal, which today does not seem worthy of the guests' rank. I reassure her. We are here not to feast but to enjoy one another's company in this holy place. Equicola cannot refrain from uttering a detested name: "Tolomeo Spagnoli hates us for having had him condemned. He and his brother Alessandro are turning Italy upside down."

"Perhaps it is ingenuous of me," I say softly, "but I must ask myself how he has won the pope's favor."

Equicola reacts to this prompting. "He took away from Mantua a wagon loaded with sacks of gold."

"What a thief!" Bandello remarks.

I hint that in my opinion, Tolomeo Spagnoli matters little to the pope. Leo pretends to esteem him in order to use him as an indirect spy; the pope knows that Spagnoli's accomplices in Mantua keep an eye on our every movement, and this makes us feel uneasy. Leo has not forgiven us for granting refuge to the duke and duchess of Urbino, and he must hold against us many other things that we will never know.

Castiglione joins in the conversation. "The bad thing is that Tolomeo, being with the pope, never ceases his evil work. And he is such an expert liar that often he makes his listeners even doubt the truth."

"He would deserve a nice dagger thrust, which would free us of him," Equicola murmurs.

I take exception. "Signor Equicola, we cannot become assassins in order to rid Mantua of a traitor. Even betrayal must be fought with fair weapons. Signor Castiglione, dear friend, you should return to Rome and try once more to regain the pope's friendship for us."

"My lady, I have tried everything. My hand has cramps from all my writing to you and to the duke of Urbino, trying to follow the pope's hazy notions day by day. Ever since I arrived in Rome, in May, just after the death of the Magnifico Lorenzo, I hammered ceaselessly, taking every opportunity to mention the return of the della Roveres on a thousand different pretexts, but the pope's only reply was to incorporate Urbino among the possessions of the Church. He considers my lord Francesco Maria untrustworthy, his natural enemy, even if at times he makes a show of referring to the duke more benevolently. Urbino is a source of hatred for him, that calm but deeply rooted hatred of his."

"Precisely because the times and men are our enemies, you must return to Rome," I insist warmly, and I add that only he, with his generous way of speaking, can dismantle the treacheries constructed by Spagnoli; only he can pierce the pope's aversion to its distant roots and transform venom into honey.

Castiglione heaves a great sigh and bows his head politely. His distress continues, but his opposition is relaxing. The moment has come to press the secret spring that would change the tone. I ask my gentlemen to give us news of Raffaello and of his new work in the Vatican. The shift of subject succeeds. Castiglione's eyes light up at the thought of his friend, and he starts telling about the loggia frescoed with Bible stories and decorated with stucco, and he says that this work is wondrously beautiful and perhaps the most beautiful thing to be seen today copied from the antique.

"Signor Castiglione, would you kindly eat, please?" at that moment Tortorina, my maiden, says. "Unless you wish to fast in honor of San Raffaello."

All laugh. Equicola then takes the floor, to praise the constant jubilation of Rome. Our correspondents inform us daily how the pope is constantly at festivities, plays, the hunt, and, above all, how conquered he is by music. He has ordered a concert of forty-two excellent players. And a singular thing: Leo the Tenth laughs superficially at every sort of jest even if the wit is not of great artifice; but when it comes to music he demands nothing but the best, and he takes profound delight in the metaphysical essences of sounds.

"You are fortunate, Signor Castiglione, that you can live at a court of such pleasures," Iva cries, "but how will our court live without its perfect master, Count Baldesar?"

"Am I not here? And do we not have with us Matteo Bandello?" Equicola says with feigned offense. "He, even though a monk, can truly keep you merry with the mad tales that come into his mind."

"Fra Matteo," Tortorina says, assuming an ingenuous expression, "the other day you did not finish your story as the hour was late. You have not told us what your Sempliciano did after putting Togna on the bench."

Bandello bursts into vast laughter, his face pink, and he declaims: "He kissed her bosom and her long, fat, and rough breasts—"

I stamped my foot under the table. "Matteo Bandello! Not here! Every now and then you randy men try to elude my control." I turn again to Castiglione. "What do you say, Signor Baldesar? As the pope is so hostile, we are reluctant to send our Ercole to Rome when the moment comes, to the great school of theology. I am thinking of sending him to the Studium of Bologna, where Master Peretto, our Mantuan philosopher, teaches."

Equicola, who cannot bear Pomponazzi, asserts that this bizarre man is more Jew than Christian and quotes erroneously his book on the immortality of the soul. I have read it, and I have often repeated to myself a concept of his that struck me: Virtue needs no reward since its reward is virtue itself.

Equicola raises his hands to heaven. "Good God! That does not seem to me the proposition of a good Christian; I catch a whiff of diabolical pride." And, as if hurling an anathema, he cries: "Get thee behind me, behind me!"

I restrain his tirade, assuring him—what is true—that Cardinal Sigismondo has assured me Master Peretto is a good Christian. My son Ercole, respectful but resolute, affirms that he would gladly go to the school of Bologna. He knows one can study well there, and besides, that city is not far from Mantua. At every opportunity, in a short time, he could come home. I remark that this is not the chief reason that would lead me to choose Bologna. Immediately Ferrante, in a sharp tone, boasts as little boys do, that he will go farther off, to Spain, to the court of the emperor Charles the Fifth. And he calls me as his witness.

"And I? Where will I go?" Livia suddenly burst out, with her promptness of speech that displeases me more in her than in the others, perhaps because she resembles me and should not.

I answer that she will stay in Mantua, in a happy house of nuns, perhaps this same Santa Paola. She and her sister Ippolita have been granted the grace of being brides of Christ. More gently

I say that our family now counts on their prayers, and I hope they will help me live amid the painful turmoil of the world. Both girls bow their head, nodding assent with a pride that seems to want to dominate their bewilderment; emotion throbs in them, and perhaps an ill-tamed sense of rebellion. I remain pensive for a moment, amazed at feeling a twinge of remorse for what I have said. Ippolita has become used to her vocation, but Livia is still stung by the merciless reminders of her future. At that moment my protective instinct flares up, and I promise Livia that I will have her take singing lessons from our best court musician; we will train her voice. She raises her face, more amazed than pleased; she does not believe me.

To the Most Illustrious and Excellent Signora Isabella, Marchesana of Mantua, My Lady

From the Field of the Cloth of Gold, Near Calais

After six years I do not know whether or not I have been forgiven for a letter of mine from London full of unguarded pages that I subsequently begged you not to read. Finally I lack the heart to resist, and I assume that a woman of your character would surely have found a way to convey her outrage, or I would somehow have heard of it. I am not one of those people who flinch at enigmas. Indeed, I like enigmas; the play of words attracts me when the thought is freely concealed in it. But a more inspired idea now makes me summon my courage again and, I believe, forever. You will not doubt this feeling, I hope, which calls my soul toward yours and at times almost drives me mad in a solitude full of sorrows. But how is it possible not to see; when the light strikes us clearly, how can a lucid mind be deceived? Finally a sudden thought blinded my eyes with truth. For, my revered lady, refusal means rejection, but as far as I know, you have never rejected my letters; you have not bundled them up, sent them back to my hands, the seals perhaps still unbroken. You have saved those pages. I sought a sign from you, and for a long time I did not realize that this was, in fact, your sign, our pact: silence. How much suffering was spared, how much sleeplessness overcome, how many questions allayed by the mere thought of your acceptance.

Forgive this joyous excitement. Guaranteed by your repulse, my freedom is now complete. It is exciting to ask myself what can have been pleasing to you that came from me: the information about new or unknown things; the attempt to satisfy in advance your appetite for knowledge, something I know you love supremely. Or do you prefer the argument you surely raise against me, against my devotion and admiration of your free, imperious spirit, merry, at times savagely resolute? I want to write you, my lady. From today on you cannot save yourself anymore. Knowing I am accepted, I will tell you everything, or much at least, of what happens around me, and I will compare the universe with you. The world is bloated with events, and I know you sense it. Shall we compete to see who can foretell them, with intuitive mind?

I am here at the Field of the Cloth of Gold, as this place has been called, scene of an extraordinary meeting between my king, Henry the Eighth of England, and Francis the First of France, to discuss the familiar subject of European peace. Six miles from Calais lies the county of Guînes, an English possession in France, and here we are camped. Nine miles from Calais, in the town of Ardres, are the French.

It is sad to think how sometimes people are not in their right place; it is as if there were black gaps in a shining sky. How well you would fit here, dear queen, so human and proud, to temper these sovereigns' spirits at the meeting in the French camp, where a hundred tents have been raised, of gold, silver, brocade, velvet. The king lives in this tent city like a Mongol emperor, in a kind of palace of silk and gold, all spangled with the lily of France. We English do not easily allow ourselves to be outdone. My king has ordered a palace of painted paper, boldly set on a foundation of bricks, and has entrusted the supervision of its construction to our great cardinal, Wolsey, his most trusted adviser. The cardinal's imagination has outstripped his king's, and he has created a palace, half in colored canvas and half in glass, where columns of pink crystal alternate with gleaming windows, a true stage scene, magical in its appearance. The men who move on this illuminated set, among its iridescent glints, are dressed in gold, decked with gems. And with equal pomp the men come from the tents decorated with the French lily.

Never again will people be able to admire such a sumptuous display: trumpets and trumpeters, troops in dazzling overgarments beneath the banners, and men rushing on every side among the tents of satin and velvet, their pinnacles surmounted by slender pennons. Perhaps you alone, with your accurate, direct gaze that can victoriously fix images in your mind, can imagine the regal splendor of this encounter and understand immediately how a shadowed air could breathe among tourneys, parades, and noisy banquets. For the more we see the two kings exchange gifts, publicly embrace, and ride as equals, followed by their four hundred guards, the more some vague suspicions seem to circulate. Or (perhaps I know it well and would like not to know it) behind our two sovereigns, so full of jollity, physical sturdiness, royal splendor, and ambition, there is someone who is directing the thoughts of all. I am sure you are already saying his name. Yes, it is Charles the Fifth, the emperor, who managed to gain the title through the wise employment of two tons of gold against the ton and a half of his antagonist Francis. Charles is also young, but youth is depicted differently on his worn face.

I must inform you that at the royal joust my king was knocked to the ground before hundreds of simpering ladies and gentlemen. Francis won; Henry had to bear the humiliation. If you had only seen the glorious audacity of the king of France! But Henry, shrewder, has already set a date to meet Charles at Calais, in two weeks. This very young emperor knows how to use moderate words, and he already knows his job so well that he advances calm and quite concrete proposals, supported by an exceptional man, his secretary Gattinara.

From the intrigues of this earth to the debates over heaven. Have you heard anything, my lady, of the revolution threatened by the writings of Brother Martin Luther? I believe you have. The Augustinian friar of Wittenberg for years has been preaching violently against the Church of Rome, and in the Curia it is known that Pope Leo, in his way, is aghast at those cold but fervent criticisms. It seems he actually said to one ambassador: "I would give Bologna to silence this monk."

It is doubtful that he will be silent. That preacher is somehow tireless in his mind, his studies, and his reforming determination. A born theologian, at thirty-seven he has already glossed the Psalms and the Epistle to the Romans of Saint Paul, and has written books, and sent outcries of protest against the Roman Church, in a tone capable of making the whole Christian world blanch. Surely your brother-in-law, the most reverend Cardinal Gonzaga must have spoken to you about him. Three years ago, with a determined act of revolt, Luther nailed to the door of the Church of All Saints in Wittenberg, where he lives in the Augustinian convent, the thunderous ninety-five theses of his dispute on ecclesiastical indulgences, proposing those theses as an occasion for public debate.

I will tell you, my lady most beloved in spirit, that there is a kind of resounding beauty in the Augustinian monk-reformer, though I do not share his doctrine. And surely for the German church, enormous wealth has been fatal, driving the nobility to parcel out among its members the church's offices, especially the posts of canon in the cathedral chapters. The young canons cause great scandal with their lascivious and opulent living; on the other hand, the humble clergymen have no prebends or even a fixed salary, and they must live by expedients, not all of them religious. And further, is there not also a determined aversion, I would say almost inborn in the race, in the blood of the German people against the pope and the Roman Curia? Rome is attacked not for reasons of faith but because of the assignment of benefices and the imposition of taxes made by the authority of the pope. And what pebble was it, my lady, that risks becoming a frightful avalanche? Close to us and—it seems impossible—only a few years ago it was the preaching of a Dominican, subcommissioner general of Archbishop Albert of Brandenburg, who had been given the right to sell indulgences for the fabric of Saint Peter's. To be sure, the offerings of the faithful would never have gone toward raising the greatest temple of Christianity; they served to pay the debt Prince Albert had contracted with a bank to obtain from Pope Leo his appointment as archbishop.

It is superlatively scandalous that indulgences are granted not only to the living but also to the dead. If, to have one, the living must confess themselves and repent, for the dead the oblation itself suffices, and further, the indulgence can be applied to a specific soul. To follow the sermons of the Dominican Tetzel, I assure you, is enough to make you shudder. There is a quip going the rounds, more or less to this effect: "When the money falls into the box, the soul springs, blessed, out of purgatory." And this has prompted, and still prompts, laughter, scorn, and revolt. The Wittenberg friar immediately published a blazing sermon on indulgences and on the remission of sins.

I have too many things to tell you, my lady, about this great earthquake that has begun to shake the foundations of the authority of papal power and of the Holy Roman Church. Are we to hope that before our eyes we have the reform that for all these years the best minds have demanded, to remove the many incrustations of error that have formed within the Church? What could happen, in the onrush of a wave, too lashing for our holy and benevolent religion?

You will recall Erasmus of Rotterdam; I spoke to you about him when I had the ineffable joy of living in the same house in Venice, where both of us were guests of Aldus Manutius. This beacon of European culture, friend of so many scholars, author of the ebullient *Praise of Folly*, a satire on the presumption of scholars and the scandalous immorality of the clergy, after having spent some years in London and having taught at Cambridge, is now in Basel, engaged in the famous editions of the New Testament and *The Fathers of the Church*, which he is still studying, in order to complete his work.

I tell you these things, my lady, because some legends are being repeated: Though Erasmus is perhaps the greatest man of culture in our time, in Italy, except in the academies, he is not especially praised. And a spirit like yours cannot dismiss him from your mind. Imagine, now, what the uprisings of the Wittenberg friar can have meant in the world of a man like Erasmus. At the beginning Luther's polemic appealed to him, the invective against the Roman Church found him in agreement; but then the revolution became too violent and disturbed him deeply. A certain cynicism on the reformer's part, a hostility toward culture faced Erasmus with a constant inner conflict, as he believes in culture above all things. Reading his letters, you sense his effort to reconcile Luther's Christianity with the Christianity of Catholicism.

To see that great spirit painfully seek equilibrium, arriving at the verge of compromise, distresses Erasmus's true friends. And yet a legion of fanatical rebels calls him roughly into the fray, and he will have to make a pronouncement. All the cultivated men of Europe and all its politicians, too, and even the populace are anxious to hear his decision. But Erasmus can think only that the accumulated study aimed at rediscovering human clarity will be flung into the void under the Lutherans' attacks. These are deaf times, filled with grim warnings and provoking such distress of intellect and soul that there is no one who is not uneasy.

My lady, I would so like to know if the core of these things that agitate the world interests your imagination. Looking through the window, supported by slim glass columns, in my little room here at the Field of the Cloth of Gold, in this contest of ostentation between two kings, like something in ancient history that would demand a Titus Livy, I feel in anxious suspense both for those not commited to a true and good accord and for the more distant rumbling of the storm. What do you think about this? Would you trade your rational, benign God for the inexorable God who prescribes the iron rule of predestined grace for each of us?

Luckily we English do not believe in Luther, and our powerful Cardinal Wolsey is a great enemy of the reformer. So you and I are on the same side. Nevertheless, I will admit that I understand the vacillation of Erasmus, though I hope he will decide for man's culture as the center of life. We are on the side of the Ciceronians and the Virgilians, the poets and artists who are today reconstructing the Christian Olympus, and how could a Michelangiolo or, even more, a Raffaello be taken on by a Luther?

I write the name of Raffaello with a grief beyond solace. I must tell you that I left for the Field of the Cloth of Gold not only out of dutiful obedience but also in order to breathe a different air from the air Raffaello breathed during his short and miraculous life, which ended this year in windy April, not three months ago. I know how much you loved and love his divine works and his privileged brush. How many times, in the room of the School of Athens, have I admired that painting which is among the most rational and poetic creations of

thinking man? In my sorrow I consider my great fortune of
having seen him often in Rome, walking through streets and
squares with an assertive step, discoursing with a little group
of artists and friends chosen by him for company or as
associates to work with. It seemed that prodigiously revived,
some noble figures of a restored Greece were visible in the
sunny air of Athens. I also saw him painting in his studio,
where silence always fell as he set to work, and I have seen the
singular, sacred melancholy of his refined face, which became
gradually more serene, as the brush progressed, as if the man
were penetrating the meaning of existence and arriving at a
confine where he could pause to meditate. He seemed
detached from the earth, and yet he remained wholly earthy,
especially in his risky and most ardent loves.

Once I was even allowed to attend a meeting of men of
learning and witness a debate, rich in subjects, between him
and Signor Baldesar Castiglione, the Mantuan knight, whom
you know well and who noted down ideas on some papers of
his for a discourse to be addressed to the pope. Raffaello was
proposing a great map on which the monuments of Rome
would be depicted and, with it, a book that would tell their
history through the centuries, certified by the testimony of
writers, poets, chroniclers of all time. It was to be at once an
inner history and an architectural lesson on ancient Rome, in
which questions would be answered about the values of
spaces set in carefully studied relationship, a work to remain
eternal as an invention of reason when it becomes the poetry
of a civilization. He emanated a majestic clarity of intellect
mixed with austere tenderness, and thanks to the latter, the
man was not unloved, as often happens with men of
excellence. Only we, having seen and heard him, can testify
to the truth: In dying, Raffaello took with him a good part of
our life, and we have gained little compensation. Indeed, we
are oppressed by the thought that there are fatal events
where prudence and knowledge and affections are of scant
avail.

With these words I am coming to the evidence of misfortune,
and I would not wish to make your dear eyes shed tears. I will
say that this place of painted canvas and crystal that houses me

as I write would seem the last place to speak of losses, here where I seem to be in a fairy tale of knights where everything appears wondrous, fantastic, even if ephemeral. I do not know if it is licit for me to express adequately my condolences for the loss of your Illustrious Husband, which occurred in March of last year, to the bereavement of all his people. It would be my duty to do so, and I am taken aback by my inertia; but I believe that my dismay is justified. I have no right to intrude, even for a moment, into your most sacred and tested sentiments, of whatever sort they may have been or may have become. I grieve to write such words, which I submit to your judgment, so that it will be your sacrosanct decision whether to scorn them or not. Rest assured that whatever your verdict, even though I shall be ignorant of it, I bow to it with infinite respect and suffering.

And now I must actually speak of you yourself, for a reason I have left to the last, though it should have preceded all other subjects, prolusion, not epilogue, the reason for my writing you from here, from the Field of the Cloth of Gold, amid such dubious splendors. Coming from the Roman Curia, to which I am to return the moment these festivities end, I made it my duty to warn you. Beware, my lady, beware of our supreme head, who can in a thousand ways affect your person. He does not love you; he detests your ability to sense and to build, especially now that you govern the state in the name of the young marquis. You are under strong suspicion because of your son-in-law, Francesco Maria della Rovere, hated in the Vatican above all others. But the supreme Jove who would like to seem meek and holy does not have a consistent spirit: He vacillates; he pretends to himself; he hides and keeps hidden from others his real opinion. You, my lady, must send to him a great gentleman who will not play at hide-and-seek but will discourse with him, with presence of intellect; otherwise, you will derive no advantage. And if you ask me for a name, I can think of none except that of Count Baldesar Castiglione. In confidence, for him it would be no slight matter because he would have, in daily consort, an incalculable number of irritations. But being the man he is, he would be able to bear them.

I will not go into the questions that have made him whom I mention your enemy, but I implore you with all my heart to take care. Your son is barely twenty, and in these days, among these corrupted people, he needs the most acute counsel, the very kind of inspiration that can come from you; if I were in your son's position, I would follow your dictates, whatever they were.

I am convinced I am giving you a proof of friendship, and what I am about to reveal is a further proof, it will surely seem grave to you (and it is), and from it you can deduce how the air of the Roman Curia has become poisoned against the Gonzaga court. Shortly before leaving, I was informed by a man famous for his maliciousness that some very detailed letters had arrived from Mantua; referring to one in particular, without revealing the sender of the sly report, this man told of a conversation someone had overheard on the subject of Signor Rozone, your son's former tutor, killed in Bologna years ago by an assassin never discovered. They insinuated that you, shut up with your son in the most sealed rooms, asked him with special severity what he had to tell you about that crime and if he had anything to do with it. The marchese Federico is supposed to have answered with vague annoyance. At which you admonished him sternly, with these very words: "Marchese, you can deceive me, but you will not deceive God," suggesting that you truly considered him guilty of having armed an assassin's hand against his old master. Naturally I denied this story; I absolutely do not believe it, and it is not to believed, it is only palace gossip, and I silenced the man, reminding him of the punishment that could strike him for his slander. I hope he has repeated around the city what I said.

It is difficult for me, now, to resume the joyous guise I wore when I began this letter, having discovered that you have accepted my pages, even though with inclemency. I do not wish to seem presumptuous in protecting you, but I urge you again: Take care, my venerated lady, and be sure that these warnings I have given you are true, and when I am again in Rome, I shall not fail to watch over your affairs.

I would like to know you are happy. Is it true that you are changing your apartments and will leave forever those rooms in the castle where I saw you that one time in my life? I will have to provide my own answer to this question, and this is known by

> *your devoted slave*
> Robert de la Pole
> *born in England*

From France, the twenty-fifth of June, 1520

DURING A WHOLE night I felt the repeated shock of the slander the Englishman had reported to me, ending his letter from the Field of the Cloth of Gold. Gradually, as I turned it over in my mind, including the name of Federico, it became more and more cruel and hard to bear. My son was the object of a perverse accusation, manifestly false, as the writer declared, having rebelled against it. But I appeared as one who, having called God to witness, asserted that falsehood by my own doubt: I, his mother. So the very slanderers considered me more terribly perspicacious than any other and endowed with such cold strength that I ignored the wicked accusations made against those who wield great power. As for slanders against the powerful, I would return to them later with more philosophical attention. Meanwhile, Federico was entitled to his innocence.

Apart from that conclusion, painful though attended by every consideration, the letter in jagged handwriting was stirred by gusts of folly, at times merry, at times disconsolate, typical of people of the far north. And also with gusts of wisdom. Excellent and opportune were his counsels; mad, the lucubrations about my accepting or not accepting those fanciful pages of his; all a soliloquy, for that matter, of rather ingenious ratiocination. Nevertheless, I was not displeased that he had written me after six years of silence, treating them as if they had been days, or that he wanted to write me still. As it was understood that I would not answer, his vocatives did not irk me, nor did I care if he defined me in somewhat bizarre terms, like "savage." On the other hand, I enjoyed his bits of stories about his island of England and his king, which are a great novelty for us. I would have liked him to dwell on those subjects. Everything that he narrated of the Field of the Cloth of Gold resembled some epic tale, revealing at the same time a story worthy of a romance.

I was irritated, on the contrary, by his way of introducing the heretic monk Martin Luther onto the stage. He paid that monk too much attention; I disagree with that man as far as is possible. Another subject is that of his beloved Erasmus of Rotterdam, who still does not enjoy great standing among the Italian scholars, accused of being Ciceronians, especially those at the court of Rome, except for our friend Jacopo Sadoleto. It is curious to remark how these people of the English island are often subject to blind rages and do not know the full, if slow, brooding of Mediterranean spirits. But above all, this much was certain: With Leo the Tenth our position, the Gonzagas', at the Vatican court was no longer one of favor, and someone was needed there to defend our cause, and this someone could only be our Baldesar Castiglione. For some time I had insisted on this new ambassadorship, but the clear insight of one who lived in the Curia reassured me that my choice was right and useful.

When I think again of that rapid decision of mine, I am still stunned by the thunder of Jove the Inexplicable. Baldesar had been in Rome a mere two days when a miracle occurred, something I cannot fathom. The working of the pontiff's mental machinery is a mystery. All of a sudden, as if concluding internal ruminations, Leo the Tenth announced to our ambassador his intention of offering the marchese Federico Gonzaga the command of the papal troops. The pope asked who held authority for him in the governing of Mantua, and this was a strange question as there was no one in Italy who did not know of my regency. Nevertheless, though dumb struck, Castiglione behaved like the man he was: prepared for anything. He tried to plumb the situation, to make sure it concealed no pitfalls. He then reminded His Holiness of my position, established by the testament of my husband, Francesco Gonzaga, and that I governed, coadjuvated by the counsel of Cardinal Sigismondo and Lord Giovanni Gonzaga, my brothers-in-law. Quite benevolent, and as if he were saying something already aired between us, Leo spoke of Francesco, of beloved memory, affirming that he had been very fond of the marchese, and he even attempted to suggest he had moved against the duke of Urbino because he had been forced to, and he said other things, perhaps invented on the spot, from some dark stirring of humors.

When Castiglione's report arrived, I nearly fainted with joy. It seemed impossible. We were tormented by the near certainty that the pontiff was hostile to us, and here, suddenly, we were faced by an offer of great dignity and honor, a princely command we would never have dared hope for, still less propose. The pope's only insistence was secrecy; no one but I was to know of it. This secrecy, which on his side he often transgressed, was a curious mania of his. In every matter, even the most trivial, he wanted to be assured of the complicity of silence.

THAT late June was resplendent. In the castle currents of triumph were flowing, and when I looked at myself in the glass, I saw the image of a queen, encompassing the infinite pride of a mother and the pride of a chief of state who sees fortune hovering, wings outspread, over the turrets of the castle. My son Captain General of the Church, a youth who still had not been invested with the fiefdom by the emperor, who had still to prove himself in any armed conflict, who was still a ward. And how his father had suffered for that command, even though he was the victor of Fornovo! The Gonzagas were prevailing, their weight was being felt in Italian affairs, and in that moment, considering the State, I was brimming with energy, happy; my son regarded me as a goddess. From that July on I was unable to find peace. I was gripped by an ardent desire to live to the full the hours of my day and, at times, of my night. I supervised my household with a kind of fever; I imposed new disciplines, alert to a collective formation of an exemplary court.

Castiglione continued writing his concrete, very beautiful letters. Every day he trudged to the Vatican and lingered in substantial conversations with His Holiness, who bade him, cleverly, always to tell the truth, for he knew everything anyway. Some sly figure was reporting to Rome from Mantua, conveying in careful detail everything that was being done or not being done. Lately they had reported that I, Isabella, was saying nothing but evil about the pope. But I knew these partisans of Tolomeo Spagnoli well; they informed him of the Mantua gossip hostile to us Gonzagas, and he saw that it regularly reached the pope.

Just when Castiglione's letters were coming in most thick and fast with the latest news of Federico's command, the envoy's young wife died of a childbed fever. Pirro Donati, our Baldesar's great friend, rushed to inform me. That day I was greatly distressed by some outrageous talk being murmured about us at the Vatican court. The pope was complaining even about my Ferrante's boyish gibes against him; he had also been told about the destruction of the sash with the Medici arms, and it was not recalled that these were the words and actions of a mere child of twelve. Leo sent a special messenger to his godson, and Ferrante replied sensibly; with great smiles we assisted him, pretending

to jest about how a child had become so important that he had
to explain his words to a papal messenger.

Things took a strange turn. Leo did not withdraw his offer to
Federico, but he began to impose conditions, create obstacles,
raise doubts so that we were led to think the offer was not truly
sincere. I was in a state of touchy irritation, suspecting that Leo
intended somehow to humiliate us, when Pirro came with the
news of the death of Ippolita, Castiglione's wife, and with a choked
voice added that he considered it necessary for me to write a letter
"to that poor husband so deeply in love with the gentle creature,"
barely twenty. I estimated all the despair of my ambassador, and
I confess to myself that his grief alarmed me. What if Castiglione
were to be distracted from his delicate mission, now endangered?
What if he could no longer concentrate on our dealings with Leo?
So, at my secretary's urging, I dictated the letter. "And we beg
you," I said, after formulating the usual condolences, "once you
have given free rein to your immediate sorrow, to return as soon
as possible within the confines of reason, and since neither tears
nor laments can mend such loss, dispose your spirit to patience,
and the sooner you show your soul's manliness, the better; and
you will earn our deepest gratitude. . . . "

I had never seen Pirro's pale face flush from brow to chin or
his eye, always benevolent toward me, gaze at me from such a
distance. When I finished dictating, he rose, and lowering his
eyelids, he commented with unusual emphasis: "The signora
Ippolita passed through this world like a rose held against the
light." And with a half bow he left me.

August was waning, an August of not intolerable heat. I wore
a loose dress of Alexandrine blue, its white sleeves decorated with
little palms embroidered in red and gold, and I had pearls and
rubies at my throat. It was a new style, but at that moment I felt
uncomfortable in it. My gentleman's reproach had reached me,
and his remark sounded critical of my dictated words to Castiglione. This would not make me change them; with all my heart,
I still wanted my ambassador to throw off the mantle of his grief,
to return to our cause, and to be more alert than ever to papal
ambiguities. For that poor, very young wife I had to admit I felt
compassion, but superficial enough to allow me to stamp my foot
impatiently on the floor, and then I was ashamed; but I had no
time to reprove myself, because my women entered, followed by
Equicola, who had written a poem to be sung with dancing, and
they asked me to listen to it. What drove me to chastise them all

together? Music and dance, indeed! They should collect their veils, before going to vespers.

"In church," I ordered, "we will pray for the blessed soul of the lady Ippolita Castiglione."

FEDERICO'S captaincy soon became a prickly subject, and that uneasiness was surpassed by a direct grief, as strong as it was implacable. My cardinal brother died suddenly, at the age of forty-two, through some unknown cause, because I cannot believe the eel of Comacchio, eaten out of season, was fatal to him. It was the very beginning of September. I admired Ippolito desperately, his bright and distant intelligence, his irresistible and command-ing strength, but now nothing in me was moved. I had to think back to the picture of him as a prodigious boy singer and re-create in my mind those tones pure as irradiated crystal that surpassed all professional singers; then, finally, I wept. But in those tears there was no suffering. I realized how estranged he had become when, summoning him, I mentally reassembled our great Ferrara family and called up the adamantine Ercole, my father, and the always present Eleonora of Aragón, woman of unforgettable charms. Of the six children whose exuberance had filled the Este palaces, two, Beatrice and Ippolito, so blazing with life, had gone; one, Ferrante, consumed his days with his unfortunate half brother Giulio, his fellow conspirator, in a sealed prison of that castle that had seen them young and free setting out to conquer the world. The youngest, the pale Sigismondo, had lived an uneventful, calm existence, without glory, in a high and silent palace. So that left the two of us: the two oldest, strengthened by our years. Alfonso grieved at the death of his cardinal brother, who had supported him with such severity and detachment. But Alfonso, too, had learned by now; his forty-five years had seen harsh changes and the troubled entanglements of family life and politics and the uncertainty of the future. We wrote each other firm words, almost totally formal; still, each of us could recognize in the other the capacity of our hands, skilled in unraveling deeds and opinions.

Yes, the game I pursued was becoming destructive, through the constant jolts to my heart, this subterranean battle I was fight-ing with Pope Leo. At this time in the Vatican hints were being dropped by a man who proved to be of great help and on whom I could rely. In the enormous papal household of six hundred and eighty-two people, this man held the position of private and personal secretary to His Holiness, a man unearthed by Castiglione, who immediately won him to our side. His name was Pietro Ardinghello. Thoughtful and devoted, this papal servant liked to help princes and potentates and also to earn substantial compensation because, as our ambassador said, he was very fond of good things. He was privy to Leo's slightest reflection and seconded him, thrusting him ahead with light little taps, never giving the pontiff the impression of being forced. Ardinghello was the sort of man we needed.

Amid a thousand doubts and a thousand hopes I opened the letter from Rome dated August twenty-seventh. After the first enclosure, the "Stipulations for the Command" that the pope offered us, we came to an obscure point, dramatically obscure. And even more prominent were the Latin letters, written by the hand of Baldesar himself, of the second enclosure, which was immediately called the secret policy. It ratified a clause that was, in fact, to remain deeply secret, and forever, between the pope and Federico. In it, my son, marchese of Mantua, pledged himself to defend the Church and take arms personally even against the emperor, if required. We had only to consider the Gonzagas' position as vassals of the empire to realize the extreme danger of that pledge, with the risk even of being driven from our State, especially under an imposing master such as Charles the Fifth was proving to be. This policy, if known, could be our utter ruin.

Thus my life proceeded from August to December in a separation from myself in everything that did not concern Federico's command. I was barely touched by the death of Cardinal Bibbiena, my dear old Moccicone. Undecided, yet opposing every warning with fearless ploys, I was consumed in months and months of true agony, while I waited for the definitive signatures on the stipulations. Castiglione, who was very sure of the pope, had, however, to hear himself told how the king of France had advised His Holiness against taking Federico into his service, considering him a youth too fond of enjoying himself with women and lacking in military experience. European politics in those days suffered harsh changes: The rivalry between Francis the First and Charles the Fifth was opening an ever wider road to war, and Leo seemed to make his choice, falling in on the side of the emperor.

Finally on the eleventh of December the stipulations of the command were signed at the Magliana villa, but, as usual, under cover of secrecy. Leo wanted to await the opportune moment to make the command public. The policy, signed and sealed by Federico in my presence in our palace at Porto, was now guarded in the Vatican archives by Pietro Ardinghello. More than six months had still to pass before the captaincy would be announced before the consistory: On July seventh Leo then proclaimed the pact, and there was a beautiful celebration in Mantua. The bells never stopped ringing, fireworks traced in the sky the allegories of our earthly joys, and the cannonades of our artillery presaged future victories.

My anxiety did not disappear; but it relaxed, and I succeeded in participating in the reality of each moment, and so I was certain that no one spoke of the secret pledge, either in Rome or elsewhere. I had not lost—quite the contrary—the habit of spending some hours alone with Federico and training him, without seeming to, keeping my distance from any sort of facile prompting. I took pleasure in seeing him move with authority now that he had the title of Captain of the Church; even with Prospero Colonna, the grand general of the imperial armies, he could behave firmly, though always respectfully. And he had immediately named his court, more military than princely, eager to display his valor now that hostilities had resumed between the French and the Spanish.

THEN he began to elude me, and it was not difficult for me to guess why. Already the previous year, with his sister Eleonora and with Elisabetta, he had gone to Venice for the Feast of the Ascension, taking with him a young married woman whose Christian name is the same as mine. I did not delve too deeply into those private matters; but my conviction was that for a youth of twenty it was a good thing to decide upon a love affair that would complete his personality, and it seemed to me discreet and acceptable, this connection with a woman of noble house, a wife and mother. He should enjoy himself and learn about love; in the meanwhile, I would calmly study his marriage possibilities, the tie that could best help him and the State. I happened to encounter the cavalcade that this lady and Federico were leading through the city, followed by a retinue of brilliant young people. We greeted one another politely as courtly rules decree. I looked too long at Federico and the knights around him to be able to gaze much at the woman, wrapped in a cloak of blue-green velvet spangled with golden stars. I could tell she was tall from her seat in the saddle; she was blond and haughty as a duchess, and sweet-faced, but there was a bright flash of arrogance in her blue eyes.

If I ask myself why I did not immediately catch some warning signal, I can only answer that in those days I still wore the regent's

crown firmly on my head, though in April we would celebrate
Federico's investiture as fifth marchese of Mantua. And our dialogue had been so intense, so deeply shared through the wearing
conflict with the pope that I felt I was my son's sole ruler. Furthermore, what attention I had free I devoted to a new building.
For the first time, after so many years of life among the ancient
walls, I was changing my dwelling place.

I was having built for myself a new, cool residence, outside the
castle but not far from it, within the enclosure of the Bonacolsi
family's old houses, near the little Church of Santa Croce, in a
vast space under the boundless sky. I would be almost at the
piazza gate, on the ground floor, in a suite of communicating
rooms forming an L, and I wanted their atmosphere to be both
gay and serious. Along the outside walls of the rooms there already ran a beautiful loggia of slender arches, with frescoes that
depicted the famous cities of the world. Two more loggias lightened the construction beyond the courtyard, and in the middle
a handsome garden flourished; at the end a little hidden door led
to another secret garden, all mine, also with a short loggia, thickly
covered with jasmine. Gardens and vegetable plots were on every
side, with great trees, limes, planes, fruit trees, roses of all colors,
in an ordered array among statues and fountains.

I understood why Francesco had wanted to spend his last years
in the palace near San Sebastiano, buried in the countryside. Not
only are we masters of farmlands, but also our times no longer
confine us to the fortified enclosure of castles. Poetry, Latin and
vulgar, the study of the ancients direct our spirits to mild living
and make days in the sealed walls of our towers insufferable for
us. I came out into the open. In Rome I had seen palaces and
villas of supreme architectural elegance, like those conceived for
some of the great cardinals and for Agostino Chigi, which illus-
trated how easily the mind is opened to beauty. I would renew
our way of being in the world. New cuts of clothes, hitherto
unknown settings of jewels; I would collect musicians to re-create
the harmonic moments of modern inventions. This time I would
finally return to studying Greek grammar. My head was a dizzy,
buzzing nest.

After the great bells and celebrations of Federico as Captain of
the Church, the arrows began to whistle. The pope could not
tolerate the duke of Urbino, though verbally he consented to the
duke's staying with us; in reality, he wanted to drive the duke
out of Mantua. And so we had him leave. Months before we had
been obliged to guarantee, through Castiglione's words, that Fed-

erico, when it was a matter of political loyalty, would not consider friends or relatives, not father, or mother, brothers or sisters. Now we were being put to the test.

I found Eleonora in the Porto villa, where she and little Guidobaldo and my peerless Elisabetta had witnessed Francesco Maria's humiliated departure. My daughter still bemoaned her fate, compared her brother triumphing in his captaincy with her poor, fugitive husband. She was expecting to be banished also, and she saw herself astray with Elisabetta and the boy, persecuted by the house of Medici, refugees and mendicants. Unfortunately all these forecasts were fairly probable. Only the greathearted Elisabetta considered the situation with her usual, frank wisdom and begged Eleonora to be patient and to accept what was ineluctable. For her I fought with the pope, with Castiglione, with Federico himself, and I gained permission to keep the duchess of Urbino in Mantua. Only, to make less display of our hospitality, we moved them, delegating them to the Sabbioneta branch of our family, requesting their city palace, which was sufficiently comfortable, for the duchesses.

But Eleonora did not cease her lamentations. She did not love that husband of hers, who, for that matter, was not very lovable, but she felt bound to be on his side in any case. She found it heroic to support him against the others. I was the first of these others, held guilty no matter what I did, and judged according to a hysterical religiosity, worthy of a reformer, if not actually of a Lutheran. I asked myself how and why Elisabetta held her so dear, suffering with her the familiar exile from the land of Urbino and pitying her, knowing that Eleonora lacked the compensation that Elisabetta herself had: the company of her husband, Guidobaldo, ardent in wounded passion. Perhaps this comprehension of others was the secret that made Elisabetta the friend of people as dissimilar as Eleonora and me.

As a mother I was beginning to notice that my conversations with my son took place at long intervals, but I interpreted that increasing rarity of his presence as a sign of growth, of independence. Federico questioned me always, in his usual way, and so invigorated me, but now it seemed his questions no longer revealed the leaping nature of his thought, perhaps ingenuous. He began to ask me about the secret pledge. He wanted to know if it was not really dangerous for him to have signed it, committing himself to move against the emperor even in person if this was necessary for the defense of the dignity and authority of the Church.

"Against the emperor?" he complained stubbornly, as if it were the first time he had come to reflect on this possibility. "Fight against the emperor? Me? His vassal? How could we pledge ourselves to such a thing?"

"The pope," I replied patiently, though a bit amazed, "wants to be quite sure that Mantua, one of the gates to Italy, is well defended against all powers."

"For Leo the Tenth the word of the marchese of Mantua should be enough."

"In politics, my son, one's word counts for little; you have to sign your name."

But Federico seemed unconvinced, and after pondering a moment, he went on: "Truly, Mother, do you believe that the secret policy, in the pope's hands, will not become a trap for me?"

"Not for the present. Leo and the emperor have reached an agreement. At the moment there is nothing to fear."

"Perhaps I made a mistake, pledging myself to those Medicis," Federico continued, hesitant, harping on the matter.

"Do not be afraid," I said to him one day, raising my voice. "Remember, it is always well to be allied with the Church because if the Church wins, she wins, and if she loses, she still wins."

The effect of Federico was immediate; he loved certain curt sayings of mine. In fact, he laughed. But I could not dispel the thought that he might have revealed to someone the secret of that policy and this person must have frightened him. Who was his confidant? One of his courtier friends? His woman, perhaps in an unguarded moment in bed? I had to prepare myself for anything.

THE FRENCH, now determined to react openly to the imperial and papal accord, rapidly moved against Parma, and this would be Federico's first military campaign. At court the talk was of nothing else, and everyone would have liked to be present at the fittings of his uniform and the ceremony of investiture of the Captain of the Church. It was not easy for me to have the doors of the audience chamber kept closed, with guards placed at them. With me I kept only a few of my girls, those whom Federico liked particularly. Equicola, man of letters always prepared, was naturally present. I wanted that rehearsal of the ceremony, which would then take place in the field, to be something unforgettable for my son. And also for myself.

Never as on that morning had Federico, at twenty, been so splendid, and that splendor gave me an almost physical joy. The ceremonial dress, slightly Spanish, underlined the grace and agility of his young manhood. The girls gathered around him "like happy nymphs at the vesting of Mars," said Equicola, amply exclamatory as usual. I hushed him politely; I was not in a scolding mood that day, and everyone, the pages first of all had realized it.

THE GIRLS are all astir over Federico. They buckle on his cuirass, adjusting the bandolier. One of them hands him his helmet, another his sword, and all together they blandish him with words and gestures. One compares him to Paris for his beauty; another, to Achilles for his valor. Tortorina insists on touching his chest, over the heart; Barbarina, Iva, and Lavagnola ask the first kisses of the hero. In jest I urge Federico not to listen to these sillies, and more slyly he answers: "Were you not the one, Mother dear, who taught me how beautiful it is to serve and entertain women?"

Equicola thus has an excuse to assert emphatically: "It is your fault, my lady. Every day, dazzling queen, you surrounded yourself with the most beautiful angels. Who can withstand such charmers?"

With a look I recall the girls and turn to Captain Soardo, our old and glorious Gonzaga soldier, inviting him to have Federico repeat the words of the oath to the flag, which he will have to pronounce before the troops. Again Equicola intervenes as the officer unfurls the banner. "What enemy could compete with the marchese of Mantua? Hear my prophecy: God has sent Martin Luther upon this earth so that you and His Holiness, together can defeat heresy and earn the palm of glory."

My heart is beating as I read the words embroidered in gold: *Leo X Pont. Max. ad dominum cum tribulater clamavi et exaudivit me.* Impetuously Federico seizes an end of the banner with his left hand; with his right he draws his sword, and in his schooled voice he repeats: "We, Federico Gonzaga, fifth marchese of Mantua, swear fealty to the Holy Church; to Pope Leo the Tenth, and to all his successors."

As any mother would be, I am moved, but I manage to contain myself so as not to diminish the celebratory tone of my young captain. All present cheer. I order the doors to be opened, and the hall fills with people acclaiming Federico in the name of the Gonzagas, in the name of victory.

His sword drawn, my son comes toward me, with an assertive stride. "With God's help," he says on the spur of the moment,

"I will fight against all our enemies. I will renew the glory of Fornovo, I will drive the French from Italy, I will conquer France, and I will arrive at Paris."

My God, what a pang I feel in my heart. I seem to be hearing his father as he set off against the Serenissima, and a few days later he lay prisoner in the Torresella in Venice. But Federico is twenty, and his youth justifies him. I raise my voice calmly. "Do not waste too many words, my son. France is not such easy prey, and the French are brave fighters. For the present let us be content with the Parma campaign. Displaying oneself requires no courage, but it takes bravery to act when war demands action."

We are left alone. Perhaps Pirro Donati, alert to my inner shifts of mood, has had the hall emptied. Federico sets sword and helmet on a stool and kneels at my feet in his usual way. It always makes me feel a surge of warmth, that gesture of his; I observe that he does not abandon himself to it as often as formerly. But Federico speaks devoted words to me, promises he will fight like a paladin only for me and in my name.

I laugh, flattered, and I gaily call him a liar; he is so handsome, so bold that I am gripped by the anguished thought of losing him.

"Federico, my own Federico, do not expose yourself too much, be careful; do not rush in unprepared. I will be trembling for you at every hour."

"Dear Mother, can you not consider me a man? I am a soldier. I must win my days of glory. Isn't this also one of your lessons?"

"Federico, my soul," I murmur, "I am afraid for you. Ever since you have been without your master at your side, your Rozone, I have always been afraid. He would have protected you against everyone."

Federico's features alter in a faint, nervous twitch. "Rozone again!" he says casually.

"Federico!" I cry. "Tell me the truth. Do you know nothing, truly, of the murder of Rozone? Your hands are clean in this crime; that is the truth, my son, is it not?"

He stands and looks at me with an expression of pure innocence. "Mother, you know it well. I myself ordered a strict inquiry into his death." He comes closer, takes my hands, and lifts me from my seat to embrace me; then he speaks again, his face close to mine, in his irresistible, persuasive tone. "Dear Mother! Am I not the mirror of your soul? You see into my heart, Mother dear, beautiful Mother! I am your Federico. I will always be everything for you always!"

Whatever I might glimpse in him, his voice would erase from my mind any disturbing thought or presentiment. To savor the divinity of hope, with an effort, I believe him, and joy is my reward.

To the Magnificent and
Most Excellent Signora Isabella,
Marchesana of Mantua and My Lady

*F*aithful to my decision, to write you when I cannot prohibit myself from doing so, here I am, my truly venerated lady, in the hope that these pages will not be a source of irritation. After my journey to the Field of the Cloth of Gold and after a stay in my own bright green and silver gray land, that Suffolk of broad plains, I have returned to Rome. And here I live in the troubled times that rack this city when its pastor and pontifex maximus leaves us. It would be futile for me to tell you of my great desire to converse with you, a desire painful through its impossibility. But I have not forgotten that between you and me only the pact of silence can exist.

I am happy, however, to tell you that I now learn much about your present life, for during these past months I have become intimate with your friend and servant, that man of supreme talent, the supreme gentleman, your envoy here in the Vatican, Count Baldesar Castiglione. And though he is a man of great discretion, in speaking of his masters, he does not fail to give a spirited account of your acute way of counseling the young marquis of Mantua, whom I met as a comely boy, the ward of Pope Julius, here in the Vatican.

I had been back in Rome only a short time when, last July, Lord Federico's captaincy was announced in consistory. I realized that through an abrupt shift of opinion, which is, however, consistent in Pope Leo's character, things had been reversed: The pontiff now favored you and protected you just as he had formerly been suspicious of you in the wavering of his political ideas, and in the end he was definitely turning in your direction. I was proud as if it were my own concern. I then followed the events of the imperial and papal campaign against the French, and I witnessed last November the furious joy that overwhelmed our pontiff at the news of the conquest of Milan and the enemy's withdrawal from Cremona. Never have I seen Pope Leo's round, plump face so bright with happiness as on that day. He could not stop talking; to everyone he read the missives from the field in Lombardy. He did not know he was preparing himself for death.

Restless in this excess of contentment, on the twenty-second of November, he decided to go to his beloved Magliana, and all of us at the Curia were invited there to celebrate with him. Those were clear days, not even cold, but heavy with sirocco. The pope felt no discomfort and could hardly contain a joy as pressing as sorrow. Toward evening a group of Swiss soldiers arrived, belonging to that same corps that had fought in Milan, and the tawny glow of their torches brightened the villa and its broad courtyard, which you will perhaps recall: a gently sloping space, surrounded by dark, harmonious little houses and closed off at the end by the charming two-story building with the arched portico and the cross windows and the circular fountain in the center. From window to window the pope looked out, accompanied by the torches held high by servants; he leaned forward, exultant, heedless of the night's damp cold rising from the river; and he blessed and greeted soldiers and household with repeated festive waves. The next morning he had a fever and was taken from La Magliana to Rome; in the space of a few days the fever worsened and killed him. He has just passed the age of forty-five, very young for a pope. We were all amazed and did not regret him.

I wonder, my lady, if you have been told. Leo, of the house of Medici, who had drawn on the great papal treasury without stint to surround himself with incredible luxury, died poor. He was given a modest funeral, and an inept preacher pronounced a sermon more wretched than any village vicar's, for that man who had so appreciated the refined orations of the most celebrated Latinists of the Roman University. Leo apparently had squandered the entire treasury of Julius the Second, as well as his own income and that of the next pope. The coffers were found empty; crowns and tiaras were missing. The bustling swarm of Florentines who had peopled Rome and looted the Vatican is now in suspense, sniffing the air, and at times some of them dart away like flights of scared birds.

Everything looked threatening, but now, through the intervention of the lord governor of Rome, it seems peace and quiet have returned.

You will surely know that each of us has his candidate for the papal throne, as I know you have. We English favor Cardinal Wolsey, with his authoritative, perhaps excessive vigilance over our king, as royal adviser, a man of decision in all things, including his own unbounded ambitions, of which the highest is the papacy. It was perhaps his advice last September that led my king to send Leo a special envoy, the bishop of Bath, John Clerk, to present the pope with a work of my sovereign (Henry is a good theologian), bound in gold cloth and decorated with the most elegant illumination. It is a polemical tract against the Wittenberg monk, a lifely confutation of the Augustinian reformer, entitled *A Defense of the Seven Sacraments Against Martin Luther*. Leo the Tenth uttered words of great gratitude and replied with a triumphant bull conferring on Henry the title Defender of the Faith. The title was highly appreciated at the royal palace in London and inscribed by the sovereign's command on the royal coat of arms.

Our ambitions thus aim directly at Cardinal Wolsey. And what about yours? I know that in a generous gesture full of enthusiasm, you have pawned your most famous jewels to help Cardinal Gonzaga, your brother-in-law, along the path to the papacy. Nothing excites me and rejoices me more than the glowing vitality of hope that surrounds your actions with a special light; it would be a wondrous thing to see you here in Rome, full of grace and benevolence, an angel at a pope's side. And rest assured, my lady (and I confide these words secretly because there is the risk of ending in the Tower of London for simply having imagined them), that if my wishes were to conflict with yours, I would retire before you. Though all is agitated and obscure, since no one is prepared for this election and the cardinals rush to the conclave with an air of alarm, I believe that neither our candidate nor yours has any likelihood of victory, even if there is never any knowing what can happen. The solemn intriguer for the present is Cardinal Colonna, of the imperial party, and one thing is quite certain: He does not want another Medici.

I have changed house, but the evocative words "fourth floor fifth window" still obtain, remember. Now for my duties I still go and work in the palace opposite the one you blessedly inhabited. My home is in one of the little houses behind the Borgo, which belonged to Raffaello, and as I go from room to room, I seem to sense the hovering of that great spirit. It does not frighten me but rather affords me perfect company.

I am seated at a long table in this moment, under the pale lamp, and you will forgive me if I speak to you a bit about myself. I have greatly feared that one of these days I would receive a packet containing my letters or at least that one I hoped you would never read. Nothing has arrived, and now I can consider the pact between us sanctioned, the pact of consensual silence. At this table, driving my pen across the paper, I even have a consolatory shame, thinking thus, and my only fear springs from the remorse at my meditations too youthful for me and too happy for my condition. My temples have gone gray, and every morning I beseech God to grant me the sobriety that befits my age.

Most sweet lady, pray also for the health of my soul. For me you must be a great sin, if at the very sound of your name my soul explodes in an ineffable festiveness, with no rational explanation. But where can any sin be in this abstraction of feelings that has no place and no logic? All those who have loved you and still love you are beyond my reach. If I am jealous and envious of anyone, it is Count Castiglione and Signor Mario Equicola, or the courtier closest to you, your confidential secretary, Pirro Donati. Judge for yourself the devotion of my warm feelings. I could also call it "pure." But what, in us men, can be defined as pure?

I do not wish to subject myself to any such examination, first of all out of respect for you. What I need now is one of those pardons that I ask from time to time as

your slave for life
Robert de la Pole

Rome, the twenty-third of December, 1521

Postscriptum: This very day I have received an unexpected and fortunate sign. I encountered your image in a youth of about sixteen whom I met face-to-face in the rooms of the Venetian ambassador's palace. Seeing him with the most reverend Cardinal Gonzaga, your brother-in-law, I recognized him at once as one of your sons, Ercole, also because he was wearing the bishop's habit recently given him by Pope Leo. Never has a young man of that age seemed to me to express so well with his bearing his own substance in the company of others. He resembles you as much as a man can resemble a woman and, though little more than adolescent, with a certain solidity that suggests, by contrast, your divine lightness. I would gladly have approached and spoken with him, but he turned his gray eyes to me with such interrogative steadiness that I was embarrassed and went out, barely able to keep my features motionless and remote and "English," as my friends here would put it. All day I have remained shaken and ecstatic. But how distant you are from me, my lady. It seems to me that I cannot reach you, not even with my thought.

R. de la Pole

T HE EMPEROR CHARLES the Fifth received a great and quite unforeseen gift from the Deity. Immediately after Pope Leo's decease, among the agitated cardinals of a conclave influenced by an indirect reaction to the heretical preachment of Luther, the confused but real necessity arose for a pope who would be a strict theologian, at least as good as the Wittenberg friar. Amazing, but logical, then was the election of Adrian Florensz, cardinal of Tortosa, a native of Utrecht. It was known that he had been Charles's tutor when the emperor was a young princeling. My brother-in-law Sigismondo Gonzaga, who had entered the Sistine Chapel seeking an opportunity to advance to the throne of Peter, referring to the ties between the new pontiff and Charles, remarked, "It can be said that now the emperor will be pope, and the pope will be emperor." Disheartening but true.

And we felt even more disheartened, especially I, who had let myself be overcome by the too ambitious hope of a pontiff from the house of Gonzaga without realizing what weak esteem our candidate enjoyed. My income was not scant, but I lost much money in Rome; I still had to redeem my jewels, and I postponed some of the work to be done in my new apartments of Cortevecchia, which were devouring so many ducats. Federico did not stint my expenses, but not even he could go beyond a certain point. Brought up with a taste for beautiful things, he desired them firmly, seeking everywhere unearthed statues, paintings, precious objects. But things far from beautiful lay in store for him.

Though this new pope was still a long way from Italy, he occupied my mind, appeared to me in nightmares in my fitful nights, as more exact information about him was reported. He was sixty-three, and the crown did not attract him; he had accepted it rather than offend God and the Church with a refusal. Pale, a bit hunchbacked, with large white hands and sturdy legs, he loved especially the study of theology and meditation. He was so severely religious that others were led to foresee a true reform of the Church and a hard battle against Lutheran heresy. One idea hammered insistently in his brain: a crusade of all the Christian princes, reconciled, to liberate the Sepulchre of Christ from the Turks.

The fact that in his ascetic severity he saw ancient statues only as idols or remnants of paganism mattered little to me, but I blanched at the mere thought that he would soon come from Spain to Rome and with him would arrive all the problems of the state of the Church, including the military ones. Almost surely he would confirm Federico as his Captain General, and equally surely he would learn of the secret policy whereby my son had pledged himself to take the field in person against the emperor. And if Charles the Fifth were to learn this, how would he react? Would the word "treason" be uttered? I trembled, and with me Federico also trembled at the thought of the rift that might open beneath our feet.

A second thought followed logically: to recover that document guarded by Pietro Ardinghello in the secret archives of the Vatican. Castiglione was bidden to act promptly, and in support we sent him Franceschino Gonzaga, our ambassador and kinsman. At whatever cost the policy had to come into our hands. The new pope had not yet begun his journey; some months would go by before he reached Rome, and the city was settling into the disorder of interregnum. It was the right time to act. Even if we were drained by the great expenditures made to raise Sigismondo Gonzaga to the papal throne, at whatever price we had to carry out the enterprise. Every day Ardinghello seemed more inclined to the proposal of our Castiglione and Franceschino Gonzaga: For a thousand ducats he would purloin the policy from the secret archive, though the sum seemed small to him.

Covertly things proceeded. The arrival of Hadrian the Sixth was delayed by the bad weather his ships encountered at sea, and the *sede vacante* was extended, so there was time to perfect the agreement, and in the end Ardinghello consented to steal the damned document. Franceschino Gonzaga came in person from Rome to Mantua, to my Porto residence and handed it over to me. My hands were shaking as I took the paper. I read it greedily to make sure it was actually the one that Federico had signed and sealed; then, looking our ambassador in the eyes, I tore it up; the paper crackled as it was ripped. I had a bronze basin and a lighted taper brought to me. Piece by piece, as if performing a propitiatory rite, I burned that document, unable to repress a genuine explosive laughter of happiness. "The danger that such a document could become known is so great that it did not seem safe even in my hands." Thus I wrote Federico, not thinking, in the gaiety of the moment, that these words were a confession that inculpated us. Luckily those words are buried in our archive.

Hadrian reached Rome at the end of August, saddened by the destiny that made him pope. He began at once dismissing his predecessor's entire court, and our envoys said that the Vatican had been transformed into a monastery. He sent the academicians away, and every man of letters, because of his severe hostility to the study of the ancients, and with every means he set about reforming the Curia. Toward us the new pope was fairly benign, confirming Federico's captaincy and, after only ten months, adding the title of Captain of Florence. Paolo Giovio, the papal historian, came to Mantua in the name of Hadrian, with the standards and batons of the command. This time we had taken care to add to the articles a protective clause; in fact, in very clear words, it was stated that Federico, under whatever circumstances, would never have to fight against the emperor.

BEFORE eight days of that September of 1523 had gone by, Hadrian the Sixth, pope for barely a year and a half, died in Rome, felled, it was said, by the thought of the immense task that loomed over him. In Milan, meanwhile, the emperor's favorite turned up: Francesco Sforza, brother of my nephew Massimiliano, who was spending a kind of exile in France, almost forgotten. And not for a moment did I harbor the idea of celebrating a new duke of Milan, second son of the Moro and of my sister, Beatrice. I no longer trusted my enthusiasms; the illusions of another return were remote by now, remote the flattering and reckless gaiety of Massimiliano's brief time. Inexorably that time had ended; recently gone, too, was the man who had so inflamed us ten years before, the enamored Spanish viceroy Raimundo of Cardona.

I ask myself how it is that our Bandello, so drawn to the events of contemporary life, has not yet narrated, at least as far as I know, the novella of Brognina, protagonist of one of the most dramatic stories that have unfolded around us. I would like to suggest it to him, in a summary along these lines:

"There lived at the court of the illustrious lady Isabella, marchesana of Mantua, a very beautiful maiden, one Brognina by name, sought after and worshiped by important men, including the powerful bishop of Gurk and the viceroy of Sicily Raimundo of Cardona, general in chief of the imperial armies. She was not one who lived only by reflected light. Her whims took on a rare feminine humor, where obedience and disobedience mingled, and she clearly proved this by suddenly abandoning the court to take the veil. But she soon wearied of the convent and after a few months ran away as her temperament demanded. Cardona, more enamored than ever, in his delight at regaining the hope of having her, settled on her a dowry of two thousand gold crowns, but the young woman in great secrecy vanished again. Finally she gave herself to her suitor, perhaps at Lendinara, where the general had brought her, in the vicinity of his military encampment. And thus, some time afterward, Brognina, in an agreeable and comfortable residence near Goito, gave birth to a male child; then, after a month, she gave birth to another: a twin birth of unusual interval, whereupon he, Cardona, left for Naples. A rich and noble wife awaited him there, a woman beautiful of face such as never had been seen.

"The damsel's adventures do not end here, for Francis the First, king of France, having settled in Milan, was enraptured by the beauty's story, and he had her abducted. But when she was set free by men loyal to the viceroy, who always kept her under surveillance, she courageously returned to Goito and from the marchese Francesco of sainted memory obtained permission to baptize her sons in the Cathedral of Mantua. To the first she gave the name of Guadalcair, in Spanish style, and to the second, Brogno, so that the glorious name of her family would not be lost. The godfather was Bernardo of Bibbiena, and there is no knowing how he remarked on this sponsorship. The conclusion of the story was propitious. Invited to go to Naples, Brognina faced the long journey with the two four-year-old boys, and having arrived in that magnificent city of queens, she deftly placed herself in the center of a great scene by marrying Gutiérrez de las Padilla, a nobleman of Cardona's household, who had assisted her in the very long journey from Goito to Naples. She then was assigned a fief outside the city, where she lives today, respected and revered, always showing how good fortune arrives ever at the right moment. And here ends my story."

To be sure, Brognina was not an empty head on a full body. I realized that from the way, at our receptions in Mantua and Milan, she used to put her hands over her white face, flushing with embarrassment to the brow, without scorn and above all without disgust, in the whirlwind of the fiery, tempestuous words of her suitors. She sensed the boundary of her female existence, beyond which there was only the embarrassment of her glory. Federico fortunately was never caught in similar snares.

I hear myself uttering these words, and I know I am lying. I wonder whether I should have said, "If only it were a Brognina!" The time is coming for me to examine this insidious woman my son chose, this Isabella Boschetti, of a family arrogant to the point of treason, kinswoman of Alberto Boschetti, beheaded in Ferrara for complicity in the conspiracy of Don Giulio. Impoverished feudal lords, a bad breed. She, naturally, was still a child at the time of the conspiracy; later, while still very young, she married a distant cousin of ours, Francesco Calvisano Gonzaga, of a good but not excellent position. As for Federico, everyone believed it was a twenty-year-old's caprice; but time passed, and every day he became more and more closely bound to her. He took her always outside Mantua, to be closer to her and to put distance between her—I wish I did not have to say this—and me. She flattered him, glorifying his enterprises, seconded him in his princely presumption, and she kept an eye on me; one of her people, surely my enemy, kept her informed in detail on my days.

And still, Federico walked in my footprints. He resembled me in his avid reading; for example, from the field of Parma he asked me for three books at the same time: the *Orlando Furioso* of Signor Ludovico Ariosto, the *Innamoramento di Orlando* of my dear Matteo Maria Boiardo, and the *Innamoramento di Lancilotto*. When my friend Chiericati of Vicenza spoke to me about the extraordinary discoveries of Antonio Pigafetta, who had sailed around the world with the Portuguese Magellan, I thought how much those stories would delight my son. A few months later Chiericati sent Pigafetta to me in Mantua. It had been a long time since I so enjoyed myself. The traveler, with his penetrating speech and Vicenza accent, told such an unusual tale of his itinerary that my enthusiasm spread to the whole court. Federico immediately wanted to know more and promised the bold voyager to pay for the paper in order to have the narrative printed. Prompt in generosity, my son has no fear of making gifts and spending, like me, thought I have always counted and re-counted my funds. He is entitled to openhandedness and the wholly male privilege of satisfying himself with every gesture he makes.

At the end of December Federico returned from his successes in the field at Pavia, but he did not come and live at Mantua. He withdrew to Marmirolo, though the weather assailed us with cold and fog and the trees in the garden were wrapped in straw and rags to confront the winter frosts. I have never been fond of Marmirolo; it is an old villa, often renewed to meet the requirements of the princes' merry life. It has been enriched with paintings, statues, infinite furniture, and rare objects. It has an

unparalleled park and an immense pool with fish big enough to
be caught and an aviary with walls painted by our own Lorenzo
Costa. But there is a lack of harmony in its vastness, overdecorated
with joking allusions to those young lords tempted by sensual
malignity.

The men of the Gonzaga house have always favored Marmirolo,
the women less so, perhaps because of the amorous legends that
have surrounded it for centuries. Federico laughs when I say these
things, but now he is shut up in there, emerging only for hunting
parties in the nearlby forest of Fontana. And this Boschetta, as
she is called, is always with him, almost taller than he, of too
great proportions to be a harmonious woman. At first sight she
seems affable, but her amiability is only a kind of pride, between
contempt and triumph; she dresses in a showy fashion that pleases
men greatly because over our modern style she drapes mantles
of satin and brocade or little capes of velvet edged in fur, and she
often lets her hair fall loose over her shoulders like a king's daughter. On her head she places diadems in the Roman way or great
brimmed hats that extend to cover her shoulders; my Elisabetta
wore them about twenty years ago. These hats are extremely
irksome, but they heighten the face, in the shadowy area around
the head. They say she possesses very precious jewels for a woman
of private condition.

I AM IN my new apartment, surrounded by every sort of comfort, here in Cortevecchia. Federico was delighted when he saw it, but he never lingers to enjoy it in my company. I stroll beneath the city loggia, where it is never cold because it is exposed to the sun and sheltered from the wind. When the fog comes down, torches are lighted, and the contrast between the gray air and the yellowish light surprises our gaze with a festive effect. We have music either in the rooms toward the church or in the great hall frescoed by my dear Leonbruno, his brows always knitted, but still an excellent painter. In the lunettes around the ceiling he has depicted hunting scenes, including Lavagnola's famous feat, when armed with a pike, she confronted a wild boar. Since such light grace directs his hand, I told Leonbruno to pay special attention to the villages and countryside in the background, which he has done as if he were portraying nature herself.

Our subjects, admitted in small groups to my new apartment on audience afternoons, rejoice to see me so well and splendidly lodged. I have reconstructed here my most famous chambers: The Studiolo has emerged a place of rare elegance, and so has the Grotta, both with walls and ceiling paneled in inlaid wood, gilded by goldsmith-carpenters. And against this ground the strong, pictorial truth of my pictures stands out, and the collections of little ancient bronzes and the rare objects aligned on the shelves gain new prominence. These perfect spaces are divided and joined by Gian Cristoforo Romano's door of porphyry and red granite, intervaled by white marble medallions with carved figures, and thanks to its dimensions and its design, this door apparently has the power of revealing the character of those who enter, as the frame possesses its own interior proportion. The study adjoining the bedchamber is my place of work, where in the little cupboards I preserve rare books and secret documents in chronological order, and next to it is the room of the clocks. Here, long ago, I began collecting these mechanical instruments. Their accuracy is of little importance to me, and I rarely summon our engineers, to bring them all to the same time.

I was here, in fact, in my private study when Pirro Donati brought me the news that the new Medici pope, Clement the Seventh (successor of Hadrian the Sixth), had told our ambassador of his intention to confirm Federico as Captain General defender of the Holy Church. No one would ever have suspected the foul smell concealed behind these devout words. Mantua hailed Federico, who came to visit me with his court of well-outfitted youths, admired and criticized by my girls in their familiar, playful tone. In the Cortevecchia rooms, bright with colors and ornaments, these twenty-year-olds moved about with ostentatious elegance, too well trained in court ways to make a show of pride and yet proud to be young in the suite of a young lord already distinguished by so many honors. And he, my son, in the center of the company, did not utter one word of apology for having shut himself away for so long at Marmirolo, never seeking my counsel.

I listened to him, amazed to learn how much he had changed. He told me that for Marmirolo, in fact, he had planned a "maze of construction," but now he wanted a completely new residence, perhaps designed by Giulio Romano, Raffaello's leading pupil, invited to Mantua from Rome. Federico spoke much of this house of his, a single story, to be built on the model of a Roman villa, on the terrain covered with lime trees and surrounded by laughing waters, that area called the Tè. And he seemed certain of one thing. Yes, once in Mantua, Giulio would remain at court. His architecture, powerful, Roman, would transform the city, and from it everyone would derive the honor and joy that he, Federico, now received from his military ventures, which had won him so much approval. The Parma campaign and then Pavia, even more, had not been triumphs and bore not even a distant resemblance to Fornovo. Federico was too shrewd to boast of them openly. He told how as a votive gift to the Madonna, he had donated to Santa Maria delle Grazie a wooden statue made to the measure of his body, later to be decked with armor being made by the Milanese family of Missaglia.

"Mother dear," he said, joking, "I cannot do as you did when I was born, offering that Madonna a solid silver infant of my same weight. But both will look well in that church, the babe and the captain in armor; they will keep each other company."

With the usual intimacy he again took his place on the dais of my seat, turning his head upward, charmingly. He was so young, so untouched that he wrung my heart; there was no sign of what happened to him when he was far from me, in the hands of that giantess. So it was natural for me to bring up the subject of matrimony, and I mentioned a very beautiful daughter of the king of Poland, who might be sounded out.

"Mother," he said, "do these seem times for marriage? But go ahead and maneuver, as you do so well. Then we will see." And he added gaily: "Oh, dear Mother, do you think I will have to teach my bride how to love me in Italian?"

He was happy, and I did not dare afflict that bold twenty-year-old. I recalled the letters he had sent me almost daily from the field during his first military campaigns and my distress, almost terror in finding in them my own turns of phrase, my use of language, my ways of opening and closing sentences, my logical reasoning. It would be dreadful if he had looked to me only in order to imitate me.

These thoughts of mine overflow with such passion that I hardly know how to recapture them. But I can relive my fright when, in mid-January, I heard the news Pirro Donati came to report, with consideration and dismay: Someone in Milan was spreading the word of an illness of Federico's that made his urine red, and neither the imperial troops nor the pope could budge him from Mantua.

I thought back to the days of my husband, Francesco: the repeated humiliations that had kept him a voluntary prisoner at home during the terrible days of Julius the Second; the wretched pretexts; the accusations of cowardice and ineptitude circulating among the troops and chiefs of state. Would they now be repeated, imprudently stirred by a young man of twenty-four? To allay my distress, I sent Pirro to Marmirolo; I wanted truthful news. My secretary came home puzzled, to say that Federico was quite well and had guaranteed, with great laugher, that he was hale and hearty. He mocked those who would send him into the mud of midwinter, when the masses of dirty snow were melting, after having chilled all Lombardy this year. He planned to travel to Rome and pay homage to the new pope; this was also the advice of his court.

INSOMNIA seized me. During the day I observed the slightest things that happened around me, the dispatches that arrived at random, because my friends were not always very assiduous. Even Equicola, official singer of my praises, was seldom seen at Cortevecchia, though he never ceased extolling that new residence of mine that inspired writers and poets. I was overcome by sophistic passions. I set myself to copying Ciceronian epistles, which I had read aloud at court, or I dressed myself always and entirely in white with ciphers of gold and of black velvet in relief, rare dresses that only Elisabetta and I could wear. Soon I began to fear I was a prisoner even in the new apartment, open onto green spaces, with so much sky above it. I should go away, uproot myself if possible. I was recalling that next year was the jubilee. Rome was always my goal.

And in Rome there was, ready, completely refurbished, the palace in Via Lata, given back to the della Rovere family immediately after the death of Leo the Tenth, when the whole duchy returned to their hands. My Elisabetta and my daughter Eleonora were living now in their handsome palace in Urbino, surrounded by faithful courtiers, and Francesco Maria, more grouchy than ever, kept changing military commands, first here, then there; for the jubilee none of them wanted to move apparently. Thus I would be mistress of the Roman residence, where I would take with me a carefully chosen retinue, not too numerous. My cardinal friends and Pope Clement himself had sent word that they were awaiting me with joy. But it was not sure that I would leave.

October was ending, and the autumn was milder than is usually our fate. The sun took on a strange, chill, golden hue; the vineyards became heavy with grapes; hunts followed one another, every day troops of horsemen and ladies rode through the city to the sound of bugles and horns. In those days there was talk of a feast, called an "invention for the house of love," that Federico was giving for courtiers and gentlemen in that locality known as the Tè. Equicola, my secretary, was of the band. And with him, awaited and legendary guest, went Giulio Romano, now some days in Mantua and much honored.

I have always been a glutton for reports of feasts and gatherings, as even my bizarre Englishman, Robert de la Pole, was aware. I have ways of keeping well informed when I choose. Here I was not so much curious as anxious. One of my ladies, I will not say which, noble and beautiful, not an excellent but a discreet observer, told me about the feast on the meadows of the Teieto. I record only the most salient episodes.

The guests, about fifty in all, were crowded into two great river barges, bedecked with brocade and yellow velvet, which slowly glided among the canals. They got off at the island, where, in a sunny little dell, servants had spread out thick carpets to protect the feasters from the dampness; all around, in a semicircle, seats and cushions were arranged, and on low stools covered with white linen were placed silver trays laden with food, every kind of the excellent game found in our opulent Mantuan countryside. In the air, barely stirred by a light breeze, the notes of the musicians wafted, and against that harmonious background all the company joked and laughed. Renzo and Bigino, Federico's silliest pages, discovered a lizard, fleeing and cold, and to the cry of "Salamander! Salamander!" they set to hunt the animal, to throw it into the fire and see if it truly passed through flames without being burned. The lizard escaped, but conversation about salamanders went on, the way such things develop among people who know the art of enjoying themselves. Federico, looking at his Boschetta, remarked meaningfully that the salamander is lucky, for it passes through the pyres of passion and remains untouched, knowing none of human torments.

Boschetta (who was wearing a satin and velvet dress of two shades of green) drank in these compliments, and Equicola expanded them. Federico, meanwhile, went over to Giulio Romano to ask: "And you, Signor Giulio, what will you invent? Here we are not rich in marble. How will you manage to raise the vaults and arches of Rome for us?"

Giulio Romano answered that from the water surrounding this island of paradise the dwelling that the marchese had asked of him would rise. "We do not need marble." He added, "The palace will not even seem to have walls but will emerge from the rural happiness of the meadows and the river. This will be a place where man's life will proceed in conjunction with the energy of nature."

The artist expressed himself freely, filled with inspiration: Trees would serve as wings for the facade; the building, low like a Roman house, would breathe in the countryside through a series of arches.

"No," he concluded, "I will not use blocks of stone or slabs of marble. I will use this humble mud; I will transform it into a rustication that will suggest the earth's renewing strength, season after season."

There was more music, the pages passed more goblets of Verona wine, and Giulio Romano, pointing again to the spaces on the horizon, said to Federico: "The house will be well oriented, and everywhere there will be your emblems, first of all, the salamander."

I listened to this account. I saw Boschetta in the role of a favorite, not a very considerable part, and no remarks or witticisms from her were quoted. The triumph belonged to the artist and, with him, to the lord, who had stimulated the tension that generated original methods of building a new work. My informant, cleverly questioned, declared she had not noticed any excessive demonstration of amorous servitude in Federico except that he was more amiable and fanciful in attending his woman than the other gentlemen. And how could he have failed to be, he who had graduated from my school?

I thanked the informant with a generous gift that made her eyes sparkle. I reflected at length, calling up the usual dream of the triumphs of Federico, chief of state, captain in war, great patron of artists and instigator of their inventions. Against my expectations, however, the future was assuming hazy outlines, vacillating forms. Now I well know why: I was uneasy, and I was even wondering if my informant had deliberately suppressed something, to spare me, or to deceive me. Cottony clouds were descending, the air had a gray breath, and we were assailed by news. One of the many turns of events exploded, the kind that disintegrated the politics of those years. Francis the First came down into Italy to take Lombardy back from the Spaniards. Milan had already fallen, the French were moving on to besiege Pavia, and the pope suddenly took sides with the king of France. Charles the Fifth, his infinite pride irked, at that moment decided to strike a mortal blow at the supreme head of the Church. Luckily for us the secret policy had been burned to ashes, and no one could force the Captain General of the Church to fight personally against the imperial troops.

Meanwhile, Federico had had to come back with his gleaming cavalcade of honor from Bologna to Mantua, breaking off his journey to Rome. Clement himself had issued the order for him to stay put and prepare himself for war. Repelled by all these bellicose plots, I had two carriages prepared, and with a very small escort, I left for Ferrara, to visit my brother Alfonso. The two of us had such faith in our reciprocal strength that we felt like allies even when our states were not, especially now, when the pontiff was joining the French.

At Ferrara I lived in the rooms which for twenty years had always been set aside for me in the Lion tower, all draped with tapestries and carpets, and with the famous canopy worked in golden pomegranates, which had once belonged to the duchess Lucrezia. Now, five years after her death, I saw her children: Ercole, sixteen; Ippolito, fifteen; and the handsome Francesco of eleven. Eleonora, nine, impressed me because she repeated the features of Cesare Borgia, her uncle—sharp, almost vulpine, a bit gloomy—a child destined to the convent because my brother would never allow her to be humiliated by refusals of marriage offers because she was her mother's daughter. Her father envisioned her only in an abbess's habit.

Ferrara sent fresh blood to my heart. My conversations with Alfonso were clear, without dubiety. Alfonso took an ironic view of the withdrawal of the imperial troops from Milan, suggesting they were afraid of not being able to defend it. As for himself, he was making good preparations just in case; in a low voice I confided to him the secret of the burned policy and Federico's regained freedom of action. He approved. He asked me about Castiglione, who in the matter of the secret policy had displayed a cleverness equal to his intelligence. Yes, he was truly excellent, but now he also was leaving me, sent as papal nuncio to the imperial court, to Charles the Fifth in Spain. I had not even bidden him good-bye in Mantua, and there was no knowing when we would meet again because he was leaving in haste, given the urgency of the war in Italy. I chose to go through the grand courtyard, which I remembered crowded with guards of honor and courtiers, and so it was still. The steps of Benvenuti's staircase, which I had climbed, holding the hand of Pico della Mirandola, still seemed too high.

I REALIZED AS soon as I went back into my bed-chamber. There was something awkward or, at least, disturbed in the order of the objects on my little tables: The book on the inlaid stool by the bed showed a crack which was widening into a flaw. The book was a collection of Cicero's family epistles, which, if I woke up in the night, I read with a spirit far from scholastic. There I sought reflections of the thought, not to say the errors that the great man tried always to evade. I picked up the book, and I perceived the reason for its altered appearance: Between the pages someone had inserted a folded sheet of paper, an unsigned letter in a falsified handwriting. Feeling my hands suddenly limp, desolate, I promptly placed the book under the pillows and called my Jacopa with the two young maids, her helpers, to undress me. None of the three, as I observed them carefully, glanced toward the stool. I dismissed them and slipped into bed, measuring my movements. This was not the first time I had received messages of this sort. The unsigned denunciations of my courtiers and my ladies were frequent, and I made short work of them all, throwing them into the fire, not allowing people to believe that in an anonymous guise they had the right to importune me with unpleasant suggestions. This time, however, I lacked the nerve to perform that act of destruction. My own uneasiness created a complicity with the writer; I unfolded the paper, and I regretted it.

MOST EXCELLENT LADY

Your son is betraying you; he is completely and badly involved with his Capitana. The writer heard, unseen, a conversation between her and your son and feels obliged by his loyalty to report it to you, word by word. Obviously I cannot sign this letter. I will be brief. She, the Capitana, is obsessed with the idea that her Love wishes to marry, as is the duty of all princes. And she hints that you are pressing the question, to accustom him to the idea of his matrimonial duty. They were in their little hexagonal sitting room, the scene of their amorous meetings, and she was insisting on the usual subject. "You are sorry not to have gone to Rome, are you not? You dream of the horse races, the tourneys, the Roman ladies. And you do not realize that someone was forcing you to make that journey for another secret purpose." He replied that these were fancies of hers and that there were no secret plans. She raised her voice. "Sooner or later the pope will make you send to Monferrato for your Maria, whom you unwisely married when you were nine years old. This Maria Paleologa is fifteen now, she is a woman, and she wants her husband. You are pledged to her." In a teasing voice your son explained: "I was going to Rome for political reasons; I have never gone to pay homage to the pope since he confirmed my position as his captain." The Capitana would not give way. "But isn't your marriage political, too? The mother of your bride, this Anne d'Alençon, isn't she a close relative, practically the sister-in-law of the king of France?" Your son said that he was against France, but she replied harshly: "There's never any knowing how these things will turn out; alliances often change." Our marchese, continuing his apostolate of patience, went on: "My dearest, I will send my ambassador, Signor Cappino, to Casale Monferrato to speak with the Paleologo family. Rest assured, I have no thought of ratifying this wedding contract. The time of war is approaching. The king of France will soon join his army in Italy. We will have infinite battles. Marriage, indeed!" Here the Capitana repeated that he had failed to take his mother into consideration and that you foster that Maria of Casale Monferrato. Remaining calm, your son informed her that his mother had suggested quite a different match, with the daughter of the king of Poland. But she insisted that you, signora marchesana, want only to confuse him with this princess; in reality you will obligate him to keep his word with Maria. He went on shaking his head. Then she rose, in a fury. She reminded him that he had attained his majority three years ago, and she underlined her words: "It is your mother, the marchesana, who governs; everything passes through her hands: she opens the dispatches, she judges, she deals with the ambassadors, she decides. And everyone in Mantua knows her iron hand, in ruling. The late lamented marchese Francesco also knew it well."

She succeeded in making him lose his temper, poor youth. But he defended himself, saying that he fears nothing and is on his guard. His father always exhorted him never to be the slave of the marchesana in matters of state, and for all his life he will respect the adr.ıonition his father left him and repeated to him before dying. Many of her words flew before, as then happened, there was a reconciliation on which it would be futile to dwell. Your son confessed himself the slave of love of his Capitana. This is the warning of one who takes your affairs to heart, which is to say

A FAITHFUL SERVANT

I savored it all, the perfidious unsigned letter, distiller of wormwood. That paper burned my hands, not openly insulting, but terrible because it answered my suspicions and the doubts that I had kept to myself. It told the truth.

I had stubbornly rejected the thought of a Boschetta hunter of prey, one of those women who lay their hands on powerful men, especially when young. I had pictured a woman in love experiencing a romance, a suitable teacher for Federico, who at times could seem a bit slow. Now before my eyes reality was revealed, a reality I had feared and repressed, a prince prodded by an ambitious woman who was my furious enemy. I thought of Francesco, warning my son, covertly turning him against me, and in the very last days of his life, when I thought he was at peace; on the contrary, even as he was appointing me regent, he was bequeathing to his son a heredity of hostility. So I had never been forgiven for having seen beyond the obvious things. In Federico my living image was this: a woman greedy for command, who wanted to maneuver him to her own ends.

I clenched the paper in my hand as I questioned it, to understand what evil purpose drove the writer. Who was he? Surely not some subaltern woman steeped in hatred old or recent; the letter emanated a brisk nastiness that was all male. One of Federico's courtiers? But which, and why? My first impulse was to call immediately my natural ally, my son. Immediately I came up against the image of him suddenly my enemy, and I withdrew my hand already reaching for the silver-voiced bell.

Meanwhile, it must be established if the scene was truly observed or if that odious portrayal was invented on the treacherous paper. True or false, however, I should betray no sign of having read it; I should speak of it to no one, not even to my Pirro Donati, the man of all loyalties. I should not inspire compassion. Boschetta would laugh triumphantly if she knew I was plunged in torments so cruel as to leave her freedom for every sort of game. To pretend she had been slandered, to place herself on a level with me would be easy for her, and she would reduce Federico to apologize for my wrath, with mortification and sorrow.

My son, I concluded, whatever his role was, should be saved in order that I be saved. I got out of bed. I flung the paper in the fireplace. The fire was low; the thick paper burned badly. I added a little bundle of twigs to kindle a good, voracious flame that would destroy every trace. I dragged myself back toward the bed. The sheets scented of jasmine received an exhausted woman.

WINTER that year was sullen, but in my Cortevecchia apartment it could be faced better because the rooms, of medium size, were mostly exposed to the sun, with the vast fireplaces always lighted. It was a new spectacle to look through the leaden windows at the trees outlined with their surviving leaves or at those drawn by their stiff, thin boughs and branches. Nature seemed closer here, not abstract and distant as from the loftly halls of the castle. I went to visit the apartment of the guards adjacent on one side to the walls of my chambers and on the other to the outer part of the palace. I felt the square against my shoulder, I listened to the footsteps of the sentinels and those of the populace, echoing under the tall arches of the palace, which had belonged to the Bonacolsi family. I heard the sturdy Mantuan speech and was warmed by the testimony of so many lives nearby, each with its own story.

On a morning of winter sunshine I was alone in one of the little rooms that give onto the secret garden. A fanciful snow was falling at intervals on the shrubs; in those rooms that measured six feet by six, heated by great bronze braziers constantly fed, I was looking at some lengths of stuff unfolded on the tables, displayed to me by a merchant from Bergamo. A brocade of gold on cut velvet challenged me with its price, but I have never been economical except when circumstances imposed economy on me. I asked Equicola, who had just arrived with excessive compliments, if he liked it.

"The sun moves in it; you will be a pyre of light, my lady," he said with hyperbolical enthusiasm.

I felt an impulse to be contrary, and I answered him a bit sharply: "I do not know if I can buy it. For the new apartment I have sacrificed my court. I also had to forgo a picture of Perugino."

I had forgone it, in fact, leaving the painter's wife free to sell it to whomever she pleased; and all of a sudden I decided not to economize: I bought the gold brocade and another dress, and yet another. Someone would pay. I addressed Equicola with ironic concern, inquiring about his health; I had not seen him for some days and had feared he was ill. Informed that his health was good, I asked him if there were important dispatches beyond those that Pirro Donati would collect in the chancellery; the war in Lombardy was much in my thoughts.

"There is nothing urgent, my lady."

"Then how is it that you are here?"

"I felt nostalgia for your lovely face and a desire to kneel at your feet, my queen!"

"These declarations of your love are becoming more and more rare," I remarked.

"What? Am I not the author of the rules for loving you well, the decalogue of Isabellian worship? Am I not the one who, at every opportunity, has exalted you to the heavens?"

With a wave of my hand I dismissed him. Calling the merchant, I told him what I had chosen and instructed him to take the stuffs to the wardrobe and then stop by my steward. I would pay the debt in three installments. I cast a glance beyond the window; through the leaded panes I tried to discern my girls moving in the garden. I heard monotonous male voices distinct in the clean air, remarking: "Good for Ippolita; one point for Lavagnola," and then a conclusive cry from Trotta: "Enough! This is boring! We are dying of boredom!" Approaching the panes, I could make out two of my old gentlemen, Ippoliti and Guerrieri, wrapped in their furs, trying to joke with the girls and make them laugh. Sullen, grouchy, they turned their backs; they said they were cold and would go into the kitchen to warm themselves with a *sorbir*, a hot broth with wine. They fled, one after the other, and their dresses rustled along the passage. The gentlemen slowly turned toward the little door of the secret garden and went out, not speaking.

I had decided to choose the stuffs by myself, so as to avoid futile yearnings and even more futile envy among my young women. In the hall of Leonbruno there were people of the court. Some notes could be heard, a singing exercise, but the voices sounded thin; visitors must have been few that morning, and the snow and frost had something to do with it, but not everything. I recalled other icy winters when my rooms were filled with friendly people, who drank hot spiced wine and crowded the windows of the castle to look down at the skaters flashing over the ice of the lake. I was forced to admit that today my girls were bored, and I had announced in vain that for carnival new pages would arrive from Modena and Reggio, and new gentlemen of the chamber. "Children and old people," Lavagnola had muttered. A promise escaped me: a young people's ball if the war situation allowed it.

"Oh, dear lady, why not invite the duke's men?" Tortorina had asked, clapping her hands. "Did you know that Lord Federico's courtiers have decreed they will admit no one to their company who has passed the age of twenty-four?"

The little door opened, and Pirro Donati looked in, with a warm and gentle smile. He had nothing in his hand. I asked him if the day's dispatches were in another of my rooms and where, and with a grave expression he answered me: "The chancellor Lanzoni would not give me the letters. He declares there is nothing important."

A genuine plot against me did exist. Equicola had been sent to explore my reaction to what was going on in the chancellery. So I was soon enlightened.

"Nothing important the chancellor declares?" I cried. "And yet all the roads of Italy are being traveled by hundreds of messengers sent in every direction. Of course, thre are important things, Pirro. We will go to the chancellery. Or rather, no, I will go alone. If there is to be a storm, they would misdirect it at you. Instead, I want it to be all mine."

I flung my fur-lined cape around my shoulders, and I went out the little door at the end of the secret garden to avoid the audience hall, where someone might have stopped me. I reached the little stair leading to the upper floor, and I passed through the hall of Roman statues, between two lines of marble creatures; the white arms made gestures of warning to me, but I paid them no heed. Reaching the offices, I advanced straight toward the chancellor.

"Signor Lanzoni, what are our agents doing these days? Dispatches seem to become infrequent, and yet these are days crowded with events. In a moment like this are our people asleep? Tomorrow the Bourbon or the Frundsberg with their Landsknechts could be in Verona. Will we continue to be ignorant?"

Confronted like this, Lanzoni was caught off guard; beneath his clump of hair his olive face now turned pale, gray.

"We are all too wide-awake, my lady marchesana," he said, making an effort to be polite. "True, never as in these days have dispatches been so frequent. We haven't time to reply. Soardino is ill from overwork."

"If this is true, if you are not lying, where are these dispatches? I want to see them with my own eyes."

From livid Lanzoni turned deep red. He had fallen into the trap. He stammered some vague words. Then Carlo Silvestri intervened, an old friend of Tolomeo Spagnoli's, a man with a malignant, misogynist's face. He bowed, bending double, and unctuously, with false respect, assured me that I should trust him, our papers were well guarded.

"Who gives the instructions?" I asked sharply.

Secretly Silvestri was jubilant. But he maintained an anonymous voice as he said: "The lord marchese wishes to have everything that arrives; then he makes the annotations in his own hand. The replies go out every hour. The documents are listed and stored in the archives according to the date of arrival."

"We have orders to give no one the papers of the chancellery," Lanzoni added, courageously.

I know from whom that order came: Equicola. My secretary would pay for his insolence, his abuse of authority. But Silvestri was already reacting. "Your Ladyship will forgive us, but the orders come from the marchese in person."

I felt a scream in my bosom, painful. I took a few steps, to regain my demeanor, and at the same time I was thinking: "Federico! Federico obeys his father against me. Federico is setting me aside, and he does not know what terrible disasters can come from a reaction not tempered by prudence. Without me, Federico is risking destruction."

At that moment Federico entered the chancellery agitated, almost terrified. He had the air of a child, guilty but stubborn. He came to me, politely kissed my hand. I saw him as he was: handsome, but spoiled by adulation and presumption. The clerks' eyes were fixed on us. The pain of defeat alternated in me with a mother's compassion. I mastered myself, and I mastered my suffering.

"Federico," I called to him, "I have been looking for you, my son. I've been looking for you, perhaps too impatiently, but you know my character. I was in a hurry to tell you that I am leaving. The jubilee year has been inaugurated, and Pope Clement has invited me several times. You cannot have forgotten that. I plan to say many prayers and do much penance so God will assist us."

I held out my hand to Federico, and he grasped it with the usual respect. I resumed walking, bound to him thus, and I continued my words as I left that hated room that had seen me humiliated, even worse than I had been humiliated by my husband. I explained that in Rome there were many things awaiting me to be done. The question of the new cardinal of the house of Gonzaga, our Ercole, had remained at a standstill, and as our own Ferrante was now well established at the court of Spain, nothing could be more useful than some friendly conversation with the imperial ambassador. I had gathered some strength; I could permit myself my usual animated tone.

"Rest assured, my son, that I will not spend all of my time on devotions and affairs of state. Many cardinals have already written to me, announcing great festivities. I intend to take young and beautiful people with me, expert in singing and dancing. We must conquer Rome as in the days of Leo. Ah, have you heard? Prince Vespasiano Colonna wants to marry young Giulia, your cousin from Bozzolo; I must concern myself with this marriage. Cardinal Pietro Bembo has also promised performances of new plays. We will do Mantua honor. I have invented a new motto that will provoke talk. On a black ground, picked out in gold, in Roman numerals, the figure twenty-seven, *ventisette*, or *vinte le sette*, the enemies, the sects, are vanquished. Do you like it?"

Federico listened, wary but dumbfounded. "You are the mistress of everything, my lady mother." And after an anxious pause: "But who will pay all the expenses?"

The swelling of my eyes was spreading to my face. I managed to muster more courage, and I said with a dull voice and painful irony: "The marchese of Mantua, naturally. Who else?"

VI

Roma, Roma

Room of the clocks
the year 1533

MANY AMONG THE machines surrounding me have marked off the minutes of searing loneliness that fell upon me that day of deep snow. They know how you can believe you are drowning, and even thoughts lack the strength to rise against that mortal state. I had devoted twenty-five years of carefully devised inventions to raising the son of my womb, the son of my spirit, to creating his legend. He who was to have been a virtually perfect man had eluded me with a clumsy scene, leaving me exposed, the target of a band of clerks. By a hair I had saved my dignity. Later, reflecting on the Federico of that time, I concluded that he was too young, not yet sufficiently disenchanted to judge the true measure of what is human. The robbery—felt as a right—of the young from other beings is instinctive, and their acerb minds support them. And wasn't it also possible that between him and me two youthfulnesses were in conflict: the youthfulness of years and that of the mind, interlocked adversaries?

Age no longer frightened me. I was as curious as I had been at twenty about every living thing; I wanted to discover harmony even in the deformity of existence. Deformity: I say this word, and I feel within me a singular fascination of secret horror. I have always studied whatever is outside normality, perhaps the better to understand what normality consists of. Why do dwarfs arouse in me a twisted tendency to amuse myself, making fun of them? I have only to recall my favorite dwarfs like Delia and Mantello. They were misshapen creatures, marked by an obscure power, and yet I suffered for their unhappy lives, and often I helped and supported them in instinctive charity. I must confess, in me there is a greedy pull toward counterfeit depictions. I was greatly excited, determined to learn everything about the monster of Ravenna, whom I saw in a drawing, though I did not dare have a copy made for myself: a hermaphrodite with wings instead of arms, a horn on his head, a beaked paw, a frightful eye below the knee.

Many astrologers and soothsayers and even the heretic monk Luther interpret the appearance of monstrous creatures as a sign of immeasurable catastrophes. Often I have observed this, and often, always gripped by that incomprehensible fascination, I have sent for passages of ancient or modern works, seeking in them horrifying descriptions of animals or of men, cyclops or human dragons with crested backs. Mamia, a little bitch of mine, whelped a dog with eight feet, attached to limbs, two bodies, and a single head, I had it desiccated to preserve its memory. I rushed at once to see the monster cast ashore at Porto Catena by a flood, stirred by the storm from the depths of the lake; another time I ordered a detailed description of the monster that the current of the Po dragged to the bank of the river in the vicinity of the Monastery of San Benedetto.

With my friend the master of philosophy Pietro Pomponazzi, I spoke at length of these beings without future, all or almost all destined to live briefly. For him this sort of miracle was the work of motor intelligences coming from some astral movement; in a given century, he said to me, a human monster can be born parallel to a strange event such as the creation of a new religion or a great historical upheaval, and we must not be amazed since both the one and the other are governed by those same motor intelligences that proceed in one direction. An acutely logical explanation, which, for me, surpassed that of Cicero, who considers our amazement dictated by our awareness of the wonder, observing that if we were accustomed to unusual things, we would attribute to them more the significance of possible and natural things and not of wonders. And didn't the nature of Federico have also a wondrous aspect?

I was pregnant with him, and (this happens to almost all women in that state) I had got it into my head that I was going to bear a monstrous creature. It was the blessed Osanna who reassured me, my beloved saint, whom I still visit in spirit, going to pray at her tiny hermitage, where there is barely space for four people and where a low window overlooks the garden, framing the pure, brief loggia of paradisiacal dimension. At the prompting of her confessor, she referred me firmly to Saint Augustine. The lofty Church father wrote that man does not have the right to judge peoples of strange blood or strange individuals because only God, creator of all things, knows who must be born and how to distribute, in its different manifestations, the law of universal harmony.

A great serenity comes from the word of one who knows God.

And in fact, I no longer thought of the horror of generating a monster, and Federico was born, of perfect form. How I would have liked to learn from the blessed Osanna whether deformity of the soul is also decreed by God and whether Federico, rejecting the interchange of spirit he had had with me in long, daily harmony, was within the reason of nature.

She, my saint, was no more; my courage was a weight I had to bear. And I had to continue, as challenger, with the determination to emerge victorious.

A BSTRACT, THE WINTER landscape on the shore of the sea. I arrived in Pesaro in February, with all the cavalcade I was leading to Rome. We were to meet Elisabetta, coming down from Urbino, moved by the affection that in more than thirty years of friendship had never waned. We wanted to be alone, a wish ever more rarely granted, without witnesses, the two of us together. We had met on the grand staircase of the Pesaro palace of the Sforzas; she was accompanied by Guidobaldo, quite a likable adolescent. But after the greetings and refreshment we went outside; I took Elisabetta into my new carriage, and we drove slowly along the beach.

The day was turning windy; our heads were wrapped in elegant folds of very light Bolognese veils, which protected our heads and ears and soared around us, light and filmy. We laughed, seeing ourselves attired in almost the same style, and we recognized each other also in this trivial thing, the way we were: I, educated to contain myself, and she, who contained herself naturally in her complicated modesty. We conversed about our family and about Eleonora; my daughter's health was delicate, as her husband had transmitted a grave disease to her. And surely she did not accept it out of love. In recent times her religiosity had become accentuated by her insistent reading of sacred texts, which she pondered and, in the secrecy of her rooms, perhaps annotated. At times, with her spiritual women friends, she spoke of religious reforms. Perhaps religion helped her in the depths of her spirit and instinctively led her to choose such company.

Elisabetta and I got out on the beach as the wind grew calm and a pale sun forced its way through the gray clouds. We walked slowly, pausing from time to time. Brief, white-rimmed waves broke on the waterline. Elisabetta spoke with animation, looked at me tenderly and gaily as she had in Venice more than twenty years earlier. She was happy that I was going to Rome, which I so loved. Not she. Her memories of Rome were full of anguish; she preferred her Urbino. There, in her handsome palace, she lived in a pleasant circle of friends: They made much music of viols, voices, and clavichord; they were reading and discussing *The Courtier*.

"Rome helped me greatly at another time," I said. "I could no longer stay in Mantua. I was dying of melancholy."

" 'Melancholy thoughts finally corrode the spirit, and they have to be vanquished.' You said that once, Isabella. Do you remember?"

"I didn't know how true it was then. But today I know. I know that truth so well that I am going away, far from my home. But now I will amuse you."

I told my dear one that I had had the Mantua women work with their needles almost to exhaustion, and now I was bearing new inventions that would overwhelm. All the courts would be talking about them. Elisabetta brightened; she loved dresses and original combinations, and she determined to have some Roman artist draw my styles for her. Suddenly, still smiling, she confided to me that her time of exile had always been alleviated by the thought of me and my way of living in the world.

"And what about me? When I have to drain a bitter draft, I think of you, Elisabetta, and everything goes down more easily. Now more than ever. Federico has shut himself off from me, he is distracted, his mind forgetting all but the summons of another woman, and perhaps he no longer loves me. But you, you have been loved always, adored by your husband and the men of your house."

She turned grave.

"I have never done anything for them, except suffer exile twice, whereas you, Isabella, have fought and saved your State with the force of your intelligence."

"Oh, Elisabetta! I have been made to understand in every possible way that for a woman intelligence is a curse, and it must be paid for dearly."

Again we laughed, completely relaxed, looking down upon male foolishness; we mirrored each other, united as never before, in the past, in the present, and for the undefined time into which we were advancing. We repeated together our favorite motto: To arrange well each time of our life and wait for happy days. She spoke to me again of Eleonora, of her two little girls, sisters of Guidobaldo, and of how good and courageous my daughter was; she had long lost her habit of weeping. I confessed to Elisabetta that Eleonora seemed more her daughter than mine, and for this reason, through her, I loved Eleonora singularly.

Elisabetta thought for a while and then uttered the right words: "We never know why we love and how we love."

We were walking on the sand, near the margin of the waves. Every now and then we would stop and look at each other, clasping hands discreetly. We felt the absence of our friends, distant or gone, and our current thought made them live with us. We begged each other for another meeting; it was understood that when I was on my way back to Mantua, I would go out of my way and take the road to Urbino.

Our veils tangled in our farewell embrace. Elisabetta motioned to a gentleman following us and leaned on his arm. I climbed into the carriage and turned to wave to her. To the last I was nourished by that smile.

WE HEARD a heavy blow followed by a thick hail of stones. The carriage stopped, and the brief procession creaked to a halt with it. Pirro Donati rode up beside my door and said: "Have no fear. We have caught him." From a little hill, the outriders were dragging down a young man of medium height, red in the face, his mouth twisted in an expressionless grimace. He was not a beggar but a peasant, in humble but clean clothes. They pushed him roughly, threatening to have at him with their whips and knives; he was unarmed, except for a little stick. They told him they would lead him into my presence. As he approached, I thought with what tenderness and for how many years his mother had devoted herself to this poor wretch. There was no telling why he risked punishment with his crazy stone throwing. Pirro immediately tried to question him. The boy stammered, choking and befuddled, gurgling now and then.

"The king is prisoner; he is no longer master of the world, he has lost the battle, the soldiers are all running off. Now we can do what we like, can't we?"

"He's raving," Pirro said, "a poor fool."

A heavy voice interrupted him, and a huge man appeared. "I beg you, I beg you, my lords, my lady, do him no harm. He is my brother, a mindless innocent. But he isn't wicked. No, I swear it!"

In his deep dialect the man had a strain of profound pity and anguish. He went toward his brother, put an arm around his shoulders, and continued. "Ever since those horsemen from the Lombard lands stopped to refresh themselves at our tavern, he has lost his mind. He keeps repeating their words constantly; he sees prisoners everywhere and fleeing soldiers."

Pirro asked him what he was talking about.

"What? Your Lordships don't know? The king of France is prisoner; he lost a battle at Pavia; the French soldiers are in flight. At least that's what the horsemen said."

Pirro made him repeat his words amid the general silence. We set the two brothers free, and they went off, the bigger one admonishing the stone thrower, who kept turning toward us with his crooked laugh. We stared at one another, dumb struck, speechless at that news. There could be no doubt it was the truth. It was too heavy, too bare and brutal.

We resumed our way. We had only just passed Narni, the countryside lay deserted, and some time went by before we saw a wayfarer coming up from the south on a little Spanish mule. His clothing suggested he was a student, and in fact, he told us that he was on his way to his lessons at the Bologna Studium. Pirro spoke with him, but the young man knew nothing and seemed much amazed by the news of Pavia. Great events were taking place, and it had been our lot to hear their announcement from the twisted mouth of a lunatic.

The rout of Pavia, Francis the First a prisoner: The world was shattered. I don't know why I gave orders to urge the horses faster, as I huddled up in the corner of the carriage, as if to evade a looming threat, my eyes trained on the road. Two more days we spent journeying, endless, and we received nothing but confirmation of the Pavia defeat. On the third morning we crossed Borghetto; as we gradually advanced, we encountered patrols of soldiers and wagons of civilians heading for Rome or coming from there. The city, we were told, was teeming with armed men, and some implied that it was madness to take so many ladies and maidens into that swirling confusion. Unintimidated, I bore it all with the necessary patience, alert to the dubious situations in store for us. Nothing happened. Eight miles outside Rome a squad of guards came toward us, armed with lances, sent to escort me to Pope Clement. They were amazed to find us so close to the city, and they urged us to hurry.

Rome was invaded by the Colonna supporters, who, totally on the imperial side, rejoiced in the great defeat of Francis the First and rapidly hunted down the Frenchified Orsinis. At San Paolo without the walls, where the Orsini troops were encamped, there had been heavy fighting. Now the survivors fled toward the city, pursued by the Colonnas, and the inhabitants of the city were gathering their households together and barring their doors. The pope had dispatched guards to enforce peace, and he would succeed, perhaps with the help of his Swiss. The captain of our escort expressed the opinion that soon the factions would reenter their strongholds.

We reached the battlemented cube of Porta Flaminia in the afternoon of the third day of March. Our little procession with its papal escort entered beneath the arch and deployed in the open space beyond the walls. Pirro headed for the office of seals, followed by the dwarf Morgantino, who waddled after him in a clumsy imitation. I leaned out and realized that my girls, from the opened curtains of the other coaches, were making great signals to a cavalcade that had just arrived.

"It is Signor Pietro Bembo," Lavagnola cried, peering out from the other door. "And there is also Signor Franceschino Gonzaga, our ambassador!"

The two gentlemen, both of them, came toward me, and all gaily exchanged greetings. We asked for news, and they made a show of great good humor, perhaps to reassure us. In reality, the Colonna men had fought both at San Paolo and in Campo dei Fiori; many dead lay in those places. But now the city was calming down; armed squads of papal guards were patrolling the streets.

We told how we had learned the news of the French rout at Pavia, and Morgantino played the role of King Francis as prisoner but without making us laugh.

Monsignor Pietro Bembo climbed into my carriage, which he praised highly for its comfort and spaciousness. I explained that it was a copy of the one brought from Hungary by my brother Ippolito; for a good craftsman it would not be difficult to build another, similar. With us came also Lavagnola and Camilla Gonzaga. Thrusting her head out of the door, Camilla ordered the girls of the other coaches to draw the curtains and not to peek outside. Glum faces on all sides.

Once the police control ended, Pirro mounted his horse, and the carriages moved off. Via Lata was near. The wheels turned with a low, steady sound on the straight street, long and empty. We passed beneath the arch of Portugal and finally reached the palace of the duke of Urbino, meeting no one. I thanked Bembo, always admiring his regal politeness, and I charged Franceschino Gonzaga to tell the pope that we would come to him as soon as our wagons arrived, which were two days behind us. Greeted with pretty compliments, we entered the palace and established ourselves in the rather cramped rooms, nor was it easy for our cooks to prepare us a modest meal.

An extended silence, marred only by the water vendor's cadenced cry, and the gilded white spring sun accompanied my waking the next day. I thought of Elisabetta, and I imagined her looking southward from her window, as if to follow my progress. In fits I was assailed by my suffering for Federico, and I rediscovered the harsh savor of this alarmed flight that had driven me thus far. Now I knew it. This escape was another voluntary exile, the flight of a refugee. Baskets and coffers filled with dresses, embroideries, jewels, and every sort of ornament could not change reality. My maternal existence felt polluted by filial betrayal; I could not accept it. Behind my son the female diabolical Boschetta lay in ambush, the woman I had till now dismissed as if an intrusion like hers could never have any connection with me. But it was useless to shut all those doors; I had to face reality: Federico loved her.

To My Most Illustrious and Excellent Lady, the Marchesana of Mantua

*A*ll in great haste, today, illustrious and most dear lady; I am about to leave, as I will explain in this letter. But first, I would speak with you as if I had encountered you by chance in the Vatican rooms or in front of the Pantheon, where you will surely go to pay your homage, beneath the pierced dome, at the grave of that supreme inventor of painting who was and is our Raffaello. The moment I learned, from your Franceschino Gonzaga, that you were about to arrive, I was grateful to God for the moment of surging joy he deigned to grant me. I would have done nothing to place myself in your path, I swear; I would have roamed about on my own, to see once more old things and new with the hope of spying your carriage and of standing to look at you from the distance. And then?

And then I cannot say how the spheres of destiny would have acted. Happy only to know you were near and people would speak to me of you, I would not have forced them. And instead, here I am, in my office, choosing which papers to take away with me. I have been recalled to London by Cardinal Wolsey, who has been shaken, as is all Europe, and struck by the defeat of Pavia and no longer knows what to think. We English are at this moment the great mediators with Charles the Fifth, and we press the suit of the pope, so compromised with the French and the Venetians; but at the same time the expansion of the emperor's power over all Europe, harmful also to our island, which the emperor can reach with his fleet, arouses no slight apprehension in my king. And it seems to me that our ambassador in Rome, the bishop John Clerk, shows enlightened intelligence, as he has more than once asserted his conviction that Italy should be freed from French and from imperials alike by the confederated Italian states, which liberation, if it took place, would restore peace to the world.

Henry, my king, has sent his envoys to Charles the Fifth,

impatient to learn what the emperor will do with his
magnificent prisoner, the king of France, heir to the chivalrous
legends of the paladins. Between the lines of the king's
dispatches I seem to read that he wants Francis liberated to act
as a counterweight against overweening imperial ambitions. In
this tangle of information and illations, I have been hastily
recalled to England. I am further obliged to leave as I must
seek knowledge of the highly uncertain state of my family,
which lost in the Battle of Pavia its last representative and
legitimate descendant: Richard de la Pole. He fell in the field,
fighting at the side of Francis the First. To explain briefly, he
was the count of Suffolk, a "White Rose"; for years he had
been living in exile in a village in Lorraine, poor and
uncomfortable, because he was suspected by my king, who
always feared his probable claim to the throne of England if the
Tudors failed to produce heirs. But you must not think that
such dynastic pretensions could now come to me, the
descendant of a very distant collateral branch, as far from the
throne as from the moon. And indeed, Henry and the
scrupulous cardinal Wolsey and the ambassador Clerk for years
have considered me worthy of their Tudor trust.

In short, they are sending me to London when I would wish
only to be in Rome. I do not know how long I will stay there,
but rest assured that all my skill will be directed toward my
return as soon as possible. Perhaps I may find you still in this
beloved city. I do not even know what my mission will be;
some have whispered that an appointment awaits me in Spain
at the imperial court, where our friend Castiglione is now
living. But much as I love Signor Baldesar, at this point my
place is here, Italy, Rome. And you are the ideal queen of this
land of my spirit.

My only lady, two hours remain before my departure, and
misfortune decrees that I must separate myself once more from
the hope of seeing you. Perhaps this is a good thing, for I will
thus be spared your cruelties, which would wither my capacity
for hoping. And hoping for what?

I enjoyed speaking to you at length of Erasmus and of his
singular defense of culture, for him the only real bulwark
against those politicians poisoned by their desire to possess our

beautiful Europe and against heretics like Luther, quick to deny culture or, indeed, to revile it. I am confident that my king, a man of very cautious actions, is not such a politician and is not himself tempted by a desire for total command. I will write to you quickly as soon as I am in London.

I beg you, my lady, in Rome take care never to go out unless escorted by armed guards. The danger is not great for those who are locked in their houses or those well protected. Actions are still expected from the Colonnas against the Orsinis, and Cardinal Pompeo will give a great provocatory feast to the cry of "Empire, Spain, Colonna!" At the slightest sound seek safe refuge, and make sure that the people always following you are trustworthy and prepared for everything. These are no longer the times of Leo the Tenth, though these derive from those.

What dress will you wear on the first day you go out in Rome? I wonder why I imagine a pale blue velvet with a red mantle lined with fur, or else a garment of black velvet, paneled, on a gold ground with white sleeves and collar elaborately embroidered. Am I frivolous enough? I must tell you a secret: I think of commissioning a portrait of you and I will have it done by Sebastiano del Piombo, a most excellent painter. As soon as I am back, I will tell the painter what to do, working from a copy of your profile by the supreme Leonardo. Yours will be the image I can crown triumphantly; I am

your slave forever
Robert de la Pole

Rome, the third of March, 1525

My dear lady, do not call this, and the other letters that I send you, alibis; it is true, however, that I clutch at external events rather than narrate to you my temptations, a tale you might consider offensive. Know only that they exist and that I combat them, taking refuge in beloved stories.

R. de la Pole

T HE DEEP COLOR of the June sun is differ-
ent in Rome. I feel the wonder of moving about in a place
never before imagined: the magic gardens of the Colonna palace,
resembling the backgrounds of paintings. From the Square of the
Santi Apostoli they rise in terraces, as the legend describes the
gardens of Babylon, up to the crest of the Quirinal Hill. There is
a merry solemnity, an Olympian laughter in this place that, of its
kind, has no equal. Groves cover the hilly rise, giant pines, slender
cypresses, their gathered branches swelling, and sumptuously
fringed palms, gay orchards, well-tended vegetable gardens, clumps
of heather, and fountains at every turn. Whole hedges of roses
divide the spaces, alternating with huge bushes of jasmine that
waft perfume from their starred corollas. Every now and then,
amid the greenery, gigantic Roman arches are glimpsed, columns,
pillars, carved cornices, and scholars debate whether these are
the ruins of the Baths of Constantine or of the Temple of the Sun.
At times, stepped ruins, benches and shell-like niches compose
corners worthy of a pastoral fable. The scented silence, the faint
breezes are enhanced by the choral or solitary singing of a whole
bird population. I wonder at being here, with my girls, the dwarf
Morgantino, and a few members of my household; all the others
of our company are still lodged in the duke of Urbino's palace,
where we were rather cramped. It was Cardinal Pompeo who
offered me this paradise all to ourselves because the Colonna
families have gone to spend these hot days in their castles around
Rome. For us they opened the beautiful pavilion behind the church,
adjoining the Santi Apostoli palace; the walls are thick, a protection against winter cold and summer heat, as in our Ferrara and
Mantua castles. The rooms are comfortable and charming, and
the great ground-floor arches onto the gardens have, as a background, a spacious grove of olives. I rest beneath the porch full
of sweet shadow, rereading poetry, Virgil or my Petrarch.
    As in the days of Leo, life in Rome repeats the rituals and

customs of festivities and conversations. One or another of the cardinals comes to visit me; they offer me collations and suppers prepared on allegorical themes. Frequent plays and cavalcades, and every day the sacred functions, which I enjoy more than usual. The Santi Apostoli palace has windows that look into the church, and so I often go to those windows to hear the most beautiful sacred music from the chapel or to listen to my favorite singers. I am enfolded in a strange languor that only the games of my girls can dispel, and the lively, humanistic discussions with my visitors. Among them Paolo Giovio is often present, my friend with the open Lombard spirit.

But why do I compare my other Roman stay with this one today? Yes, things change. From the field of Pavia we have also heard the cry of a civilization's defeat. A French king taken prisoner, and so many gentlemen of great value killed. Galeazzo di San Severino is dead, the most handsome and valiant knight of our century. No one can imagine how, in his day, Galeazzo filled Milan with his spirited strength; where he breathed, women also breathed easily, benevolently attracted and curiously placated in their rivalries. I can almost hear again that debate about the paladins, Roland and Rinaldo, and my sister's shrill voice as she took the side of Roland, hero of war, and my own voice, more full and studied, defending Rinaldo, hero of love. Without knowing it, we two sisters were fighting for Galeazzo, I seeing him in Rinaldo, and she, in Roland, and both of us cheering him on.

I try to take a deeper breath, and I think of that Englishman Richard de la Pole, relative of the eccentric Robert, who still surprises me with his jagged writing; this other paladin, too, has died under the banner of the lilies of France, at Pavia: welcome news to the Tudor Henry the Eighth. Pretenders always inspire dark thoughts in those who rule. Luckily he, the Robert de la Pole who does me the honor of proclaiming himself my slave, says he is as far from the throne as from the moon, and it must be true. Odd fate, he was rushing off to London as I was entering Rome; time ticked, synchronizing the sharp separation of two distinct fates. This Robert does not lose heart; he says, "when I return," and here I ask myself what I would have done if I had seen him again, what I would have accepted in agreement or disagreement with my spirit and my reason. But since he is gone, let him go ahead to his misty England. I would like to add, "And may he never write me again!" But I do not add that; I feel such levity from those letters in the jagged hand that put me under no obligation. I have—and not only now—the suspicion that this Englishman is very clever. His way of making me believe myself free could be a sharp shrewdness. But to what end, if it is understood that I will never answer him, and this understanding has lasted for so many years?

> *And so time passes, and in the glass*
> *I see myself proceed towards the hostile season*
> *towards the unpromised and my hope*

as Petrarch says, and both of us could repeat it.

ONE OF the faces I see constantly near me is that of the duke of Sessa, ambassador from Spain, a fine-looking man with pompous affectations, totally absorbed in his fidelity to the emperor. It would be easy to conclude that he has little to do and spends his time spying on me, but on the contrary, he is minutely informed on every big political development and also on the petty concerns of everyone. Tetchy, he complains if one day, thanks to some errand that takes me elsewhere, I am less willing to play with words, so then he goes about saying to everyone: "Madama is in an ill mood and does not see me gladly." With him one has to take care in speech, especially, in the "open jest" we like. At the summit of his loyalties he places Charles the Fifth, and he frowns upon our freedom of expression in anything that might refer to the emperor.

I continue to be annoyed with my son Federico, who sends me scant news of his dealing with matters of state and writes me at length about his new building at Marmirolo or begs me to collect some antiquities of quality for him or urges me to supervise the two doors with magnificent frames which he has ordered from an artist in marble. It is even more irksome for me to learn all about him from figures in the Curia; often Datario Giberti, quite a talker, comments on the marchese's dispatches, assuming that I am kept informed on every subject. As a result, I know more about Mantua now than when I was a few steps from our chancellery. I keep watch over that son of mine, but with caution, and I note that he is reaping the fruit of much repeated teaching, but sometimes he does this in the wrong way. To stick always to the safest path, especially if it is also just, is wise, but not in every instance. Nor can I refrain from mentally giving him advice. My general idea remains steadfast: We should not have denied passage and victuals to the transient troops because the Mantuan forces are not enough to hold out, especially when the foreigners are armed to such an extent. What the marchese does not allow freely, the soldiers would seize with force, to the great harm of the country and its subjects.

Also to the pope I keep illustrating this position of our state in the event of war, and between sighs, he seems to approve of it. I wonder if, in his place, I would have approved a captain general defender of the Holy Church who spends his time in his villas amid hunts and balls, music, feasts, intent on spending swollen joy, consuming life, while immense disasters can be ripening. And yet, no matter how much you debate the subject, the reality, harsh and solid, is this: A little state like ours can save itself only through inaction or a series of slight, cautious actions.

MY ROMAN life during those two very long years is filled with contradictory events. I hardly devoted myself to anything beyond meditation on the daily shifts of politics. I even forgot to display the dresses I had brought with me, and I dressed only to be in keeping with the grand encounters that took place in Vatican.

I was far from being distressed when I learned that through a chance accident (a messenger's death) a conspiracy was uncovered, a plot to rob the emperor of his chief general, the marchese of Pescara, husband of the lady Vittoria Colonna, and then, if possible, to drive the imperial troops from Italy. In Milan my nephew Francesco Sforza, despite his title of duke, lived a humbled existence beneath the searing contempt of the Spanish. To free the city from that foreign bullying was the idea of Gerolamo Morone, the duke's chancellor. He devised a very weak plan: to lure away the marchese of Pescara, victor of Pavia, who raised to heaven and broadcast on earth his complaints against Charles the Fifth, guilty of holding him in scant esteem. A league of Italian states was planned, with the future help of Francis the First as soon as he was liberated. That perfect, insidious weaver of events Louise of Savoy, mother of the king and his regent in France, secretly abetted every step of the conspirators. Pescara was offered the crown of the kingdom of Naples; covertly pope, Florence, Venice, Ferrara, and, above all, the French king seemed in full agreement.

I have often asked myself how Morone and his accomplices could have been so ingenuous as to believe that the marchese of Pescara, bloated with Spanish honor, would join that dark cabal. Only his wife, the poetess, believed him a bold and angelic spirit. As soon as events fortuitously precipitated, the imperials were warned by their own general. Duke Francesco Sforza, accused of base treason, sealed himself up in the Castle of Milan, to evade capture; outside, the supporters of the absurd conspiracy were persecuted.

Dismay and alarm rattled the chancelleries of the Italian states, and as if by a thunderbolt I was struck by the news of certain words Morone was reported to have uttered about connivance with the marchese of Mantua. I protested that it was entirely false, well knowing the ruthlessness of those foreigners; a mere nothing would suffice to make them set up a military garrison in Mantuan territory, the equivalent of decreeing our country's ruin.

The duke of Sessa came to reassure me; I replied, also to him, that it was all an invention of that wretch Morone; Federico, a young man of such excellent disposition, would never have so deviated from his mother's counsel. Tears of tenderness mixed with anger started from my eyes, and the ambassador saw them and went off to tell the story everywhere as testimony of my loyalty to the emperor. I gave myself the satisfaction, however, of also telling him that I suffered for the duke of Milan, my sister's son; a natural duty obliged me to grieve over his misfortunes. I so insisted on this point that the ambassador considered himself bound to console me, reminding me that my nephew the duke had friends of great authority in the emperor's train and they would find a remedy.

Clement talked and fumed. The discovery of Morone's plot, which at first had terrified him, now seemed to prompt outlandish thoughts in him. Secretly he sent Federico a proposal: In the complex pattern of political negotiations, there would be a way, in the pope's view, of having Federico become duke of Milan, while Mantua would pass to the constable of Bourbon, my other nephew, son of Chiara Gonzaga. And, again according to Clement, this procedure would give Italy general peace. Our Giangiacomo Calandra, Federico's wise adviser, went to some trouble to refuse, but then what did the pope do but offer Federico the crown of Naples? Calandra, in difficulties this time as well, replied that these were the thoughts of the young, who had active imaginations, and he pursued more concrete matters such as the renewal of Federico's captaincy, now expiring.

OUR SURPRISE at all these amazing events was no reason why our daily custom of inventive pastimes should cease altogether. The June of that windy, unstable year led us to the pope's vineyard on Monte Mario, Clement's guests, though he was not present. The day promised to be festive, first because of the company; I was taking with me my most high-spirited girls and two ladies-in-waiting, Camilla Gonzaga and the duchess of Camerino. In a long arbor's shade thickened by boughs laid on the roof, a table had been set up. I myself sat in the pope's place, between the imperial ambassador, the duke of Sessa, and Cardinal Cibo; facing me, I had Datario Giberti; our own Franceschino Gonzaga and other gentlemen, some of them quite young, completed the group. At Clement's wish I was given his plates and his gold cutlery. A magnificent silver service was arrayed on the cloth, dotted with little embroidered roses.

The food was very delicate; the wine, very cool. The dwarf Morgantino, who had given himself the title of Esteemed Pander, furtively delivered here and there little amorous notes that were read aloud and commented, often with Latin tags. The musicians played flutes, harps, and little drums in the Roman style. We were having a merry time, and as I laughed at a quip of Pasquino reported by Cardinal Cibo, I called him mad. Thus we fell to talking about madmen. The duke of Sessa defined the world as mad and was reproached by Giberti, who with ironic vehemence asked what the emperor would have said of this opinion. There was a general outburst of hilarity.

"Laugh! Go ahead and laugh!" the Caesarean ambassador threatened, pretending to joke, and in a prophet's voice, he added: "You'll see!"

But there was no restraining Giberti, and he declared that the maddest madman of all was Charles himself. The ambassador rose to his feet to answer.

"Take care not to insult my emperor!"

"There is someone else who calls him a madman: the Florentine secretary Niccolò Machiavelli."

"The Florentines are insolent by nature, and they, too, will pay."

"But how can he be anything but mad?" Giberti continued. "He takes the king of France prisoner, his declared enemy, and then he frees him with a treaty that will never be observed because we all know it's impossible. What's madder than that?"

The duke of Sessa did not conceal his irritation. "Mind your tongue, Signor Giberti, and say this to His Holiness, who listens to you so carefully: If he persists in his alliance with Francis the First and the Venetians, the emperor will destroy him."

Giberti said something very seriously: "In this war, my lord, the freedom of Italy will be decided."

Cardinal Cibo, young and gifted with good voice, broke up the gravity of the conversation, singing a song that went: "For those who want war, peace is made; for those who want peace, war is made." He did not mean to be allusive, but I considered it wise to intervene, with my best womanly grace, and I urged the guests to enjoy the splendor of that vineyard; the pope's invitation to Monte Mario should produce only a serene happiness.

I had my usual success, and I exploited it to rise and invite all of them into the shady little piazza at the front of the villa, which, still unfinished, stood as Raffaello had designed it, within the wooden scaffoldings, surrounded by dark patches of pines. Stools and benches had been arranged around the open space, and all sat where they pleased.

"The play! The play!" the girls burst out, clapping their hands.

It was not a play but a mimed action, a political allegory, of the kind that had been popular for some time, for I had seen it performed also in Castel Sant'Angelo. At the sound of tambours and fifes, the company of players comes out, with comical fires, big saucepans, and huge forks, and they pretend to hit each other on the head. As they dance, they fight in a preordained fashion, paired or in fours, in amusing interweavings. Swinging bloated yellow bladders, a group of devils arrives; scorning the pans and the fire, they improvise an orgiastic dance of their own. A high trumpet shrills; the sounds cease; the dancers stop abruptly. From the back a tall man bursts forth, wrapped in a dark cloak, his face covered. He cries: "I am Friar Martin Luther!"

The man in black, holding up a book, furiously chases the devils, hitting them on the head, as he keeps shouting in a ridiculous nasal voice: "Gospel! Freedom! Fire and iron will purify Rome, the new Babylon!"

These words are echoed, in cadence, by the emptying of the bladders, with obscene noises, as the devils prick them one by one, leaping and running. As they take to dancing a sprightly *moresca*, the devils press the feigned Luther in a narrowing circle and strike him with the pans, amid endless contortions, jokes, and somersaults. In the end a big black dummy remains on the ground, split in two by the fury of the dance.

Laughing, all applauded, although the vulgarity of the pantomime's theme left me somewhat dubious, and then a great flash of lightning exploded in the sky and thunder ripped the air just above our heads. The stormy announcement was followed by confusion. Musicians and dancers vanished; the guests rushed to seek shelter; faithful to my principle of summoning calm in those who have lost it, I found myself suddenly alone, still seated on my stool. At that moment from the end of the garden Pirro Donati arrived, running. It began to rain. He dashed toward me to fling a cloak around my shoulders, and he dragged me to the portico, still unfinished.

We were standing, pressed against the wall of the villa, under an arch. The rain poured down, a sudden storm. Pirro, beside me, was immobile.

"Something very serious has happened, signora." He spoke in gasps. "Pietro Ardinghello has killed himself, with poison."

The rain beat at us, isolated, and the arch seemed draped with thick fringes of water. I heard Pirro's voice, breathless, at my ear: "I came at once to inform you. I wanted to put you on your guard, if anyone was to ask you about him, signora. Ardinghello had no other course. Clement demanded the policy signed by our marchese for Pope Leo. They have discovered everything; they even know the sum the secretary received from us, a thousand ducats. They would have sentenced him to an infamous death, for treason."

I said, in a whisper: "Did he speak before dying?"

Pirro answered with a reassuring no.

"And the pope?"

"He said only: 'That man sold me for money.' "

"A thousand ducats!" I murmured. "A man's life is worth a thousand ducats!"

I bowed my head, but against the black anguish that assailed me I managed to rebel. I turned my thoughts to concrete things, and I replied, underlining my words: "Castiglione will not open his mouth. Never. And no one will dare say we acted in the wrong, regaining our policy at all costs. Times are becoming more and more cruel; Federico could not jeopardize the State. And now it is certain that Charles the Fifth will soon be the most powerful man in the world."

"What a tormented death, what a lost soul," Pirro repeated, as if to himself.

At this point I dismissed that image of the poisoned man; I was thinking of the future.

"Pirro," I said, "to everyone and at whatever cost, we will deny that we ever had any dealings with Pietro Ardinghello."

*To the Most Illustrious and Magnificent Marchesana
of Mantua, My Lady and Sovereign*

*M*y venerated and intrepid lady, I know you are still in
Rome, at this moment the place closest to the fires
raging in the world, and to Rome I send this letter, which a
trustworthy person has promised to deliver to you. Do not be
surprised to see the envelope has two seals, mine and that of
the secretary of Cardinal Wolsey. I have crossed the Alps again
to go to Venice on a confidential diplomatic mission. Forgive
me if, for the present, I do not speak to you of it. You know
with what keen favor my king follows the cause of the Italian
states against foreigners, be they imperials or French, and it
was on this very subject that I was charged to arrange a
Venetian colloquy. But then, passing through the blessed land
of Lombardy, I betook myself almost instinctively to the siege
of Milan, and now I am at the League's camp at Marignano
among papal forces and Venetians, with a fervor I did not
know could exist in me.

It is already dawn, a beautiful July dawn. The lantern still
gives me light in the army tent where Signor Francesco
Guicciardini of Florence, lieutenant general of the army, has
lodged me and where I await my horses and my groom to
leave for Venice. This early-morning pause in a life so torn by
the change and overwhelming succession of events invites me
to the thought of you or, rather, brings me closer to you, flying
over the still-sleeping world. If any spirits are awake, I am
pleased to imagine that yours is among them.

It is a moment of many burdens, this moment we are living
through, my lady. And I do not know if in Rome you have a
notion of those grave matters I guessed at, having had some
clues in London when I received orders to come to Italy after
the departure of Guidicci and Gregorio da Casale, my king's
gifted envoys. I know they are constantly in motion, alert to

the development of our policy. And I am overjoyed to repeat to you that I have come to Italy to display England's benevolence toward the League, though Henry could not openly declare his association with the antipapal alliance for many reasons.

Unfortunately the course of money governs the course of decisiòns of state. In fact, Cardinal Wolsey clearly explained to me that the king, profoundly suspicious of Charles the Fifth, who from our island observatory looks to be the future master of Europe, must move cautiously because at this moment he has no motives for a sensational rupture with him. Furthermore, there are financial considerations to be pondered, first among them the fear of losing our credit with the emperor and especially the notable question of the Low Countries. A war would block English credits and would spell the total ruin of our cloth industry. Nevertheless, King Henry has sent to ask the emperor to dissolve his Italian army, maintaining your nephew Francesco Sforza as lord of the duchy of Milan. If it is any consolation to you, rest assured that many of us are working toward a favorable solution of this conflict. Cardinal Wolsey's motto is: "Gain time without disheartening the Italian confederates."

Today, or rather yesterday, I had an encounter that I believe I must write down, to record it. Signor Guicciardini did me the honor of inviting me to dinner, having as fellow guests Signor Niccolò Machiavelli, secretary of the Florentine state, Captain Giovanni de' Medici of the Black Bands, and your friend Matteo Bandello, the creator of adventurous tales. I believe our Lombard storyteller means to entrust to his pen a memory of this meeting, but I wish to give you my simple account, assigning to everyone his speech as do those who write for the theater.

So, in good company, we ate roast beef and drank crimson wine; Signor Bandello praised the goodness of the food, observing that Giovanni of the Black Bands is not idly called the Great Devil, and as a devil, he needs red meat if he is to fight well. Signor Machiavelli said that he hopes the Great Devil will not become more choleric than he usually is, at least not with his friends, to which Bandello replied that the

Florentine secretary, given his constant office as thinker, should require very light food, perhaps butterflies' brains.

"Signor Guicciardini," said Signor Giovanni, in a deep, laughing voice, "thank me for having allowed you to dine. If it had not been for me, Signor Machiavelli would still be in the field, trying to bring the three thousand foot soldiers into line."

Guicciardini agreed. He considered that his friend Machiavelli had not really proved himself in his new way of deploying troops, whereas Signor Giovanni had simply to order a roll of drums and the soldiers, promptly in formation, fell into step properly.

"I am learning," Signor Machiavelli reasons aloud, "that the art of war requires practice; what seems correct in writing is quite different in the field."

But the other, Signor Giovanni, replies: "Secretary, you know well how to write, and I know well how to be a soldier. These Black Bands of mine have stirred up their share of fear!"

"And I know well how to sleep," Bandello concludes. "After this good dinner I dream only of a cot." And he goes off toward his tent, followed by the Great Devil, who, amid hearty laughter, teases him to tell his latest, vituperative tale of the joke played on Fracasso da Bergamo, who, in his vanity, seeking to perfume himself with his master's scents, ended by spreading dung on his face.

So there are three of us left, and I ask what the others think of the war. Signor Machiavelli and Signor Guicciardini, in brief words, give me a clear view of the situation. In Milan the Spaniards seem confused, so this is the right moment to attack them, immediately; otherwise, those beasts would be reinforced. The duke of Urbino, in his constant uncertainty, arouses doubts. The day before yesterday he and his troops went as far as Porta Romana, and if they had attacked the castle, Milan would surely have fallen; but the duke came back again, and no one knows why. And this morning he refuses to approach Milan again unless at least five thousand Swiss arrive as reinforcements.

"Francesco Maria is a della Rovere," Signor Machiavelli comments. "He hates the Medici; he will never be a good captain for them. His spirit is too embittered by the memory that Leo took Urbino from him and forced him into exile for years."

The Florentine secretary stands up and paces nervously about the tent; then, in the grip of a fury, he explodes: " 'We will wait for the Swiss,' says the duke of Urbino. These damned mercenaries are our festering wound. It may seem to you an impulsive man's dream, but in Florence, when the news came that Giovanni de' Medici was raising an army to make war, a mad hope surged in my heart. You know well, Signor Guicciardini, how long I have been preaching that we must have an army of well-trained citizens. Only the good citizen will be prepared to fight for his homeland. The mercenary's is a profession of violence, sack, rape."

"Your idea is beautiful but a chimera," Signor Guicciardini answers slowly.

Both are shrouded in a tragic bitterness.

We go outside and stroll a bit in the camp, among the tents, where the soldiers are lying in a state of inertia: Some are dicing; others are in a drunken sleep; others quickly hide stolen booty.

"Signor de la Pole, as a foreign gentleman and as our friend," Signor Machiavelli says to me, "look at these soldiers. They are becoming weaker and more corrupt every day. Give them a little more time, and they'll be worse thieves than the Spaniards."

We walk on, we climb up a rise, a little bump in the plain where a grove of poplars has been planted.

"Think," Signor Machiavelli continues, "if a redeemer were born for Italy, with what love he would be welcomed, with what thirst for vengeance, with what stubborn faith, with what piety, what tears. This barbarian dominion stinks in everyone's nostrils."

Signor Guicciardini looks at his friend, with his frank and desolate face, and replies: "We have no time to wait for miracles. I tell you this: I do not mind toiling, making enemies, being slandered. If the duke of Urbino does not attack, if the Swiss do not come soon, I will go and attack with these wretches and with the banner of Signor Giovanni leading us. We are numerous enough to take the Castle of

Milan. Once Milan is taken, it will be possible for our bands to seize Pavia and Cremona. And when their lines of communication are broken, for the Spaniards it will be all over."

The Florentine secretary's face seems to narrow, and with heartfelt intensity he says: "May fortune hear you! Signor Guicciardini, you love your country more than yourself!"

Signor Guicciardini waves a salute, a sign of faith in something higher, then disappears among the tents. Signor Machiavelli observes me, sees that I am pensive. I tell him that I am wondering if Cardinal Wolsey was right in affirming that the league against the emperor should be presided over by our king, Henry the Eighth; a new vigor would then be imparted to the fighting. Who knows if this prophecy has any probability of coming true? He does not answer me. A little later we say good-bye, and I return to my tent.

I have chosen to report to you this meeting where I was present, so you can realize how sadly the destiny suffered by strong men can be expressed today, as they still exert themselves to dominate in the name of a few, impassioned hopes. As I told you, I was unable to sleep all night, sensing imminent disaster; I do not know what and where; my heart aches every time I think of you in Rome. How can you, so delicate and beautiful, manage to live far from your home? What is there in Mantua that keeps you away? Or what is there in Rome that you prefer to have near? My mind is made up: I must return to Rome to see or at least to know. No one will prevent me. I am at your feet, not to ask permission but to ask one of those many pardons that bind me to you. My groom has arrived. Before turning out the lantern, I beg you: Take care, my dear vision, my lady. Against what? Against everything.

your slave forever
Robert de la Pole

From the camp at Marignano, on the ninth of July, 1526

TAKE CARE against everything, I repeated a little later, when the Colonnas offered their hateful "insult" to Pope Clement. But take care how? It was a beautiful late September day when the mercenary bands of the Colonnas burst into an unarmed Rome, unprepared and aghast: wild men, somehow desperate, good only to release in raids and looting their wrath at being under command. Pirro came that morning to inform me that the Colonna rabble were rushing down from the Quirinal Hill; it was said they numbered five thousand, armed and fierce men. I collected my women; we locked every door, then stood still, to listen as the yells came closer to the Santi Apostoli palace. Those devils chanted the cry "Colonna. Empire. Freedom," and vaunted their determination to reach the Vatican and depose the pope hostile to the emperor. Behind the windows, in the crack of the nearly closed shutters, we peered at the square and the troops, eating and drinking, reducing it to a receptacle of rubbish. Into our rooms came Ascanio Colonna and Cardinal Pompeo, who reassured us completely. We would never suffer any harm; there were Spanish foot soldiers outside the door of our palace. We had to accept such defenders and, with them, Vespasiano Colonna, whom I had received in my apartments last July, when I was witness to the contract for his marriage to Giulia Gonzaga, a beautiful girl of our house, of the Bozzolo branch. On several occasions Vespasiano had conducted negotiations with the pope on the emperor's behalf, and Clement had trusted him, whom he considered and loved as a son.

Sated with food and drink, the immense horde of mercenaries remained in the square like wild beasts in repose; at a command all stood up and began running wildly toward the heart of the city. And then the horrible sack of Saint Peter's ensued, and of the apostolic palaces; the mocking of the pontiff, imitated by lurid buffoons, who pranced around in sacred vestments and cloaks; and the loot of everything, the papal offices, the houses of Giberti, Giovio, Sadoleto completely emptied, doors and windows shattered, the beautiful porcelains in shards, the draperies and wall coverings shredded, the Raffaello tapestries looted and perhaps torn or destroyed. The populace did not make a move, not only out of fear. They remained indifferent to the ruin of their supreme leader, whom they had long loathed for his parsimony, regretting the free-spending days of Leo.

Anxiously we asked one another what could have happened to Clement, and we were told only later that he was in Castel Sant' Angelo, in safety, while the heavy artillery of the fortress swept Borgo Nuovo. The sack lasted all day, and it was only toward evening that the Colonna's bands retraced the road toward Marino. It did not seem possible to us; we were stupefied and outraged, incapable of saying a word. I sent a message to Vespasiano Colonna, warning him that he would not see me at his marriage to our Giulia, which was set for the next days. The hard face of that Colonna, almost the equal of the ugly snouts of his mercenaries, was too repellent to me. I informed the pope of my decision. Back in the Vatican again, he wandered among its destruction and ruins; the poor man thanked me.

At that time my son Ercole, reflective and clever at his age of twenty, entered my view. I had summoned him in haste to Rome; the pope invited him to a very private audience. With him I made my entrance into the Vatican, where the rooms bore the marks of the Colonnas' jackals, though they were tidy now and still impressive. Giberti came forward to meet us, complaining of the Colonnas and then of the pope, wavering between one indecision and another. We were joined by our ambassador, and as always, I asked news of Mantua. Federico had hinted to Count Lodrione, the emperor's envoy, that if the imperial soldiers were to decide to cross Mantuan territory to join the Bourbon in Milan, he would grant them passage.

I became pensive. We were faced by a grave demand and, precisely because it was grave, unavoidable. Federico chose the lesser evil, and yet a vague uneasiness disturbed me. Franceschino Gonzaga described to me my son's exuberant gratitude for my advocacy in the Vatican, my zeal for the Gonzagas' honor and glory, and, in particular, my invaluable justification to His Holiness of the necessarily rather unwarlike actions of his Captain General. Now, however, the marchese believed the time had come for me to return to Mantua. In the general upheaval that lay ahead, he feared for my fate and said as much to all.

"He is afraid for me?" I asked.

"Yes. He suspects new disorders will break out in Rome, like that of the Colonna bands. Here there is constant danger."

I turned to Ercole, with my inventive way that so amused my children: "You hear that, Ercole? Your brother is concerned for his mother. You must reassure him as soon as you are in Mantua again, and tell him that I am very well here." I laughed gaily and added: "I am not a soldier, and if there were really any danger, I would already have taken horse and galloped off at top speed."

At that moment we were introduced into the audience chamber, met by Giovio and Sadoleto. I bent toward Franceschino's ear and whispered to him: "I have hope that today the pope will give us good news." And so it was.

God, what moments those were! I began to breathe faster when Clement invited Ercole to sit beside him, keeping his head covered, as is the right of the princes of the Church. First the pope discussed the complicated political situation of the day, which made him more and more uncertain; then he came to the praises of the "eminent and trusted" house of Gonzaga, which could no longer remain without a cardinal after the death of the most reverend Sigismondo, might he rest in peace. Ercole had a generous impulse: He confessed himself undeserving of such honor because of his youth. For a moment I was aghast. I had only to study his face, animated by deep fervor, to realize how beautiful his sincerity was and how it pleased the pope.

"Yes," Clement said, in fact, "you are a bit too young; you are twenty. But your spirit is strong, and in these stormy times the Church needs support. It does us good," he added, "to feel the faith and the strength of the young close to us. My heart is filled with anguish. But I intend to perform an act that seems to me right to offer to God: I will leave Rome, to go to Spain and then to France, to speak with those two stubborn kings, Charles and Francis, and I will make them understand that mankind's true necessity is peace."

Ercole's eyes, similar to mine but wiser, sparkled. "Holiness, yours is a great inspiration!"

"A great madness!" Giberti muttered behind me.

I could not contain myself, and I said to His Holiness that he did not know the spirit of those conquering warrior princes. In a moment of rage or caprice they would hold him prisoner.

"What of that?" Clement added. "And what even if they killed me? Why should a prince not hold captive my poor body? Before I set out, I will leave instructions for every eventuality. If something were to happen to me, the cardinals here in Rome will immediately name my successor. No man can stop the life of the Church."

His words vibrated with great faith, and Giberti's low muttering, "Madness! madness!" irked me considerably. I realized that on Ercole's face, as his passion faded, a rational coldness had descended. Modestly, but with an adult's vigor, he debated with the pope and gently brought him back to reality, soberly portraying to him the probable state of anarchy in a Rome left to its own devices. The pope sighed but praised my son's counsels with the desolate tone of one who sees a dream wrested from him. Then, turning to us, he bade us keep secret Ercole's cardinalate until the other cardinals were ordained. My son, however, from that moment was a full-fledged prince of the Church. And he was given the decree, tightly rolled up, with the pendant papal seals.

Gliding on air, I crossed the rooms painted by Raffaello. For the first time I allowed my son to precede me, and I was following him at a distance, with triumphant joy, gazing at him. Conceived by me, he had been my son Ercole, and, desired by me, Cardinal Ercole. Now he walked ahead of me with the brisk and grave tread that becomes the princes of the Church; I sensed his rising power, and at that same instant, I seemed to see him escape, without turning back.

To My most Excellent Lady, the Magnificent and Illustrious Marchesana of Mantua

From the Castle of San Giorgio

Yes, you have read aright, dear lady, dear in all things. From Venice I have come down to Mantua, accompanied by a letter from the Venetian Senate introducing me to the marchese your son as informant—which I am—of the king of England in the course of this war unleashed by the imperial forces against the League of Italian states. I am in Mantua, and at every moment I imagine seeing you come out from your new apartment in Cortevecchia, the old court, which as it is yours, could now be called Corte Beata, Blessed Court. But I will give some kind of order to my extraordinary tale. From the Serenissima I have betaken myself to the court of the marchese Federico, as I was interested in following closely the war plan established by the League to prevent the Landsknechte from crossing the Po. Suddenly descending from the Chiese valley, these twelve thousand Lanzi are making a broad maneuver to elude the Venetians and then rapidly go and join the Bourbon troops in the Milan countryside. Here I have been received with every courtesy, though there is a shudder of perceptible apprehension running through your court. They have lodged me in the "white chambers" of the castle with the finest grace in the world.

I arrived late yesterday, and this morning I climbed up to the rooms of the chancellery to greet your Calandra, soul of the palace's offices and my old acquaintance, and some celebrated observers and envoys like the duke of Urbino's Agnello and the Florentine republic's Borromei. Other names encountered so often in documents and heard frequently are now matched with faces in my mind. But you are right to hold Signor Calandra in your esteem; his discourse expresses an ever wakeful interest in things, which gives him little flashes of intelligence from time to time, perceptible on his face. His tall figure is well articulated and somewhat scornful, but scornful

of petty things, as he is devoted to serious tasks. While he
listens, he bows his head slightly, reflecting, suddenly turning on
you the gaze of his pale gray eyes. Now what do you say, my
lady? Have I drawn a good portrait of a man so familiar to you?

I am happy to move like this among your people, in your
house, free of the magic terror of coming upon you. Ah, I was
forgetting! In the chancellery three lieutenants of your son the
marchese were also present: Ludovico Guerrieri, Paolo Luzasco,
and Carlo Nuvoloni. This last was complaining of the
quarrelsome captain of the League, Signor Giovanni delle
Bande Nere, who has made memorable scenes: Apparently he
has called the Mantuan infantry ill armed and worse trained.
Calandra shrugged. A man like Giovanni delle Bande Nere
must be forgiven his extravagance and eccentricities; he is
wrathful, but in battle he is full of bravery and sweeps the
soldiers along. Not even the least of his men would refrain
from following him into the most reckless attack.

I wished to pay my respects to the signor marchese,
reminding him of our acquaintance during his stay as a boy in
Rome, but he is ill and is staying at his Marmirolo villa, which
he has recently enriched with new construction—so I have
been told—on a design by Michelangiolo; I hope he will soon
regain his health, which, as he is twenty-six, will quickly be
restored, as those of his household are confident. You must
have received word that he has been obliged to issue
arrangements for the passage of the imperial troops through
Mantuan territory, imposed on him first by the Bourbon and
more crudely by Georg von Frundsberg, the great Lutheran
leader of the Lanzi, a huge man who has been described to me
as strong as a bull, a blasphemer, and a violent fighter.
Imagine, around his neck he wears a gold thong because, he
says, he will personally strangle the pope with it. Frundsberg,
then, asked the marchese for permission to cross the Po at
Borgoforte, but here at court it is already being said that the
German will have to give up the idea because they will not let
him find the boats. Meanwhile, at Soncino, the duke Francesco
Maria della Rovere is encamped with Giovanni de' Medici, and
together they have made a plan: to let the Swiss and French
remain on the Adda, while keeping an eye on Milan and the

Spaniards; the Venetians, with Signor Giovanni, will pursue the Lanzi.

Probably during these last few hours the plan has undergone changes, but you, who know these places, can foresee everything better than I. The notion I draw from my various sources of information is that the Lanzi will be allowed to advance into the Serraglio; afterward, finding no boats at Borgoforte, they will be forced to march along the embankment toward the Po at Ostiglia, where they will be overtaken by Signor Giovanni. He will attack the rear guard and ruinously disperse the main body of the army before it can join up with the Bourbon's troops. May God assist them, for their cause is just.

At dinner with your Calandra, both of us sated with war talk, we discussed matters of art and of painting, for we were in the new rooms of the castle, redone by the marchese Federico, near those you once lived in; to be specific, we were in the Hall of the Suns, very handsomely decorated. We talked of you and of your generous actions on behalf of the glory of the Gonzaga house, and these gentlemen never ceased praising you with the greatest devotion.

Calandra secretly hinted to me of your work in Rome for the cardinalate of your second son, Ercole, and they consider you have achieved a stupendous result also for your third son, Ferrante, having won permission from the pope for him to accept a commission as captain in the imperial army of Charles the Fifth. Your good sense, my lady, must be equaled only by your courage; otherwise, you would not expose your youngest son to the risk of having to fight in a war against his oldest brother. But you are sure that this will not happen, and in one way or another you develop your arguments on your own.

During the dinner in the Hall of the Suns I led the talk to your new apartment, and Signor Calandra immediately offered to have me visit it. I concealed my joy. After consulting the others, he decided to give me as companion a singular person whom they call the Scholar Page, his real name being Bertino of Alba. The general opinion is that no one equals him in the understanding of painting and sculpture. He is old for a page, twenty. You will not know him, for he has been here only a few months, ceded to the marchese Federico by the lord of Guastalla at the request of Giulio Romano, who finds him a peerless expert in searching out every sort of rare object, ancient or modern. Singular though he is, I am sure you will be pleased to have him at your command. He is a tall, very thin young man, who scorns tight-fitting dress and wears on his head a little hat with a scrawl of a plume. Irregular face, significant nose, head covered with black, smooth hair, but it is his eye that strikes you, deep-set, black, and shining; it seems composed of many inner eyes, gleaming, each ready for a revelation.

The Scholar Page, then, silently led me into your new residence. November is almost over; a great shifting fog steals the palace gardens from our gaze. And in the fog a voice began to emerge from my companion, a warm voice, a deep and modulated bass with sudden flashes, ironic or merry, and with penetrating firmness when he illustrates the works of the artists. From the loggia of the city, light as your footstep, I entered—and I hope this does not displease you—your rooms. There some women were tending fires in the fireplaces, a lively blaze that fought off the menaced humidity in the air. I was seized by a strange access of youthfulness on seeing your places, your velvet-covered chairs, the little tabourets and the big inlaid tables, the stucco decoration, the paintings in that air gilded by the glowing lamps—it was a dark day—which licked with tongues of yellow light the silver candelabra and vases. But this was nothing compared to the Studiolo and the Grotta, where paintings of Mantegna, Costa, and Perugino emerged boldly from the atmosphere, their forms dancing and fleeing in the brief space, divided by the clear marble doorway; a true creation of genius, said my young scholar, and he included that goldsmith's work that covered walls and ceilings, in the Grotta, cadenced by your metaphysical emblems.

My legs almost buckled at this testimony of your life, my most beloved signora. I pretended to listen to my companion, who moved about, pointing out from time to time with a rapid phrase the little bronzes, the rare statuettes, the geometrical cities depicted in inlay, and finally, flinging open the door of the cupboard near the window, he showed me the

Michelangiolo sleeping putto, whose weighty grace heralds that
great master's future work. We passed then into the secret
garden, whose forms the fog transmuted. In it, all was vegetal
specter; only the hedges branched out here and there among
the bare little twigs of the climbing plants. How different it
appeared from the place described by our Castiglione, "divine
garden, flowering in May with ruffled jasmines and roses,
green with little fruit trees." Through the wisps of fog I read
your queenly declaration on the cornice that runs all around
the wall: *Isabella Estensis regum Aragonorum neptis, ducum
Ferrariensium filia et soror, marchionum Gonzagorum coniux et
mater*.

At this point I sank into a wondrous, bizarre enchantment in
which I am still living. My companion's eye stared at me so
intensely that my cheeks flushed. He is a necromancer, I
thought; he has discovered my secret. Instead, I heard his
voice, lighter now and perhaps with a hint of tenderness
matched with irony, inviting me to the discovery of something
both mysterious and sublime.

"Sir, are you not an Englishman?" he asked suddenly. "The
wonder is nearing us, summoning us. Do you wish to reply?"

It was clear. Nothing in his mind connected me with you.
My secret saved, I could breathe. I declared myself immediately
ready for any revelation.

"Follow me then," said the page, and he quickened his step.

We climbed stairs, grazed walls of narrow passages,
encountering only some few servants, who greeted us. Thus
we arrived at an ancient, enormous door. The page rummaged
in a purse, took out a key, and with some effort turned it in
the lock. I found myself in a hall illuminated by a muffled light
that entered from three big arched windows. The roof was in
part supported only by some beams, and the floor was of
rough, cracked bricks. My companion took a few quick steps
and pointed ahead.

"Look!" he said.

My eyes rested on the great wall facing me, suffused in an
even light, and I saw an extraordinary depiction of a battle that
sprang violently from the wall, a sturdy arabesque, fantastic
and cruel: men in cuirasses and helmets, with enormous

winged crests, swelling with plumes or else decorated with
ribbons or embroidered, fringed fillets, which flowed over their
shoulders, covered with the iron of warriors. Against the dark
blue background the swerving of the ponderous horses and the
armored men was caught at its most vigorous moment, and
from the fissures of the helmets, pierced in front like masks,
the distant eyes cast glances, frightened and yet stubborn, of
those preparing to die.

"What war is it?" I asked, with scant breath.

"Worse than war. It is a tourney, depicted in the area where
the fighting is thickest and the madness of killing triumphs.
See how inexorably the swords are raised and the men fall;
here cruelty is haughtiness inspired only by a pride in killing in
cold blood, with none of the fever of conquest; it is an
explosion of man's natural rapacity. The tourney is a poem
dedicated to luxury, regality, the funeral pomp of heroes, and
it does not lack the assent of the superhuman and yet real
ladies, whom you see up there, peering down, under the
canopy. They are shown absolutely without fear, made abstract
by their own value exalted by the knights, blond, in dresses of
regal form, touched by infinite mortal delicacy. The painter was
unable to complete this fresco. He no longer believed in the
fairy tale of past centuries; he denied the epic that surrounds
the name of the paladins, considering it a futile rite of blood. In
this vision the artist comprises only the horror of the haughty
cavalcades, the terrible constriction of the armor that seems
sealed to the bodies, torturing them; and he dresses in the
costume of chivalry his Triumph of Death."

On the wall where the figures seethed, I could make out
episodes of wounding and waiting, now and then released
from their steely stiffness. I asked what genius had painted the
fresco. The page smiled his assent.

"Yes. He is a genius. It is Pisanello." Then he added that I
deserved something more and I would have it.

He headed toward one corner and returned carrying a
ladder, swaying because of its height. He went again toward
that corner and brought back another, just as tall and also
swaying. He set them side by side against the wall, taking care
to choose places where less fresco remained. Carefully he

tested the two ladders, and pointing to the more solid, he invited me to climb, as he scrambled up the other with agility. Emotion and curiosity led me to climb, in such a way, my lady, I assure you, that it was only when I found myself on the top rung that I realized I was suspended on high, very high. What would you say if I swore to you that my romantic nature had a jolt and I was so fired that I imagined myself languishing at the feet of that mortal triumph, so close to your house?

He whom they call the Scholar Page flung down his cap, baring his thick inky black hair. He winked a moment, and pointing his very long finger at the upper part of the fresco, he urged me to look; he would explain later.

Along the frame of the scene, at the level of our eyes, a magnificent frieze unfolded; amid stems of very long, swaying flowers there was a succession, very thick, of round collars, each closed with a trefoil clasp and sealed with a pendant bearing a bird with opened wings, alternately facing right and left. Though I could not believe my eyes, I immediately recognized the ancient collar of Lancaster, which I had seen carved on the family tombs, and here it was reinforced by that superhuman pattern, repeated dozens of times in the frame of that extreme battle. Then I truly had to cling to the ladder, uncomprehending. My companion laughed his shrill laugh, and his eyes shone, and his face was transformed by a kind of combustion.

"That's enough; we can climb down," he said.

When we were on the ground, we sat on a dusty bench. I was all questions. The young man told me of his discovery of this ultimate masterpiece, of his inquiry among the courtiers of every age, the wardrobe attendants, the stewards of the palace; all he could learn was that the hall once known as Pisanello's had had its roof staved about fifty years ago, then somehow patched up. One thing was obvious: These paintings had been abandoned long before they were finished, and no one could say why.

"Pisanello! Have you never heard that name?" He was disappointed that I did not know Pisanello, the painter who had illuminated the northern Italian courts a century ago, the favorite of every prince, worshiped by all, lords and potentates.

And why, now, this abandonment? Why did this great work stand so scorned?

The Scholar Page was filled with wrath, and it seemed he spoke to unburden his resentment. He had asked an elderly courtier who esteemed painting highly the reason for such neglect of a work displaying all the signs of genius. There was no reply. But the court painters? Mantegna, especially Mantegna, painter of the house of Gonzaga—had he seen the fresco? There was not a word that led the page to think so. It was known only that the moody painter roamed constantly about the old rooms of the palace, seeking forgotten art objects in the areas inhabited or not, but there had never been a word from Mantegna. The Scholar Page winked again, "The envy among geniuses?" he asked himself, sarcastic, fierce.

"But what about the collars? The collars of Lancaster?" I insisted.

He had searched for information also about them, he explained, in the chancellery, among the dispatches from England.

"Shifting packets of papers, I found a letter from King Henry the Sixth of England. That school Latin, that chancellery language is something only the English can employ. This king of yours was greatly pleased that his very dear counselor had been welcomed and entertained, one John le Scrop, passing through Mantua, and in gratitude the king granted the marchese Gianfrancesco, then reigning, license to confer on fifty of his subjects the royal device, the collar painted in the frieze."

The page mechanically brushed off some dust, and as if he were continuing a private discourse, he said: "How long will we have to wait before this painting is recognized and loved, though it is unfinished, damaged, mortified by neglect, though it is one of the great human expressions and sends us a terrible appeal? You, my dear English lord, don't you sense a flood of thought and emotion overwhelming your mind? Do you not suddenly remember the existence, contemporary with our own, of so many distant peoples, so many men who have shared war and death? Perhaps the collar of the *S*'s sent by Henry the Sixth, king of great England, to the marchese Gianfrancesco

Gonzaga, lord of a little state, is a sign of warm friendship, and he announces it with that almost affectionate Latin letter; but Pisanello is a man who has arrived at the extreme sufferings of existence, and he transforms the celebration of that gift (perhaps a tourney had been arranged among the fifty knights honored with the English 'devisement') into an incomparable feast of death."

My young companion fell silent. I jotted something in my notebook and drew some details of the elegant collars, the Lancasters' "devise," of the "Red Rose." As I told you last time, I am distantly related, through the Yorks, to the "White Rose," but to me these now-ancient divisions are remote, these rancors cultivated and spattered with blood. The collar, the medallion with the swan and its opened wings, the *S*'s—I drew everything with care, feeling a clot of warmth in the gray cold that penetrated through the big windows.

The Scholar Page was very much at his ease on that bench, his arms and legs crossed with innate elegance. After a long silence he cast a glance at my drawings and with his thin finger indicated some points to be corrected. Then we moved again along the corridors, down the little stairways; coming out into the open, we headed for the castle. On my companion's face the signs of rebellion were visible.

"And what about Mantegna?" he said, all of a sudden, in a low voice. "Doesn't it seem strange to you that he must, in any case, have seen this Pisanello? Did he perhaps try to blot out the other through neglect?" He added a few more sentences, announcing to me a journey of his to Turkey, to broach a certain trade in jewels which promised to be propitious: He preferred jewels, even though he loved painting; he wanted to spare himself thrills of the mind. He entered the fog of the castle gardens after a long, warm, but absent farewell. I was already on the drawbridge, getting my bearings.

Now I am in my chambers, have been here for hours, alone, under the light of a lamp, writing you. The day died before its time; the groom, having lighted the fire, has served me my supper. I feel overwhelmed by the impressions, all so various, of your house, the fairy tale of our time, gem of our thought, and by that wall, surely almost a hundred years old, unknown, which yet seems to threaten our future. What am I doing here, unable to read in my soul by the light of Your Clarity? And are the Lancaster devices that follow one another above that warlike Apocalypse a casual encounter or a summons from the great island of Europe? I believe in signs. I often have the sensation that something suspended over us would like to reach us. I feel ill and unhinged.

Lady of my soul, hear this moment of pure sorrow that cannot explain itself. You are far away, but thank God, you exist, and if I were close to you, I would also know what to believe. Why do you act always as if I did not exist, leaving me to fill my world with suppositions? Dangerous currents form and induce in me a weariness beyond remedy. Tonight I will sleep on the rug beside the fire, as our great dogs sleep in the castle of Suffolk.

Dawn of the twenty-sixth of November

My lady! My lady! News has just come that Signor Giovanni de' Medici has been wounded at Govérnolo by a shot from the Ferrara artillery. They are bringing him to Mantua, to the palace of Signor Aloisio Gonzaga, opposite your court palaces. I will fling on a cloak and rush to see him. Everything is precipitating. The Lanzi have crossed.

Evening of the same day

I lack the courage to live, but not the courage to write you, my revered lady. This day has been the most grievous I have spent in Italy, and it will never be possible for me to forget it. This morning, shortly after dawn, the news reached here of the wounding of Signor Giovanni de' Medici. It was snowing. I arrived in the great square just in time to encounter a procession of men, mourning and furious. They were walking on each side of a closed litter where their captain lay. No one heeded the snow and the lashing wind. Signor Giovanni's distraught soldiers inveighed against ill fortune. Last of all, alone behind the litter, came Signor Pietro Aretino, the man of letters. In his angry bass voice he called his friend's name and ceaselessly spat imprecations and curses, releasing in them the violence of his anguish. The curses seethed with insults against the cheating whore that Fortune showed herself to be, the putrid trollop who had allowed this catastrophe. All cried, in rhythm, "Giovanni! Giovanni!" and from time to time, they repeated in louder voices, "Who will now say to us, 'Follow me and do not precede me'? . . . Who will ever give us back the best soldier of all time?" And those hoarse cries had a tragic ring that made them unbearable.

The men stopped outside the palace at the end of the square, then entered. I did not dare follow them; they seemed so closely joined, an anguished family that rejected anyone else.

Now I have come back to my rooms, and I feel the solitude like a heavy air, hard to breathe.

Evening of the twenty-ninth of November

My lady, once again I pick up my pen for you. At the hour of vespers I went to the room where Signor Giovanni was lying, stretched out on a camp bed that he himself had asked for. He seemed very pale but aware. His awareness was terrible; into my mind flashed Pisanello's spectral horsemen and their moribund gaze from the depths of their helmets. A gentleman still wearing his cuirass was standing by the bed, and I recognized the duke of Urbino. Paler than the wounded man, he bent over him and exhorted him in a fraternal tone to confess himself, showing that the valor of the spirit is equal to valor in war.

A strange smile spread on the face of Signor Giovanni, who replied clearly: "I have always done what I had to do. And I will do this, too."

To the confessor monk he had the strength to say that, being a man of arms, he had lived like a soldier; if he had been a priest, he would have lived like a priest. At that moment your son came into the room. He approached the wounded man and begged him to ask for something, a favor suited to the style of them both.

Giovanni answered: "You love me, because I am almost dead. Love me still when I am dead completely."

"Your valor, which has won you such glory," the marchese said gravely, "will make you not only loved but adored by everyone."

Signor Aretino, seated on a bench at the head of his friend's cot, cast his eyes around, staring, as if he had lost the will and the strength to cry out. But every so often he gave the impression that he would explode in his raging grief.

Darkness fell quickly; the lamps were lighted. Signor Giovanni said something to the Aretino, who took up a book from the bench and began to read softly; I could not discover what book it was. At that flow of words, somehow comforting, though who can say why, Signor Giovanni dozed off a little, then woke, and asked to be read to further, and again he fell asleep. The doze caused by the mortal wound was invading him, but his vigor caused him to stir again now and then. At a certain moment he said: "I dreamed I was healed. If I am well again, I will show those Lanzi how to fight, and I will avenge myself."

His household spoke no more and tried only to catch his eye to convey their loyalty and their distress. Every now and then someone would start weeping, and someone else would lead him outside. In the corner of the window the marchese Federico had taken refuge, pensive and sad. He did not recognize me, nor did I attempt to be recognized. And that subdued reading, those choked tears, that dazed waiting in everyone made me feel an intruder, spying on the secret between life and death, and I came away.

Here I am, before you, distraught by this death that seems to deliver Italy over to the Spaniards and the Lanzi. The sorrow at the loss of Signor Giovanni becomes all the more harsh as it penetrates inside us, and as we are oppressed by the news that floods into the chancellery, where I sought your Calandra's confident words. There is great confusion. The least perceptive heave a sacrilegious sigh, thinking that the war is moving away from Mantua, indeed, from the whole Mantuan region, because Frundsberg's troops have crossed the Po at Ostiglia. The more informed fear unspeakable disasters. Many of our people have seen these Lanzi face-to-face, armed with harquebuses, crossbows, and swords, blasphemous people who sing the praises of Luther in that disjointed language of theirs.

I tell you all this, my lady, because there is no time to lose. Whether you answer me or not, I must help you, no matter what happens. I am rushing back to Rome, after entrusting this letter to Magrone, an outrider formerly in the service of Signor

Castiglione, and whom I have encountered here by chance. Whatever you may think of me, I am prepared for your every thought. I will suffer anything, provided you may be soon again in your rooms, painted bright with the harmonious arches of the divine loggia of Cortevecchia curving once more over your head.

Farewell, farewell. Until Rome. Have no fear: either of seeing me or of not seeing me. I shall be there.

Your faithful
Robert de la Pole

Mantua, the thirtieth of November, 1526

I RAPIDLY STARTED up the narrow, spiral staircase that climbed into the tower, from time to time mistily lighted from the narrow slits. But after a brief dash I stopped, breathless; there were limits in following impulses. I was no longer capable of the headlong pace that too often had sent me up to the turrets of the Castle of Mantua, to seek an all-embracing view of my city.

"Remember your years!" I said to myself. "And don't pretend all the time." My whole person rebelled in an immediate reply. On the contrary, I had to forget those years, especially in this trial. I climbed with a more sedate step; the tower was high but not very high. We were soon on the terrace and, as the crow flies, close to the Campidoglio. And from there, promptly, the tolling of the Patarina trapped us. Rome was showing herself off, superb, below us, all red roof tiles, cloaked in a splendid glow; it was May, and the sun's shafts breaking through a light haze poured rivers of gold on the walls and the roofs. We moved from one spot to another, I found again the city diminished by the new perspective; our ambassador Franceschino Gonzaga pointed out to us the different places, the palaces and churches, identifying each one. But the ambassador was very anxious. He hovered around me and never ceased his warnings and pleas. Federico, his master and my son, had written him another tormented letter, urging him to bring me away; I was to hesitate no longer and set out for Mantua. I listened to him, but I was more alert to something inside me, a profound worry accompanied by a temptation.

Franceschino was of the opinion that we, my court and I, could still find the road to Ostia open. The danger was worsening; for two hours the Capitoline bell had not stopped sounding the alarm. He pointed out to me a little swarm toward the meadows of Nero; it was the advance guard of the Lanzi and the Spaniards, preparing perhaps to attack the Leonine walls. We should escape, wasting no more time, immediately, taking the only free road. I answered clearly, without bewilderment or pique; the duke of Urbino's envoy had informed me that the army of the League commanded by Francesco Maria would arrive before evening.

"And what if it doesn't arrive?" Franceschino Gonzaga replied. "These damned imperials will spread through the city like a river in flood bursting the embankments. Leave, my lady, save yourself from this horrible threat. Do as your son the signor marchese says. You know how worried he is about you and how much he loves you."

"No!" I cried, with a violence that shook my whole body. "It is useless to leave and, above all, dangerous to go away from Rome; the lands around the city are overrun with Spanish and German armies. Here I feel safer. The Santi Apostoli palace is the only refuge for me. We are on land of the Colonnas, the imperial faction; they are much loved by Charles the Fifth. Nobody will dare do us violence."

"That is true," our ambassador concurred. "But don't you find it suspicious that the Colonna families have all rushed off to shut themselves up in their castles in the Alban Hills, well defended every one? Though they are partisans of the emperor, they are unwilling to wait in their Roman palaces for the Lanzi's attack."

I was about to answer when, from the spiral stairway, Pirro Donati appeared. He informed me that Signora Felice Orsini was at the door, seeking asylum in our house. Panic had exploded in the city. The pope had lost his last opportunity; he had been unable to raise from the city's inhabitants the three hundred thousand ducats the Bourbon demanded to spare Rome.

"Tightfisted! Mean!" Franceschino said with an anger that rose from his heart. "And the city is bursting with gold."

Pirro told us that according to the last reliable news, it seemed that the constable of Bourbon was scaling the slopes of the Janiculum. The Romans had gone crazy. All were looking for a place to hide, themselves and their possessions.

"Signora marchesana, make up your mind," our ambassador begged. "This is your last chance."

Pirro added his exhortations. All were truly anxious about my fate. But I felt somehow sheltered by a singular certitude of my destiny.

"Pirro," I said, "tell Signora Felice Orsini that we are happy to welcome her. And then we must prepare ourselves for the first onslaught. We will give asylum to all the women who ask us. Come!"

I quickly reached the entrance hall of the palace; I crossed it several times, breathless, in haste. In front of the main doorway we had to run up a bastion in masonry: artisans and volunteers with spades and hods of mortar and bricks worked rapidly and with strict precision. Meanwhile, the fugitives filed into the palace with baskets and bundles. One basket overturned because it was too heavy; gold and silver dishes fell into the dust.

Pirro came to me and said softly: "This is the greatest danger. The gold will attract the looters to us."

Some men followed the women and insisted on also being admitted. I rushed to the door determined.

"Only the women!" I decreed. "There is room only for the women! The men can go and take up arms!"

In the confusion some men slipped inside anyway. Meanwhile, I summoned my secretary, and from my purse I counted out ten gold ducats for him to give the armorer, who had brought sacks of gunpowder. The pikes had to be counted, there should be fifty of them, and we should remember to pay sixty ducats to the seneschal. It took Pirro and me a while to count, and my purse became lighter. From the square some men advanced, led by an officer. They were resolute men of the populace, loyal to the Colonnas, enlisted for defense. This little militia was to be stationed behind the bastion, at the main door and in the vestibule of the palace; if we rewarded them generously, they would not abandon us. Everything seemed to me set in motion, and I went back inside.

IT IS impossible to describe how disheartening a crowd of fugitives looks, huddled with their bundles on a stairway. My girls, under the command of the brisk Camilla Gonzaga, run toward me like a flock of sparrows, trying to outshout one another. I understand there is no more room, the halls are full, and the stairs threaten to collapse under the weight of the refugees. I order my own apartment opened, reserving only two little rooms for myself. The rest is quite large; everyone will find a place. I give precise commands: It is pointless to shout, forbidden to weep; all the girls must look after the children. I stand outside to speak further with Pirro, and someone comes up behind me: I turn and I am facing the Venetian ambassador Domenico Venier. Hoarse with fear, he greets me and, dissimulating his fright, in an almost joking manner, asks if I will give refuge to a friend like himself.

"So Venice also asks for help?" I say. "To tell the truth, we offer asylum only to women, children, and the old. Ambassadors, whatever may happen, will be respected."

"By the Lanzi? You have never seen them; otherwise, you would not say that. Signora marchesana, give me refuge, I beg you. Here you have armed guards; the palace is fortified. In all Rome I have not come upon a soldier with a pike."

"You must not believe that Palazzo Santi Apostoli is the fortress of Mirandola. We must hold out for a few hours. My nephew the constable of Bourbon and my son Ferrante, imperial captain, have just sent me two similar dispatches. They are at the gates of Rome. As soon as they enter the city, they will send armed men in our defense."

"This is why I want to stay here with you. If the imperial captains protect Your Ladyship, no place is more safe than this."

"Come in. Your friend Grimani is already here, and the envoys of Ferrara and Urbino." And I lead him, at my side, into a private room, not yet too crowded. He receives a bench and a mattress.

I cross the salons, the little rooms, the galleries. Everywhere people are huddled against the walls, the children clinging to their mothers. Under the dark cloaks I can glimpse family jewels, donned in the haste to escape. Each refugee is carrying coffers, caskets, bundles of every size. The people are frightened and dazed. I approach the most exhausted, to cheer them. I tell them all that we have to hold out only for a short time; I urge them to be calm and patient. The old are distressing in their weakness. The girls' eyes are of those who are prepared for every violence. Some, almost immobile, clutch the objects they have brought with them: boxes, candelabra, silver pieces wrapped in cloth, a cage with a jade-eyed cat, as if to make sure they have close to them the cherished objects from home. I push the door of the chapel. A fanatical priest is ranting in the midst of a group of old women.

"Pray! Down on your knees! On the ground! Pray! God's thunderbolt is about to strike us sinners!"

The poor women, crushed beneath those threats, fling themselves on the ground.

I know who he is: a certain Friar Lorenzo, famous in Rome as a master of invective. I call him to me and order him to cease his preaching and to recite prayers softly, to console those poor women without alarming them. He pretends to give in, but his pale eyes do not reassure me. I wonder how much store he sets by his apocalyptic inventions, perhaps the only powerful thing he has ever possessed.

In the rooms of the state apartment the crowd has been jammed for hours. People actually lie in heaps, the Chinese carpets stained by the urine of the children, and perhaps of the adults; the odor is already poisoning the air. The drive to act urges me on in my inspection; the imperative to help, to save thrusts me forward, and from that imperative I draw an extraordinary ease in assisting others. I even smile, glimpsing one of my girls in the arms of a page in a dimly lighted entry; Signora Camilla points her out to me with a reproachful whisper: "At a time like this!" On the contrary, I would like to reply, these are the very times when this natural, youthful vitality strikes the right note. Couldn't she feel how strength came from staying well alive just when life seems at its most undesirable? Worn out, late in the night, I find myself back in my room, and I fall on the bed still dressed. In my mind clouded by sleep thoughts continue to stalk.

I WAKE early in the morning, prepare myself very simply, slipping on comfortable house shoes. I write in a little book the expenditures and a date: fifth May, 1527. My Camilla comes, to tell me that the prothonotary Pirrino Gonzaga, our kinsman, has arrived, sent by Pope Clement with a message from the Vatican. Before I can reply, she runs off. Nor can I restrain my girls; they also run out and, a moment later, come back with Pirrino. His long black cassock is white with plaster.

"I managed to get inside. They pushed me through an aperture still open in the bastion," Pirrino tells me. "The other two priests have remained down in the square, waiting for me. If you look out, you can see them, still laughing."

Pirrino Gonzaga stands before me; he bows and kisses the hem of my garment as if we were at a reception in the castle. He assumes an adult demeanor as he repeats his message: "Last night there was a consistory in the Vatican. His Holiness publicly named cardinal your son Signor Ercole Gonzaga. But then they could find no one willing to set out amid the dangers of the war, to go to Mantua and take the cardinal's red hat to the newly nominated prelate. His Holiness thought then to send it to you, with his blessing. I assumed the obligation of delivering it to you in person, and I swore that I would pass even through an army of Landsknechte. But there was no need. Rome is empty; only occasionally somebody pops up, then runs off to hide, slipping along the walls."

My joy is too great to be expressed. My heart fills with new hopes, and they do not seem too rash to me. I tell the young prothonotary to thank His Holiness devoutly; I intend to deliver the hat in person to my son Ercole when I return to Mantua, if God grants me that grace.

"We have all wondered why you haven't left already, signora," Pirrino ventures.

Consoled by Ercole's red hat, by the thought of the pope in consistory with the princes of the Church, intent on praying, I reply that someone perhaps has decided I should stay in Rome. He asks if I am afraid.

"Of course, my dear nephew, I am afraid; I am not mindless. My fits of courage don't last long, and I have to keep renewing them, hour by hour."

As I clasp the folded white linen with delicate care, a bombard shot explodes, then another. The Capitoline bell begins to ring, with accelerated strokes.

"Forgive me, signora marchesana, we must go back to the Vatican. Apparently this evening or tomorrow morning the pope will withdraw into Castel Sant'Angelo."

He bids Camilla and the girls good-bye, then hastens down the steps, pulling up his cassock to be able to move faster; he has gone down only a few steps when he turns and says to us gravely: "God assist you!" And he disappears.

From the windows we follow the three young clerics as they rapidly leave the square, heading for Saint Peter's.

EVENING was approaching. People were crying out in the palace, and it took time to hearten them a little. Crossing one room, I discovered some refugees tearing the brocade and the tapestries from the walls, to use them as blankets. I ordered that nothing be touched; for the moment it was easy to make them obey me. But for how much longer?

Our ambassador Franceschino Gonzaga, who had not abandoned us, came in great secrecy to my chamber, accompanied by two circumspect men.

"These are our most able and boldest informants," he said to me, when he had opened the door a crack, "the brothers Pietro and Sebastiano Gherardi, Roman citizens, devoted to the house of Colonna. They are trying to observe all the movements in the city, using certain special methods of their own, and it would be very difficult for them to be discovered."

"We move over roofs," the younger said, Sebastiano.

He explained to me briefly how, with some other Romans, they had set up a network of observation that covered the whole city, from roof to roof. In the few places where that aerial path broke off, such as between the two banks of the Tiber, they made use of signal lights. The latest news told of Spaniards and Lanzi massed at Sant'Onofrio on the Janiculum. The constable of Bourbon had already deployed his army: Captain Georg Frundsberg facing Trastevere from Porta San Pancrazio; Philibert d'Orange at Porta Pertusa; Ferrante Gonzaga aiming to take Porta Sant'Angelo. He, the constable, would attack at Santo Spirito, the road leading straight to the Vatican.

The other brother, Pietro, reported, in his turn, other information. It had been learned that the Bourbon, speaking to his soldiers, had stirred up their fever for looting and their hatred against the pope, who once again refused to pay three hundred thousand ducats for the army's wages. They had to act fast. The troops of the duke of Urbino were a mere sixteen miles away, and within twenty-four hours, or thirty-six at most, they could fall upon Rome, locking the attackers in a vise. The only salvation was to sack the city rapidly, at once. And he had concluded with these words: "Rome will make all of you rich. We will attack tomorrow morning at dawn. Our watchword is: Take the city or die!"

This is what the Gherardi brothers told us, and not at much greater length, but still sufficient to describe the tattered, blaspheming Lutherans, who swore to destroy the Antichrist. The pope was in no danger; Renzo di Ceri and his troops were ready to escort him to Castel Sant'Angelo, an impregnable fortress, defended by powerful artillery. All our hopes lay, then, in the duke of Urbino and his foot soldiers. The two brothers ran off as soon as they could, to return to their positions and keep watch through the hours of the night.

The sky announced a violet sunset, shading into pink. I shut myself in my little chamber, and still too upset and tired to fall asleep, I went to the window over the Santi Apostoli square. No one was in sight; I examined the houses, and they seemed to be bulging with people and with wealth, perfect lures for those greedy hordes about to pour down on Rome from the Janiculum. Time passed slowly; the sunset colors were now turning ashen; the fog gradually insinuated itself between one wall and the next, filling the spaces with gray. I could not tear myself from the window. At the end of the square I thought I could discern something that moved cautiously. I made out a man, then two, three. Two remained in the shadow, against the wall of a house, the third, dressed in black, advanced with halting steps and was then alone in the middle of the square.

The man looked up, keenly; he seemed drawn perhaps to a last glint of sunlight, and he came a bit farther. I suddenly thought I recognized him: that long, pale face; the dark line of the eyes; the almost violent expressive tension. I drew back abruptly. I felt certain it was he, he, the English Robert de la Pole. He had said in his last letter that he would come, but five months had gone by since then. More than once I had looked for him in the Vatican or peering among those who stopped to watch me ride through the streets or pass in my carriage. Now he was here. What did he want from me, or rather, what did he want for me? I felt insulted and yet touched by a secret little imp of happiness. I took refuge in a corner of my room, and meanwhile, I prayed him to go away, to take shelter, to save himself; our defenders at the bastion could easily have fired. These were no longer kindly times we were living in; we could think only about survival. And why, then, did I leave him there, foolhardy and alone; why didn't I hold out my hand, as I had done with so many people: envoys, ambassadors, secretaries? Wasn't he an envoy of the powerful king of England? But I kept repeating to myself that his world could not come toward me, could not mingle with mine. I moaned in anguish, and over that anguish rose life's imperative to prevail; it was not even significant that he was a loyal friend, who had accompanied my existence for so many years, though from a distance. Wounded and trembling, I ran to the window, opened the shutters, which creaked in the silence, and I searched on all sides. The square was empty.

I HAD no idea what time it was when I woke, with a start, from the sleep that had seized me by surprise and felled me at some moment in the night. I realized why; as I turned my head toward the window, which I had forgotten to close, a gray wall, compact and cottony, stood between me and the world. I recognized the fog. It resembled Mantua's on certain November days, it was so still and dense, though not icy as it is in our parts. How there could be such fog in Rome, at the beginning of May was something I did not even ask myself. It was there, too, to threaten.

There was a knock at the door, and Camilla's voice came from outside, calling me. I got up, opened the door, and my cousin peered in, her eyes swollen from sleep. She was bearing a steamy bowl, a bit of broth she had procured for me in the kitchen. Behind her Pirro Donati told me he had counted the refugees as they were sleeping. In a space that seemed more and more cramped, there were about two thousand people; half were women, and the others were old people, children, the court. I charged him to go down to the larder master; out of prudence, they should lock up all the provisions and set half the flour apart as a reserve supply. If there was to be a long delay before Ferrante attacked the city, there was no telling when he would be able to devote himself to his mother. Pirro announced one of the Gherardi brothers, the roof men; he was bearing the latest news. I nodded permission.

Immediately the younger of the informant brothers came in: Sebastiano. He had a regular face with a certain adolescent quality, but his very black hair and something scornful about his lip made him more mature. The news was this: In great haste the pope had gone into Castel Sant'Angelo through the passage that links the Vatican with the castle, dragged there, you might say, by his household and by Monsignor Paolo Giovio, and protected by Renzo di Ceri and his soldiers. There had barely been time to blow up the undefended part of the corridor. The Lanzi had entered at Santo Spirito and were advancing beyond Porta Leonina, disemboweling all the people they could. The constable of Bourbon had been killed by an harquebus wound in the loins at Porta Torrione, and the German horde no longer obeyed its captains' command and was spreading through the streets. Four or five thousand crazed people were pressing between the Church of the Traspontina and Porta Castello; some flung themselves into boats, others into the river itself, seeking an avenue of escape. Two Lanzi had been seen, waving the imperial standards, arriving beneath Castel Sant'Angelo, their German yells hymning Martin Luther; a bombard shot had blown them to bits.

I sent away the women who were crowding in the doorway to listen. This was only the beginning. The tale would become more and more frightful. If the defenders had not put up some resistance at Ponte Sisto, those damned hordes, rushing like a flood toward Parione and Ponte, would soon overflow as far as Campo dei Fiori and Piazza Navona and, from there, through all Rome. I could only repeat: With the Bourbon killed, we had lost the one general who could stem the savage fury of those predators thirsting for loot. And what of Ferrante? I shuddered with anxiety for my twenty-year-old son at the head of unruly troops. I thanked the young Gherardi, beseeching him to bring me more news quickly, and I gave him some gold pieces. He put them in his pocket without glancing at them and disappeared. Spontaneously I wanted to set out and inspect the palace; Pirro warned me that my hair was still undone. Seeing me in disorder, the women would take fright; they would believe the imminent catastrophe allowed no time for feminine care.

HE IS right. Collecting my hair in a simple black net, I gather my group of women and go out. The rooms are in turmoil; the atrocious news has reached every corner. People cling to the windows and stare into the void; at any moment they expect to hear the Lanzi's drums. In the square, a great silence.

I give orders to distribute a little food, scarce though it is. We have only a little soup made of various greens picked during the last few days up in the vegetable gardens of the Colonnas by some foresighted, venturesome servant. The long coordination of turns proves a piece of luck, the regulated shifts of so many people in the ground-floor hall, with cups and bowls. The hours pass in the waiting for food, which makes us forget our waiting for the catastrophe.

A cry that seems to come from a thousand throats echoes in the palace. All are staring at the house opposite, where an armed man has appeared; he flings a child down from the window. In the livid air forms can be discerned fleeing, horrible scenes, women grasped by the hair and killed. The Lanzi with mad laughter slit the throat of anyone trying to escape. The cries pierce the walls. Suddenly a band of Lanzi approaches, running in front of our palace, hurling incendiary torches. With a loud, unanimous yell, the refugees move away toward the inner walls, as if driven by horror. Guns crackle, thick and close, and from the stairs one of our defenders cries that they are attacking the bastion. Terror spreads beneath the painted beams of the ceiling. With joy I identify the shots fired from our bastion, consistent, well-aimed shooting.

"Courage, courage," I say, "this is our defense. Have the windows barred. All of them, except the one for the sentry and those of my chambers."

I did not believe I would have an immediate result. But on the contrary, semidarkness is reassuring, and it is reassuring to obey an order. The noises outside are more muffled and mingled. Some of the women unburden themselves in weeping; others remain immobile, as if paralyzed. The children, infected by the adults, are rigid with fright, sobbing. In me a calm arrives from some unknown place, temporary but sustained. I manage not to tremble. I hear again my words or, rather, my exorcisms: "Nothing will happen if you remain calm. We are well defended. Those demons will not be able to dent our bastion; they lack the artillery for that. There, the shooting has stopped; they have given up the idea of attacking us; they have gone away. We will strengthen the bastion even further; we do not lack arms and ammunition. And soon my son Ferrante will arrive with his soldiers. We will then have nothing more to fear. It is only a matter of waiting."

I see Morgantino creeping along the floor, frightened, and I call him: "Morgantino! Come, show your talents to these ladies and these children. Hurry!"

Mechanically, as if I had wound him up, the dwarf unfolds his comical somersaults, and he is also invigorated by his own obedience, redoubling his skill. One by one the children stop crying; they are quiet and alert; some of them smile. The men, meanwhile—the ambassadors, the agents, the envoys—have joined Pirro Donati and are helping him nail planks to bar the windows. We see reddish fumes of smoke among the crossed planks, but no one dares ask the reason for them. Many of the refugees, exhausted by the tension, sink into sleep, overwhelmed.

The time is never completely consumed. Now, flanked by Camilla, who proves to be quick and brave, I am driven ahead by an inexorable wind that leads me to climb the stairs, floor after floor, to pass through halls and rooms, along landings. I go, return, climb, descend, retrace my steps, extend an arm to calm a quarrel, arrange to give a little bread and wine to those who did not receive soup and are hungry. This drive never leaves me. I cannot say how many times I go down to look through a window at the bastion while the new culverins are being set up, and then up to the turret, where we are collecting piles of rocks to hurl down on anyone who ventures too close to our palace.

Pietro Gherardi knocks at my door, his face tense. He has seen. His story is horrible beyond bearing. There is something demoniacal about the slaughter, a tragic drunkenness of blood. No one can escape now; the streets and the houses are piled high with corpses, which those madmen kick ignominiously. The fog that drifts all around stimulates this army of scoundrels, isolating each in his own inhumanity. Yes, there is news from Castel Sant'Angelo, words lowered in a basket by the besieged. Also up there, alarm is infinite. The gunners refuse to load their pieces, will not light the fuses, but stare, dazed, at the horrendous spectacle that unfolds in the streets and alleys below them. They are afraid of striking their own houses with their bombards, their own wives, children. Only one has given proof of bellicose courage and has lighted the fuse of his bombard, firing mercilessly: that Florentine goldsmith Benvenuto Cellini. They say that he flung himself at the feet of Clement, asking to be absolved for the deaths he is causing. Inside the fort cardinals, papal household, and priests all are in prayer, and the pope is suffering an unspeakable anguish, hoping only in the arrival of the duke of Urbino, his invoked rescuer; apparently he glimpses the duke at every point of the horizon, and he prays, he prays also, desperately. Meanwhile, the slaughter continues.

My girls gather around me. Hell has been unleashed in the palace. Nothing new has happened, but the people scream to release their fear, or they cry out invocations of unbearable dread. Best not to listen.

Shooting bursts out near us; the noise rises again; I prick up my ear.

"Silence! Be quiet! No one must approach the windows," I order. "Have faith in our defenses!"

In the distance, from time to time, the Lanzi's panting and growling can be heard. They are attacking the houses of Pompeo Colonna toward the Torre delle Milizie. Suddenly I hear Pirro, in the next room, calling to those of the bastion, ordering them to cease fire. I run to the window left unbarred, my girls after me. The fog has thinned; in the milky air a little banner moves, with the imperial colors, fixed to the helmet of a soldier, who is running across the square, heading for our palace.

"Alessandro! Alessandro!" Camilla cries, recognizing her brother, Captain Alessandro of Novellara.

They throw down a basket tied to a rope, and he jumps into it. Slowly, swaying, he is pulled up to the level of the unbarred window. And he is at once in his sister's arms; I and my women surround him, with trepid eagerness.

"Where is Ferrante?" I ask him.

"Ferrante is safe and sound. He sent me to reassure you, signora marchesana. For the moment he cannot leave his command post at Ponte Sisto. He thinks to come to us this evening, or tomorrow morning at the latest. I am here to serve you."

AT TWO in the night Ferrante's trumpeters make themselves heard, and to us they sound like angel musicians.

"Lord Ferrante is coming! Lord Ferrante is coming!" the girls repeat on all sides, embracing one another.

Instinctively I run a hand over my hair.

Ferrante. Can it possibly be true? I rush toward the great staircase. The fusiliers have stopped shooting. Alessandro of Novellara goes down to the entrance, sword in hand; and Pirro, with one of the young defenders, removes the iron bars from inside the main door.

I am on the first landing of the stairs. From outside some sounds come, as if they were opening a passage in the bastion, the noise of uprooted iron. I see the two leaves of the door sway, then open wide.

"Ferrante!" I call.

In the vestibule with the little columns a Spanish captain appears, pompously dressed, though quite dusty and tattered. He steps inside and introduces himself, putting his hand to the hilt of his sword and bowing.

"Alonso de Córdoba, imperial captain and commander of the Spanish forces."

After him, with heavy tread, his sword already unfastened, a German captain enters. He has a conqueror's face.

"Johann, captain of the Landsknechte," he roars.

The girls, who have gone down a few steps, come back up toward me, very slowly. I call again, in desperation: "Ferrante! Ferrante!"

"Mother, I'm here! Here I am!" my Ferrante replies finally, and he appears.

Simultaneously the Spanish and the German captains cross their swords before him, blocking his way. Then the Spaniard says: "Lord Ferrante Gonzaga, swear upon your honor as captain that you will not oppose the payment of ransom by all those who are in this palace."

The German adds: "No one will leave here until he has paid for his life."

Ferrante draws his sword and swears, as those two have demanded. Then he pushes aside the two swords, which are withdrawn before him; he runs up the stairs and takes me in his arms. I feel immersed in a lake of tenderness, so heartrending that I can barely maintain my role as proud queen. I put my hands on the still-soft shoulders of this twenty-year-old son of mine, and with my eyes I graze his head, those thick, strong curls that make him resemble a Roman portrait. He whispers into my ear that he would have wished not to see what he has been forced to see. I hug him still tighter. My girls gaze with veneration at the young companion of their carefree days, now a cuirassed Saint George, with all the powers of salvation. I lead him off with me, to comfort him; to Alessandro Gonzaga I entrust the two captains left at the bottom of the stairs, and I forget to take my leave of them. They have made Alessandro, too, guarantee their ransom, forcing him to swear.

I DO NOT raise my head. I stand with my neck straight and my back, as I was taught in my childhood, but I do not look up. What would I see except the arched vaults of this ground-floor hall emanating force, force that, no matter on which side it stands, inspires at this moment only revulsion? So I have deliberately reduced the range of my vision. I well know that at the end of the hall there are the refugees, huddled together into a single mass of terror. All my senses are tensed toward the space in front of this table, where we have been sitting for three days, deciding the fate of two thousand people. Each of them must pay ransom in order to be released to safety under the escort of German and Spanish soldiers. The sum is decided by the five of us, who are, besides me: Alonso de Córdoba, Johann, the German, Alessandro Gonzaga, and my son Ferrante, weary but heartened by my presence. Each captain is guarded by a soldier of his trust, standing behind his chair. Behind me there is no one; my Pirro Donati roams about the room, and I lose sight of him every now and then. At this point we know the city has been set afire. The glow of the flames filters through the windows and at times illuminates the hall with shafts of smoky light. I cannot help hearing the subdued weeping of those poor people who trusted me. And if I am to be useful, I must not allow myself to be corrupted by pity.

Now there is a moment's pause; the captains and their guards have gone to eat. I have not moved; where could I go, dear God? I hear the scratching of my girls at the door. They arrive; politely they ask permission to enter; they sweetly make some fuss over me, and they offer me some bread smeared with garlic, which they are carrying in their baskets. At the sight of the bread the refugees dart across the room like lightning and fling themselves toward the table, shouting in a single voice that they are hungry. Pirro Donati hastens to comfort, to allay; he guarantees that each will have a share, and he leads men and women back to the far end of the room, as the distribution begins. One young woman, who has remained near me, asks how I managed to choke down this stuff; garlic nauseates her. Patiently I extol the purifying virtues of garlic, which can keep away even the Black Plague. The girl, frightened, runs off, crying, "The plague! The plague!" It takes some time then to calm everyone.

From outside come the cries of the looters, circling our walls like rabid wolves; hour by hour it is becoming more difficult to ward off this rabble. Word has spread that in the Santi Apostoli palace there is more than two million in gold, and a roar bursts from the throats of these devils. The captains come back, and the Spaniard says that two thousand Landsknechte had already gathered at Campo dei Fiori to move and attack our palace; but just in time the prince of Orange appeared, first among all the captains in dignity, and he firmly forbade any hostile action toward us. Our house was to be considered the house of the emperor. We are in a privileged situation. No palace, the Spaniard repeats sarcastically, is safe from the sack: the palace of the chancellery, the Cesarinis', the della Valles', the Colonnas'. And after the sack, abductions, killing of men and women without distinction of rank, and insane tortures.

The Spaniard urges me to leave. He promises I will have an escort to make sure I arrive at the Tiber safely. By boat I can reach Ostia, and there go by sea to Civitavecchia. Ferrante also begs me to flee; the German raises his eyelids over the icy blue of his eyes and studies me. It is clear, all of them would like to be rid of me. How sibilant my voice sounds as I thank them and declare that I will never leave this palace except as the last woman, after all the others have been saved.

The German reacts and says curtly to Ferrante, "Enough! Your mother goes! Away!" and he continues in his choppy, halting Italian, saying that I must not intervene any further; it is their right to set the ransom amounts, and women know nothing of the rules of war.

Fiery, Ferrante reminds him that he is addressing the marchesana of Mantua. The man shrugs his shoulders, as the Spanish captain intervenes.

"Three days have gone by, and look at the slim booty!" He points toward the wall where riches of every sort are amassed: silver objects of every size, candelabra, gold coins, little sacks of jewels, gold and silver brocades, silk garments embroidered in pearls, luxurious furnishings. "It takes more than this to arrive at two million in gold!"

I am silent when Cristoforo Del Bufalo enters. Facing the table, he raises his arms and swears up and down that he has no money with him; he rushed from his house at the last moment, bringing nothing away. He is ready to sign a note on any bank in the city.

"We want good coin, not paper," the Spaniard says, with irony.

The German flies into a rage; he is determined to have the man tortured. Speaking up, I insist on being guarantor. It is useless to ask Signor Del Bufalo for what he does not have. It seems to me wiser to be content with the note on a bank. The treasurer will draw up the obligation in proper legal form. But the Spaniard, in his high-pitched voice, says slyly: "Signor Del Bufalo is on in years; he is ill. Accepting notes from him would be a risk. He might die the moment he is outside here."

"Gold, gold! Only gold and jewels," the German yells louder.

The Spaniard now urges Del Bufalo to write to his relatives; he can have two days' time to pay the two thousand gold ducats.

"They would never give it to me! Never! My relatives are mean to the marrow. Misers!"

"We will help you find the right words to convince them," the Spaniard answers.

Del Bufalo seems almost dead; his whole body is trembling.

"Signora marchesana, believe me, it is the truth. I do not have that money with me. And no one will give it to me."

"Ferrante," I say then to my son, "accept Signor Del Bufalo's note. We will charge the two thousand ducats against your share of the ransom."

Laughing, the Spaniard adds: "Signora marchesana, your son will have a beautiful collection of scraps of paper!"

The guards thrust Francesco Mellini forward. He is a man of some presence, not old and not young, narrow lips in a full face, an air of violent, treacherous passions. The German reads his name on a paper and, in his slow but very clear speech, declares that freedom for himself and his family costs ten thousand gold ducats, plus, of course, all his silver and jewels.

Mellini enacts a scene of angry desperation. He has no money; he is a poor man, not a thief; he would have nothing left to keep his family from starving. The German, with cruel amusement, suggests a discount of five thousand ducats in exchange for his four daughters, beautiful, haughty, sullen, two of them hardly more than children. Mellini writhes like one possessed, and I blurt out: "Don't you understand? Don't you know what these people do to girls? No reason restrains them. You are rich enough to pay any ransom without impoverishing yourself, but you complain like a pauper. If you and those like you had accepted the proposals of the Bourbon, who asked three hundred thousand ducats from the pope to spare Rome, we would not have come to this. Pay, Signor Mellini. Madman that you are, pay in the name of God!"

Pitying himself with the tone of a beggar whose life's blood is being sucked from him, the miser undoes his jacket and pulls out, one by one, some little sacks of gold coins that he had tied around his waist; the treasurer opens the sacks on the table and counts the gold pieces.

I turn to Alessandro Gonzaga. "Sir, give orders that the girls of the Mellini house be entrusted to your sister Camilla and taken to my chambers, where they will stay until it is the suitable moment for them to leave. And let no one dare molest them."

The Spaniard pales at my scathing tone. "Do not exaggerate in acting greathearted, my lady," he says softly. "The Gonzagas, the people of your house, will also receive a generous part of this ransom. And not only your son but also your kinsman Captain Alessandro of Novellara will have his share."

"Beautiful scraps of paper, as you said yourself a little while ago," I reply scornfully.

OUTSIDE, at the approach of evening, the campfires were being lighted again; in the fog that had thickened once more, the glints of the fires seemed to resemble the fires of hell, and the sound of the Lanzi's singing and their inhuman laughter was more gloomy. I could almost see those blasphemous people walking through the streets, wearing the sacred vestments ripped from the sacristies, and miters on their heads, as they pushed and shoved poor naked priests with horrendous curses, forcing them to kiss the Lutherans' hands bedecked with the bishops' pastoral rings.

Ferrante touched my arm to give me courage. And I, who felt strangled by fear, just barely found the strength to give him a sign of understanding, to assure him that a space of ours existed, far from that damned world that was closing in around us.

ON THE thirteenth of May, at dawn, my refugees, mercilessly fined but alive and well, left the Santi Apostoli palace. The last of the women under the protection of the Spanish soldiers had been escorted outside the Nomentana Gate, where relatives were waiting. Once again I entered my chamber. The chill penetrated my bones, but finally I could wash. I donned traveling garb, seized a veil. Out of mere habit, I cast a glance at my image in the mirror. I was haggard and drawn, no longer myself; but I cared nothing for that. I was leaving. Ferrante and Alessandro Gonzaga were accompanying me to Ripagrande, where broad boats were ready to take me to Ostia. From there, with a Genoese galley of Andrea Doria, I would go to Civitavecchia by sea, or perhaps to Pisa. From the Tyrrhenian to the Adriatic, cutting across the peninsula horizontally, we would ride as far as Pesaro. I would not go by Urbino; since last year my Elisabetta had entered the great silence.

We would reach Mantua by way of Ferrara. It is quickly said. I repeated that itinerary to myself like a promise to strengthen my blood: I was going home, home! I was ashamed of the breath of happiness that enfolded me when the jasmines of my secret garden appeared to my mind's eye; they were not all that close at hand, I reminded myself sharply. I stood in the entrance; I was waiting. Servants and porters were loading boxes, baskets, bundles into the carriages, all my belongings and those of my court. Lined up behind me, my girls did not speak, they seemed afraid to go out. Alessandro of Novellara reassured them, and they started off with him. Ferrante came toward me; he said to me that along the street, all the way to the Tiber, his harquebusiers were arrayed in double file, with those of the prince of Orange. We need have no fear.

I saw the people of my household pass before me, the envoys of Ferrara and Urbino, and the Venetian Domenico Venier, disguised as a porter with a chest on his shoulder. He kept his eyes lowered beneath the gray wool cap. My dwarf, Morgantino, overtook him on the last step of the staircase and gave him a kick in the behind, telling him to get a move on. Venier, furious, gave him a withering look but did not lose his place and began to walk faster. In the vestibule, cluttered with refuse and waste, desolate evidence of fears, the dwarf swaggered vaingloriously. With malicious delight he declared: "I'll be able to say that at least once in my life I kicked the behind of an ambassador of the Most Serene Republic of Venice."

I prepared to scold him, but he eluded me with a somersault and ran to hide behind Lavagnola, already beyond the main door. He clasped her hand like a little child wanting to be led, and he turned to look at me, pretending to weep; but I was unable to muster even the shadow of a smile. We could go. All were safe. God had granted me this favor. Before I also went out, I called Ferrante, who had gone off to make sure the guards assigned to follow me most closely were well armed.

"Ferrante," I said to him, "my son, before leaving this palace, give me your notes."

His dubious gaze clashed with mine, steady. Obediently my son took from his coat a packet of notes on various banks signed by some of the refugees. As soon as I had the papers, I began tearing them up, one by one, into little pieces, which I then dropped on the piles of filth. Ferrante, protesting, tried to stop me.

"Mother, you were the one who made me accept those notes. You didn't rebel when they accused us of sharing the booty. You did that to deceive the captains, didn't you? As long as they believed I was their accomplice, they wouldn't consider me an enemy, and so my word retained its value."

Ferrante insisted timidly on the necessity of the laws of war, however hard and cruel. Then he had to listen to me. I saw he was surprised when I reminded him that the prince of Orange had not demanded ransom, even though he was the supreme leader, a great gentleman but not rich. We Gonzagas would never profit from the sufferings of that unfortunate city. He was to follow my counsel. I knew what I was doing and what I foresaw. I finished tearing up the papers. Then I also went out into the square.

I was received by a gray air, veiled by a fine, smoky dust that penetrated the eyes, pricking them. And where was the square? From the windows it had been impossible for me to form any idea of the ruined palaces and houses, the enormous heaps of charred rubble behind the few facades that were still standing. Rome had no splendors left; the sky was a dirty curtain; there was no longer anything that was not soiled, shabby, lifeless. I lowered my eyes, and following my household, I entered a corridor flanked to the left and right by lines of harquebusiers in light cuirasses, in battle array, with firearms, swords, daggers. Their staring eyes made them abstract: a depiction of machine men, mercenaries, instruments of misfortune. Their cuirasses reflected the glow of the fires.

WE PROCEED in silence. No one speaks. From time to time we hear a crackling, a dull thud, distant cries, and also cries nearby, the neighing of a solitary horse, the baying of crazed dogs, whimpers of exhaustion. The sound of our footsteps is the only real thing that confirms our condition as survivors. Desperate, to keep from screaming, I murmur softly to myself: "All this ruin! This monstrous ruin! My God, nothing is left alive! There is no one left!"

With a desolate tone, which he tries to make simply informative, Franceschino Gonzaga answers me to break the silence that oppresses us: "Those who are not dead have escaped. We must hasten, my lady; let us walk faster."

"My heart is shattered in my breast," I say, gasping. "And what of the pope?"

"Still shut up in Castel Sant'Angelo. A prisoner, to be truthful." The Mantuan ambassador sighs. "Perhaps he will never again have captains and soldiery in his service. They are even saying the emperor wants to appropriate the lands belonging to the Church. The pope will become chaplain to all the potentates."

The hand of Charles the Fifth is now pressing upon us without respite. But if Rome, the first city of civilization, has been ignominiously degraded, mankind itself is being degraded. To our left a wall collapses; in the cloud of settling dust, a beautiful column appears, beside a broken arch. I seem to hear a great sorrowing moan, but I cannot tell if it is an animal's or a human being's. I slow my pace, but I perceive only that silence, that destruction, that disintegration of a living creature in its death throes.

The white geometry of our studies and our culture is disappearing under the blows of perverse people of diabolical spirit, who in destroying also humiliate. The pain of so many innocents, those children slashed in their beds with sabers, those sick people drowned in the Tiber, the many young girls and nuns raped and killed, men and women ferociously tortured—who decreed all this grief, beyond healing? Had we really been such sinners, to deserve it? And now, who would find it useful?

I shake my head, to dispel a rebellion that risks turning into blasphemy. Resolutely I take my companion's arm and continue to advance along that sinister corridor among those distant sounds of death.

We come to Ripagrande; the boats are at the jetty. Before starting down the gangplank, I look around. The landscape is everywhere the same, on this side of the Tiber and on that: dust, ruin, desolation. I remember that radiant morning of another May when, a new bride, I found myself for the first time before a Roman building, the virile arches of Catullus's villa at Sirmione, crowned with green, facing the blue of the lake; and my ecstatic cry, "Rome, Rome," was not so much a cry as an appeal to the youth of the spirit. That name broke in my throat.

VII

Rather
Than Die
of
Melancholy

"I'VE GOT A a primiera!" I cried, laughing loud. "See! I have four cards of different suits. It's very clear! Give me your stakes. I win everything."

With a sweep of my hand I gathered in the coins of the stakes, and I laughed again; before me had formed a little hill of small coins, the ones we call *da elemosina*, for alms. Everyone in the barge drawn slowly along the bank of the canal by sturdy mules was dumbfounded, staring at me.

"What's come over you?" I asked.

My cousin Camilla answered: "Isabella, this is the first time we've seen you laugh since we began our journey. May God bless you."

"We can't play any longer; we've run out of coins," Domenico Venier, the Venetian ambassador, complained, "and here no one will change our gold."

"Pirro, change His Excellency's gold for him," I said to Pirro Donati. "In Ravenna you changed some money. Come on, everyone, we'll continue our game."

Before looking back at the cards distributed by the dealer, I had caught the yellow splendor emanated by the fields of the immense Po plain, thick with nearly ripe wheat. In a few hours we would reach Ferrara and, from there, home. Still alert to the play, I followed within myself that lighthearted yearning that bound me immediately to the reality of my surroundings. Of the month of May, after the thirteenth, I retained only a piecemeal memory: At Ostia we stopped for many days—I could not count them— in the uncomfortable lodging of the fort, almost without eating, because the local inhabitants kept their provisions hidden, in fear of the Lanzi's raids. Informed by someone, Ferrante sent us from Rome a great raft with bread, flour, oil, and wine. And finally the heavens tired of pouring down rain.

I found myself aboard ship. Then I landed at Civitavecchia. I cannot say how I decided to continue by land, entrusting our baggage, soaked chests of silver plate, dresses, ornaments, books,

to a ship that, escorted by the Genoese galley, would take it all
to Pisa. We rested at Corneto and from there on toward Viterbo
and by the road to Orvieto and Perugia as far as Cagli, Pesaro,
Ravenna. I was wearing only riding dress, I endured without
suffering the hardships of the journey over the stern mountains
through the uncertain season, and it was only the ache of weariness that made me realize I was alive, at least in some part of
me. The other part remained in a mute area beyond my reach,
nor was it possible for me to reconstruct any wholeness for myself.

In Ravenna I was overtaken by the first gusts of awareness. In
the boat I had laughed at that lucky stroke in the game of primiera,
which has been my passion since childhood, and more and more
clearly, to my own surprise, aghast, I began asking myself what
everyone around me—the women, boys, gentlemen, even the
suite of almost a hundred horses—had been doing for an entire
month. I seem to have gone forward thanks to mechanical thrusts.
I must have appeared out of my senses if, at my laughter, they
all thanked God as if for a miracle. I felt stimulated just by repeating the names along the route that at this point in our journey
had a familiar ring: by canal to Ferrara, then by river from Stellata
to Sermide, to Govérnolo, to Mantua. I glanced at my riding dress
of fine gray flannel with little gold epaulets; I had nothing else
with me save my purse, my white veil, and the package containing
Ercole's cardinal's hat. And I felt light, being stripped of all other
possessions.

I picked out Ferrara, spying the four towers of the castle, and
a cavalcade came to meet me, led by Ercole d'Este, Alfonso's oldest
son; my brother was in Milan at that moment. The riders escorted
us from the embankment, occasionally raising their bannered lances
in greeting. I found my familiar Margherita Cantelma and Alda
Boiarda on the gangplank, ready with joyous welcomes. I slept
in my usual rooms at Porta Leone, and all of my childhood filled
my bosom. When it was time to leave the next day, I cannot
remember who whispered that at Sermide Boschetta would pay
homage to me.

Boschetta did not present herself at Sermide, but the whole
town was standing on the embankments, waving branches of
good omen. And so I was in Mantuan territory, and I wrote at
once a letter to my sons, arranging how and where we should
meet: At Govérnolo I would deliver to Ercole the cardinal's hat
that had cost me so much passion. But I saw Ercole before then,
dressed in scarlet, grave and happy, at Stellata, and together we
joined Federico at Govérnolo. There, on a little dais of packed

earth near the course of the river, my second son knelt, and I placed the hat on his head. None of those present could repress tears of genuine happiness. My cardinal, accompanied by Federico, entered the Duomo with all the nobility, and I went to Sant'Andrea to venerate the relics of the Precious Blood, unable to appear at a solemn ceremony in my humble, dusty dress.

The populace seemed to love me more tenderly in that attire. All were rejoicing. Nothing could be heard except the sound of bells and voices crying, "Isabella, Isabella." So many people crowded to touch my hand that Jacopo Tridapale, our gentleman, exclaimed it was like being at poor Rome's jubilee; a fit gripped me for a moment, casting a pall over the vivid light. At that same moment someone greeted me in the name of my daughter Eleonora, and for the first time in my life I spoke of her as my soul's delight.

I glanced from one face to the next, among those who pressed close to the head of my horse to applaud me; never had anyone seen such public happiness. My miraculous salvation was considered an example, a terrible adventure happily concluded in which everyone had participated from the distance; the triumph was thrilling, as it united me and my sons before the people, and I would never forget how Federico and Ercole bowed humbly before me on that little square of packed earth at Govérnolo, diversely grateful and adoring. And yet a weariness not so much physical as spiritual exhausted me, as if in a tedious convalescence. I was happy not to have to climb stairs, as I entered my ground-floor rooms at Cortevecchia. Cool, scented by the groves of limes thickly planted around, they welcomed me, but I no longer had the heart to do anything, neither to laugh nor to cry.

When I woke, a whiteness tending toward indigo blanched the sky. Instinctively I got out of bed very quietly so as not to wake my women, sleeping in the next room; I took a lantern from the shelf and lighted it. I crossed the apartment, the entire loggia, and I was in the secret garden. I could just make out the little domes of the trees and the apricot aflame with its fruit, perhaps ripe. The space, framed by the geometry of the wall, smiled at me. What sweet air. I reviewed the depictions of my achievements. I ventured a game with myself: at every painting or motto, a comment for my immediate use. *The musical pauses*: Patience is an angelic exercise that can become diabolical. *Twenty-seven*: *Vinti le sette*, the sects defeated; we never finish defeating the conspiracy around us. The candelabrum with a single light, *Suffict unum*, "and can I be that one"? *Nec spe nec metu*: Hope is a secret impulse, all the more intoxicating if you pretend to be indifferent. As I was joking with myself, I heard a sound and I did not have to ask myself who it was. The white, affectionate face came forward.

"Pirro!"

"My lady, is that you? The night watchman informed me that a little light was wandering around here, and I flung myself out of bed. Alone like this?"

"I was playing, Pirro, I was joking with myself a little, to regain my balance. Let us go into the Grotta. We shall see how my musical instruments are after more than two years of my absence. It is possible that strings will have to be changed, at least for some of them."

Pirro, amiably amused, led the way and opened the inlaid doors of my cupboards. I found my flute again, and a recorder, I tried out a lute, a harp, two viols. The tuner had to be summoned because I heard some dissonance in the instruments. As I delicately replaced them, my hand touched a little picture. I took it out, curious.

"Maria!" I exclaimed. "Maria Paleologa."

Was it a warning, a reminder? Maria Paleologa, Federico's bride, the daughter of Anne d'Alençon. Maria was beautiful, as her mother was, crowned with flowers like a little nymph, an oval face with high cheekbones. What madness had driven Federico to marry her when the contract did not stipulate the wedding for the present? Had it been Anne who wanted her daughter a bride at the age of eight, or had it been a whim of Federico's? And this marriage was still valid today; Federico was bound to Maria; in the eyes of the Church he was her husband.

Swift as roes, my thoughts raced, discordant, away from that image, but were drawn back to it, by strong attraction.

I UTTER the name of Maria Paleologa, and behind her the face of our ambassador is outlined: Giovanni Francesco Capi, known as Cappino, that alert, wiry, pale-skinned figure, with strong links to families of the far north, for he himself originally came from Novara. Our man, he is of the patient and truthful kind. He reports to me on his journey to Casale Monferrato, undertaken a few months after my arrival in Mantua. I think that the rediscovery of that little portrait on the first night of my return home was an imperative sign. "In November I set out on the road to Casale again." Thus Cappino begins his story, in his smooth, calm tone, a secret informant's. At the castle he was introduced into a room sheathed in hangings, where in a great curtained bed a boy of thirteen was lying, wan and impatient; a housekeeper tucked in his covers. His mother, Anne d'Alençon, lively and enthusiastic, was trying to console him.

"The doctor says you will soon be able to get up, my son. Are you happy?"

At that moment she became aware of my envoy. "Signor Cappino, have you just arrived from Mantua? We are happy to see you, as you know." She turned to her daughter, who was at the window, and called her: "Maria! Signor Cappino is here, your husband's messenger. Let us hear what he has to say to us."

Maria moved from the window and came forward, with a reticent step, not speaking. An inner door suddenly opened and a little girl of fifteen appeared, Margherita, Maria's younger sister. She said in a loud voice: "Yes, I've finished it! I've really finished it! Come, Maria! Mother, you come too! Please come!"

Noticing our Cappino, the girl greeted him gaily. The three women disappeared into the next room, leaving our envoy all alone with the boy, who, silent, lowered his eyelids on his pale face. After a few moments two chambermaids entered, carrying on outstretched arms a nuptial coverlet of pale yellow brocade embroidered in colored silks and threads of gold and silver; the arms of the Paleologues and the Gonzagas were interwoven in the center and in the corners in a branched drawing in tapestry point. Behind the triumphant emblem stood the three Paleologue women. Anne d'Alençon indicated the coverlet to Cappino and to Bonifacio.

"Look at the work that my Margherita has executed with her women. It is the most beautiful nuptial coverlet ever seen. And you look at it, too, Maria. Don't turn your head away; it's yours."

Maria spoke, rapidly and ironic. "It's beautiful, magnificent, a true nuptial coverlet, but in twelve years I have never had my husband at my side, not even for one day."

Anne replied: "A husband like Federico Gonzaga has to be merited, my daughter. He is not only a man of valor, courtly and amiable; he is something more. He resembles his unparalleled mother, one of the great women of our time. And why do you think I and your father, of happy memory, would choose him among all the princes who were asking for you as wife? Federico is the best of all, different from all; he is unique."

Margherita spoke up, the young, impulsive, ardent child: "When he came here to Casale to marry you, he was all dressed in white and silver, with long, long coppery hair. He was always festive, smiling. Do you remember, Maria, when he gave you the ring and called you his beautiful little bride?"

Maria became impatient. "I don't know how you can remember such things, Margherita! You were only six at the time!"

Anne laughed. "Margherita has a lively imagination; she's still a child. For her Federico is something out of a marvelous fairy tale, to be told over and over. But you, dear daughter, must think of the future. Mantua is a reality, a court full of life. There are poets there, and musicians, painters. Every day there are feasts, and something new is invented. Federico confided in me that he means to have a little palace built on the lake, where you and he can live by yourselves. The design will be by that great master Giulio Pippi, the Roman, very famous; and the little palace will stand in the gardens near the castle, toward the shore."

Maria rebelled. "Words, dreams, Mother. He's repeated the same things to me for years. What sort of bride am I? A bride made of paper, dispatches, documents, and signatures, not of actions. Federico promised to send for me when I was sixteen, but two years have gone by since then. And what message does Signor Cappino bring me today? From his face I know I will not go to Mantua this time either. Everything separates us."

"Everything unites you!" Anne blurted. "The will of the pope, the benevolence of the emperor, the consent of our kinsman the king of France, the wishes of the people of Mantua, and the true affection of the marchesana Isabella. She is your best ally."

Maria rebutted again. "The emperor, the king of France, the pope, his mother, the people. You see? It is the others who want me, the others who would force his hand. That's why Federico doesn't love me. There is only one thing that could matter to me: for him to come to me on an impulse of his heart. He is my husband, you have ordered me to love him, and I will obey you always."

Anne's eyes rested on her daughter; they expressed a stubborn tenderness. "Now we will let Signor Cappino speak, and we will hear what he has to say to us. And you must not lose faith. Federico will come soon, be sure of that; you dwell in false shadows. One day you will have forgotten them all. Signor Cappino, I beg you, speak."

Cappino tried to assume a nonchalant tone. "Madame, the marchese Federico loves you and remembers you always. But your mother is right, you must be patient. My lord at this moment is oppressed by grave military commitments and still cannot set the date to come to Casale."

The marquise Anne's pale brow frowned, but only for a moment.

"He will come," she declared firmly. "Never fear, Maria; he will come."

THE INVITATION was unexpected. My son entered my rooms, and in his flatterer's way he insistently asked me to come on Christmas Eve to see the little play with talking animals that some of his household were preparing in the stables of Motteggiana, the beautiful Gonzaga villa near the Po, opposite Borgoforte. This was a very, very old peasant farce handed down from one generation to another, a kind of ritual, part theater and part magic. I did not know what to think, so to find out, I said yes. I would go in a closed coach with a little group of my women, all of them excited by the unusual festivity. Federico seemed happy that I had consented.

In the evening as the flurries swirled low over the countryside, streaking the ground diagonally, we came to Motteggiana. In the darkness of the black night we could barely discern the elegant proportions of Luca Fancelli's building, whose chimney pots seem Oriental in design and make this residence a fairy tale site, enhanced by the grace of proportion. My son was awaiting us; some spiced wine had been prepared, and the usual *sorbir*. Then we went down to the handsome, spacious stables, like a low nave of a church, and we took our seats opposite a manger fitted out as a stage, with drapery of brocades and a carpet on the platform. Peasants, servants, grooms, messengers, and workers were seated on benches and bales of hay arranged in a row. In the manger around a wooden Baby Jesus, there were four children with head masks, depicting the cock, the ox, the ass, and the sheep. Some musicians of Federico's court were playing folk music, Christmas chants, simple songs easily sung. When the music ended and the singing ended, the children came to the front of the stage. The cock made a shrill sound cock-a-doodle-doo and announced: *"Puer natus est, puer natus est."*

Immediately another boy, assuming a deeper voice, almost mooing, asked: *"Uuhm, uuhm, ubi? Ubi est?"*

It was the sheep's turn. *"Baaa, baaa. In Bethlehem. In Bethlehem!"*

And the ass began, partly braying: *"Hee-haw! Andemus! Andemus! . . ."*

To this interweaving of animallike voices, the children alternated their movements with graceful skill. In the end they joined together their various crowing and mooing and baaing and braying.

"Jesus is born! Jesus is born!" cried a chorus hidden in a stall, and the whole audience echoed the cry festively.

Federico followed the scene with a tense emotion I had rarely seen in him. After the performance one of the child performers, the one who played the ass, was the first to jump down from the stage, take off his animal head, and come running to Federico.

"Father, Father, did I do it well? Did I?"

Federico bent over him with great delicacy and declared that he thought he was hearing a real ass. In the laughter that united them, I recognized father and son, a very close resemblance.

"Alessandro," Federico said, "greet this lady. She is the marchesana of Mantua, my mother."

Not the least intimidated, the child greeted me in courtly fashion, looking into my face. He was pretty, with that childish sweetness that seems a sudden miracle. I responded to his greeting. He turned and with great naturalness went to the other children, who had not removed their masks and were clowning among themselves.

"Federico," I said, "what does this mean?"

"I wanted to present my son Alessandro to you, Mother. Will you forgive my plot?"

I laughed.

"Your son is beautiful, but he does not resemble you," I decreed.

It was not true. Indeed, except for the lighter color of his hair, the child looked to me like my own son at the performance of the *Formicone*, and my heart was pounding. But that resemblance, attractive though it was, made me suspicious and aroused in me a wave of new anxiety. I sensed a presence between us, almost palpable. To whom should I attribute the idea of this meeting, if not her, the wily Boschetta, who, even though she was absent, loomed over that scene? She had unleashed her attack, sending me that beautiful and lively child, who made my heart melt. I would gladly have kissed him and taken him into my arms. How long had it been since I had embraced a child of my blood? By now all my children were grown up.

At that moment of reflection Alessandro flew toward me and put his little hand on my dress, as if to warn me.

"Signora, signora, we must go. The animals must remain alone on Christmas Eve. At midnight they talk with the Baby Jesus. If you spy on them, you die."

"You really do die!" the other children repeated, in chorus, as they came closer. "We must go! Let's go!"

In their voices there was a terror, half joking and half real.

I rose, to go along with the joke. And everything seemed to me of welcome simplicity: the stableful of animals, the actor-children, and even this little Alessandro, for whose sake they had dared plead before the throne of the emperor Charles the Fifth, virtually defying me. I was moved to pity for this child used as bait. An ambitious woman dared put her own son at the risk of being rejected, gambling with me to win me over and tame me. I tasted a furious contempt for Boschetta, and at the same time remorse sank deep into my bosom. I had to betray my son's hopes.

Alessandro was still there, before me; his pure eyes suspected nothing. I bent over him, I held him in my arms, and mentally I asked his pardon for having to be his enemy.

To the Most Illustrious and Excellent Madama Isabella, Marchesana of Mantua and My Lady

From Orvieto

*M*y lady, venerated with eyes full of tears, I do not know how this letter will sound; I am struggling in a state of dazed horror, which, almost a year after the events that provoked it, has diminished only just enough to give me strength to raise my pen and set it on paper. You must know everything about me, signora, even if I do not know whether any of it matters to you. But having lived through the same period of misfortune in the most wretched place in the world, by which I mean Rome, we are somehow comrades in suffering, though comrades at a distance, as fate has always decreed for us. And first of all, tell me, or tell the air at least, if on the evening of the fifth of May you were that shadow I thought to see at a window of the third floor of the Santi Apostoli palace, a delicate, womanly form outlined against the glow of a light burning in the room. Promptly you disappeared, and the light was put out. Driven by an impulse to see more, I came closer below the windows, but an harquebus fired from above, aimed at me. Then the soldiers who were escorting me, frightened by the immediate risk, dragged me away. Responsible for their lives, I was obliged to follow them. I could not sacrifice those faithful men of the pope, but I beseeched them to leave me alone in that square. I assure you I was throbbing with shame and wrath, having come to save you, having glimpsed you, to be then forced to turn back to Castel Sant'Angelo, even though at the last moment. Vain desires, betrayed loyalties, new sadness to add to the sum of misfortunes.

We breathed the same poisonous fog during those May days, and you cannot imagine how I prayed, sorrowfully, offering myself in humble holocaust to God or how I later embraced a young man, a certain Sebastiano Gherardi, who had himself

hoisted by rope onto the southern bastion of Castel
Sant'Angelo, to descend from there again during the night, he
bore news from the city. Grim, haunting news. Only one bit of
information was reassuring, the tale he told of you at the
ransom tribunal in the Santi Apostoli palace, the great regulator
of those unhappy bargainings, magnanimous toward your
refugees. Some days later we received news that you had left
by river, escorted to the barges by the troops of the prince of
Orange and your son's Spaniards. You were going home, and
this comforted me. At least you would be far away from the
continuing mockery of the Lanzi; you would no longer see
houses being sacked for the second or third time and many,
many people still being murdered. At the last sacking they
even tore the nails from the buildings and stabbed to death the
few servants remaining there to weep.

Who is to blame for such wicked horror? His Holiness sinned
in his indecision, not realizing the infernal wrath of the
emperor, so inhuman as to harbor the idea of a total sacrifice of
the city and of all us inhabiting it, including Christ's vicar on
earth. To give the world a proof of his strength, to measure
himself against a power one would have thought beyond
attack: This is what Charles the Fifth wanted to demonstrate.
And now, if you could see him, our pontiff, dressed in his
humblest clothes, having fled from Rome to this little city of
Orvieto, an impregnable citadel but where the archbishop's
palace is almost uninhabitable, it is so decrepit. The pope's
court, including us foreigners, lives on the charity of some
compassionate faithful; our clothes are wretched and stained,
the imperial punishment weighs heavily on us.

Today, however, is a day of clearing skies. It seems that
Charles is about to set aside, little by little, his vindictive wrath.
And Clement has finally understood how dangerous it is to
make any agreement with the French, so to their urgent calls
for a new league against the emperor he will reply with a
declaration of benevolent neutrality. Meanwhile, we are
besieged by famine. Would God the pope had the heart to go
down to Viterbo, where conditions of daily life would be less
fierce.

I have further reason to grieve. In Orvieto there has arrived,

unexpectedly and secretly, a messenger from my king, Henry
the Eighth, who implores Clement to declare invalid the
marriage with Catherine of Aragón. There is a whole,
complicated story of documents, bulls, and dispensations
granted in his day by Pope Julius of sainted memory, and it
may be that my sovereign's arguments are justified, even just.
But all is bristling with sharp spikes around this afflicted
pontiff, who, with a bench, an unsteady table, and a few straw
chairs, grants audiences, sad and very patient.

My lady, now that we have emerged from this swamp of
death, I want to return to the pace of my story with you (I
refrain from saying "our," as you see), to tell you what
happened to me in the five months after that reckless cry of
mine that was to reach you from Mantua, that "I am coming at
once," which implied a presumptuous "to save you," the
language of an incorrigible paladin. In fact, I took my leave of
the marquis your son, who seemed to me very upset, though
most courteous, and I flung myself on my horse, then, with my
groom, Beltrando, sought mile by mile the shortest and safest
routes toward Rome. Our plan changed constantly, but every
day, by a great deal or a little, I was coming closer to you.

There would be no use in my describing to you this journey,
slightly insane and laden with forebodings. The fierce wintry,
rainy season forced me every now and then to stop at some inn
and to let the season exhaust its temper. In January I had left
Chiusi behind and was proceeding southward when, at a bend
in the muddy downhill road, my horse had a bad fall, and I
with him. Beltrando came to my aid. Some people from the
locality turned up, and they had a house not far away. They
succored me and lodged me, in a big, bare room on the ground
floor, with a fireplace black from smoke. My left leg, however,
had suffered a bad fracture, which caused me pain. This same
pain made me lose count of the days, and some time went by
before a healing physician arrived, who tormented me in a
thousand ways and wrapped me in a perfect labyrinth of
bandages. The damage was great, and I am no longer young;
everything was against me.

Luckily I had a little money. My lady, excuse me for
mentioning this detail, though it is necessary for daily life. The

room was furnished better and heated; I had white covers, warm and scented, appetizing foods; Beltrando was settled in a real bed, set up in one corner. My hosts were serious people, cordial in their way. Sons, daughters, fathers, mothers, uncles, aunts, children, relatives, grandparents, a tribe that took turns tending me, to the great satisfaction of my good, but lazy, groom. A little boy, by the name of Rosalino, kept me company. His mother, Albatra, prepared my meals, and at evening, with a benevolent but unsmiling expression, she entered my room with a light step and gave me an infallible potion to make me sleep. The hours never passed, and my leg was not improving. I was restless, I sent Beltrando to all the nearby hostelries for news, and when it was certain that the imperial army would encounter no further obstacles and was advancing straight toward Rome, I became delirious. Nobody paid any heed to what I was saying, also because I was raving in my native tongue.

One night I was wakened by some thuds that I seemed to hear, and I observed from beneath my eyelids. I seemed to be dreaming: At the end of my room there was a high, narrow opening that at least two people could pass through, and beyond the opening a kind of grotto yawned, its sloping ceiling illuminated by torches. Shadows were coming and going in that reddish smoke, and some were carrying on their backs statues, vases, objects of unfamiliar shape. Two bronze arms, advanced, fixed to a base; bare, held upward in a votive gesture, hands open, they followed the shadows in silence and left by the big door. Rosalino came to my bed and, turning, he murmured: "He's asleep. Yesterday evening he drank the herb."

As he disappeared, I saw, advancing from the depths of the cavern, a tall statue, erect on a pedestal, as if it were being carried in procession. It came in my direction, proceeding so slowly that I could distinguish every detail of it, a figure, surely not Roman, but perhaps Oriental, in any case, nothing I could place in my mind with definite attribution. It seemed made of colored terra-cotta; it had great eyes, wide and staring, outlined in black. The hair was long, parted in the middle, curled, with geometrical waves; the dress was a long, loose tunic. The right hand clasped a flower, a lotus perhaps; and the left, a fruit. I could not say if the figure was male or female, god or goddess. By now it was close to my bed, always looking at me with open eyes. There was a moment (but surely I was raving) when the divinity leaned forward and, with the lotus flower, touched my foot. Suddenly the sharp pains stopped, and I sank into sleep.

In the morning my well-being persisted. I could even move without feeling lacerated. The end of my room was walled up as always: nothing betrayed any sign of the magic apparition. I asked Beltrando where he had been that night since I had not seen him in his bed. He became confused, and in the end he mentioned one of the daughters of the nearby innkeeper who had invited him to drink. I tried to make him talk about our hosts, but he had little to tell me; they were a big family of people who worked hard on the land.

It may be that I had a hallucination, and from the hallucination ecstatic visions were born, of very remote origins. Or having obscurely perceived the symptoms of healing, my consciousness invented a healing god. Perhaps. But after that night I began really to improve; the physician came back and was surprised to see me on my feet. Cautiously I asked if in that area there had once been some divinity's cult, perhaps in very ancient times, or if they recalled any remote religions. Amazed, he replied that he knew nothing, but he seemed upset. I kept the vision to myself, and my questions, and for that matter only one thought was constantly besieging me: to be in Rome, to hear about you (and I was praying you had gone home). I managed to remount my horse, after having rewarded and thanked my hosts; as I was giving the kindly Albatra a diamond ring of mine, I noticed her great eyes, of a steady, fixed black like those of the lotus-flower statue. I was so well I could let my mind range freely.

And so, after adventures and encounters pointless to narrate, I found myself in Rome, and assisted by skill and luck, and by my inner frenzy, we entered the fortress of Castel Sant'Angelo. And from there, with two guards I had beseeched and lured with gold, I dragged myself before the Santi Apostoli palace, as I have already told you.

I pick up my pen again after a few minutes' pause. The

weariness and the emotion of those searing adventures so oppressed me that they robbed me of the strength to write. Our old days, our old Rome seem centuries away. Never, in all our lives, will we find again what we had. Never, climbing again the steps of the Vatican, will we feel that restless, silent intensity that descended from the rooms where Raffaello was painting the School of Athens, to the Sistine Chapel, where Michelangiolo was creating his world of sybils and prophets on the ceiling. Never more will we see the young assistants and disciples of the two painters, shod in felt shoes, tiptoeing up and down the flights of stairs that connect the two floors, pursuing the unique moment that united and separated the two geniuses, releasing them to their freedom. Sacred spell, gift of a God obscurely vindictive, who lifted us to the spheres of genius before allowing us to be struck down.

I am afraid, my lady, of telling you sad and unhealthy things. Everything that happened "before" the misfortune of Rome seems to me to contain the germ of a threatening sublimity. I still do not know how right it is to divide up time like this and declare it guilty. What if we were to rebel and to put a little fervor in penetrating the meaning of today's events? A frivolous thought now crosses my mind; it concerns you, and it brings you closer. I would like to know whether your baggage, so rich and gay with dresses and adornments, after it was stolen by Barbary pirates from the Genoese ship taking it to Pisa, was ever restored to you. I know that your son Ferrante tried to ransom it with the help of the imperial forces. I hope very much that you have had it back. But in spite of everything, I like and am strangely refreshed by the description of you given me by one of those captains of the prince of Orange, who saw you set out from Rome on the barge for Ostia with a dull little dress, hardly ornamented, your hair gathered in a net, with a white veil over it, and in such noble despair that everyone wanted to worship you because you had taken upon yourself the suffering of all. And so I worship you.

On the fourth of January, 1528

As I am about to sign my name, a hypothesis strikes me: If I had known what lay in store for you and for me in the future, would I have had the courage to send the first letter I wrote you? If you will allow it, I will make an egoistical calculation: I will add up the impulses of the spirit that have so often exalted me, measuring them against the sorrows undergone. The result is that today I find myself greatly indebted for that generous light that I have been able to gaze upon, that I still see in you, living and radiant in my own weft of days. I bless you, and I commend myself to you; accept, I beseech you, both benediction and pleas.

Your Excellency's

devoted slave
forever
Robert de la Pole

IN WINTER, THE FIRE is our friend. In the little stuccoed hall the lighted hearth stimulates daydreaming if you follow the consumption of the enormous logs or the arabesques of knights and ladies depicted, and transfigured, in the marble frame. Before me, my son Ercole made an effort to conceal his uneasiness; at every moment I knew he pictured the pope shut up in the fort of Orvieto, in that humiliated poverty, and yearned to join him, to share his mortified days. To bring him closer to me, I told him about the Christmas festivity and the performance with the talking animals.

My son sorrowfully remarked, "Signora Boschetta has emerged from the shadows; she wants great things, at this point. Even these half-pagan festivities serve her to maneuver feelings."

"That woman will ruin Federico and our State," I affirmed.

"It will not be so easy for her, dear Mother. A marchese of Mantua is pledged to the legitimate succession. And we are here to remind him of that."

"Federico still refuses Maria Paleologa as his wife. He has sent to Casale a brutal message that 'these are not the times for weddings.' He decided this without seeking my advice. And meanwhile, he reveres that other woman like a queen and every day feasts in grand style with the court in their House of Love at the Tè, ignoring the hardships of our people. God knows how the people have suffered for months now from the pestilential fevers that cannot be dispelled."

"The city," Ercole said quietly, "is full of libelous writings, as never before, and almost all are directed against my brother. The populace has never expressed the satirical ideas against the Gonzagas that they are muttering now."

"She, she is the one who is provoking it all. She knows Federico cannot refuse the wedding with Maria without dishonor, and she is fomenting some obscure plot. Strange rumors are circulating."

I felt a pang, and from a box I took a little pill Giusto of Udine and I had made, camomile pounded up with a very small amount of poppy. I could not help complaining: "Why is my son betraying me, Ercole? When I was rescued in Rome, I thought I had regained my place in his heart. I hoped to be able to help him in everything."

"You must not surrender, dear Mother. You have never surrendered."

"I want to defend him against that woman, but she has powers I cannot combat. I saved his father; but Francesco was a strong man, and Federico is weak."

"Where logical principle is of no use, then you need astuteness. You have said that many times, Mother."

These words for a moment brought me back to myself. Someone knocked at the door. It was Iva, my girl; she put a fur around my shoulders. I rose and informed Ercole that I was going to San Lorenzo to hear a special mass.

"The sun today is beautiful. Pray for my forthcoming journey, Mother."

"It seems the Roman sun," I remarked; then I corrected myself. "No, it's paler." I could not keep from saying, in a rush: "I am happy to be here: I am tired of wandering, even if my thoughts run on."

I bent my knee before that prince of the Church, barely twenty. As I kissed his hand, I sensed a very faint scent emanate from him, and I recognized the famous hand pomade of my herbalist.

During those days fearsome speeches were circulating, swollen with exclamation points. I realized I had to go into action and could not do otherwise. Accompanied by only one of my women, I climbed in the castle, up to the Hall of the Suns, one of my old rooms redone and repainted by Federico's order. I found him there. A great table of veined marble was draped with stuffs—satins, velvets, hides—and covered with statues, rolled-up drawings, and many other objects of furnishing that my son had surely chosen for himself. Federico seemed agitated: he was accusing the captain of the guards and one of the officers.

"And so will you let him get away from you!?" he declared in a loud voice. "Well?"

"The Agnelli brothers are already in prison, closely guarded, my lord," said the captain.

"Yes, but Francesco Calvisano has escaped to Modena. Set everyone and everything in motion. I want him here, dead or alive; make the Agnelli brothers speak. I want all of them in my hands, all those guilty of taking part in the wicked conspiracy."

The two officers nodded and saluted, before hastening away. Federico, seeing me, changed expression. He rushed toward me and offered me his arm, that I might lean on him.

"Forgive me, Mother, they didn't announce your visit to me. Thank you for coming to console me."

He led me to a seat covered with yellow velvet and immediately repeated the movements of his adolescence. He drew up a low stool and crouched at my feet.

"You are ever my dear mother. Ah, if you knew everything! I am being attacked by events!"

I kept silent. I was waiting for him to explain himself; the news was too little and too uncertain for me to venture into that swampy terrain. Agitated, Federico stood up and paced back and forth in the room, as his father used to do. Finally, he stopped and came back toward me.

"Think, Mother! Poison! Yes, poison in my house. It could have reached me. The count of Calvisano has demonstrated his villainy!"

He walked some more.

"They wanted to offend me, to strike what is dearest to me. And yet she, Signora Boschetta, is harming no one. Her only wrong is to love me."

"Calm yourself, Federico. Thanks be to God, there are no victims apparently. Why don't you tell me, in an orderly way, what happened?"

"They made an attempt on Signora Boschetta's life, with an ampoule of poison, substituted for her usual elixir. They meant to kill her, you understand? And the prime culprit, the leader of the conspiracy, is Francesco Calvisano, her husband."

"Federico!" I admonished him. "Consider things clearly; do not let wrath blind you. If a husband has chosen to punish his wife, to avenge his long-outraged honor, there is no intention of revolt against you. It is something between husband and wife, criminal, to be sure, but nothing to do with you."

"She could have died!" Federico exclaimed, so desolate it was frightening.

"But she is not dead. Signora Boschetta is protected by the gods."

"I know certain things. They plotted an out-and-out conspiracy, I tell you. I must expose and punish them. If you had seen her! If you could see her now! She's lost all her color; she's languid, unsteady. She says she still hears those cries that saved her from the poison; her terror will not leave her."

"This is a hard thing to get over, true. Tell me how it happened. Who discovered the poison?"

"It was Achillina, her chambermaid, absolutely trustworthy. She glimpsed the ampoule in her mistress's hand, and its shape seemed different from the usual, and when she went to the shelf, she realized that the stopper left there was round instead of a pyramid shape. She flew to the signora Boschetta and was just in time to snatch the ampoule from her and fling it on the ground. The liquid wet the edge of the rug and almost singed it. The mark has remained, horrible evidence. Unfortunately it is impossible to examine the liquid because Achillina struck the ampoule to the floor."

He told me all this in agitation, still trembling at the peril his woman had been in. Suddenly he rushed to my feet and flung himself into my embrace. It was a while before he became calm.

BETWEEN castle and palace the story of the plot with all its ramifications of loves and hatreds and jealousies fascinated and upset both court and populace. Little groups of courtiers and of citizens with grim or anxious faces would collect under the arcades, in the corners of drawing rooms. I found myself confronted by a Federico so distraught, inflamed, and entirely liege to his Boschetta that I was turned to stone. Must I confess? The tale of the poisoning did not convince me. Secretly, silently, stealthily I began my own investigation, consulting the one person on whom I always relied, Pirro Donati. My intuitions, confirmed day by day, I kept mostly to myself, not confiding all of them even to him. The direction they had taken was too dangerous. First of all, I wanted to learn the truth about the most important testimony, that of Achillina, Boschetta's chamber woman, who had saved her mistress. With slow encirclements, Pirro managed to penetrate the court of that woman who called herself queen of Mantua. But Achillina was no longer there. She had left suddenly to take refuge in a Franciscan convent at Solarolo in Romagna, a personal fief of mine; we could not go and speak to her there without alarming those who were surely on guard. The only way I could find was to talk again with my son, and at length. He would unburden himself to his mother. Toward evening I climbed up to him again. He had no further news.

"What were you saying the other day, my son, about that certain grave matter?"

"Her cowardly husband, the leader of the conspiracy, and the

Agnelli brothers, especially Giovanni, are part of the plot. And there are more serious implications, with distant roots, and this I know for sure, I tell you. There is a powerful woman involved."

"A powerful woman?" I asked in a stifled voice. "Is that possible? Here at court, a powerful woman, behind a conspiracy?"

"Not here in our house. But just think a moment. Wasn't Giovanni Agnelli our ambassador at Casale Monferrato? Isn't he a devoted friend of the marquise d'Alençon? Haven't he and his brother Gerolamo constantly sung the praises of Maria Paleologa, my so-called wife?"

"A Paleologa?" I asked with an amazement that, to gain time, I prolonged much more than natural. "A Paleologa? But who?"

"I don't know; it doesn't matter. One of them: Anne, or her daughter Maria, or both. They've been harboring a stormy jealousy, and they thought that if the signora Boschetta were to disappear, my marriage to Maria would be saved. That French mother is capable of anything; in her view she may have acted to open the way to Mantua to her daughter. Maria, poor victim, never ceases her laments for a moment, tormenting everyone. And she doesn't know what to think of this horrible act. The marquise d'Alençon must not believe herself invulnerable. Once the proof is in my hand, I will order a trial—immediately!"

Using some little business of mine as a pretext, I sent Pirro to Solarolo, and I bade him discover if Achillina's family had made any recent, considerable expenditure. A few days later my gentleman returned, alarmed and amazed by my intuition. Not only had the girl's family bought a valuable property, but she, Achillina, had allowed herself the luxury of paying a good dowry to an excellent convent. The story was that the contessa Calvisano had given her a large sum in recognition of the good service she had rendered for more than a decade in her household, and that made everything credible. My suspicions, on the contrary, began to take root, and Pirro shared them, as he hesitantly asked for new orders. I replied that for the moment we would not move. The vital witness had been placed out of reach; no one could question her, especially in private. It would have been risky to arouse attention. I surely did not want to cause painful scandals, nor did I want to entangle Federico in such blatant deceits.

"We will stop here and forget," I said to Pirro, and he replied that he had already forgotten.

I hadn't. I could see clearly. The conspiracy proved, by unmistakable evidence, never to have existed. Perhaps, a suspicion of a conspiracy more desired than plotted by Boschetta's husband had given birth to the episode of the suspect ampoule smashed on the floor by the maid so no evidence would remain. But not a word could be said. The only harm, at the slightest hint, would be to us; Boschetta was too firmly entrenched in Federico's heart for him not to believe her. Now that I guessed how things had probably gone, I had to wait and act at the right moment, in another way. It was not long before we learned that Francesco Calvisano, the husband, had been killed by the blow of a sword in his refuge in Modena. Meanwhile, Federico raged. He felt no constraint in asserting to his cardinal brother that he would never marry, would never give the Gonzagas a succession if his marriage to the Paleologa were not dissolved. Revolted, Ercole would not accept the idea and refused to gratify him; the cardinal was filled by my own cold anger.

The poor pontiff was caught in the middle, assailed by dispatches. Still in Orvieto, he measured this whim by the standard of his fugitive wretchedness. At the beginning a glint of hope for us: Clement was opposed. He loved and respected his sister in Christ Anne d'Alençon, whom he could not imagine guilty. After endless tergiversations, driven by his nephew Cardinal Cibo, who demanded the liberation of the Agnelli brothers, his intimate friends, the pope found a way out: In a very discursive brief he granted powers to resolve the matter to the archdeacon of Gabbioneta, a man who easily lent himself to the Gonzagas' wishes, as I knew all too well from the days of Francesco. And so the dispensation, the dissolution, was quickly written and signed by the archdeacon, and there followed immediately the pope's brief from Orvieto. In very limpid Latin, Clement declared himself certain that the Paleologue women, mother and daughter, *"procuraverant propinari venenum"* to the signora Isabella Boschetta, and this was an impediment to the consummation of the marriage between Maria Paleologa and the marchese of Mantua. I felt pity, since it was so laughable, for Federico's recommendation to the archdeacon that the brief be "modest" and that it leave "intact the friendship between the two houses." God only knows what he thought to save.

The intrigue became even more entangled. By Clement's brief, Federico was free, even if the two Paleologas were ignorant of everything and actually sent an ambassador of theirs to Mantua to insist the commitment be maintained. I thought of Anne's grief and outrage and of the violent humiliation bowing the head of the twenty-year-old Maria, before the archdeacon who presented himself in person at Casale, with the papal brief. I prayed constantly for those two women, martyred by a calumny of such gravity. And meanwhile, I kept an eye on Boschetta, who was sharpening her weapons.

Politics, in the following months, invaded much of the European scene, as we anxiously awaited the signing of the peace, the treaty that was called "of the two ladies," Louisa of Savoy and Margaret of Austria. Charles the Fifth meanwhile had already set out to reach Italy, with the intention of having himself crowned emperor by that poor, desolate pope, only recently back in his lacerated Rome. And there was someone very eager to meet the emperor; Boschetta, draped in her new role as innocent victim, kept hourly watch over the sovereign's steps, as she brooded on her secret plans.

Federico invited me to the castle; he wanted my opinion of that great painter from the Veneto region, actually from the mountain of Cadore, Tiziano Vecellio, who had agreed to make a drawing for a portrait. It was said that the emperor had also asked to have the artist paint him during his journey in Italy. I went to see Federico gladly, also to have more court news, which arrived only at intervals, and scantily, in my rooms. Federico was in the Hall of the Frieze, and a page was helping him arrange some red satin over his cuirass; I remembered Federico's first investiture, before he set off against Parma.

Signor Tiziano, a man of about forty with brusque dignity and vitality of spirit, was at an easel, where some rolls of paper were fixed.

"Dear Mother." Federico greeted me affectionately. "You are well. Better, indeed, every day. Sit facing me. If I can see you, my expression will become more amiable."

He led me to the velvet chair and made sure that I was comfortable. My girls took their places a bit farther back, on some benches; they were curious about the whole thing; they relished the comings and goings from room to room of so many young people.

With a face showing smug contentment over some unknown matter, the archdeacon of Gabbioneta said to Federico: "His Holiness was extremely pleased by the liberation of the Agnelli brothers and by the exemption you have granted them from any confiscation of property. He says Signor Giovanni has written him that they are absolutely innocent of any misdeed and have been slandered by malicious persons."

"They are free now," Federico said curtly. "We are not interested in this talk, and you, Archdeacon, make them realize they have been lucky, thanks to our Holy Father." He changed the subject and, with interest, addressed his painter: "Signor Tiziano, have you seen Giulio Romano's paintings at the Tè Palace? Do you feel in his drawing the power of the supreme Michelangiolo?"

"For me," the artist said calmly, "every force in painting bursts out in the invention of color."

My son went on to something else. He pointed to the arrangement of his dress and seemed hesitant. "The cuirass and the baton are right, but I'm not sure the folds of the stuff fall properly."

The painter replied soberly: "For the present I will only make a sketch."

"But, Signor Tiziano," Federico resumed, "have you forgotten your promise to do my portrait soon and also a Saint Sebastian? And the painting of the nude women should already be finished."

"It is well advanced."

Signor Tiziano was drawing. The archdeacon went to the easel with a familiar manner. "Maestro Tiziano, tell me something. How can you work with all those naked damsels you have around you? Aren't you afraid of too much distraction?"

"That's my business," the painter replied sharply.

"Signor Tiziano," Federico said, still pursuing a thought of his own, not listening to the others, "you have an excellent hand. You are an artist without equal today. I want you to paint the twelve Caesars in my private study. You must surpass Mantegna."

The painter, as he went on drawing, remarked: "The good artist must surpass only himself every time he picks up the brush."

From a side door my second son, the cardinal, entered, and all stood up to revere him. He greeted me with eager solicitude and seemed happy to find me there. He said to his brother: "I have just received a message from His Holiness. Pope Clement really takes the destiny of our house to heart. He hopes to see you soon happily married, and as bride he would propose the young sister of the king of Navarre."

"If Your Excellency will allow me," the archdeacon of Gabbioneta intervened, "I should explain that proposals are becoming numerous. Charles the Fifth has mentioned the name of the daughter of the duke of Cleves and has pledged himself to write to his aunt Margaret, asking her to act to ensure the success of the betrothal."

"I have heard," Ercole then said, "that the daughter of the duke of Cleves has been promised to the duke of Lorraine."

Piqued, the archdeacon replied briskly: "That is true, but the contract has not been signed. There might also be the daughter of the duke of Bavaria, very beautiful, eighteen years old, and rich."

"We know the virtues of the candidates," Ercole said with a smile. "We could add also Caterina de' Medici, Pope Clement's favorite niece."

"Of course," the archdeacon assented. "Caterina has the dowry of a real queen. The duke Alfonso, your uncle, wanted her for his oldest son; a pope's niece can always be useful, at least as long as the pope is alive."

Ercole, warming to the discussion, said to Federico, as if to reassure him: "Dear brother, the pope is fond of you. I am sure he would be overjoyed to see Caterina de' Medici enter the house of Gonzaga. We will speak about it."

"And we must not forget Julia of Aragón!" The archdeacon began again, to take upon himself the most important role in this delicate conversation. "Julia is the daughter of a queen of Naples, a niece of Charles the Fifth. True, she lacks a great dowry, but Charles would assign her lands in the Cremona region."

Putting down his chalk, Signor Tiziano concluded: "Signor marchese, there is no prince in the world more desired than you are. I have heard this also from Signor Pietro Aretino, your friend, who preaches about you not like a Peter but like a Paul. For today I have finished."

He put aside the papers, arranged the pastels, pencils, and everything else, cleaned his hands with a cloth, bowed, and went out.

Federico was deep in talk with the archdeacon. Ercole sat on a leather stool near me. He studied me carefully. "Mother," he murmured, "you have not said a word. I do not understand you. And I am tempted to think it is far better for me not to understand you!"

FEDERICO did not take part in the coronation of Charles the Fifth in Bologna. He had become embroiled in complicated pretexts: He could not allow Bonifacio Paleologo, the fifteen-year-old prince of Casale, to precede him in the ceremony, bearing the imperial scepter, as was the boy's ancient right; or perhaps Federico feared that his presence might arouse excess suspicion in Francis the First and impede a possible marriage plan with the daughter of the king of Navarre. And there were other reasons, perhaps more trivial but no less irksome. The first was the one he did not confess:

Anne d'Alençon would be in Bologna, and he did not want to meet her.

I was obliged to go, and I made my usual grand appearance with my company of girls (now no one called them *donzelle* anymore, in the Italian fashion, but *damiselle*, Frenchified), quick and keen after a few lessons from me. They wore stunning dresses, various hairstyles, each devised with genius by my experts, who amused themselves with bold inventions for our hair. And all of them wore hoods of white velvet I had designed, edged in ermine.

I was hardly in a mood to enjoy myself in Bologna. But we were comfortable in the handsome palace that housed us. There, as it was December, great fires burned night and day to keep us warm, and gentlemen came in droves to honor us and converse with us and to listen to my musicians, who, at intervals, sang some new compositions, like the Petrarchesque madrigal, for unaccompanied voices, on the verses of Pietro Bembo, "So contrary to love nor so fleet." To tell the truth, the probability of coming upon Anne also made me uneasy.

In any case, I had decided to leave Bologna quickly, and it seemed obscurely necessary for us to be away from there. On the morning of the imperial coronation, the twenty-fourth of February, 1530, Spanish horsemen rode through the streets, cheering Charles and throwing gold coins to students and populace. Later my girls, already in order and adorned with their fur-edged hoods, leaned out the window, exchanging quips with the knights who came and went in the street. The Bolognese students and the Spaniards, in loud voices, expressed their enthusiasm; then some of the hotter heads began quarreling. Soon there was a brawl, swords appeared from their sheaths, and blood flowed. The sheriff arrived and collected the wounded.

Sharply I ordered the windows closed. "These Spaniards will never stop slashing our people," I said to myself sorrowfully; but it was also true they had been provoked, and my girls had had something to do with it. "I have given you freedom, but you do not know how to be free. The first of you who plays the nymph with an Italian or a Spanish knight will be dismissed from my court," I declared, irritated. That twenty-fourth of February was somewhat cold, a pale light fell on the red bricks of the palaces, and the colors and gold of the trappings gleamed. The Church of San Petronio, which was to substitute for Saint Peter's in Rome, with the same names given to the chapels, vast as it is, could not hold all the imperial and princely retinues.

We made a triumphant entrance because no lady had such a

train as ours, of beautiful faces and brilliant dresses; but the heat of the tapers, the crush, the clouds of incense wearied us. Alert to the magnificence of the ceremony, we followed Clement the Seventh, still pale from all his suffering, as he bravely bore the triple crown and the cope embroidered in gold and studded with rubies. Charles the Fifth wore a simple deacon's tunic as a sign of humble submission and served the mass said by the pope. How haughty that submission was. You had only to look at the emperor's face to read there his implacable determination that nothing could ever affect. Abstractly glorious was the moment of the coronation. Clement took the crown, held it over the head of Charles, and, like a good priest, spoke, in his cultivated voice, the ritual words in the name of the Father, the Son, and the Holy Ghost, with the augury that "overcoming the ancient adversary and every vice, you may live justly, mercifully, and piously." Charles knelt and bent his crowned head, with proud devotion. At this point there rose, thrice repeated, the acclamation of those present: "Long live Charles! Long live Charles, lord of the world!"

The emperor kissed the hem of the pope's garment. Everything glowed in the ancient church, its every corner illuminated, and the power of that spectacle swelled with a truly imperial resonance. I could not help recalling how this pope had been impugned by the harsh determination of Charles and how he had been humiliated and crushed to the ground and threatened by a proposal—perhaps even opportune—to call a council.

"Long live universal peace!" the congregation cried all around me. But what did that peace mean for us? Living beneath the iron fist of a powerful monarch who would never stop burdening our people with taxes, tributes, demands for money, more money. The words "Freedom of Italy" were drowned in those cries of praise that, in great waves, accompanied me as the procession passed along the central nave of the church, to file out into the square. I walked a bit stiffly, but another stiffness struck me, a sensation of jolting someone, as there was a sudden swaying in the long line. I thought immediately that I was near Anne d'Alençon. A short time before, I had seen her son Bonifacio, holding in his hand the scepter he was to consign to the emperor. I seemed to feel my every fiber shrivel at some unknown radiation. No, Anne d'Alençon was not near me. I knew none of the prelates and monsignors surrounding me, trying politely to keep their proper distance from us, and yet the radiation persisted, and for a moment it no longer seemed distant, but familiar, intimate, from head to foot.

* * *

SOLEMNITY did not weigh on the Tè Palace that Giulio Romano displayed, its masonry still fresh, not yet decorated with all his paintings, during the visit of the emperor Charles. The active March air enhanced the colors and underlined the arched design of the great loggia toward the garden. The two broad basins of purest water reflected transparently the branches starred with barely tawny buds; only a few bushes were wearing their first veil of green. I was struck, as by a chord of bass notes, by the image of Charles the Fifth, who stepped upon the dais covered with carpets in the center of the loggia; his lanky figure, richly cloaked, his long and colorless face, the prominent jaw were in contrast with the shape, of Roman sturdiness, tending to rotundity and fullness, of that house that had risen in the midst of the Teieto woods. But it was true that plunged into Giulio Romano's choreographic fairy tale, the emperor became closed in himself, more isolated and more awesome.

WE GO up toward him, Federico and I, hand in hand, at our natural pace, and the old breath of youthful vigor makes me the equal of Federico's thirty years. We have often rehearsed the ceremony: My son is to leave me at the edge of the dais and proceed until he can kneel before the emperor. Charles smiles, signals him to rise, embraces him. A courtier approaches, and from his hands Charles takes a parchment heavy with seals. He reads it in his pure Spanish. Some words rattle in my ear: "For the loyalty and devotion he has shown toward our person, we grant our most beloved Federico Gonzaga the title of duke of Mantua."

Our great audience of gentlemen and ladies cries out: "Long live the emperor Charles! Gonzaga! Gonzaga! Duke! Duke!" All the crowd, dressed in silk, is vibrant with happiness. His every gesture showing his great self-confidence, the emperor comes toward me and holds out his hand. He speaks to me with truly regal affinity, still in his Spanish, which he slows harmoniously so I can understand better. I will not forget that sovereign tone.

"You are a true queen, signora marchesana. Your son is lucky to have a mother like you. . . . We love you very much, and we consider you the only great woman there is in Italy."

That hand of his transmitted a stubborn energy. Charles moved off with me through the rooms, all stucco and paintings; with a truly regal step we crossed the shining floors, and at that moment I myself forgot, and I hope that behind me Federico was also forgetting, our disappointment of the previous day on learning that none of the lands we had so insistently asked for would be granted us, neither in the Cremona region nor toward Venice. A great title, much good benevolence, admiration, and honors. Nothing else. The emperor holding my hand with such rigid politeness was a potentate who conceded nothing, and that light contact, as he flattered me, made me rebel. I seemed to sense that the plan for Federico's marriage, a few words barely uttered, as if my son would marry only thanks to him, concealed a trap, something unpleasant, perhaps evil.

We stopped to observe the paintings in the Hall of Psyche, which portrayed the classical myth with unrestrained, seductive voluptuousness. Without comment Charles ignored it, his head stiff. Still in cadence, we entered immediately the Hall of the Horses, with the portraits of our most celebrated chargers. Fires burned in all the fireplaces since the building was not yet thoroughly dried out, but in this room whole tree trunks were ablaze. Tables decorated with flowers, laden with foods, followed the line of the walls. The emperor took his place near the fire, on a little throne raised from the floor, alone at a little table, and he ate with remarkable voracity. Around him the cup bearers and the carvers moved cautiously, under the command of a Spanish gentleman. But what was happening? A child, perhaps a little page, eluded the order of the ceremony and advanced with a silver amphora, ready to pour wine. He did not reach the imperial table but was politely stopped and led back. I immediately recognized that innocent child used as bait, by his pink cheeks and his pure eyes; it was Alessandro, Federico's son. Boschetta, greedy eyes flashing, followed him with her gaze, and the perilous ray of her smile passed impudently from Federico to the emperor and to her son. Charles noticed and frowned; he bent over his golden plate and resumed eating at a faster pace, without raising his eyes.

I had feared it, and then it happened. Before leaving Mantua, Charles said that he had designated as Federico's wife his niece Julia, daughter of one of the many dethroned queens of Naples, who lived in Ferrara. This imperial bride was almost forty and was said to be ugly; to me she seemed neither ugly nor beautiful, but rather haughty and querulous. It was also said that she was ill, and sterile as well, at least in the physicians' opinion. Federico

had believed that this sacrifice would bring him the lands of Cas-
almaggiore, Spineta, and the others around Cremona that he so
wanted. None of this proved true.

It would already be a great gain if Charles were to give her a
dowry; we should not expect so much as a peso. It was pointless
to be angry, but I was angry. The marriage to Julia, ensured by
her great relatives, marked a victory for Boschetta. With her own
hands, she would direct this older, sickly woman, who had no
chance of bearing children. Once appearances had been saved,
the emperor could be besieged; there was a greater possibility of
having him recognize Alessandro as heir to the dukedom of Mantua. Two days after the signing of the nuptial contract with Julia,
Charles signed a decree that Boschetta welcomed as a hope. If
Julia, the almost forty-year-old bride, did not produce legitimate
Gonzaga sons, then Federico was allowed to name any natural
son as his heir. In other words, Alessandro had not yet been
declared legitimate, but he could be one day. At Marmirolo the
court of the new duke dared celebrate the future victory of love.

T HE MANY HONORS shown me by the emperor irritated some people, and in fact, my son no longer came to Cortevecchia, or if he did come, he discussed vague matters or perhaps joked; he never dealt with any substantial question. Taking advantage of the free periods that I could allow myself, I collected my suite and set off for Ferrara. I arrived there, feeling my old energy come to life. I boldly faced the Benvenuti staircase and stopped at the first landing, as Alfonso came down to meet me and give me his arm.

"I'm no longer young enough," I said, laughing, "to run up these stairs, not even to meet you."

We recalled our races on those steep steps, and it came out that I had won many of them against my brothers. Painful images returned to me, and I suddenly suffered the ache that had not lost its capacity for torturing me. On the staircase I saw my other brothers, and especially, running and scampering with us were the beautiful and unruly pair Ferrante and Giulio, now, for almost twenty years, confined a short distance from where we were, in the highest tower of the castle. They lived, by Alfonso's grace, in two adjoining rooms, and some people claimed to have glimpsed their shadowy forms behind the bars of a window toward the Giovecca. It was difficult for me to make a show of happiness when I imagined the shadows of those prisoners.

Alfonso meanwhile was leading me to his new little rooms. On one wall a painting seemed to herald something sunny; its power of radiance was so mighty in stirring me that I was prompted to say that this "Bacchanal" of Signor Tiziano could be the envy of any monarch. The painter had put into his picture the calm, full happiness of my brother's life. As a young man Alfonso had not known that happiness but only outbursts, almost brutal, of physical strength that then made him withdraw into himself, brooding. Gradually he had matured in a proper way, and now he was enjoying the pleasures of balance. Raising my head toward him,

I asked if it was true that he had married his beautiful Laura Dianti.

Alfonso remarked that the courts never tire of gossip; he had no idea what he might do in the future, and this was the truth.

"In any case it will be done well, and forgive me for this curt manner of mine. You govern excellently, brother. Perhaps you were right not to want to burden yourself with a third wife."

After a little while I assumed a dispassionate tone and said: "Alfonso! You have been very close to the emperor in recent times. Do you really believe that Charles will agree to legitimize Boschetta's son? That woman is determined; she wants Federico to name her little bastard as his heir immediately."

Alfonso reacted. "Don't tell me, sister, that you are the only person in the world who doesn't know the emperor's reply!"

I nodded gravely.

"Well, what Charles said was this: 'I would never do anything so base for all the gold in the universe, and not even for another realm that would double my own.' "

I was relieved and mortified. Alfonso came and sat down beside me.

"What is going on, dear sister? You are unaware of something everyone in your court has already discussed."

"Nothing reached me about the imperial reply to the legitimization proposal. Now you will understand why I have come to Ferrara to see you. It is like death, to feel so cut off, not knowing what's going on around me. You are the only one to whom I have the courage to tell the truth."

Realistically I expounded the facts, sensing the weight of my words. I confessed that shortly after my return from Rome Federico had again closed the doors of the chancellery to me. Sometimes he sought my advice, but in private, without witnesses. Yes, by now I was *extra muros*.

"It is not possible!" Alfonso exploded. "A woman like you! Is your son so foolish not to take advantage of your judgment? I have had you as my ally in critical moments, and I can truly bear witness that your wisdom is almost prophetic. Your Federico infuriates me. How can he forget that you possess the Este intelligence?"

I fell back on a kind of family irony. "Leave fury to me, brother. Conditions these days produce such situations. I care little, provided our affairs proceed with order and provided that nothing is known outside our house and that we suffer neither harm nor scorn."

"In this you display your intellect all the more, Isabella. You were right to come here. I will open my chancellery to you; every document concerning you will be shown you. Today, to begin with, you will learn some news that will shake the palaces of Mantua."

"Tell me at once," I insisted anxiously.

"Yesterday, after a fall from his horse, at Casale Monferrato the young marchese Bonifacio Paleologo died suddenly. The succession now passes to an uncle of his, Giovan Giorgio Paleologo, mortally ill, as everyone knows. Maria and Margherita, the two daughters left to Anne d'Alençon, will divide Monferrato between them, with all its riches. And to think that Maria was repudiated by your son, who, further, accused those gentlewomen of having tried to poison his Boschetta."

I felt as if I had been summoned by a trumpet's blare. I said, excited: "Let's not dwell on past mistakes! Do you really believe Federico's marriage to Julia of Aragón matters a great deal to the emperor?"

"That is another foolish thing Federico has done," Alfonso replied sarcastically. "He signed the marriage contract before the emperor's eyes. And Charles will never allow his position as ordering force of the world to be belittled."

"It is true, but the marriage with Maria Paleologa existed before; it could not really be dissolved. None of us likes this Julia, who is simply an intolerable imposition of the imperial will."

Alfonso looked at me for a long moment.

"Thoughts are whirling in your head; I can almost see them. You are thinking of going back in time and in action, making Federico free again, and giving him back Maria. You are a true Este, sister dear. You should rule a kingdom. You deserve a reward."

He reflected for a moment and sat at the table, writing something on a sheet of paper, which he then gave me, unfolded. It was an order to his Ferrara agent in Mantua, Anteo Rinuccini, to come to me secretly and tell me what he knew on every aspect of the matrimonial situation of the duke with no reservations or reticence.

"Signor Rinuccini, intimate member of Boschetta's court, is actually my faithful subject and very shrewd. He will inform you, at my instruction, now and always. But you must not breathe a word of these conversations to anyone; I will never speak of them either. In your thoughts you are already rushing along the road to Mantua. You would like to be at Sermide at least and perhaps farther on. Isn't that true, my tempestuous sister?"

I WASTED no time on reflection. As if driven by Alfonso's affectionate incitement, I returned to Mantua. The court was in a state of upheaval. I had never seen so many people in the Leonbruno Hall or in the other rooms along the loggia. Preceded by trumpets, a deputation of the people was announced, coming to send word to the duke, informing him how much his subjects loved Maria Paleologa and how they wanted her to be duchess of Mantua. Silkmakers, embroiderers, tailors, stitchers, capmakers, and the artisans of the other schools had sent their representatives, and all of them approved what Panizza, leader of the hatmakers, was saying. With them were two jurists, who gravely observed how I listened to the voice of the people, when addressed to me, while the duke remained in his Teieto palace. The two learned doctors, after long consultation of the codices, expressed opinion that Maria was the duke's legitimate wife and the marriage was to be respected.

Slowly they dispersed, as if with the desire of witnessing other events of court, the artisans of the corporations and then all the other citizens and courtiers, after communicating to me that hope of theirs. Later, when everyone, even my women, had withdrawn, I went out into my secret garden; there, introduced by Pirro, Signor Rinuccini appeared.

Perfect beauty, whenever it reveals itself, interrupts at least for a few instants the flow of time, fixing a single, unchangeable moment. And so it was with the young man of Ferrara. The full-bodied color of the setting sun illuminated an astonishing exemplar of mankind at a moment of the day that always takes us by surprise. And I was reminded of all that had been said about an incomparable portrait of him that apparently had been secretly painted by Signor Tiziano, in which the youth was holding a glove, probably by Ocagna. The young gentleman sat at his ease on the stool I pointed out to him; he spoke of Alfonso with words of great respect. Confronting the subject squarely, he assured me that there were no maneuvers on the part of that perfect lady who had the honor of bearing my same name or on the part of the duke Federico, though much of their talk appeared daily in little satirical sheets that could be read, stuck up on the columns of the palace and in other places.

"Even that," I said to myself. "I'd wager the humblest artisan of Mantua knows the situation better than I do."

A good courtier, but with a certain summary air, Rinuccini began to praise Federico's personal devotion to me. An expression of Federico's was constantly repeated: "My mother is a great woman." At times, however, the young man tempered his remarks on Signora Boschetta by firmly adding, "Not everything, however, depends on her." Once, when the couple was bathing in the Grotta del Tè, Rinuccini was posted as guard outside the entrance, and since the space was narrow and resonant, he overheard their talk. In a somewhat bitter tone Boschetta kept repeating, with emphasis, how important Monferrato was, a very rich land and of great military significance, and she concluded that this was a lesson she knew by heart.

"And you think I don't?" Federico said. "But I love you, as everyone knows."

Laughing in her usual way, which seemed caressing and was persistent, Boschetta answered that his love was, after all, not so evident. It would be that only if her son were legitimized.

"It's futile," Federico answered. "Charles the Fifth is the emperor of scruples. He absolutely will not recognize Alessandro as the legitimate heir of the Gonzagas. I obligated him to me, true, because of that niece of his. But the people also have their voice. It will be against me unless I marry Maria; she seems part of some legend, alone, fatherless, slandered."

"Why would you deceive me, my lord?" Boschetta said, accentuating her coy and enigmatic manner. "Do not lie. You have taken information, but I also know everything. Soon Cappino will go to Casale with a friendly message for the marquise Anne."

"A diplomatic mission approved by my brother the cardinal."

She interrupted and changed the subject. "Federico! Federico! That Frenchwoman! Her! Have you forgotten the terrible moments when Achillina snatched the ampul of poison from my hands—"

"That story is over," Federico said sharply. "Your husband, the chief conspirator, is dead. A good stroke of a sword has freed us from him. Now you are mine without impediment."

There was silence. Perhaps the two had succumbed to an access of love. But soon Boschetta's voice was raised again. "How can you believe, Federico, that the proud kinswoman of the king of France will welcome you with open arms and forget the accusations which caused her daughter's marriage to be annulled?"

Federico replied, controlling his voice, "Don't you yourself say no one can resist my spell?"

"Try it then."

He said he was ready to try at once; he called her his Psyche and went on, with other murmured words not audible outside the Grotta.

Signor Rinuccini confided in me that Boschetta's love was rather obstinate, as she tried to ensnare Federico more and more, but his impression was this: Just as before, Federico opposed, even in his own thoughts, the name of the Paleologa and accused her of poisoning without any evidence, as was publicly known, so now, obsessed by his repugnance to marry the ugly Julia, he saw Maria as a beautiful young wife, who was also mistress of half of Monferrato.

I did not tell my visitor he was right; indeed, I gave him a friendly lesson on the absolute necessity of Federico's marrying Julia of Aragón, as his signed contract obligated him. He himself, the duke's friend, would not want us to find the imperial troops again at the gates of Mantua, would he? No, he would not want that at all, agreed the handsome youth, so in love with himself that he seemed absent.

I dismissed him and watched him go off through the garden with a nimble step that matched the elegance of his limbs. What a lovely wave he addressed to me and what a smile in his blue eye, shifting and luminous! It would be too much if he were intelligent, too, I murmured to myself. He had not brought great news or secret information, but he had been sufficiently indiscreet for me to assure Alfonso that his man was serving me properly.

I FIND myself in a mood of incitement and intolerance. I can command nothing, not even what I see unfolding as a clear sequence of actions. I must await my moment. I had quite a different informant in Cappino, the Gonzaga envoy to Casale, who was devoted to me in the name of everyone's peace, he used to say. Jesting and totally committed to his task, he knocked at my door before leaving for Casale and confessed to me that he was very uneasy because of something new and so absurdly shameless that it was almost comical. The duke was sending him to Monferrato with this message for the marquise Anne d'Alençon. "My master, the duke Federico Gonzaga, has decided to annul the annulment of his marriage to Maria Paleologa. He wants all to be forgotten and to consider your daughter as his one, real wife."

My devoted Cappino remarked that if the marquise Anne did not have him drowned in the Po, it would be only out of the greatest kindness. She would not even allow him to open his mouth.

I wished him safe journey and good luck.

I liked this maneuver very much indeed; it was a triumph for me and an irrevocable defeat for Boschetta. After Signor Rinuccini's indiscretion, I was convinced that Federico's egoism now weighed relentlessly also against Boschetta and would finally prevail.

Cappino returned a week later, and just seeing him in such high spirits, I had before my eyes the face of Creon, after his return from Delphos, facing Oedipus. Cappino had a great deal to tell. In a room still draped in mourning (the boy Bonifacio had died barely a month before) he had been received by Anne d'Alençon, in deep black. Seeing our ambassador, the marquise wept and resumed the subject of her great grief, still not assuaged. Fate had struck down her husband and then her son, and now it was preparing to take her brother-in-law, Giovan Giorgio. To be robbed of the men of their blood: this was the fate of the last Paleologa women. Moved, Cappino plunged in without much forethought. He spoke, in the name of Federico, his regret at the sudden death of young Bonifacio, and finally Cappino said that the duke of Mantua would have liked to be at her feet, as if he were at the feet of his own mother.

"My lord duke loves you above anything in the world; for him you have always been the lady of his heart."

Anne had remained speechless.

"Lady of his heart?" she repeated sadly. "Kneel before me? He who denounced me publicly as a poisoner? If he wanted to dissolve his marriage, Federico could have done it without recurring to such monstrous accusations."

"It was the fault of evil counselors. A woman perhaps," Cappino said casually. "Young people make these mistakes. But in his heart his devotion and love for you are intact."

Anne seemed to brighten by degrees. "I was so fond of Federico, and I would always have been understanding. A man who has received every gift from nature. Of course, he wanted to feel free, as so many youths do. But to wound Maria's heart like that! She is not yet twenty, and it is as if life has abandoned her."

Encouraged by the unexpected tone of her speech, Cappino said that life would return to the young princess; Federico was repentant and would do anything to be forgiven. Anne began to reflect, and the dizzying whirl of her feelings and thoughts was almost perceptible. Cappino was dismissed with polite words. They would meet again the next day, after mass.

All night the Mantuan envoy lay awake in agitation. He thought he would have to defend himself against new accusations all too justified by the old ones, but he was now aware of the sweet pride, the secret fondness of Anne for Federico. He did not understand her. Toward dawn he decided to impose on himself an infinite caution. Was this great lady perhaps laying a trap for him?

He was received in the same room draped in mourning. The marquise Anne was not alone; with her, both daughters greeted him, the lily-white Maria and the dazzling Margherita. An innate skill prompted Cappino, after the most devoted greetings, to make some reference to Federico's uncontrollable jealousy.

"Jealousy?" Anne asked, dumbfounded.

It was known, Cappino replied, that Princess Maria had been asked for by many great lords: the duke of Milan, the prince of Orange, among others. Like a magnet, Casale Monferrato attracted the ambassadors of all Europe. How was it possible not to be jealous?

The two girls remained dumb, and their mother said, vaguely, that these things were true, but far in the past. Then Cappino, as his character would have it, plunged headlong. "Madame la marquise, forgive me if I dare ask a question: If we supposed that the absurd accusation of poison had never been made, how would you feel about our duke? Would you still choose him for your daughter's husband?"

"Signor Cappino"—Anne reacted—"Federico is Maria's husband! I have always refused to accept the brief of annulment sent by the Roman Curia. Jurists of every studium, on being questioned, have declared themselves in agreement with me. Maria is the true wife of Federico Gonzaga, duke of Mantua. And, in all conscience, could never be the wife of anyone else."

"In that case, illustrious lady," our ambassador urged, "I can tell you that my master is happy to proclaim himself your son-in-law. I am here to tell you that from him."

Anne's face covered with a deep flush as she exclaimed: "Do you wish to deceive me again? In every court it is known that Federico has signed a new marriage contract with Julia of Aragón, the emperor's niece. What have you come to propose to me, my lord ambassador?"

Cappino changed his assault weapons but without retreating. He approached the matter in a roundabout way. He observed that

Anne herself had said as much: The marriage contract with Maria was valid, and therefore, the contract with Julia of Aragón could not be valid. For that matter, the papal brief of annulment had never been published; it lay, carefully preserved, in the Mantuan chancellery.

The dialogue was prolonged, but always a variation on the same subject. Anne blurted out her words, repeated them tirelessly, in this guise or that. Cappino insisted always on his duke's repentance and fondness; the princesses, in their vital immobility, followed the two speakers. And suddenly every knot was undone. Anne called Maria by name, held her close, briefly summed up what had been said, reminding her how many suitors had asked for her, desired her, princes and dukes, and how many paths were open in her future.

"Express your thoughts, Maria; have no fear."

The pale creature's cheeks turned pink in her alabaster face; her voice dim with emotion, she said that she had long decided and that her decision remained, now and forever: "Either duchess of Mantua or nun." She spoke this sentence without fear, as if she had repeated an axiom, and she lowered her eyelids, weighted by her own courage. Cappino told me how proud this sight was and how unusual. The three women dressed in black up to their chins in the room draped in mourning seemed to move against the black setting, and only their hands and faces, faintly flushed, betrayed their aspiration to an unreachable happiness, suddenly very near.

AT CAVRIANA in July, Umbrasia, my herbalist, who in the search for products of nature was welcome company, followed me along the rows of vegetables and flowers, in the gardens where we gathered herbs to be distilled for unguents and medicinal waters or those to be dried and scattered on our food in winter: balm, sage, rosemary, marjoram. Adding to these herbs cloves, nutmeg, and cinnamon, we made extracts, to be sprinkled in the inner rooms where fires burned and smelled of wood: cypress, laurel, pine, and fir. Now the summer wafted from the countryside and made us light, as we stooped to choose the aromatic stems. On my head I wore a broad straw hat, and to my girls, a bit distracted by the summer breeze, I gave lessons in how to decipher the herbaceous alphabet as Umbrasia called those natural choices of ours.

At a nearby galloping of horses I turned. Federico, rapidly slipping to the ground from his saddle, greeted me gaily. He had no people of his court with him, only one groom, who stayed to hold the mounts. I saw my son climbing up the little hill that rose toward the line of cypresses. When he reached me and was reverenced by my immediately electrified girls, I asked him why he had come without any other escort. His visit took us by surprise; nothing was prepared to celebrate him.

"It is a celebration just to see you, Mother," he replied merrily. "It is beautiful to look at you, like a splendid Hygeia among your disciples, as you uncover beneficent plants. Only, as I came up, I discovered all too many lettuces; they don't agree with me."

All the girls laughed because it is well known that lettuce diminishes men's amatory prowess. I said that good herbs heal any ailment; it was all in knowing how to find them. As for him, I was sure he had drunk far too many philters.

I handed my wicker basket to Umbrasia and leaned on the wrist that Federico held out to me; we advanced, with easy steps, and secluded ourselves on a little half-moon terrace, where we sat on two benches of dressed stone. I looked at my girls, who had remained farther down, collecting herbs; I drew a breath and said meaningfully: "Well, my son, what do you have to ask me?"

"There's no hiding anything from you. I always say you are a sorceress. In any case I have two bits of good news: The pope, after much talk, is finally prepared to declare my marriage to Maria Paleologa perfectly valid, and Maria is more determined than ever to declare me her legitimate husband."

"But the emperor?" I asked. "Surely he will not want to hear your arguments."

"Exactly. Now for him the only valid marriage is with Julia of Aragón. In fact, he insists that if I chose to dissolve it, my honor as a prince would suffer."

I thought of our people; the Mantuans also had displayed their wishes without moving that inflexible ruler. The voice of our people counted for nothing with Charles. It was useless even to mention it.

Federico, seeing me pensive, made a gesture of impatience, as if he were also following my reasoning.

"Mother dear, help me. Please, think of me. I am in the greatest anguish. I put all my hopes in your hands. Advise me. Free me from these torments."

"What?" I quipped. "At your court is there no person of sound counsel? Is there not Carlo Nuvoloni, your sole friend, or someone else even more to be trusted?"

Not the least bit offended, Federico assumed that flattering manner of his. "Must I come out and say it to you, Mother? No one is of such sound counsel as you. Only you can save me."

I adjusted the shoulder of my dress with the movement that Dionisia, my Ferrara housekeeper, would have called a maidservant's. I concentrated, alert and meek; the coil of my thought began to tighten. After a moment I spoke, as if to put my reasoning into words: "The emperor likes to judge with his own mind. The emperor, as we all know, is miserly. The emperor is very religious and strict, like no other monarch, about things concerning the soul."

A moment's pause. Then I went on, more rapidly. "We will need an excellent ambassador, but not one who has a familiar tone; we need a tenacious, indeed an invulnerable but convincing orator. Our Cappino, no. He would be no good with Charles. Soardino. Yes, Soardino. He was so long in Venice; he learned his lesson well there. Do you want sound advice, Federico? Listen to what I say!"

I rose and slowly declaimed: "Most Holy Majesty, my lord and master, the duke of Mantua, is suffering the worst torments in the world. His confessor has roughly reproached him for having promised himself to the lady Julia of Aragón as his marriage to Maria Paleologa is still valid. His confessor has threatened him with excommunication and, for the present, refuses him absolution. My master's conscience is deeply troubled. He lives in fear of hell. All day long he prays; his tears are destroying his youth. In your hands lies the peace of a soul that would not be damned."

Federico came over to me, seized with enthusiasm.

"Magnificent, Mother! Magnificent! If necessary, I will go around in penitential sackcloth. But will the emperor really believe in my troubled conscience?"

"It is all up to you and to Soardino. Expanding the notions I've suggested, you should be able to make yourself believed. And even if Charles were to have some doubt, his religious principles are too strict for him not to accept those of others. Remember to insist that you are not acting out of greed for land or possessions, but only for the salvation of your soul. The whole discussion must be absolutely religious."

"You are a great inventor, Mother dear. I will summon Soardino back to Mantua at once. Then I will report everything to you."

He kissed my hands tenderly and rushed away in haste. I heard the two horses being urged to gallop.

IN SEPTEMBER in my study "of the Cimmerians" (so called because of the frieze of warriors in damascened helmets) I was paying attention to the lesson that Umbrasia, now an expert musician, had learned from Alberto da Ripa of Suzzara, now called to France to the court of Francis the First. How academic it must have seemed to the new girls of my court, whose immature little voices named the notes and measured their duration. Later, with the accompaniment of instruments, they would put them in tune. I was relaxing at those first steps in musical education when Pirro came to my side and with considerate composure informed me that Federico had fallen in a faint; he was in his palace at the Tè and had not completely come around.

In a moment I was at the door, to give orders to Umbrasia: She was to collect our vinegars and everything else of use in such a case, and she was to rush at once into the courtyard, to the carriage ordered in great haste. After a few minutes my four horses were galloping toward the Tè, very swiftly. Federico, on a camp bed, was lying in the still-unfinished Hall of the Giants. He had been taken ill in that room, and they had not dared move him. From a little door, closed in haste as I entered, the flutter of a peacock blue skirt was disappearing, Boschetta's surely.

The urgency of reanimating my son was so imperative that I almost felt no apprehension, or I buried it in the depths of my spirit. The compresses of linen soaked in aromatic vinegar and some good essences restored his color and movement. Then I became frightened. Federico wept on my heart, invaded by every terror, hot with a high fever.

"Mother," he said to me, gasping, "a disaster has befallen us, the worst possible disaster. My wife, Maria, is dead."

I supposed he was delirious, and I glanced briefly at Anteo Rinuccini, but bowing toward me with discretion, the gentleman signaled that it was true. Again I peered at Umbrasia, a silent consultation between us. We gave Federico a calming syrup. His features reawakened, and little by little they became composed again.

SO THE misfortune has truly happened. As I keep my eyes constantly on my son, Anteo Rinuccini tells me in a low voice the whole story. Federico was here, curious to see how that fanciful painting was proceeding, Signor Giulio Romano's last invention, partly painted and partly only drawn on the walls and on the curved ceiling; an imperial messenger, introduced by a page, turned up in great haste. Completely breathless, he announced that he had come from Casale and was going to His Imperial Majesty, bearing terrible news. The princess Maria Paleologa had died in the space of a single night. No one knew the cause: a destroying fever, some said, or a seizure of the heart. The mother seemed turned to stone; the sister, ceaselessly dissolved in tears. He, the messenger, could not stay further, having to reach the emperor as quickly as possible; on his own initiative he had stopped to inform the duke of Mantua. Signor Federico slowly paled, then, all of a sudden, fainted. His pages stretched him out on the camp bed that Signor Giulio Romano used to rest on, and meanwhile, several had rushed to call the doctor; but we, Umbrasia and I, had got there ahead of him.

Federico can now raise his head, utter some broken words. "Mother, mother," he repeats. "God is punishing me. God is just. I lied too often to her and to my conscience. I accused Maria falsely, and I did not even have the courage to go and beg her forgiveness on my knees: always envoys, letters, intermediaries, written words between the two of us. I was never at her side. Oh, Mother, I killed her, my beautiful, sweet, innocent bride."

He sinks back on the bed and bursts into long sobs, he who never weeps. Before beginning the task of healing that pain, I let the tears flow. I think of Anne, of her inhuman desperation, of all the dreams she has cherished about that marriage of the young girl. I cannot think from what point I might raise the funereal veil that has been spread over us.

IT WAS not I who acted this time; another woman, by surprise, took my place.

Federico had just gone back to his chambers, surrounded by a dumb struck court, displaying a contrite countenance. I myself exhorted him to send an envoy to Casale. I was sure he would stir himself and go in person; but he lacked the courage, and this time perhaps it was a good thing. If he had humiliated himself, asking too many pardons, the splendid view of him in all the courts of Europe would have been dimmed. Maria, in death as in life, would have lost her husband.

Cappino, all aghast, went. The good man was truly distressed at his sad mission. Through the whole journey he racked his brain, seeking convincing words, and he could not connect them. When he reached Casale, Anne sent word that he was to be patient. She could not receive him because first she had to be able to breathe again. The poor ambassador felt mortified and also could not understand why the marquise sent her secretary to be with him, meaning to be courteous. That secretary was a man of experience; in the great hall of the castle he pointed out many gentlemen and the envoys of the greatest lords of Italy and of Europe, who had been waiting for hours to be presented. There was the ambassador of the duke of Urbino, that of the duke of Savoy, the marchese of Saluzzo, the count Palatine, and even the envoy of the king of France. All these potentates had their eye on the last Paleologa, Margherita, now sole mistress of the splendid and strategic land of Monferrato.

When the religious ceremonies were over, Anne called for Cappino, who bowed at her feet, kissing the hem of her dress.

"My master! My master! If you could see him! He lost his senses at the news. He is suffering the worst agony in the world. God chose thus to deprive him of such a dear wife!"

Anne looked at him, her eyes with their dark lids widened, and she murmured: "Wife. Maria knew she would be a wife only in name. She was not granted even a brief time of joy. Her twenty years were marred by false hopes. Day by day she consumed her courage imagining herself happy."

"And now, when she would have had everything," Cappino said, disheartened.

"It was late, too late." Anne resumed, shaking her head. "I should have fought for her, well before; I should have gone to Rome for her, flung myself at the pope's feet, sought the emperor's help, or to Mantua, to speak with the marchesana Isabella, my great friend. Could they have refused to listen to me? But our pride deceives us. Pride always prevents us from being natural and true. The fault is mine, entirely mine. Maria should not have had to wait like that for happiness."

Cappino was speechless in the face of this implacable self-accusation. Anne did not allow him to reflect. She solemnly made the sign of the cross and addressed the ambassador again, with determined words: "And now, Signor Cappino, we will wait no longer. Listen carefully to what I am about to say to you. I am prepared to give Federico Gonzaga, duke of Mantua, my second daughter, Margherita, as his bride."

Our ambassador was so overwhelmed that he did not even have the strength to collect his thoughts. "Madame," he said. "Blessed lady, can what you say be true? The duke, my master

. . . the joy of everyone . . . but is the la
ment?"

With gentle vehemence, Anne replied:
I know her heart."

With endless questions I besieged Cap
Casale about that choice which changed
the tale of that inconceivable scene, he w
and reminded me how the marquise A
have Federico write her and ask for Marg
out referring to her own hasty offer. Sure
her daughter's spirit well because that sa
fore the ambassadors of all those rulers,
bling, declared her obedience to her motl
to choose a husband among so many pi
voice, she said, "The duke of Mantua."

Thus Cappino returned to Mantua, "
griff," as he said in jest, and Federico,
savored the joy of an imminent bride, e
than the other, who would bring into t
ancient marquisate of the Paleologues.
descendant of this illustrious house, ha
he was on the brink of death, and n
his own.

Room of the clocks
the year 1533

THE YEAR 1530 is still so near me that I have only to extend my hand and I touch it. It is dense with events and upheavals. It brought the coronation of Charles, the emperor, and the title of duke to us Gonzagas, the ecstasy and death of the bride Maria Paleologa, the arrangement of a new wedding with the second Paleologa, Margherita. It could be said that Federico was a favorite of fortune.

But in this story there is something more than what I grazed or penetrated. We would have to go back, to another year, 1516, when Federico found himself passing by Casale to meet Maria, and he appeared dressed in white in the splendid challenge of his sixteen years. Now I understood all the unconscious forces of affection he had attracted. The eight-year-old child Maria, her sister, Margherita, aged six, entered into their matrimonial fairy tale like the infants they were, but the mother, very young and very beautiful (I had seen her well myself that same year as I returned from my colorful pilgrimage in Provence), had been swept up in Federico's magnetizing wave, and without knowing it, transforming herself first into Maria, then into Margherita, she had become bound to him.

How otherwise to explain her absolute refusal to repudiate, for any reason, Maria's wedding contract with a man who had shame-fully accused her mother of being a poisoner? Anne, so proud, so stern of spirit? And even more, how to justify the hasty offer of the second daughter to Federico, amazing our Cappino so? She trembled at the thought of losing touch with a young man who had appeared to her as a paladin of angelic grace, perhaps the only man to desire. A three-cornered secret thus united the Paleologa women to Federico, a secret of attraction, never acknowledged but compelling. And wasn't Anne the most inscrutable point of the triangle, obscurely pure, joined with her daughters in a complicity of love? I will never mention to a living person these hypotheses of mine that ring so true, but however it may be, I cannot but envy Anne, who will advance into future years guiding her daughter with a protection of warm thoughts, en-trusting her to the vision that has spangled her own life with light. I envy her also because I, his mother, know the whole portrait of Federico, and I know how he betrays.

It is useless to try to perceive the secrets of a human being and, worse, of a son. And I will tell the truth: Federico appeared to me humanly real, in the fullness of himself, only that day when he was sobbing in my arms, blaming himself for the death of Maria, in the hall at the Tè, under the ceiling where Jove bran-dished his thunderbolts at the giants.

Needless to say, I would give my life for my son. I am too bound to his living substance, neither in ill fortune nor good, but simply because a mother cannot elude this destiny. Unlike other mothers, I do not complain of him, I do not weep (or I weep rarely), and I can judge when and how far he has moved away from me. It is already a great deal that he retains his lighthearted loving ways from his childhood when between me and him there existed the discovery of an interchangeable identity.

I look at my clocks, and I observe how they differ among them-selves, moving farther and farther apart. I would like to confuse their times even more. If only there existed some necromancy that would allow me to find again the boy Federico, enamored of Julius the Second. Now he hardly remembers the old man, and I grieve that also the titan has been betrayed. I grieve not so much for the della Rovere pope, but because this betraying him is further evi-dence of Federico's ability to know only in words the meaning of inner loyalty. This detached examination I make on a late summer evening is the last—perhaps—that I will allow myself to make of him profoundly. In the days of my return from the catastrophe of Rome, three times I saw my son betray without the slightest distress. I repeat this to myself to be convinced of it, as I breathe in the intermittent gusts from the lake.

Will I have the courage, this evening, to examine them, the three last betrayals of this too beloved son of mine? At this point I am sufficiently wise to refrain from moralizing about any of his actions.

I have long become accustomed to the news of secret infor-mants, and I believe it is impossible for people in power, even if that power is conditioned as mine is, to forgo it. To be well in-formed is, to some extent, to reign, even if only hypothetically. In the days that followed my return from Rome, I sent one of those informants to the Doge of Venice with a long, detailed letter. It irks me even to recall it. It concerned Signor Domenico Venier, whom I was keeping with me in Mantua, while waiting for him to pay the ransom, quite small, promised to my kinsman Alessandro of Novellara. Since the Venetian had to await the money from his distant lands, I had granted him complete freedom in a good Mantuan residence, from which one day, with wife and belongings, he had fled to Venice, insisting that he had to pay nothing, a lie. In my letter I told the Doge how I had taken his ambassador under my protection, how I had shared with him and his family the days of sorrow, the flight from Rome, the journey to Mantua and, above all, how I had guaranteed his payment. My letter was mild but firm. I felt contempt for Venier.

And this is what happened. The letter, on reaching Venice, passed from the hands of our ambassador to those of the Doge; even before it was opened, the same ambassador smiled and informed the prince in a low voice that the duke of Mantua congratulated His Serenity on the liberation that Venier had taken upon himself. And thus my son annulled and denied my protests, made them futile and even ridiculous. Our ambassador accompanied Federico's congratulations with a brief laugh that belittled all my dignity, banished me from the serious discussions that count in our world of rulers.

Second betrayal. A little time went by, and I was given, by another man who venerated me, a copy of a letter from Federico to the king of France, who never ceased flattering him. Francis the First had complained of Ferrante and of other Gonzagas, who had agreed to enter the service of the emperor. Concerning his brother and his relatives Federico wrote long, confused, almost idiotic lamentations, repeating every now and then silly expressions such as "I cannot command them," "none of them obeys me" with a whining totally lacking decorum, the tone of some subaltern uttering clumsy apologies.

But most serious of all, worse than the betrayal of his mother to the Doge, worse than the denunciation of his kinsmen, treated like unruly and fanatical people who even inspired his pity, the most serious of all—and it is hard for me to forgive it—was the betrayal of himself. This, too, I discovered from a letter, a copy of which came to me through Pirro, my true and faithful friend. Matteo Cusato, our excellent envoy, informed my son of a conversation he had had with Georg von Frundsberg, the captain of the Landsknechte, in Ferrara, where the German was spending some time convalescing after a bad illness. The days of the sack of Rome were still vivid, and Clement the Seventh was still a fugitive in Orvieto, and this is what Federico Gonzaga, captain defender of the Holy Church, asks of his enemy, of the man who had boasted of carrying a golden noose to garrote the pope: "Should the marchese of Mantua dismiss his army, meant for the defense of the pope? And how could it be quickly dispersed?"

But it is necessary to hear Frundsberg, this Lutheran fanatic, as he attempts a moral theme. He speaks like a soldier and declares: "No, the army must not be disbanded now because by abandoning the pope at this moment, the Gonzagas would blemish their honor with a stain that could never be erased. It is necessary to gain time and above all avoid such a sudden blow that would plunge the defeated pontiff into grief." The German's words blaze as he confronts my disloyal son, who must truly have felt their heat. Or did he even notice? That is his nature: When he seems so ingenious in deceiving everyone, slipping unharmed through any situation, he proceeds with confidence; deceit to him seems a proof of skill.

That evening I wandered in the secret garden, and I seemed to feel on my own face the sting of the Lutheran lash. Now, here, among my capricious clocks that warn me how they are true and false at once, I can say I have learned to bear this, too: I wonder at the way my teaching has been misinterpreted. "Yes, Federico," I say, in an imaginary dialogue, "it is true, that firm line, that sense of limits that reveals the man of government, in you is slack. Though I have taught you much, you have never assimilated my lesson, and in my turn, I was not aware that the meaning had escaped you or that for you I should have invented a different, more direct language, more severe, with no trace of those logical, free elisions that I adopt with myself."

How faint the chime of the Basel clock has grown, the one with the little gilded columns. It brings back to me the name of a man so close to the English Robert de la Pole: Erasmus of Rotterdam, who still today in that city is fearlessly proceeding in his exercises of the intellect. Robert—I call him by his given name—is present to me, with that jagged writing I see here before me on these pages lying open on the ivory-inlaid table. What do I think about him, after that fearsome vigil of the sack of Rome? I see him again advancing into the Santi Apostoli Square and approaching, with a limp, beneath my windows, and now, as then, I am afraid of recognizing him. I am seized by a new temptation: to answer him. What? How? I do not know. He reaches me always with an enigmatic logic; to be sure, he knows what he loses in never asking me to write him, but he seems to insist in wanting to lose the favor of a reply in order to gain an invented favor.

Mister de la Pole, what a triumph for you, this groping of my spirit. Yes, I would have been happy to write you, like so many ladies of our world who correspond about spiritual things with men of religion, but to be frank, I do not feel you are completely spiritual in your attitude toward me, though I am aware of my age and of yours. In the air, in the air these questions hover, and these answers. The only thing I accept is to await with goodwill the arrival of your next letter. If you ever write it.

Welcoming your suggestions, I have had Pirro inquire about the Scholar Page, this character who has moved about my house without my knowing him; I would have assumed him as guide to that tragic painting you described to me, revealing to my amazement secrets of great art unknown to me. The Scholar Page has not been at court for some time. He went off to Turkey, embarked on a Venetian sailing vessel, in the year 1526. I have had someone seek out the painting with the tourney framed by the collars of Henry the Sixth of England. The arched door and windows of that hall have been filled in, to prevent the building's collapse, and we are waiting to put those rooms to some new use. I have had to postpone until another time my acquaintance with those ghosts who in my house, without my knowledge, have occupied a foreigner's imagination, peopling it with knights marked by death.

I N T H E S E C R E T garden the new girls were mak-ing a racket with their companions, the pages just arrived at court from Modena. I felt as if, beyond the windows, I had the impudent little school of Master Francesco Vigilio at the hour of their shouting play. Umbrasia, who now helped me in training this group of youngsters, spoke up from time to time in her Friu-lian contralto voice. From my midday somnolence I was sum-moned by my Pirro, coming down from the chancellery, where he had arranged to be appointed permanent archivist of the for-eign dispatches; in his mind he recorded everything or almost everything that happened, and he then informed me. I was sat-isfied with this, and I could desire nothing more than Pirro's daily, confirming visit. That day he told me that the treasurer was count-ing out and weighing, one by one, the twelve thousand gold ducats to be sent to Julia of Aragón, niece of Charles the Fifth, to console her for the canceled marriage to Federico. Thus the em-peror had decreed; as always, our gold was ending up in German coffers.

Federico, and Soardino acting for him, had performed with success the comedy of the soul pierced by thorns of remorse. It even seemed that after much tergiversation Charles had con-cluded it with one of his rare smiles. The dramatic twists did not end there. Julia the ugly had been promised by her omnipotent uncle to Giovan Giorgio Paleologo, who had been dying for a long time. What was going through the head of Charles the Fifth as he signed that macabre nuptial contract no one knew. Was he hoping for a miracle that would restore Paleologo to health? Was he also aiming at Monferrato through Julia? Or did he want some-how to teach Federico a lesson and make him uneasy? Surely it was of no matter to Charles that his niece would have to undergo such a spectral experience.

In fact, the moment Julia arrived at Monferrato, Giovan Giorgio married her, only to die immediately thereafter. So she was left with the task of supervising her husband's funeral before she returned to her mother's house, the widow of a man she had barely glimpsed.

They come in to announce Ercole, who must be in Rome in a few days' time. I can already feel his absence, the emptiness he will leave in our palaces, but I am prepared. Together, in a carriage, we head for Santa Maria delle Grazie. He says mass there, as he does every time he leaves Mantua, and I follow him devoutly; the monks perform the movements of the ritual against which the extreme youth of my cardinal son stands out. After mass, coming from the back of the church, we go and kneel at the tomb of my Baldesar Castiglione. In the first chapel on the right, the geometrical monument of red marble rises in a pyramid, cadenced, up to the statue of the triumphant Christ.

"For once Signor Giulio Romano seemed to understand the Christian meaning of immortality as ascent to God," Ercole says.

From the cloister with its little columns we emerge onto a knoll overlooking the lake, and in the water we follow the race of the white clouds. Our two outer garments, Ercole's red and mine an emerald green, compose a chord of colors, played by the wind.

"At this very moment Federico is leaving Casale with his bride. They will soon be here. I will never cease to thank the Madonna for this marriage."

"For this marriage I also said mass," Ercole replies. "I have gone to say good-bye to my dear sisters in their convents. They complain that they see little of you, Mother dear, but they pray for all of us."

"Ippolita dreams of becoming abbess."

"She is too young still, but she will become one," Ercole says. "Livia gave me this little book of prayers, which she has illuminated for me."

I take the book.

"The illumination is not perfect. The colors sing, but Livia is unable to improve her drawing."

"How severe you are, Mother. This little book is an object to love. I will carry it with me always. The illustrations of innocence will be an inspiration to me."

My cardinal son's tone of disagreement with his mother was constant and growing every day. I sensed he would probably never have thought of making a sacred amulet of those little pages blotched by his sister if I had not criticized them. He was always on the edge, in every sentence of our conversation. I said something about his *acerrimum* judgment, according to his masters, and I agreed the pope was right to summon him to his side, though I would be sorry to see him leave immediately after the ceremonies honoring the couple.

He opened his arms as if indicating a duty beyond debate. I asked him if he went to Rome gladly.

"The Church must be rebuilt in all its strength and majesty," he declared. "I am not against the idea of a council that could refashion the rules of the kingdom of God on earth. And you did well, to send me to the school of Bologna. From Master Pomponazzi I learned that reason has no scruples or fears. That is why heretics and Lutherans do not frighten me. They are men like us; they use words. The important thing is to choose the word that is the most just."

He emanated a preeminent authority, his qualities vigorously addressed to holy matters. He had passed through the secular teachings of our Pomponazzi, showing how true it is that a philosophy will never defeat a religion. He was headed surely along a road that led up: to high places, perhaps to the supreme dignity.

He understood me so well that he raised his hand, to stop me.

"Forgive a mother's ambition, my lord cardinal," I said. "And whatever may happen in the future, never forget your city and your family. Federico has great need of advice."

Ercole nodded and put his hand on mine; they were identical in shape.

"I must tell you, at least this once, Mother, that I do not approve, have never approved my brother's conduct toward you in matters of government. If I were in his place, I would seek your advice at every hour of the day."

I could not refrain from laughing.

"If you were in his place, Ercole, you would have no need of advice. You resemble me too much, my son; you are the Gonzaga with the most Este blood."

His face turned radiant. "Mother," he said, "one thing is certain: None of your sons will ever be able to outstrip you."

BRIDE and groom were on the road toward Mantua, followed by a large court of most elegant gentlemen and ladies; they had already lived the first days of their wedding. The rite had been celebrated a month before, at Casale, in the very room where Anne lay in bed, ill; no doubt excessive emotion had disturbed her. I knew everything about the ceremony. Margherita wore a white dress with silver stripes and over it a full garment of linen, also silvered, with a high collar in the French fashion, embroidered with pearls. On her head she had a white bonnet studded with many diamonds. Out of discretion, I did not go to Casale; the marriage was meant to have a subdued tone because of the recent deaths in the Paleologue family, and the illness of Anne, whatever it was, created no little melancholy. Federico displayed all his manly grace and could not help cheering mother-in-law and court, and this was conceded to him, as he was the groom. Then the moment came to set out. Though she grieved to leave her mother, Margherita exuded such happiness that only her strict education enabled her to maintain a dignified demeanor. Our Cappino said she was all beauty, enlivened by blissful amazement.

WE PREPARE our famous celebrations, and we arrange the bridal couple's apartment as my singing boys enthusiastically raise the refrain of the nuptial anthem "Hymen! Hymen!" I move about; I make notes and issue instructions on every point. The artisans are just finishing their job of setting up the great bed when Ferrante, tall and muscular, comes in, dragging Apina, my very young maid; he tries to fling himself with her on the broad new quilt; they are unaware of my presence.

"Apina," Ferrante says, "what is this? Don't you want to put the bridal couple's bed to the test? It brings luck. Don't you know that?"

The girl quickly frees herself, but Ferrante insists: "We have to make sure the bride will be comfortable in it. I'll tell you a secret: I know how to play the part of the husband better than Federico."

The time has come to intervene. I step forward.

"Ferrante! My son! An imperial captain does not jest like a silly page!"

Ferrante stands up, pulling down his tunic; as the girl runs off, he rushes toward me without the least embarrassment. "I came here looking for my beautiful mother."

He seems so joyous that my reproaches die on my lips. I ask him what the emperor, that solemn monarch, would have said, seeing him.

"The emperor?" he replies, as if throwing the ball back to me. "I've come, in fact, to tell you that Charles wants me with him as soon as possible. But what a splendid chamber you've made of this tasteless place! The hangings and the ornaments are so charming and brilliant. What will this bride be like, Mother dear?"

"She is a proper bride: beautiful, graceful, healthy, and of a happy nature. It would be time for you, too, to think of taking a wife."

"Right away, if that will please you. You choose her. But warn her that my profession is war and that I am very ambitious and proud. The emperor knows my worth. He might give me command of the fleet against the Turks or, better still, name me governor of Milan."

My son, governor of Milan? Not lord or duke, but viceroy for someone else, more powerful? I could not accustom myself to the idea that the magnificent and free city was now forever subject to a foreigner, who drained it mercilessly.

"In Milan I was happy once," I murmur. "There was deep snow, and on the snow roses were scattered." In a bright voice I say, "Then you are really leaving? Yes, arms are your destiny; the horoscopes, drawn up for you several times, pointed inevitably to feats of the sword. But I hope you will never lose the real sense of life. In a man of arms, the spirit quickly hardens, as the joints grow stiff. How fitting military life is for a man was expressed in the past, and very well, by our Castiglione, may he rest in peace. It is comprehensible that the warrior wishes to show how much his arm is worth and to gain that glory which was Alexander's and Caesar's. But cruelty is the soldier's daily bread; military squabbling is more offensive than the sword; it makes the heart dry and embittered. You must never become one of these dried-up, barren men."

"Mother, there are no women who speak to the point as you do. May I be allowed my pride in being your son? The first time I fight a tourney I will wear your colors on my arm, and I will make all proclaim you the first woman in the world."

I cannot refrain from smiling at him. I stroke his head of tight, silky curls, and I do not add that his most negative horoscope contained a sign of obscure violence. I simply repeat: "Ferrante! Remember what I have said to you. Be on guard against yourself."

MUCH later, at evening, I found myself in that same room, shining with the many lighted candelabra. Margherita was dressing for the night, closed in the dressing room, and I could imagine her beating heart. Federico was with me; he confided in me that the gentlemen of Monferrato had seemed pleased with their welcome and the magnificent banquet. They were strange people, these Monferrato men, haughty and courageous, and they had to be won over gradually. I asked, with a slightly teasing tone, if he was content with his bride.

"Why don't you ask her, my lady?" he said, echoing my mockery.

"I know you behaved very well at Casale. The report of your nightly exploits has circulated through all the courts."

"Of course," Federico went on, "I lived up to my reputation; indeed, I went a good deal further. You must forgive me this confidence."

He was slipping on a large robe of brocade, a soft plum color, hemmed with fur. On the gold bed a nuptial cover had been unfolded, of pale yellow satin, embroidered in the center and at the corners with the arms of the Gonzaga and Paleologue houses. It must have been the cover Margherita had once embroidered for her sister, Maria, preparing it, unawares, for herself. Idly I resumed the conversation and mentioned the substantial gifts Federico had bestowed on the signora Boschetta, even a property in the vicariate of the Gonzagas, with a tax exemption for that and for all her other property in the duchy.

My son's voice quivered as he insisted he owed her immense gratitude. She had accepted his marriage to Margherita, but refused for herself the marriage she had been offered, as Marquise Anne d'Alençon ardently wished. She chose to be faithful to him, even if at a distance.

I interrupted him. He did not have to justify himself; it is a prince's duty to be generous in his passions. After a pause I said, without underlining my words: "If you like, I could take your son, Alessandro, among my pages and have him educated at my court."

He turned, happy, but immediately his expression changed; he went pale. He pressed his forehead against the fireplace, gasping. I shouted toward the door, "Come quickly, someone! The duke is ill," and I ran to support him.

Before anyone arrived, he had already recovered himself. It was nothing, he assured me: emotion, weariness, the cold, the endless banquet. I stroked his brow. Love overwhelmed me; inside myself I kept saying: "Federico, my soul, be well, be happy, nothing else matters, be happy. . . ." A page gave him something to drink, and his color returned. Federico looked at me with a certain pathetic passion and said: "Have no fear, Mother. I am very well. The usual faintness, a physical defect of mine. I promise you I will live long enough to bring ten sons into the world. That is all you expect of me, isn't it?"

He spoke pleasantly, but he was dissimulating an old suffering. I also dissimulated, seconding his jest, as I wiped his brow with my fine blue handkerchief. I sensed something in him that could plunge into the bottomless ambiguity I had feared all my life, the invincible and overweening melancholy of the Gonzagas, that fascination and that mortal sorrow.

Room of the clocks
the year 1533

HOW DISTURBING the smallest of my hundred clocks is. This perfect mechanism is enclosed in the center of a golden star. I usually call it my "starred lady," because of the figure in relief on the face, a sorceress or a queen, enameled in white and gold. She wears a miter on her head, and at irregular intervals she nods. From time to time—at a distance of months or years—the clock changes its voice, chimes with a high trill or with low, tragic contralto tones. Now she sings in her highest pitch, and I know why. In this April of 1533 Federico's son has been born, his first legitimate son, handsome, healthy, vigorous. He has reddish hair like his mother, but his dark eyes, straightforward, are his father's, mine. With this infant, whose name is Francesco, the Gonzagas confront the future. As for me, I feel a sensation of happy abundance, a presage of new events, and, at the same time, a private pity that sums up all the ill-omened probabilities of living.

My papers encircle me. Many have accompanied me over the years; some are today's, like these on the little round table, sent from my little personal fief in Romagna, Solarolo. I record neatly in them the hierarchies of the town, the names of the little settlements that compose it, even the names of individual properties and farms. I specify the agricultural income of the inhabitants and of the town itself. What am I constructing on this tiny bit of land? Am I playing at power? Am I testing the workings, the mainsprings of a governing machine in miniature? No, when I receive the representatives of the community and I argue, direct, enforce, I am following these Romagna subjects of mine, fiery, at times unruly. I want to know their interests, their family condition, their character—if possible, their thoughts. Secretly I triumph when I succeed in bringing them around to my ideas (always to their own profit), confirmed in my infallibility as ruler. The mayor of Solarolo is surely no Julius the Second, but the seed of joy fructifies in me if I can subdue my antagonist in a question of water rights. So Solarolo is an intense experiment on which I can dwell even with irony but, beneath the irony, seriously. I am driven to seek out the reasons that have made me the way I am, between one occasion and the next in the course of my days. Time flows by, and it is worth thinking. I have discovered that my woman's condition is not absolutely predominant; it does not prevent me from becoming a complete person, provided I am not deceived by myself. I have learned to live without coldness and without yearning, but I never renounce rebellion and the insurgence of feelings.

Nor does my ability to think things out diminish. This is why vain as I am, however temperately, I was not shaken by the satirical writing of a man, a traitor to his own intellect, Pietro Aretino, who, having never received money or gifts from me, has charged me with being old, having false teeth and a made-up face. To be sure, all these charges are true; one by one, these devices have assisted nature, as youth has abandoned me. Apart from the fact that the false teeth are a necessity imposed by Hygeia and should be in general use, apart from the fact that no woman can sustain the authority and richness of a court dress without a great deal of red and some white lead powder on her face, the insult of Aretino, master extortionist, is that of an asp that wants to strike in a high place. My shrug did not come easily, I confess, but then I became convinced that power, even if indirect, must expect this, too: to be vituperated as if we were not human beings but symbols of what men would never agree to admire unconditionally, even a Trajan. In any case, to Aretino I will dedicate an extra garland placed on the head of my most mocking dwarf at the first feast day in our calendar, and we will give him the treatment he deserves.

It would be a very simple matter for me to take from their hiding place some papers written in a jagged hand and enter the sweet delirium of a rereading. But can I really allow myself to be overcome by such compensating weaknesses? Who knows to what truth you respond, Mister Robert de la Pole?

*To the Most Illustrious and Excellent Signora
Isabella, Marchesana of Mantua and My Lady*

*A*t your feet, at your feet, my queen! And there let me ask
you, with delighted disheartenment, another of the many
pardons that represent my history in this lost, or rather, gained
service of the soul that for so many years has been a point of
secret radiance. I am not contrite, I warn you. Too many
things, grave and mysterious, press on my heart, and I will
confide all of them to you. I feel, then, a kind warning, of a
hurricane that must reveal us, one to the other, and I wonder if
you will accept this way I speak of "us." But grave things first.
I must speak to you of what will seem to you, I will not say
frivolous but light, as another time it wondrously was. Having
taken up my pen, I am caught up in that joyous freedom I
have felt in addressing you ever since you decided not to reply
to my letters and thus allow me to wander without restraint in
the terrains of feeling and intellect where consents or
prohibitions no longer apply.

After the cruel tragedy of the sack of Rome you have long
returned to the world that surrounds your secret garden
dressed in the forms of every season, where your footsteps
enter and echo. I remain fastened to your portrait, a copy of
the one painted by Giulio Romano but revised, on my own
instructions, which portrays you as no one will ever see you,
with that fulminating and sweet eye in the elongated face, the
expressiveness always on the point of changing. In this image
you are a bit more wan than when I saw you in the castle the
only time I was granted the sparkle of your presence. But it is
you, when you look out from a secret place in your soul.

Now I return to the pardon I must ask of you, enchantress
even in rejection. It is a confession I would like to be as
sonorous as a vast organ, because consorts of organs reechoed
in chorus when I was grazed by the dark satin embroidered in
sumptuous geometries of gold, silver, and gems, and the

round, silken form of a pearl stroked my finger, as my hands were joined in prayer.

God will forgive me because he knows I harbored no guilty intentions, but you will not. You are suspicious; you might consider those intentions a bit ambiguous, that stolen contact. I hope to make you smile.

It is time to explain. This happened in Bologna, in San Petronio, at a moment now three years past, during that coronation of Charles the Fifth which sanctioned the loss of liberty for the Italian states. On orders from my sovereign, Henry the Eighth, and by Cardinal Wolsey, now vanished from the scene, I was sent, with others of the court, to represent the island of England at that dubious ceremony, and so I found myself in the vast Bolognese church near the procession advancing past the lines of ambassadors and envoys, in a soft and lagging flow that every now and then came to a halt. The tapers were burning by the thousands; at that moment the emperor was coming out into the square, impassive, wearing the crown of the kings of Italy; and step by step, slowly the groups unfolded in the order established by the masters of ceremony.

Imagine how I was fired at seeing you appear, flanked by your guards, the Gonzaga standard hanging from the trumpets. Then you proceeded toward the main door with that firm and allusive step of yours that no one can imitate. You were, or so you seemed to my eye, the only living being in the midst of a population of statues. I do not know if I prayed for you to turn your gaze, but at that moment the great procession contracted, there was some confusion, the lines jostled one another, swaying. Some were pressed together, and I found myself near you, as you held your head erect toward the beamed ceiling, but without looking around. The painful joy of your presence struck me like a wave. Holding my breath, I bent forward slightly, just enough to make sure you were real, and I glimpsed from the edge of your stiff collar, near the nape, a pearl, going by at the level of my hand. As your advance stopped, I drew the pearl very gently toward me to keep it from falling, and I kept it between my thumb and forefinger, white and round. I vowed privately that I would send it back to you, and in fact, I have sewn it at the bottom of this letter, beside my name. For three years I have kept it in a little silver box, where it shifted and rolled playfully. Now I have saved the box for myself and have put a mother-of-pearl rosary bead in it; when I am too sad, I shake the box and console myself at the faint rolling as if I heard some undecipherable talk, and this is my way of being with you.

My joy ends here. Now comes the grave story that perhaps you are not expecting. I am leaving Italy. I am on the verge of departing from Rome, as I have done so many times; but perhaps I will not return again, and I repeat these words to myself with a distress that becomes a sharp stab if I gaze for a moment at the color of the sky. Exile has seized me with irresistible imperiousness. Everything is linked with reasons beyond us and masters of us. If it did not sound presumptuous, I would say that the history of England itself is driving me. Take heart, I will write also of this; for that matter, you well know how the powerful crush the lives of those who have the fairly innocent name of subjects.

I must refer to a larger matter, to my king's life, which promised to be so radiant, the king whom I have always followed with enthusiasm and faithful passion. His name is now associated with a woman's name that is echoing throughout Europe. I met her the last time I was in my island, this Anne Boleyn, or, as they call her in the Curia, Anna Bolena, recently and solemnly proclaimed queen of England. She is not beautiful. Her eyes are big and black, however, glistening with a liquid sensuality, and in those eyes a king's heart has been lost.

For the past four or five years the Roman Curia has been invaded by brigades of theologians, priests, scholars, excellent English envoys, coming and going, laden with writings, to discuss and obtain my king's divorce from Queen Catherine. To be sincere, I have fought for him. I was pleased that my king had not only his passion but also reasons that placed him in conflict with his own, tenaciously religious spirit. For that matter, it is also true that Henry wanted a male heir for the stability of England, or rather of the Tudors, and Catherine had given him six dead sons and one living daughter. I know, this is cruel thinking; but you, my lady, understand these dynastic matters better than anyone else. Henry is still young, strong, physically exuberant, and Catherine, six years older, is by now a *mojer deforme e vecchia* as a friend, a Venetian envoy, says, an old and misshapen woman, who could never give him another son.

I was certain of this. My king had not been inspired by hypocrisy or by excessive appetites. The so-called divorce question that he submitted to the judgment of the Church was deeply rooted. Going back in the years, I remembered that when I was already at the Curia in Rome, my king Henry the Seventh asked a dispensation for the marriage of his son Henry, then a child, to Catherine, recent widow of his firstborn son, Arthur. Prince Henry came to the throne after his father's death; a youth of sixteen, he instinctively rejected that marriage, but his ministers later convinced him of that union with his sister-in-law. Therefore, his argument, which Henry has always said was a "matter of conscience," was based in his view on canon law and, even above that, on the very word of God, which forbids a man to marry his brother's widow.

Why should we not believe in his devotion as a pious prince and good theologian when he, rejecting the advice that came to him from various directions, to obtain the annulment of his marriage from an English bishop and in England, wanted only the pope, with his pastoral authority, to declare the marriage to Catherine not valid, thus allowing the new marriage? But I will not bore you with the complex question of the Roman plea that during these last years has become so entangled that it is almost absurd. And—why not say it?—also dramatic.

Our pope, Clement, is every day more under the thumb of the emperor, who like an implacable shadow watches over the judges of the Sacra Rota and will never permit that his aunt Catherine be subjected to the insult of a divorce or, worse, an annulment. Who knows? Perhaps Clement would have maintained the agreement he had already made with my king in a secret decretal, the acknowledgment of Henry's thesis. But everything will remain hidden in the abysmal archives of the Vatican. Once again Charles the Fifth has pressed his heavy hand.

Now all is changed, my lady, and things are taking a turn for

the worse. My king, as you must know, unable to obtain the
divorce from the Sacra Rota, has decided not only to marry
Boleyn but to ignore the pope and his authority; in short,
Henry has made himself pope of the English church, and to
wound me more deeply—and I repeat them for your appraisal
—these are the words the king addressed to the archbishop of
Canterbury: "We, being your sovereign king, do not recognize
higher authority on earth but only God in heaven, and we are
not subject to the law of any human creature."

How can this affirmation be acceptable? How can Henry
attribute to himself a pontiff's power? In this way the
universality of the Christian Church is lost. And who can then
prevent some pope-sovereign from proclaiming not only laws
to regulate terrestrial government but also laws to regulate
divine government? My soul is at a thousand crossroads, and
in desperation I side with my great master and friend Erasmus
of Rotterdam, who considers inane the acquisition of
overweening authority by princes. With the universality of the
Church, also the universality of Europe will be lost. Just think,
wise lady, what if Charles the Fifth were to declare himself
pope of the Spanish Church or the German? And if Francis the
First did the same for the Church in France? Men seem to be
robbing from God.

Kings grow, and collective spiritual strength diminishes. We
are in the most dire era of arrogance and pride. It is terrible for
me to see my sovereign, with the complicity of Parliament,
threaten from above anyone who does not agree to recognize
him, English monarch, the leader of the English Church. And
by contrast, how splendid are the figures of those who refuse
to submit. If I could dwell on persons whom you do not know
or know very slightly, I would speak to you of the sublime
battle that has been fought by the minister Thomas More. No
one surpasses him in loftiness of spirit, in brilliance of culture,
or in wide knowledge, and yet he is in disgrace for having
opposed in Parliament the will of Henry, who enjoined the
clergy, separated from Rome, not to issue any law without
royal permission. Thomas, like Erasmus and like any human
being who harbors some notion of spiritual greatness, is in
anguish because disorder, confusion, and error today darken

the limpid beauty of our culture. Who will repeat
Michelangiolo's words about the truly happy age at the very
early days of our century, when men could drink from the
fountain of clarity and illuminate every tenebrous error?

I am slightly ashamed, my lady, because this serious lament
of mine lacks even the power of poetic invective. I am revolted
that in a country like mine, beautiful and strong, every spiritual
virtue must be subject to the decree of a Tudor, who considers
himself God's vicar on earth, laden as he is with seething
earthly passions. I seek for myself an avenue of escape, a place
where I can retire and await the passing of the few years God
may deign to grant me still. I would not stay on in the Curia
for anything in the world. The humiliation Henry is imposing
on the Roman pontiff could be multiplied, and I would not be
witness to a total collapse, to another sack of Rome from
whatever direction it might come. Nor can I shut myself up in
a convent because my nature will not submit to a total
obedience I do not feel I can share.

For a moment I had a desperate idea: to ask of you and your
son a place in your chancellery. I know almost as much as did
our Castiglione, rest in peace, of the story of every country,
and I know how to follow their actions; Mantua would shelter
me. It was only a moment's fancy. Do not mock me for this
foolish idea, which you would never have accepted, and
rightly. The beautiful feeling that brought me to you must not
undergo transformations, not even the most natural ones. I am
not blaspheming. Divine grace has allowed my febrile nature to
approach you and live in this long soliloquy, filled with serene
moods and also with fervent remorses: my patrimony. But it
was decided that another secret, bound to a name, specific but
very far from me and from you, would in a certain way
reanimate me.

Discoursing in sorrow (but not revealing it) with a Scottish
gentleman who had come to Rome for matters concerning his
king, James the Fifth, I happened to recall a fairly brief journey
I made many years ago in that land of Scotland. The wish to
return there had always remained, not only to rediscover the
emotion of that landscape worthy of ancient legend and a
certain vivid flash of brilliance in the inhabitants but also

because certain familiar customs and characters still linger there, and the Catholic house of Stuart reigns, and monks of great intelligent studies have schools there and residence. Now, as my mind repeated these ideas, my interlocutor, who was expatiating on the unusual trades and industries and on the personages that land welcomes from foreign countries, showed me, drawing it from its sheath, a gleaming sword. He told me that it was a Scottish blade and came from an armory of a celebrated swordmaker of Edinburgh, highly esteemed by noble gentlemen, the shop founded by Andrea of Ferrara some decades ago, still of acknowledged excellence.

Can you believe how stunned I was by that name, suddenly dropped in casual conversation? I cannot tell you how we then talked of these Italian artisans, rising to become citizens in the land of Scotland. I skillfully directed our talk, and each item of news gradually assumed a kind of prehensile energy. A kinsman of Andrea of Ferrara is the prior of an Augustinian monastery, and I learned his name; I wrote him, and the answer came: That monastery was looking for a master of Latin and Greek, who could teach also some Hebrew and perhaps Italian. I invoked the name of Andrea of Ferrara, who added a link to the chain that from the days of my youth has bound me to that city, yours and ours: the bond with the masters I had and with the vision of that little girl whose gaze was straight as the blade of the sword of the Ferrarese armorer.

And so, after some months of correspondence, all is settled. I am leaving for Edinburgh. They have found me a little house near the monastery, surrounded by a garden where those blue flowers grow that only in Scotland vibrate with every subtle shade, at times so intensely that they suggest the vehemence of red.

Later

And finally this letter has been written and left to meditate upon itself. Lady of my soul, I stood up at the word "red" as if jabbed by the tip of a dagger. This color had perforce to enter into the series of farewells. It has been between us since the beginning, when blood covered my face and I saw you for the first time, and now it is brought to me by the name of Andrea

of Ferrara, creator of blades made to split the heart. Rest
assured, I am not thinking of not writing you anymore; on the
contrary, I propose to describe to you the places of Scotland
and my life there. I might even be presented at the court of
King James and be asked to do some political writing. But I
must beg a favor of you: Do not write me; do not take
advantage of my flight and cease fearing me. I feel a culpable
vanity, thinking of how you have always fled me, for more
than thirty years. It may be that my vocation is to be the
abstract slave of something I do not know.

Now it is evening, and when I recall how many times I have
written you by the nocturnal lamp, I smile. With my smile your
power returns, and with it my impulse to raise my head, to
ward off an assault that has always accompanied your name. I
confess it now: I have been much tempted by you, though
always knowing it was in vain, but I do not regret this. I have
examined my condition with the help of the Church fathers,
and I have tried to repent, at times succeeding for long periods.
I do not lament this, as I said; I would lament if I had once
tempted you, even if, in the realm of love, I could then claim a
triumphal crown. Indeed, I am so much—and so sadly—a
sinner that I would sound in glory a hymn of love. Do not
write me. That is agreed. As your—our—poet Pietro Bembo
says, love does not want its secrets revealed.

What a yearning to speak to you, discuss you, and hear you
discuss me yourself! But that is truly forbidden. Still, there is
one thing I do not want to keep silent about to you, something
completely innocent (at least I believe it so). Not long ago I
came by chance upon a letter of yours addressed to a person
unknown to me; after the inevitable pang of jealousy (all the
stronger for being unjustified), I read in it a sentence that
sketches you and makes my spirit ache. The interlocutor, a
courtly and witty gentleman, who had a fanciful name, Apollo
(and surely you know who he is), advised you to resume, to
new purpose, that determination of yours to clothe your day in
merry graces. With authoritative fancy, you replied thus:
"Apollo advises me to renew an old motto of mine and the
duchess of Urbino: to attend to the happy life rather than die of
melancholy."

I was penetrated by a revelation that flung me into the most secret place of your spirit. In order to say that, you must have known moments of bitter suffering, undergone some mortal wound in your spirit, perhaps as you were selecting the most beautiful of your brocades. No one succeeded in comforting you, or probably, you rejected any comfort that did not come from yourself. After long reflection I realized how right you were. And for this I beseech you to thank God for something extraordinary that eludes the majority of men when they want to think of women. Thank him because he has given you the gift of seeing clearly into the matters of the world, and thank him for the quality of your intellect: proud, yes, but different from the inflexibility and the haughty severity that feed the intelligence of men when they are of worth. You are led, on the contrary, to ardor, to grace, to a constant desire to foster the ordering strength of the mind, joined with the natural energy of the feelings. For my part, I thank you for enabling me to perceive what an independent female mind can be, on its own, while accepting all the ties to earthly life.

This was the only thing I wanted still to say to you. And also this: Laugh, play, sing, jest, and study and read and have pictures painted for you, beloved lady of my soul. Even if I write to you again, and at length, perhaps I will never take my leave of you with this evening's emotion, having discovered in you one of the very rare creatures that live in a freedom invented day by day, according to the lights and the shadows of your own truths.

Your devoted, dear queen,
for life and beyond
Robert de la Pole

Rome, the twelfth of September, 1533

Room of the clocks
the year 1533

THE CHIMES OF the clocks sound, different among themselves in tone and time, and the candelabra are spent as the sounds die. I collect the pages covered by the jagged hand, and I fold them with the gesture reserved for things to be shut away for an unknown time or forever. The pearl has remained, sewn to the name of de la Pole, in the little coffer where the papers of my fugitive English priest are kept.

"Umbrasia," I say without raising my voice.

Immediately, from an adjoining room where she sleeps as sentry, she appears in the doorway, raising the heavy curtain. Still young, sharpened, cheeks, nose, chin, mouth, shapely with singular refinement. For many years she has been my herbalist and my nimble-fingered musician and also my alert adviser.

"Let us sing," I say after replacing the little coffer in the cupboard. "Fetch your viol."

I have so much to say, accompanying myself in music. I have always preferred singing with the viol to recitation, which adds fire and efficacy to the expanding of the word.

"Shall we go and celebrate the rising of the sun?" Umbrasia asks. "Soon the sky will brighten; it is September, the lake is already giving up its misty white. Let us call our knights, Apollo, Demogorgon, Adonis, and Madama Blanca, Madama Risible, Madama Amata."

I grasp her wrist.

"Madama Amata's name is marred. Perhaps. No, you must not summon our academicians of San Pietro. No one must be called. Let us go, the two of us, beneath the loggia; tell them to bring us the lantern. Until the sun is high, we will sing in turn. First we will sing the song of Josquin Despres, 'Mille Regrets de Vous Habandonner.' "

"But, my lady," Umbrasia says secretly and in a low voice, "once they hear our music, all of them will rush down, the pages, the girls, the ladies-in-waiting, your knights on duty, the poets laureate. The merry dwarfs will roll about, the boatmen will wake in the ducal barges; the musicians will come running, brandishing their instruments. The garlands are already prepared for today's festivity."

I stared at her, motionless. I had no idea what festivity might still come.